D0772930

ABOUT THE AUTHOR

Brown Bear is the call sign for Navy fighter pilot Dick Schaffert. In recognition of his solo defense of an Iron Hand mission against attack by four MiG's over Hanoi, the F-8 Crusader display by TOPGUN at Naval Air Station Fallon bears his name. A survivor of the fire aboard the USS *Oriskany*, he flew 276 combat missions over North Vietnam and received 35 decorations, including three awards of the Distinguished Flying Cross: The first for rescuing a downed pilot deep in enemy territory; the second for saving a strike group by destroying a Soviet surface-to-air missile site; and the third for single-handedly defeating the four MiG. He was Operations Officer of the squadron where TOPGUN was born and commanded a fighter squadron aboard the USS *Constellation*.

He was an Operations Analyst in the Office of the Secretary of Defense, on the Ambassador's Country Team and U.S./Philippines Mutual Defense Board at the U.S. Embassy in Manila, and pursued a diplomatic career as Director of Policy Studies at NATO Military Headquarters in Belgium.

With a Ph.D. in Political Science (International Law and Political Culture), *Brown Bear* is a distinguished graduate from the National Defense University in Washington, D.C. Since leaving NATO, he has continued research and consultation in the field of international terrorism and is serving as an advisor for European law enforcement officials. His *Media Coverage and Political Terrorists* (New York and London: Praeger, 1992) was favorably critiqued by several professional journals.

FOREWORD

by

REAR ADMIRAL J. B. "REDMAN" BEST (RETIRED)

U.S. Navy Fighter Pilot
Commander, Fleet Air Western Pacific
Desert Shield, Desert Storm

Charlie is the third in Dick Schaffert's series: *Loyalty, Betrayal, and other Contact Sports.* A highly charged, fast paced novel trio presenting authenticity and political realism that leave the reader trying to distinguish between fact and fiction.

If you enjoyed the Louis L'Amour series on the Sackett Family, or Tom Clancy combining real-world political excitement with bits of fiction, you are in for another literary rush. Captain Willliams, aka Captain Orden, aka Brown Bear will introduce you to a secret organization, *Purple,* and venture into the world of terrorism, international diplomacy, arms smuggling, assassination and the contact sport of sex.

If you read *Alpha* and *Bravo,* you were introduced to the red-haired beauty with brilliant green eyes, Rita Jay; Jim Conrad, a Canadian Fighter Jock; Joe Tashki and others. Here in *Charlie,* you are introduced to El Queda and will meet tough and sexy Shreeba. You expect to meet Forrest Gump on the next page.

Charlie continues the series with a focus on terrorists and their networks, and on the failures of U.S. Administrations. It also demonstrates how our free society could be our downfall. One line replays in my mind like a song you can't kick: "The loyalty of today's politicians stops at the ballot box."

Brown Bear presents a page-turner for excitement and catapults you into one adventure after another. A guaranteed winner!

REVIEW

Famous authors have written about war without having faced hostile fire. Spy novels have been authored by people who were never involved in that line of work. Not so with Dick Schaffert, Ph.D., anti-terrorist consultant, Navy fighter pilot, and warrior.

If you search the internet or the library shelves, you will find accounts of Dick's famous air battle against four MiG's with his guns jammed. That mission earned him one of his three Distinguished Flying Crosses: Flying cover for a SAM suppression aircraft, and protecting the flank of a flight of bombers, Dick engaged the MiG's south of Hanoi by himself. Out-numbered and out-gunned, his aggressive attack prevented the MiG's from falling upon the hapless SAM suppressor or encircling the strike group. The MiG's fired hundreds of 23mm cannon shells and four Atoll missiles against Dick's elusive F-8 Crusader. In return, he launched three Sidewinders. The first passed within killing range of his target but failed to fuse. Under constant attack, he had no time to watch the flights of his second and third missiles. When other Crusaders arrived to protect the SAM suppression aircraft, and the strike group went "feet wet," Dick engaged in a deadly one-on-one contest with the MiG leader. He worked himself into a firing positions for his 20mm cannons, but they jammed. He then began a violent vertical rolling "scissors" duel with his opponent, but soon ran low on fuel. He escaped with a supersonic dive and pull-out below the red roof of a pagoda near Hanoi. For more than ten adrenaline-soaked minutes, he had outflown his adversaries--and became a legend among Crusader pilots.

I met Lt. Schaffert when he was instructing air combat maneuvering and gunnery in the F-11F Tiger, a demanding single-seat Navy fighter. He was the instructor on my first gunnery flight. I had met him earlier in students v. instructors basketball games. He was aggressive, physical, and tough. He demonstrated those same characteristics in the air, and in the debriefing of our gunnery flight. He detailed each pass made by the three of us and told us precisely what we had done wrong. He closed by saying we had all earned a "down," but it was against the Skipper's policy to award an unsatisfactory grade on the first flight. We were crushed! I found out later he earned his call sign "Brown Bear" by doing that with most students on their first gunnery attempt. We were about to get our wings and join the fleet; he didn't want us to quit learning when the end was so close.

I got those Wings of Gold a month later and left Texas smiling gleefully, knowing I would never see him again. After nine months of Navy Justice school and flight training in the F-8 Crusader, I checked into Fighter Squadron Thirteen. The Skipper informed me that I was his new Personnel Officer and took me to the Admin Office to meet my new boss, Lcdr. Dick Schaffert. For a brief moment, I died inside!

However, I soon became a Schaffert devotee. He was still meticulous and demanding, but also instructional, helpful, and correct. His flight briefings remained extremely detailed. His explanation of the maneuvers to be accomplished would be going through my mind as we flew the mission.

Late on one of those incredibly black Mediterranean nights, I lost my radio during the catapult shot. A night carrier landing without a radio requires a great deal of attention. Thankfully, the entire chain of events went exactly as Dick had briefed prior to launch. Concentrating on the instruments, I proceeded to the designated rendezvous and orbited at 20,000 feet. It was very quiet in the cockpit. I felt very much alone and was glad to see the lights of a Crusader joining on me. Dick took the lead, I locked on to his wing, and we flew formation through that pitch-black sky for the next hour. When we began a descent, I knew the carrier was out there somewhere. He flashed his lights, I lowered the hook and the landing gear. A minute later, the lights flashed again and I raised the wing. The Crusader had no flaps; the "design gods" at NAVAIR had decided to make the wing go up and down instead.

When the lights flashed again, I looked up for the first time in over an hour. There, three miles straight ahead, were the dim lights of the USS *Shangri-La*. It was the first time the carrier looked good to me at night. Dick flew my wing all the way to the "ball," then pulled out to the side so I could rejoin on him if I didn't catch a wire--but I wasn't about to screw up this landing! I caught a wire and trapped. At that moment, I wanted to nominate my boss for sainthood.

Dick Schaffert knows the spy game, first hand. His doctoral dissertation was a detailed analysis of the makeup and elements of political terrorism, and was later published by Praeger in London and New York. It came from his own counter-terrorism activities and investigations in Southeast Asia and Europe. After a tour at NATO, he became a consultant and advisor for Eastern European law enforcement agencies.

Dick's series *Loyalty, Betrayal, and other Contact Sports* is the saga of Navy fighter pilot Dick Williams in his battles against evil and corruption throughout the world. He combines his wartime experiences and anti-terrorist expertise into a gripping historical novel. Captain Schaffert is many things, add story-teller to the list. He weaves intrigue, mystery, assassination, and tension with a sprinkling of sexual encounters for his energetic character, Dick Williams. Read this book, you'll enjoy it!

Captain Larry Durbin, UAL (Retired)
Navy Fighter Pilot
United Airlines 747-400 Pilot

Over-classified files, buried in archives to cover the mistakes of politicians, leave a deep void in the recorded history of the 20th Century. They also conceal the quiet heroism of participants in the so-called Cold War. Thousands of patriots, from dozens of countries, are dead and buried under the blanket hypocritically labeled détente. This is but one of those stories. Hopefully, others will also come forward to help fill this historical void.

Brown Bear

Dedicated to Jim Conrad:

His brave heart, born from an aggressive spirit, won many dangerous battles.

But he often said it would take pure loyalty, born from true honor, to achieve the ultimate victory.

Blessed are the peacemakers for they shall be called the children of God.

Matthew 5:9

LOYALTY,

BETRAYAL,

AND OTHER

CONTACT SPORTS

(CHARLIE)

The story of a fighter pilot as told by Brown Bear
a k a
Richard W. Schaffert

Copyright © 2003 by Richard W. Schaffert

All rights reserved. This book, or parts thereof, may not be reproduced in any form without permission in writing from the publisher.

Library of Congress Control Number: 2003093554

ISBN 0-9673933-5-3

First Edition

Published in 2003
by
Erzsé Productions
Seattle, Washington

Book design by Erzsébet Czibolya

A CALL FROM THE RANCH

In his earphones, Dick heard the enemy's point man approaching the mini-transmitter he had laid at the entrance to the gorge. In the darkness between the narrow limestone walls, he could barely see Johnnie Ho on his right and the other South Vietnamese Ranger on his left. He gave them the signal. In a few seconds, the nine-man team was alert and ready to spring the deadly ambush.

Continuing to monitor the transmitter, Dick heard the point man enter the gorge. Other members of the North Vietnamese patrol followed close behind.

He rotated his field radio's frequency knob to select the transmitter placed ten yards into the gorge. He heard boots splashing in the shallow water and guttural exclamations.

He was aware of the cold water running into his boots and the headset pressing against his ears. Switching to the transmitter twenty yards into the gorge, he heard the same splashing and cursing sounds. A quick re-check of the transmitter at the entrance to the gorge produced fading sounds. All twenty-three members of the NVN patrol were now in the gorge.

Dick switched to the transmitter he had placed against the wall opposite his position. He laid the radio quietly in his lap and gripped the grenade. As the sounds in his earphones grew louder, he pulled the grenade's pin and released the trigger. "One, two, please dear God," he counted to himself, then tossed it over the boulder to the wall on the other side.

Hell on earth began with a blinding white flash. Dick pivoted to his left, along the side of the boulder. He brought the M-16 to chest-level and, still in a crouch, fired into his assigned area. The headset fell from his ears. The gorge was engulfed in violent explosions. He would never forget the sight before him. Muzzle flashes and bursting grenades illuminated the scene. The effect was brilliant strobe lights, transforming movement into slow motion. Two bodies were already down in the stream in Dick's field. A figure was raising a weapon as the fire from Dick's M-16 tore into him. Two more darting figures emerged from Dick's right side. He swung his M-16 in their direction, but blasts from Johnnie Ho's shotgun blew both of them against the far wall.

Dick was still squeezing the M-16's trigger when he realized it had stopped firing. His hand reached for the 9mm pistol in his belt. He had to straighten out of his crouch to pull it free.

In that instant, explosions to his right illuminated a huge figure lunging across the narrow stream at him. The giant had a machete raised over his head. In the staccato of light, Dick sensed he would not get his pistol out in time. The machete was coming down. He was going to die in a cold jungle stream in North Vietnam.

A blinding flash outlined the figure as it bowled into Dick, knocking him flat on his back in the shallow water. The gorge was suddenly totally black. The enveloping silence was punctured only by the groans of the wounded and dying.

Water was running into Dick's nose. He struggled to raise his head. Gasping for breath, he gagged on the metallic taste of blood. The heavy weight on his chest was impeding his efforts to breathe. He rolled on his side, and the huge body slid off.

Dick brought his hands up. His entire being froze. His chest was a mass of gore. In horror, he tried to tear the mangled flesh and shattered bone from his body . . .

"*Reechard, Reechard, aufwachen, bitte,* wake up!" Maria was shouting. She tried to hold his arms as he tore at his night shirt.

He awoke with a start, his body wet and cold, the taste of blood in his mouth. Maria turned on the bed lamp. The light pained his eyes. He struggled to focus on the lovely face framed by her fine golden hair. Tears were streaming from her soft blue eyes.

"*Mein Gott,* Richard!" she cried. "You have again so a terrible dream."

She took a tissue from the box on the night table and dabbed at his mouth. "You have bitten your lip. I get a washcloth."

When she returned, Dick sat up. He pushed a corner of the wet cloth into his mouth, exploring the cut on the inside of his lower lip. He glanced apologetically at the blood on the pillow. "Sorry about the mess, Honey."

She cupped his face in her hands. "Let *Schwester* Tiala see what you have done, *Bärlie.*"

He opened his mouth for her tender examination. "The bleeding's stopping. Hold the cloth on the cut."

"What time is it, Schatzie?" he asked quietly. "I have to be at SHAPE at six for a meeting with Frazier."

She stepped from the bed to check her watch on the dresser. "It's only three. You could sleep a couple more hours, but I'm worried you might have that nightmare again."

She felt Dick looking at her and turned her head to smile. His eyes caressed her exciting body. At thirty, she had the firm, inviting curves of an eighteen-year-old. Smooth, fair skin accentuated the glamorous posture of her perfectly proportioned, petite figure. Friends often compared her to a porcelain doll, but Dick knew the hot passion and violent desires that flamed inside her cool exterior.

The pink baby-doll did little to hide her charms. She turned gracefully and tiptoed to the bed. She wet her lips and teased him with her wide, sparkling blue eyes.

He opened his arms. She folded herself into them, saying softly: "Hold me, *Brummi Bär*, I have the perfect sleeping *Medicament* for an old Navy fighter pilot."

He pushed the key into the ignition of his small BMW and grinned in spite of the pain in his mouth. During a routine inspection, Colonel Mackenzie's Special Air Service technicians had found the KGB electronic gadget, which alerted Margo whenever he turned on the switch. Today, she'd be awaken a couple hours earlier. Dick was certain he'd see her red Fiat Spider, somewhere between his house in the Belgian countryside and the main gate of the Supreme Headquarters Allied Powers Europe.

Shortly after he reported to the NATO military headquarters last September, the KGB had assigned the buxom blonde beauty to tail Dick. That assignment might now be in jeopardy. With *Purple's* help, he'd ditched her in an airline switch last week, while enroute to deliver a million-dollar payoff to the Sicilian Mafia.

The Kremlin had arranged the kidnapping of USAF General Mack Thomas, of NATO's Southern Command, by Red Brigades terrorists in Italy. The Mafia had discovered the General's whereabouts and offered to assist in his recovery for a million dollars.

If Margo had been able to track Dick's delivery, the Kremlin would have uncovered the Mafia's deal. They would have killed

Thomas--rather than risk his being rescued. When Margo lost Dick in *Purple's* carefully planned switch in Copenhagen, the Kremlin had been denied that timely knowledge. Normally, such a failure by an agent resulted in severe disciplinary measures.

The country road to SHAPE passed under the main autobahn between Brussels and Paris. In the faint morning light, Dick saw the red Fiat waiting on the off-ramp. Before he got to SHAPE's main gate, he caught a glimpse of the blonde hair behind the wheel of the sports car trailing him. He winced as his smile irritated his cut lip; Margo must have again used her abundant charms to have her way with her KGB boss. However, Dick remembered Colonel Mackenzie's warning. The KGB had been known to ignore an agent's blown cover and simply assign an additional agent to their target. Dick must be alert for a new tail, while Margo continued on the job.

Passing through the heavy security surrounding the massive SHAPE office building, Dick parked in his assigned space. Rather than open his office at this early hour, he stopped in the cafeteria for a cup of coffee. After passing through another checkpoint, he entered the top-secret classified area and paused at a restroom to check his appearance.

The mirror reflected an imposing image. Dick's tall, athletic body was perfect for displaying the dark blue Navy uniform, with the four gold Captain stripes on its sleeves. The silver badge with the golden eagle, for service in the Office of the Secretary of Defense, adorned his left breast. Above the badge were the golden star and trident pins for command at sea and ashore. The rows of ribbons above the pins signified thirty-five decorations, which included three awards of the Distinguished Flying Cross for combat over North Vietnam. Crowning the other insignia--and most important to Dick--were the golden wings of a Naval Aviator. He'd paid dearly for those wings. They represented five thousand hours in single-piloted fighter aircraft, most of it in demanding air combat maneuvering. Those long hours--exerting extreme g forces upon his body--had been exaggerated by more than fifteen-hundred catapult launches and arrested landings on aircraft carriers.

Dick lifted his right arm to remove his gold-brimmed "cover." The sharp pain in his neck reminded him of the damage done to his vertebrae by those nineteen years of aggressive flying. They had been finalized two years ago, with his violent escape from the exploding Aura One over the Philippine Sea. The stress had been more than physical. His handsome boyish face was aged beyond his forty-five years. His wide-set blue eyes were hardened, hours of staring into the sun had etched crow's-feet at the corners. His broad forehead was wrinkled and careworn from years of leadership responsibility in hazardous situations. The set of his jaw indicated fire still tempered his proud spirit.

His lower lip was slightly swollen, but the boyish grin returned as he ran the comb through his light brown hair. After years of sporting a crew cut under his flight helmet, he now enjoyed parting his full head of hair on the right side, *Cary Grant* style.

Commodore Twillinger greeted Dick as he entered the office of the SHAPE Deputy Commander. "Had your morning coffee, Brown Bear?"

"Yes, thank you, Sir. Is the Air Chief Marshal in?"

"Frazier's in the Supreme Commander's office. He'll call when they're ready for us."

"Any idea what this is all about, Sir?"

"Something to do with your delivery of the money to the Mafia." The Commodore was interrupted by the red phone on his desk. "Twillinger here. . . . Yes Sir, we're on our way."

The short, stocky, no-nonsense British navy officer hung up the phone. He set his hat firmly on his balding head and said briskly: "Let's go, Dick. Frazier says they're waiting."

The SAS Major by the desk in the center of the corridor saluted smartly and checked their identification with the palm-print scanner. "The General's waiting, Commodore. My Lieutenant will escort you through security."

They walked down the guarded corridor adorned with NATO paraphernalia. Dick asked quietly, "Commodore, why are we meeting so early?"

"There's going to be a conference call between your President, the Supreme Commander, Air Chief Marshal Frazier, and you."

"You're joking, Sir. It's almost midnight at the White House."

"Very true, Captain, but it's only nine o'clock at the ranch in

California. That's where the call's supposed to originate."

They passed the sentries and entered the outer office. The U.S. Army Lieutenant opened the door to the inner office, saluted smartly, and stepped aside.

The Supreme Commander of Allied Forces Europe was standing behind a large mahogany desk. The Deputy Commander was by his side. Frazier stepped quickly forward and greeted Dick with a warm handshake. "Good Morning, Brown Bear, how's my favorite fighter pilot?"

Without waiting for a reply, he escorted Dick around the desk. "General Bernard, may I present Captain Dick Williams."

Dick began a salute, but the General grasped his hand. "My pleasure, Captain. It's not every day I meet someone who's bearded the lions in their own den. Mack Thomas owes you his life. I'm sorry it's taken a few days for me to talk with you about this. I needed to get Mack's story before we sent him back to the States for rehab."

A buzzer sounded and the General said: "Commodore, we'll use the secure conference speaker for this call. Please clear the outer office. I'll open the door when we've finished."

As Twillinger departed, the Supreme Commander motioned for Frazier and Dick to be seated; then he activated the switch on the speaker phone on his desk. In a few moments, Dick recognized the voice of the President of the United States.

"Good morning, Bernie. How's it going?"

"Very good, Mr. President. Hope you had a pleasant weekend at the ranch."

"Thank you, we did! Got the spring branding done early. I wasn't much help, but I surely do like swinging that rope. Bernie, this has to be a private conversation. The Secretary of State's here with me. Who's at your end?"

"Myself and Captain Williams, and here's my Deputy, Air Chief Marshal Frazier."

"Good morning, Mr. President, Frazier here. I'd like to mention that you met Captain Williams at our Aura Project briefing, during the Ottawa Group of Seven meeting last July."

"Certainly! I remember the Brown Bear. Gave Henry quite a tongue lashing. How are you, Dick?"

"Just fine, Mr. President, thank you."

"Glad to hear that. You and Frazier must realize how badly I wanted to put Aura into production, but it was too risky. That leap in technology might have pushed the Russkies over the edge. I couldn't take the chance. Your demonstrations against the Soviet Air Defense from the Philippines were too damned effective! With eight Foxbat and two satellite kills, you at least have the satisfaction of knowing you're the first double-ace in space."

"What do you see for Aura in the future, Sir?"

"It's tied to serious politics, Dick, domestic and international. My economists say the Soviet efforts in Afghanistan are bringing them to the edge of bankruptcy--the brave battles you boys fought in Vietnam went a long way toward draining their defense budget. Aura's performance has made them realize they can't match us in another arms race. I believe Moscow sees her in the same light as I do--she's the perfect defense against ballistic missiles, and anything else in outer space. If I brought her into production, the principle of mutual assured destruction, that has shielded our world from a nuclear holocaust all these years, would be shattered. Since they couldn't afford to match her technology, the Soviets might be pushed into going for a first strike. Space shuttle and other secret projects have priority on our R&D money, Dick, for many years to come. Aura will be *the* weapon of the twenty-first century. After communism has been destroyed economically, Aura will come to the fore and her technology will lead the way to a safer world. Frazier, I believe your Prime Minister also sees it that way."

"Yes Sir. She agrees with your assessment of the threat and says the full potential of Aura must wait at least one generation."

"I'm glad I had this chance to give you my view personally. I also want to express my admiration for the way your team handled the Aura Project. With that traitor Strauss in your midst, it was a miracle you and the Brown Bear came out alive. Now, let's get to the reason for my phone call. Dick, I read two after-action reports about your recent mission, and I want to start by saying *thank you!* I'm mighty glad you're back at SHAPE."

"Thank you, Sir."

"One of the reports was submitted by my CIA station chief in Rome, the other by Air Chief Marshal Frazier. I had to read them twice, because it sounded like they were talking about two different missions. The bottom lines were the same--you delivered the money to Don Paolucci and we got Thomas back in good health--but the station chief said you endangered the mission by pursuing a private vendetta, actually shooting and killing a member of the Mafia in front of the Don. He's recommending disciplinary action. On the other hand, Frazier's report says your actions were in self-defense; that you had every right to believe the Mafia would turn you over to a Syrian named Ahmad Salah and this guy you shot . . . Enrico. Was that his name?"

"Yes Sir, Mr. President. As I recall from the Aura briefing, you knew about a *Purple* agent with the code name *Red One.*"

"Yes, I did. I was very sorry to hear of her death in Manila."

"Enrico was one of the scum bags who killed her, Sir. I wasn't worried about being turned over to Salah, but I saw my chance to avenge Red One--and I took it."

"Seems to me you laid your life on the line for both her and Mack Thomas. *Purple* has confirmed the details for me, and I tend to agree with Bernie and Frazier that your courageous actions--along with those of your *Purple* partner inside the Red Army Faction--have earned you both decorations for heroism."

General Bernard smiled and Frazier added a hearty "hear, hear!"

Dick was shocked by the President's reference to Jim Conrad's covert operation inside the RAF. "Mr. President, I'm certain you realize my partner's life depends upon complete secrecy about his current position."

"Yes, Brown Bear, I do. God, how I wish we had a couple more like him, and you! You've put your finger right on my problem--it's impossible for America to thank him without compromising his safety. Proper recognition would also expose your actions, and endanger your life even more."

"Don't give it a second thought, Mr. President. If the media started digging, they might also find out about the *Friends of Thomas,* and where the million bucks really came from. Who knows where that could lead? Which would be worse, negotiating with terrorists or bargaining with organized crime?"

General Bernard warned Dick with a shake of his head. There was a pause before the President replied slowly: ". . . Captain, I've reviewed your Vietnam combat record--along with the '67 report on Operation *Trout,* where you were screwed out of the Medal of Honor for security reasons--I know you won't place your country, or your Commander-in-Chief, in a compromising position."

"I didn't mean to imply that, Mr. President. I'm your biggest fan, but I'd like to request a couple favors. It's in regard to the NATO supply of arms to Admiral Toufani and his guerrillas in Iran."

Frazier frowned, but Dick continued: "I hate to see the United States back away from him, Sir. He's a good man and could make a big contribution for us in that part of the world."

"I agree with your assessment of the Admiral," responded the President. "However, if we're to harness the evil empire, we have fish to fry all over the globe. Toufani may be one of those we have to sacrifice, but I hope you'll continue your personal relationship with him. It's obvious the Ayatollah's putting his weight behind some potent Palestinian terrorist groups, and we desperately need friends in that part of the world. Maybe you have another favor that would be easier to grant?"

"Yes Sir. I'd like to have the 1965 report on Operation *Starlight* reviewed. I want to know if we've found the leak in the CIA that cost the lives of Güla, an innocent Kurdish girl, and dozens of her friends and relatives."

"I saw *Starlight* in your file, Dick, and I'll ask about it. Incidentally, there's nothing in there yet about your being with *Purple*. The CIA report on Thomas was the first mention of that; but you know I was not one of the three heads-of-state who approved your membership. With the U.K., West Germany, and Japan already in your court, there was no need for further approval."

"Mr. President," said General Bernard, "I want to emphasize how strongly we feel about SHAPE's award recommendation for Captain Williams. He clearly offered his life for General Thomas. However, we recognize the sensitivity of the current situation. With your permission, we'll postpone our recognition of his bravery until his departure from this command."

"A fine thought, General," said the President. "I certainly agree with SHAPE's assessment of Brown Bear's courage. I'll always wonder how he was able to kill Enrico right there in Paolucci's headquarters. God must have been guiding your hand, Dick."

"No doubt about it, Sir, and I'm sure He'll do it again--when I know the CIA leak responsible for Güla's death and when I find Ahmad Salah, the Syrian who helped Enrico murder Red One."

"Sounds like Captain Williams has a pretty full plate, General," said the President, "but you'd better make a point of keeping him around NATO. With my push to put mid-range nuclear missiles in Western Europe, the Kremlin's terrorists will give our troops a bad time--Mack Thomas was only the beginning."

"We'll hang on to Williams as long as we can, Mr. President," replied the Supreme Commander. "He and the *Purple* connection are absolutely vital to us."

"I'm sure the Air Chief Marshal will keep those lines open," said the President. "Dick, I'm aware of *Purple's* pledge of poverty for their agents, and I want you to know I'll be continuing your full military pay as long as I'm your Commander-in-Chief. If you decide to revert to a normal life and return to Nebraska, let me know. I have a mission for you there. Gentlemen, it was a pleasure conversing with the free world's finest, but Air Force One's starting and I have to say goodbye. God be with all of you."

". . . and with you, Mr. President," echoed the Supreme Commander.

2

THE BELLBOY

Lieutenant Commander Dick Williams rolled the F-8 Crusader on its back and pulled its nose down to cut off the diving A-4 Skyhawk in front of him.

"Pouncer Two, do you have the Shrike in sight?" asked the A-4 pilot.

"Affirmative," grunted Dick, straining his stomach muscles against the heavy g forces tearing at his body. "It's on your nose, up forty degrees."

"No joy," replied the A-4 pilot, "stick with it. You have the lead."

"Roger that. I'm at your nine o'clock. Check gun switches on."

Reconnaissance photos had shown twelve SA-2 Guideline missiles (SAM's) on launchers at the complex twenty kilometers south of Phuc Yen. Surrounded by scores of 37mm and 57mm anti-aircraft guns, it posed a formidable threat to the USS Oriskany's strike group. Those twenty-four heavily laden Skyhawks were bearing down on the airfield from the southwest. When they arrived at their roll-in point, the SAM's at the complex could be launched from behind them. The mission was another suicide effort planned by McNamara's civilians in their air-conditioned Pentagon offices.

Dick fought to keep his eyes focused on the Shrike's trail as it sped toward a Fansong radar in the SAM complex. Yesterday his shoulder harness had failed when he landed on the Oriskany, and his head had slammed into the F-8's radar scope. His helmet had cracked, but he'd walked away with only a concussion. Unfortunately, a severe headache and occasional double vision were making today's missions difficult.

Dick and his Shrike-shooting leader had only six 20mm cannons to go against the missile complex. Normally, the A-4 would have carried a couple MK-82 bombs, which were very effective against SAM sites. However, the carriers on Yankee Station were suffering from a shortage of ammunition, and all available bombs were allotted to the strike on the airfield. Other "Iron Hand" teams from the Oriskany would be making heroic attempts to disrupt the SAM firings that were certain to come from Hanoi. They would also be badly out-gunned.

Glancing to his left, Dick saw the A-4 about 2,000 feet away--in perfect position. Denny was a hell of a pilot! He'd flown B-26's for JFK against the Viet Cong back in '62. Today would be his 380th mission over Vietnam.

They saw the Shrike impact inside the northern-most star-shaped missile site. Farther north, the heavens erupted in a mass of dirty black explosions. The 57mm and 85mm AAA batteries surrounding the airfield had found the approaching strike group.

Dick's eyes swept the F-8's instrument panel. The master arm switch was on and guns were selected. His speed was 450kts at 150 feet above the rice paddies--below the SAM envelope--he hoped!

"Pouncer Two's taking the northern site," he growled into his oxygen mask.

"Rog. One's on the southern," was Denny's quick reply.

Nearing the northern star, six missiles mounted on launchers came into Dick's view. All were pointed toward the vulnerable strike group. He broke sharply to the left, then back to the right, aligning two of the launchers. His right index finger found the comforting curve of the trigger. He brought the sight ladder down to the first missile--and all hell broke loose!

The airspace over the complex was laced by crisscrossing 23mm tracers. There must have been at least a dozen of the multi-barreled weapons hidden around the perimeter of the complex.

At 1,500-foot slant range, Dick fired a short burst. He quickly adjusted his sight picture to the launcher on the far side of the star. Ignoring the flaming messengers of death streaking across his canopy, he fired another burst into the second missile.

Then he was beyond the deadly umbrella of flak, but literally flying on the ground. He inched the Crusader up to avoid a hedge line and broke hard left. He rolled wings level on a heading of north, still at 450kts. Denny would be flying a similar pattern to the south.

"Pouncer One, turning in."

Dick acknowledged Denny's call and began the planned four-g turn back toward the complex. He got a grim shot of satisfaction as he noticed explosions rocking the airfield area. The Oriskany's bombers had broken through to their long-awaited target.

The missile complex came back into his windscreen. Dick blinked his eyes repeatedly to overcome the double vision from yesterday's concussion. The sky above him was peppered with the white puffs of detonating 37mm shells. Orange flames and smoke were billowing from the two missiles he had attacked. From his low altitude, he was unable to see the southern star.

"Pouncer One inbound."

Their timing was perfect. Denny was beginning his run from the south. They would hit the target at the same time, from opposite directions. Denny would be strafing launchers on the west side, and Dick would attack those on the east.

As he approached, the airspace above the site was again laced with 23mm tracers. A thick blanket of white 37mm and black 57mm explosions covered the complex to an altitude of at least 5,000 feet.

The radio was alive with transmissions from the strike group, as pilots pulled out of their bombing runs and attempted to escape in two-plane sections.

At 100 feet, Dick was unable to see launchers on the northern star, which was now obscured by smoke. He hadn't seen any missiles launched. There were at least four more at the site. He jerked the Crusader's nose up to 500 feet and rolled on his back. He was rewarded with a view of a missile on its launcher on the far side of the site. He snapped the nose back down, rolled wings level, centered the gunsight on the missile, and squeezed the trigger. He passed directly over the launcher at a scant fifty feet. The exploding missile rocked his aircraft.

Once again, he was over the rice paddies. Flaming tracers from the 23mm's were kicking up the mud and water around him. He broke hard left to a heading of east. Denny would be doing the same to the west.

Hanoi was twenty kilometers directly in front of him--waves of missiles were rising into the air. At least ten were approaching the Phuc Yen airfield, where the strike group was now exiting.

"Pouncer One turning in."

"Two roger." During the four-g turn back to the complex, Dick attempted to look over his left shoulder; but an incredible pain in his neck prohibited the movement. Evidently, yesterday's broken shoulder harness had resulted in more than just a concussion.

The blazing missile site came back into the F-8's windscreen.

"Bad news, Pouncer One," said Dick. "We'll have to pop-up to see anything."

"Roger that," replied Denny. "Let's go up now."

Zooming through 5,000 feet, Dick rolled on his back to look down at the target. The northern star was completely ablaze. The three missiles Dick hit had ignited the others. Two missiles were burning on the west side of the southern star, but the other four were still intact and in the clear. Flames burst from the tailpipe of one as it rocketed from its launcher and streaked westward.

"Heads up, Pouncer One!" screamed Dick into his mask. "Missile in the air--on your nose."

Denny's agile Skyhawk was halfway through a high-g barrel roll when the forty-foot "telephone pole" streaked past without exploding. Denny completed the roll and aligned his aircraft with the target.

"I'm taking the missile on the southern edge, Pouncer Two."

"Rog, I'm on the one to the east." Dick pulled the Crusader's nose down to center the pipper on the missile. "You'll be on target before me."

"Concur," replied Denny. "I'll break right after delivery."

Passing 4,000 feet, Dick's target was obscured by smoke from exploding 57mm rounds. "Into the valley of death rode the six-hundred," he muttered into his mask.

"Cannons to the left of them," responded Denny quickly.

"Cannons to the right of them," grunted Dick, peering through the dense flak. Then the missile and launcher were again visible. He made an instantaneous adjustment and let drive with the full fury of the Crusader's four Colt-Browning cannons. His 20mm HEI sparkled on the warhead of the missile. It exploded in a tremendous bright orange flame, as Dick's guns stopped firing.

Another gut-wrenching pullout and he was level over the rice paddies. He broke left, scanning the area in front of him for Denny's Skyhawk. Then he saw him--high at twelve o'clock.

"Tally ho, Pouncer One. Two's at your four o'clock low, one mile. I'm zero ammo."

"Rog Two," responded Denny. "Come on up and let's get the hell out of here!"

Dick hit the Crusader's afterburner and pulled the nose up to join on the Skyhawk.

"Heads up, Pouncer Two. Missile approaching from Hanoi."

Denny's transmission was drowned out by the loud warble of Dick's APR-27. He was targeted by a Fansong radar.

"It's on your tail!" screamed Denny. "Break left, Pouncer Two. Break left!"

With more than six g's on the shuddering Crusader, Dick snapped his head around to look for the missile. He almost fainted from the pain in his neck, but stayed in afterburner and kept the turn going. Then he saw the missile's nose and part of its belly. It was flying a perfect rendezvous on him.

He made one last desperate jerk of the stick in a belated attempt to force an overshoot. Then he was engulfed in orange smoke as the missile's three hundred pound warhead exploded alongside his hapless Crusader. His head banged against the cockpit rail . . .

Dick awoke with a start. His head had slipped off the pillow and struck the window frame of the Cathay Pacific 747. He raised his hand to search for a lump, and was blinded by a brilliant flash of lightning. It was 2:30 in the morning. They were halfway between Bangkok and Hong Kong, and had found the thunderstorms lurking over northern Laos. The huge aircraft lurched drunkenly through the chaotic skies. The pilots fought for control. Thankfully, the line of storms was not wide, and they were soon clear of the turbulence.

"Damn, damn!" swore Dick silently. "How do I get into these situations?"

A week earlier, he'd been glad to hear Colonel Mackenzie was returning from the Falklands. His SAS team had been on the islands for three months. They'd witnessed the invasion, and recorded the deployment of Argentine forces, before being withdrawn by submarine.

Dick had eagerly awaited the Colonel's return to SHAPE. Disturbed by his phone conversation with the President, which indicated a U.S. betrayal of Admiral Toufani, he wanted to expedite planned airdrop missions to resupply the anti-Khomeini guerrillas. British and French sources at NATO encouraged him with promises of support. However, the program belonged to

Mackenzie and they had to await his return.

Yesterday, the stocky, broad-shouldered, ruddy-faced Scotsman, bedecked in his formal kilt uniform, had banged on the door jamb of Dick's outer office and called loudly: "Permission to come aboard, Sir!"

His new receptionist was startled. Dick sprang to the doorway and embraced the gaunt officer. "Damn it, Mac! Where the hell have you been? You look terrible."

Mackenzie returned Dick's embrace and smiled. "Been on a diet of Falklands' rabbits and berries, Brown Bear."

"Must have been skinny rabbits. You lost ten kilos."

They released each other. Mackenzie followed Dick past the receptionist into his office. His sharp blue eyes sparkled at the shocked expression on the girl's face.

"It's okay, lassie," he laughed. "Didn't they warn you that fighter pilots will hug anything in a skirt?"

Dick pulled him into the inner office and closed the door.

"Glad you're back, Colonel. I was really worried when I heard an SAS helo went down in that blizzard on South Georgia."

"Yeah," Mackenzie ran a rough hand over his closely cropped red hair, "we lost some fine chaps in that episode; but we let the bloody Argentine Foreign Minister know the Queen didn't accept his fait accompli, of occupying the islands."

Dick retreated to a table in the corner for some coffee. "There's another reason I'm glad you're back. The President himself told me he's dumping Admiral Toufani. We have to make another airdrop, as soon as possible."

Mackenzie took the coffee and seated himself on the couch. He stared at the half-empty cup. "You must need a coffee *airdrop*, Bear."

Dick took the Bushmills from his desk drawer and passed it to the Scotsman. "The coffee's only in case the Supreme Commander walks in. You look like you need this more than caffeine."

"You're right about that," sighed the United Kingdom's Special Air Service representative to NATO. "We got caught with our blooming knickers down in the Falklands."

"I heard there was a joint SAS/SBS landing on the islands last Saturday. That should put the Queen back on the throne."

"It's more complicated now, Dick. One of our submarines put

more torpedoes into the *General Belgrado* than they should have. That old cruiser, which you gave them, has gone down with over three hundred dead."

"Damn," muttered Dick. "What's the Argentine answer going to be to that?"

Mackenzie showed him a dispatch. "We already have it. A few hours ago, HMS *Sheffield* was attacked by a Super Etendard with an Exocet missile. It scored a direct hit. The destroyer sank like a rock, with all hands on board."

Dick's face blanched. He asked thoughtfully: "How are you going to stop that? Where did they get them? How many do they have?"

"Thank God it's still May," grunted the Scotsman. "The French were scheduled to deliver a full squadron of fourteen Super Etendards and twenty Exocets to them by the end of July." He paused to sip the Bushmills, then continued: "They already have five of those planes, with at least one missile per aircraft."

"Why hasn't the U.K. already taken them out, Mac? Seems to me that would have been the first order of business."

"It was Northwood's top priority, but the Prime Minister vetoed it." The Scotsman shook his massive head sadly. "She's imposed rules of engagement that forbid strikes against the Argentine mainland. Those five Super Etendards sit in a row on the flight line at Rio Gallegos. A blind Sea Harrier driver with one arm could take them out in one pass." The highly decorated SAS officer set his coffee cup on the table and filled it with Bushmills.

"Can you stop them in the air, Mac?"

"Obviously we cannot. There are only thirty-two Sea Harriers in existence. They're doing a great job keeping the A-4 Skyhawks, which you gave the Argentines, off our fleet; but the Super Etendards can take station beyond the Harriers' range and launch Exocets whenever they choose."

Mackenzie took a stiff drink. "Once that damned thing is in the air, it's all over. Sea Dart missiles are no good against low flying targets. Sea Wolf could hit an Exocet under the right conditions, but it's only deployed on two ships. God help us, Dick, both our carriers, *Hermes* and *Invincible,* are down there! If the Super Etendards find them, our fleet will be defenseless--it could be annihilated."

"What's your good old NATO partner, the United States of America, doing about all this?"

"Well, . . . they turned down our request for AWAC's. It could have helped a lot; but, given our rules of engagement, it couldn't stop the Exocet threat. It's an impossible situation, Captain, that calls for impossible means."

The Scotsman smiled at the quizzical look on Dick's face. "Like Frazier's old saying, 'it's fighter pilot time again.' Are you ready to play?"

"What the hell could I do?" scoffed Dick. "Want me to sneak into Argentina and blow up those Etendards on the flight line?"

Mackenzie chuckled. "Damn, you are a perceptive son-of-a-bitch. I don't want you to blow them up, but I want you to get me some Czech Sematex so I can."

"You do that--against the Prime Minister's ROE--and she'll be feasting on Rocky Mountain oysters, Scotsman-style."

Mackenzie smiled. "What that sweet lass doesn't know, won't hurt her."

"Well," said Dick, "my counter-terrorism team has a little C-4, but it's under strict control. I couldn't get my hands on it without attracting a world of attention."

"That's also my problem. When I approached the Prime Minister with my solution to the Exocets, she turned me down flat. Then she issued an order placing double safeguards on our military supply of plastic explosives."

He paused to down the last of the Bushmills. "So, . . . fighter pilot, . . . here's what we're going to do."

At 4:30 in the morning, the streets in the Kowloon side of Hong Kong were deserted. It was a quick taxi ride from the airport to the fabulous old Peninsula Hotel. Its colorful lighted fountain was glowing in the early morning light.

Dick checked in, using the Edward Orden passport and identification that *Purple* had established for him earlier. Reservations had assigned him to room 535, but Dick asked the night clerk if he could stay on the sixth floor. His request was approved.

Stepping into the elevator behind the bellboy, Dick felt a sudden coldness. Only one year ago, he'd ridden this elevator during the farewell party for Project Aura. He and Jim Conrad had been on their way to room 535, to warn Joe Tashki that German commandos, working for *Herr* Strauss, were in the hotel. They had arrived too late. Joe had died from using the cyanide-laced toothpaste intended for Dick.

Unpacking in room 635, Dick grimaced as he laid the tube of Colgate by the sink. It was the same brand he'd lent Joe.

He had been traveling for twenty hours and was dog-tired, but memories of his friendship with Joe Tashki haunted him. Dick knew what would happen if he continued to think about the Aura Project. Memories of Rita, which he tried so hard to block from his mind, would invade his very soul and send him spiraling into a deep depression.

He went to the window and stared down at the fountain, forcing himself to focus on the current situation. Tomorrow, he'd make an appointment with Consuela. Picturing her big dark eyes and beautiful dusky face quieted his raw nerves. They'd met in 1966, when the USS *Oriskany* was in Hong Kong for a port visit. She was the nineteen-year-old wife of a Cuban MiG-21 pilot, who flew for the North Vietnamese. Dick had saved her from an abusive situation involving other air wing pilots. They developed a close friendship during their few days together--before the *Oriskany* returned to Yankee Station.

He'd lost track of her, but they had been reunited last year by an accidental meeting during the Project Aura termination party. She was working for an arms dealer in Macáu, and was on holiday in Hong Kong. After one glorious night together, Dick had been forced to flee to Europe to escape Strauss's killers.

Now, they would again be reunited--this time with the survival of the British Fleet at stake. Dick went to bed, pulled the covers over his eyes, and fell asleep.

The faint rapping on the door woke him. He rubbed his eyes and looked at his watch. "Ah, damn! It's four in the afternoon."

The rapping continued. "One moment, please," he called.

Dick climbed from the bed and went to the door in his T-shirt and shorts. He ran his fingers through his tousled hair and peered through the view finder. It was a bellboy pushing a cart laden with silver covered dishes, a bottle of champagne, and a vase with a single flower. The bellboy's cap was obviously too big. His face was obscured by the brim and his falling hair.

Dick opened the door and read the message on the card lying in front of the flower. "Compliments of MAC."

"Come in," yawned Dick.

The bellboy pushed the cart through the door, Dick retreated to the night table for his wallet. He opened the top drawer. Reaching for the wallet, he heard the door lock click behind him. Bellboys don't lock doors!

He pushed the wallet aside, grabbed the Beretta, whirled, and dropped to his knees. With his arm extended across the bed, he leveled the cocked pistol at the figure in the maroon uniform.

The bellboy's left hand was lifting one of the silver plate-covers. He was leaning forward, his right hand poised to grasp the object underneath.

"Freeze!" ordered Dick, in a stern voice.

The bellboy's hands stopped, he stood motionless.

"Put that lid down slowly, and raise your hands."

The bellboy responded carefully. He stepped back from the cart with both hands at shoulder-level.

"Don't move unless I tell you," growled Dick. "Now . . . very slowly . . . raise your right hand over your head and unbutton that coat with your left hand."

The bellboy's left hand went to the bottom button. Long, slim fingers began the task Dick had assigned them. The nails were perfectly manicured. A grin flickered across Dick's face. It was the first time he'd seen hot-pink fingernails on a bellboy.

The elegant fingers finished with the top button, and the maroon jacket fell open to reveal a white silk shirt tucked into the uniform trousers. The left hand joined the other over her head.

"Hold your arms straight out to the side," ordered Dick.

The jacket opened wider to reveal interesting bulges in the shirt.

"Lower your arms . . . hold them out behind you . . . shrug your shoulders . . . let the jacket drop."

She twisted her shoulders from side-to-side, the bulges in the shirt swayed seductively. The jacket fell away.

"You're wasting your time as a bellboy," observed Dick.

Then he remembered Jim's warning. Marshal-art feet are more dangerous than hidden weapons, but it's impossible to kick with trousers around your ankles.

"Raise your right hand above your head," he ordered sternly. "Now, very slowly, unbutton your trousers with your left hand."

There was no zipper. The slender fingers moved carefully down the four buttons, the trousers fell to her ankles.

Dick caught his breath. "*Beine ohne ende!*" was the German expression--legs without end. When Dick's eyes arrived at where they did end, another grin flickered across his face. Hot-pink panties peeked out from under the shirt tail. The white silk shirt was now free to cling to a sharply pointed bosom with remarkable separation.

A smile flooded his face. There was only one body like that in the world. It had been a long year since he'd seen it in all its glory. This game was too delicious to end.

"Step out of those trousers," he ordered sternly, "and those awful shoes."

She meekly complied, with her head down and her face covered by the over-sized cap. "What now, Gringo?" she whispered in the husky voice he loved.

"Come over here . . . by the bed."

She moved around the serving cart and stood by the side of the bed, opposite him. She arched her shoulders, proudly pushing the silk shirt out in front of her.

"Oh yeah!" Dick smiled. "Don't I know you?"

Her nimble fingers made quick work of the shirt's buttons, she tossed it to a chair. Once again, she arched her shoulders. "Do these look familiar, you ancient Yankee?"

Dick chuckled. "I think I saw those sitting in a Hilton Hotel stairwell, but I can't be sure. Let's check the ground floor." He motioned with the pistol at the pink panties.

She leaned forward to remove them, he caught his breath. She turned away from him, her hands went to the cap. A moment later, long black tresses tumbled down the middle of her shapely back.

Dick laid the Beretta on the night table and climbed on the bed. She turned to him. It was the same delicate dusky face, the same deep dark eyes, that had kept him awake so many nights.

He rested his hands on her shapely hips. She put her arms around him and drew him to her womanly beauty. "You Yankee bastard," she moaned, "you stood me up last year. Show me why I should forgive you."

He raised his head, his mouth found her tremulous lips, he held her tightly and fell backwards on the bed.

Their passion had been kindled during their first meeting seventeen years ago--but had not burst into flame until their meeting last year. Now, it flared again! They sought each other fiercely, exploding together with fiery energy, then ebbing slowly with the tide, then rebounding with the force of a wild hurricane.

Dick lay quietly on his back, breathing deeply to catch his breath. She moved over him, her black silky hair caressing his chest, a tender smile lighting her beautiful face.

"Not bad for a dead man."

"I'm sorry, Connie. I wanted to call you, but I had to leave Hong Kong in a hurry--bad guys were around me until the last minute."

She brushed his temples with her bruised lips. "I cried an ocean for you that night, Dick. Hotel security told me it was you who'd been murdered in room five-three-five. It was two months before I found out it was a Japanese man."

There was a catch in Dick's voice: "He was a good friend. He used some poisoned toothpaste that was meant for me."

She lowered her full bosom to his chest and teased his lips with her tongue.

Dick continued: "I called this hotel a couple times from Europe, hoping to catch you here, but no luck."

In between soft kisses on his face, she explained: "Much like you, *Captain Orden,* I generally use an alias when traveling. I forgive you, Honey. There was no way we could have safely contacted each other. Thank you for trying."

They embraced tenderly, each attempting to draw the other's soul into their body.

Finally, she raised her head and caressed him with glistening black eyes. "I was so happy when I learned you were still alive. You'll never know how deeply I fell in love with you, after you rescued me from that stairwell in '66. You tore away part of my heart when you left for Vietnam, without taking me to bed. I tried for years to forget you, but I never could. When God gave you back to me for that one night last year, I tried so hard to get pregnant. I wanted a part of you to cherish the rest of my life."

With his fingertips, Dick gently traced the small of her back and the delightful curve of her hips. He decided against telling her about his vasectomy twenty years earlier. Instead, he said: "I can imagine how beautiful our little girl would be. She'd drive all the boys crazy--just like her mother."

Her lips found his, and her tongue thrust passionately into his mouth, as she wildly renewed her desire for motherhood.

They lay quietly, side-by-side, completely exhausted. The lights of the lighted fountain below played against the window pane, casting romantic colors around the room.

Dick's fingers found his watch on the night table. "My dear bell-boy, it's midnight. What's your boss going to say? You'd better hurry down to the concierge desk."

She laughed quietly. "That's only my day job, Yankee."

"Well, give it up. It's a shame to waste talent like yours pushing dinner carts."

"Especially when I have to spend eight hours in bed waiting for a tip."

"Oh, I'm sorry, I forgot. Let's see--what's customary--another twenty percent?" He rolled on his side and began again to explore her magnificent body.

She tenderly stopped his fingers and whispered: "It's time we both went to work. It's too dangerous to talk in here, Dick. We'll have to take a walk."

"Connie, if anyone's been listening to us, that business an hour ago would have blown the fuses in their recorder."

She squeezed his hand. "Parts of me are still burning, Yankee, but you'll have to wait till tomorrow night to quench the fire."

Dick glanced sideways as the slim figure in black took the place next to him on the bench in the crowded Star Ferry.

"Anyone following you?" he asked quietly.

"My Homboldt bodyguards are sound asleep," she replied, "but let's walk to the Hilton separately. We can meet in the bar."

Dick grinned. "Do that often?"

She gave him an elbow in the ribs. "Behave yourself, Gringo. You're on my turf now."

There was a noisy party in the back of the bar. A British cruiser was in port, and the officers were out on the town. Dick seated himself at a table along the far side of the room.

He was looking at the drink card when a slight hand touched him on the shoulder. "Got a light, sailor?"

Consuela's dark eyes smiled at him. She brought a long, tapered cigarette holder to her painted lips.

"No, as a matter of fact, I don't."

She laid a silver lighter on the table in front of him. "Then use this."

"Didn't know you smoked," he said.

She leaned toward him and laughed lightly: "I don't, but how else could an old guy like you pick up a girl in a bar."

He rose and offered her a chair. She brushed seductively against him and sat down. He signaled the waitress and ordered two Jack Daniels on the rocks.

"Now that you've succeeded in picking me up," her black eyes were shining, "what are we going to talk about?"

"Let's start with how a nice girl like you gets mixed up with the likes of Colonel Mackenzie."

"I might ask you the same question, *Captain Orden.* If that's the kind of company you keep, it's no wonder someone poisons your toothpaste."

"Yeah, he's a character," agreed Dick. "I've been working with him since I reported to NATO--shortly after the last time I saw you. How long have you known him?"

She ignored his question. "Does he know we know each other?"

"No, but he told me I'd be meeting the girl of my dreams."

They paused as the waitress set the drinks in front of them. She bowed politely as Dick paid the bill, then left with the generous tip.

"Don't forget you still owe me a tip," pouted Consuela.

"You're an animal! Now, tell me about you and Mackenzie."

"I told you last year that Moscow encouraged me to have a relationship with an elderly official at the U.S. Consulate, before they sent me to Homboldt Trading in Macáu."

"Yes, I remember," said Dick.

She continued: "He gave a birthday party for me at the Consulate. Mackenzie was there. He was very charming in his Scottish kilt."

"Yeah," Dick laughed, "great pair of legs."

Consuela smiled. "Quiet down, Yankee. Unfortunately, he was as inhibited as you were--always talking about his family--but we became good friends. He has a very good heart."

"Mac's heart is made of cold steel," grunted Dick. "He never makes friends without a reason. What did he want from you?"

Consuela's dark eyes snapped at him. "I wish he'd wanted sex, but he didn't. He was working for MI-6, and wanted information from the Consulate office where my elderly friend worked."

Dick leaned back in his chair and chuckled. "The little girl from Camaguey, wife of a deceased Cuban MiG pilot, employed by Moscow, spying on America for England. How in the hell have you lived this long?"

"One day at a time," she smiled coolly, "just like you. Now be quiet and let me finish. What Mac wanted was simple, and I got it for him quickly. He asked for a few things later, mostly about the U.S. response to the British giving Hong Kong to the communists, and I was able to comply. Mac left for London about the same time that I went to work for Homboldt. He returned a couple years later, invited me to dinner, showed me a Swiss bank account established in my name, and promised me some really big money--if I'd do a little copying for him."

"Copying what?" asked Dick sharply.

"Orders," breathed Connie quietly. "Orders for weapons from terrorist organizations all around the world."

"Oh my God!" grimaced Dick. "You're really into it aren't you. Your life isn't worth a plugged nickel."

"Yeah," she grinned, "but my Swiss bank account's bigger than some corporations."

He enclosed her slim hand in his. "Where do you think you'll ever get to spend it?"

She sighed. "I was hoping in a small American town, where we could raise our little girl."

Dick closed his eyes and bowed his head. Then he looked tenderly at her and said: "Hope is the stuff dreams are made of, Honey. I'm very proud and happy to be part of yours."

"You didn't come all the way to Hong Kong to dream with me, lover boy. Let's get down to business. What have you got for me from Mac?"

"He told me to first kiss you and tell you that's what he always wanted to do--then to say thanks for the information he received last November--then to place an order with you."

"Well, . . ." Connie's black eyes shone, "you can tell him you kissed me, but you'd better leave out what went on for the next eight hours. Tell him thanks for the deposit last December, but I have no idea what he means by placing an order."

"He said it was too sensitive to communicate in writing," said Dick. "That's why I'm here. He understood from your November information that Homboldt's handling a large order for the Shining Path in Peru. Is that correct?"

"Yes, the order came from their headquarters in Lima, but the delivery's to be made in southern Chile."

"Great! That's what he was hoping for. He wants you to double the order for the Czech Sematex, if you can do it without getting in trouble."

Consuela paused, looked down, and touched her fingertips carefully together. Dick smiled. That had been Ambassador Mumfred's favorite expression of deep thought during Country Team meetings at the embassy in Manila.

"Yes, that can be done," she hesitated, ". . . without too much danger. I have access to Homboldt's shipping computers and can change the order before the boat is loaded tomorrow night. We've already processed the billing portion of Shining Path's order, so the soonest anyone could notice a problem is when the extra Sematex arrives in Chile."

"Mac says his Shining Path contact will be there to remove the extra Sematex. I hope he knows what he's talking about."

Connie's serious dark eyes brightened. "Doesn't matter! Those bastards wouldn't tell us if we sent them too much of anything."

"Yeah, but what about at your end? Won't the over-shipment be caught in a Homboldt inventory somewhere along the line?"

"Yes," she nodded. "I can keep it hidden for awhile; but Homboldt has Chinese bookkeepers, and you know how relentless they can be."

"Honey," said Dick earnestly, "if this places you in jeopardy, forget it!"

"Do you know what Mac's going to do with the stuff?"

"Yeah, he's going to save the British Fleet from Argentine

Exocet missiles."

"That magnificent bastard!" Consuela smiled shyly. "Isn't he fantastic? Always on some crusade to save the world."

"Who's going to save you, pretty girl?"

"You were there for me once before, Dick, in a dark stairwell. I'm sure my White Knight will reappear--if and when I need him."

Air Chief Marshal Edward Frazier was the consummate professional military officer. At sixty, his tall slender body would undoubtedly still fit in the cockpit of a Spitfire, where he'd began his illustrious career as an eighteen-year-old fighter pilot in the Battle of Britain. His striking angular face, with its high cheek bones, was framed by graying temples; but his full head of wavy hair was black. His aristocratic, clean-shaven chin was set firmly as his piercing dark eyes scanned the paper in his hand.

"Why the bloody hell should I allow my Studies Branch Supervisor to go into East Germany?" Frazier raised his voice in utter disbelief. "If they make you, we could lose an unacceptable level of this headquarters' secrets!"

He tempered his tone and dropped Dick's written request on his desk. "This says the purpose of your trip is to make contact with some Hungarians working at the StadtBerliner Hotel."

"Yes Sir. I have information that nine Hungarians are serving Chairman Honecker his lunch on a daily basis. Thought it'd be nice if we could listen to what the East German Council of Ministers are saying over the goulash."

"Is this your idea, or Jim Conrad's?"

Dick sipped the scotch and sighed. "Sir, I haven't had an original idea since I gave you Paula's phone number in Manila; but this would provide a deep cover if they did catch me. They'd be more likely to think I was there to enlist Hungarians, than to help Jim Conrad stop an assassination attempt on the U.S. President."

Frazier looked up sharply. "I know you have an intense loyalty for Mountie--as do I--but I can't afford to lose you."

Dick took a deep breath, leaned back on the Deputy Commander's couch, stared at the scotch in his hand, and said quietly: "It's *Eagle One* we can't afford to lose, Sir. After all the blundering idiots we've suffered through in the White House, he's finally got the Soviets on the run. We can't take the chance of them hitting him at Checkpoint Charlie."

Frazier rose from his desk, grabbed the bottle of Chivas in one hand, a sheaf of papers in the other, and joined Dick on the couch. "Talk about idiocy!" he exclaimed. "Why does he have to visit Berlin now, right in the middle of all these terrorist attacks?"

"Obviously he wants to set an example, Sir. They've been blowing hell out of our boys--the Officers Clubs at Hanau, Gelnhausen, Bamberg, . . . and even Fifth Army Headquarters in Frankfurt. His congressional opposition's clamoring for him to back away from mid-range nucs in Western Europe. This is his Hollywood way of responding to them. He's hoping the media will pick up on it, and create a little patriotic fervor back in the States."

"Fat chance of your disinterested couch-potato public reacting to anything but the weather report," scoffed Frazier. "If terrorists stuffed your President in a body-bag at Checkpoint Charlie, the news would be pre-empted by a re-run of *Deep Throat*."

The Deputy Commander of NATO's Supreme Headquarters Allied Powers Europe glanced at another paper in his hand. "Our intelligence people don't think there's much of a threat. They say Brezhnev wouldn't risk an assassination, even if it was handed to him on a silver platter."

"Exactly what our old cowboy's doing!" said Dick. "I say we'd better believe Jim Conrad's report, that a couple Palestinian crazies and the RZ--the Revolutionary Cells--are going after him."

"I trust Mountie completely," replied Frazier vehemently, "but isn't he inside a different German terrorist group, the *Rote Armee Fraktion?*"

"Yeah, but they exchange information rather freely."

"What does Jim say about the RAF's response to the President's visit?"

"No problem there. Moscow has them firmly under control. Mountie's trying to convince the RAF leadership to stop the RZ by using force, if necessary, but he's not sure he's succeeding. It'll be the last minute before he knows whether the RZ rogues and their Palestinian buddies will make an assassination attempt, . . . and whether the RAF will try to stop it."

"Is he playing a lone hand over there?" asked Frazier.

"Yes Sir. That's why I've made this request to go into East Germany. Jim's asked me to cover his back, while he picks snipers off the roofs around Checkpoint Charlie."

". . . and where would you be doing that? Atop the StadtBerliner Hotel?"

"You're very perceptive, Sir."

"Not really, Brown Bear, I read the report on Operation *Trout* in your CIA file. If you took off the head of that North Vietnamese Colonel from nine hundred meters, you must be bloody good with a Makarov. You wouldn't be trying to smuggle one of those into East Berlin, would you?"

"No Sir, Mountie has everything in position."

There was a knock on the door. Commodore Twillinger entered with a large folder.

"Sorry to interrupt. These just arrived in the U.S. diplomatic pouch." He handed the folder to Frazier. "I believe we've won the war in the Falklands, Sir."

The Air Chief Marshal spread the photos on his desk and put on his glasses. "Take a look at these, Brown Bear." He pointed with a pencil at the details on one of prints. "Isn't that the tail structure of a Super Etendard?"

Dick glanced quickly at several of the photos. They showed the smoldering blackened hulks of five destroyed aircraft, amid rows of intact A-4 Skyhawks. "Yes Sir, surely looks like it. I heard reports the Argentines only had five of those Exocet shooters. Do you know who took the pictures, Commodore?"

"They're marked courtesy of the U.S. Naval Attaché at your embassy in Buenos Aires. Guess he traveled a long way to take them."

Frazier smiled. "I'd bet the chap who torched those beauties also took the pictures. Make sure Mackenzie sees these when he returns from furlough."

3

DANNY'S CORONATION

The bow of the fifty-foot cruiser was pounding through rough waves. Dick gritted his teeth and hung on, pushing against the wood partition in front of him, forcing his aching back against the foam layer behind him.

He and Jim Conrad had been imprisoned for five hours in the false-bottom enclosures built into the cruiser's bow, but they had traveled less than halfway to their destination, Managua. Their route took them from the Costa Rican border, up the 100-mile length of Lake Nicaragua, then via the connecting waterway to Lake Managua. Their three-by-seven-foot enclosures were only eighteen inches deep. A crack, hidden by the bow railing, provided air but little light.

The first few hours had been a comfortable ride through calm waters. Then the cruiser was tossed around by a heavy storm, and a flood of claustrophobic nausea had swept over Dick. He struggled to focus his mind on the details of their trip. He and Jim Conrad had waited three years for this mission. They were enroute to kill Ahmad Salah--and avenge the death of their beloved partner, Rita Jay.

Ahmad and his Mafia partner, Enrico, had kidnapped Rita while they were running a white-slave ring from the Philippines. They savagely abused her, and almost killed her with an overdose of heroin. She was rescued by Jim and Dick during a raid on Salah's auction in Manila. It had taken her a year to recover.

Her first assignment after rejoining *Purple* had been to return a terrorist to the Philippines for trial. Ahmad and Enrico somehow found out about the mission, ambushed her convoy near the Manila airport, and destroyed the limousine in which she was transporting her prisoner. They used RPG-7's with phosphorous grenades. No bodies were recovered.

Weeks later, while delivering the White House ransom for the release of NATO's General Thomas, Dick encountered Enrico at a Mafia headquarters in Sicily. He avenged Rita by killing the thug with eight shots in the groin from her Beretta.

Ahmad Salah was also a Syrian intelligence officer. He had hidden his participation in the white-slave ring from the President of Syria. After learning the details of Enrico's death, he surrounded himself with bodyguards. An expert blackmailer, his diplomatic star began to rise. He developed influential contacts in Libya and the Soviet Union. When the Damascus regime promoted him to a foreign ministry post in Moscow, Salah eagerly accepted the assignment. Life in the Soviet Union added another layer of security from the *Purple* organization, which had pledged revenge for Rita. Now, Dick and Jim were enroute to Managua to fulfill that pledge.

In spite of White House backing of the oppressive Somoza regime, Nicaragua had fallen to the leftist Sandinistas. The U.S. President then organized and supported Contra guerrillas to attack them. When the President was re-elected, the Sandinistas also held elections. Their President-elect decided on an inaugural ceremony, mimicking the Washington celebration, and enraging the American President by inviting communist delegations into the Western Hemisphere.

Through his Red Army Faction terrorist contacts in Moscow, Jim Conrad learned Ahmad Salah would accompany the Kremlin's delegation to Danny Ortega's coronation. It was the break *Purple* had been hoping for. The jackal was coming out of his hole--Jim and Dick would be waiting.

Dick groaned as the cruiser slammed into the crest of another wave. The jarring was taking its toll on the ruptured discs in his back. He'd nursed the injury since his Vietnam days. The high speed ejection from Aura One four years earlier had sealed his fate. It had forced his departure from NATO, and his retirement from the Navy.

At the encouragement of Nelson, *Purple's* field supervisor in Frankfurt, Dick had moved to Vienna with Maria. Jim Conrad remained undercover in the RAF. They had continued to work as a team against Kremlin-supported terrorist groups, which emanated in the Middle East and transited Europe to attack NATO targets.

When Dick began experiencing periods of paralysis in his legs, Nelson had insisted that he take some time off. It presented the perfect opportunity for him to fulfill the American President's earlier request, to monitor a suspected Soviet agent at his alma mater, the University of Nebraska-Lincoln.

The person in question had fled Eastern Europe during the fifties. Highly educated, and speaking fluent Russian, *George* had spent a few months with U.S. Army Intelligence before being assigned to Radio Free Europe in Munich. He moved up quickly through the State Department ranks, and became a noted expert on Eastern Europe. Apparently not satisfied with government work, he went into academia--earned a Ph.D.--and became a Professor of Political Science at UN-L. He maintained his State Department ties and often served as a translator for sensitive materials. He was widely published. Dick had read some of his works at NATO, and often wondered how the author had gotten such accurate information about the WARSAW PACT--months before it became known to NATO intelligence.

When the new administration took over the White House in '81, the emphasis switched from human rights to reigning in the evil empire. Rapid advancement of disarmament talks was a priority. George frequently journeyed from Nebraska to serve as a front-line interpreter. Something about his perfection with the Russian language, and his personal emphasis on certain topics that were later reflected in Soviet START-talk positions, piqued the White House staff's interest. When the President learned that Dick was leaving NATO and the Navy, he personally petitioned Nelson for Dick's assignment to Lincoln--as a Ph.D. candidate in political science, and George's student.

With the goal of expanding her career to include an American license as a Registered Nurse, Maria went to Lincoln with Dick. He found himself in a political science department dominated by those who had led anti-Vietnam protests ten years earlier. It became the most distasteful period of his thirty years of service to his country. Balancing the surveillance of George with caring for his mother, who was in the advanced stages of Alzheimer's; and completing the Ph.D. academic requirements, while instructing a minimum load of 150 students, proved challenging. However, he enjoyed the youthful enthusiasm and wholesome viewpoints of his mid-America charges, and the relaxed physical requirements gave his vertebrae much needed rest.

It took only a few weeks for Maria to be completely turned off by the snobbery of the faculty. As a veteran of Vietnam--and accused *baby-killer*--Dick was treated like an outcast. He and Maria were accepted by few of the two dozen "classroom cradle-to-grave" faculty members. With the exception of George and a couple others, none had ventured beyond their protective hallowed halls of ivy.

Dick hoped for an assignment as George's graduate assistant. Unfortunately, he had to work his way through two of the worst of the former hippies before George finally became his advisor. He was then able to gain access to George's private office. Little was to be learned from his computers or phone conversations, which Dick recorded with the help of *Purple*. When George asked for help in preparing his backyard for his forthcoming wedding reception, Dick volunteered to installed some permanent garden lights--compete with *bugs*. The information gathered from that system reinforced White House staff suspicions.

By the end of the first semester, Maria had enough! She returned to their apartment in Vienna and resumed her work at the Red Cross Hospital.

Dick was awaiting the start of the second semester, when he got the Skyfone call from Nelson. Ahmad Salah was coming out! Dick was directed to rendezvous with Jim at the Juan Santamaria Airport in San José, Costa Rica.

They hadn't seen each other for a year. It was a great reunion. They had no hotel reservations, and it was the height of the tourist season, so they spent the night partying on the Calle Central. They found the old Coca-Cola depot in time to catch the morning bus to Los Chiles.

At a Jesuit monastery overlooking the Rio Frio, they worked out their assassination plan. Two of the Jesuits had been saved from a Salvadoran death squad by a daring *Purple*-coordinated rescue a few years earlier. Sources in Nicaragua had forwarded Nelson an invitation list for the inauguration. When he saw that it included Jesuit delegates from Costa Rica, he had visited the monastery and secured their cooperation.

Purple had used the cruiser, and its secret compartments, in the rescue of the priests from El Salvador and later given it to the Jesuits. They had moved it to their monastery on the Frio River and used it to visit parishes along the San Juan River, which flowed from Lake Nicaragua to the Caribbean Sea and separated Nicaragua from Costa Rica. Given the lack of roads, Lake Nicaragua was a normal travel route from Costa Rica to Managua.

The Sandinistas had invited the Jesuits to send five priests to the inauguration. After the monastery accepted, and forwarded identification papers and travel plans, they received a letter-of-invitation and authenticated photo ID cards from the Ortegan government.

At first light on a cool January morning, Jim and Dick had taken their positions in the secret compartments. The cabin walls were screwed in place over them, and the mission set sail. They passed through the Nicaraguan border check point outside Los Chiles without incident.

The cruiser had steadied in calmer water. Dick's nausea was pushed aside by blinding pain from the cramps burning down his sciatic nerves. Both legs were nearing paralysis, and he urgently needed to urinate.

Suddenly, the cruiser's engines were cut, and he lurched backwards. The silence that followed was shattered by the booming of a .50 caliber machine gun close at hand. They'd been intercepted!

"Hope those bastards shoot over the bow and not through it," thought Dick.

The firing lasted only a few seconds. Then he was thrown sideways in the small enclosure, as the cruiser was unceremoniously bumped by the police barge coming alongside.

A brief look at the Jesuits' letter from the Ortega administration abruptly changed the attitude of the young police lieutenant. He apologized profusely to the priests, had his crew transfer a cask of Nicaraguan rum to the cruiser, and volunteered to escort them to their destination.

Dick couldn't understand their Spanish, but it was easy to discern the change in the tone of the voices. The priests took advantage of the situation by having the lieutenant stamp an inspection clearance on their invitation.

As the cruiser's engines roared back to life, Dick's thoughts turned again to his most pressing problem. He had to urinate-- urgently!

The Jesuits appreciated Dick and Jim's physical limitations.

They had intended to open the enclosures for a break before the police barge appeared. Now they had the problem of arousing suspicion if they declined the police escort. The cruiser's captain resolved the situation by explaining it was necessary for them to proceed to a nearby port for refueling.

The police barge sped off down the coast line, and the priests removed the screws in the cabin walls. Jim and Dick were freed to enjoy a comfort break, a sandwich, and a shot of Nicaraguan rum. Within ten minutes, they were again locked in their enclosures, and the captain pulled into a fueling dock.

While later transiting the waterway that joined Lake Nicaragua and Lake Managua, they were boarded twice by aggressive police patrols; but the letter signed by President Ortega always resulted in immediate clearance to proceed.

It was after midnight when they dropped anchor off the city of Managua. They were on schedule. It would take Jim a couple hours to apply the disguises for Dick and himself. It began with a solution that darkened their faces, hands, and arms. Jim was an expert, but the dim light in the cruiser's hold provided a challenge.

It had been a long day for the priests and the cruiser's captain. They slept soundly while Jim and Dick prepared themselves. At last, they were ready to don the priestly robes they'd tailored at the monastery. The priest, whose identity Jim would assume, was of medium build. With the new-technology bullet-proof vest underneath the robe, the slender Jim was a close match. The priest that Dick would be portraying was more portly, so he added padding over his vest.

Their new identities were of the two priests whom *Purple* had rescued from El Salvador. During preparations at the monastery, they'd insisted on accompanying Jim and Dick to the inauguration. Jim had firmly denied their request, later confiding to Dick: "We don't need a couple heroes trying to martyr themselves for us."

The priests had finally agreed to be the two who would surrender their identities, and change places with Jim and Dick, when it was time to go ashore. They would hide in the secret compartments until the other three priests returned from the ceremony. It was important that the same five priests who had left Costa Rica returned to Costa Rica.

It was the beginning of the dry season, the night air was cool. By the dawn's early light, Dick and the Canadian Mountie stood on the cruiser's aft deck and made one final check of each other's costumes.

Jim Conrad was in his early forties. Medium-height, slim and agile, he was in excellent physical condition and normally impeccably dressed. His carefully groomed light-brown hair would be hidden by a wig and the hood of the Jesuit robe. His handsome features were enhanced by the brown stain of the disguise. His intense, deep-set, brown eyes were continually assessing his surroundings. Nothing escaped him, but his disarming boyish smile was always just below the surface. He had served with the Royal Air Force, flying off HMS *Ark Royal,* before joining the RCMP. Fluent in nine languages, and exceptionally intelligent, his first assignment had been undercover against the FLQ in Quebec. He took part in the arrest of the terrorists who'd killed the Labor Minister, and was later named one of Canada's representatives to the elite *Purple* organization--their other choice had been Rita Jay, whose revenge he and Dick were about to exact.

Their only armament would be the silencer-equipped .25 caliber Berettas taped to their left forearms. Their flowing robes would hide the weapons. Dick had sewn ribbons to the insides of the sleeves, so they could be tied to their wrists. Thus, they were able to raise their arms over their heads without the sleeves falling down to reveal the pistols. With their arms folded in a priestly fashion, they could easily free the weapons with their right hands.

As they made a final inspection of their weapons, Jim showed Dick the top bullet in his Beretta's clip. The point had been filed flat and engraved with the letter *S.* "This one's for Salah," he said.

Dick held his clip up for Jim's inspection. All the bullets bore the initial *S.* "You don't mind if I leave these in him too, do you?"

"You're certainly entitled, Bear, but play by the rules. The one closest to the bodyguard has to take him out--the other gets Salah. Otherwise neither of us will return to tell Nelson how it went."

"Yeah, you're right, but when we're finally this close, Salah's going down!"

They faced the cool light breeze blowing from the southeast. As the light improved, they could see the Masaya Park volcano steaming in the distance.

"A fascinating part of the world," observed Jim. "The Indians used to throw virgins into the lava to appease Chaciutique, the goddess of fire. The Spanish regarded it as the entrance to hell."

"Salah won't have far to travel," grunted Dick.

They heard church bells ringing in the distance, and turned to gaze at the ruins of the old cathedral about a mile to the west. They were anchored a half mile off shore. Numerous small craft were between them and the piers, where several yachts lay alongside.

The solitude was broken by the harsh sound of marine engines starting. They saw the flashing red lights of a police cruiser moving away from one of the piers.

"Well, partner," said Jim, "time to wake up our hosts and crawl back in our boxes."

Like the previous police inspections, as soon as the officers saw the invitation letter they became overly polite and helpful. The priests were asked to follow their cruiser through the maze of small boats into the harbor. They tied up to the pier behind the yachts.

A few minutes after the cruiser's engines shut down, the senior priest knocked softly on the cabin wall over Jim's enclosure. Dick listened intently as Father Figueres explained: "Mr. Conrad, we must go ashore to check in with the port authority. We'll return for you as soon as possible."

The cruiser's bow was facing directly into the rising sun, the still air provided little ventilation in the enclosures. With the heavy robes over their fatigues, Jim and Dick became quite uncomfortable. They were sweating profusely--it would be a real test for the facial disguises Jim had created. Dick felt a cramp coming into his right leg, he focused his mind against it.

Finally, he heard the screws being removed from the false wall. Dick squinted into the bright light. Jim assisted him from the enclosure. He staggered from the painful leg cramp and fell onto a narrow bed.

While Jim checked their disguises, the two priests who had returned to the cruiser explained: Their papers had been cleared by port authority officials, but the five priests had been told to remain in a waiting room--their transportation to the inaugural ceremony was enroute. When a van flying a Costa Rican flag finally arrived, the two priests had said they needed to return to the cruiser because they'd forgotten their video camera.

As Jim finished Dick's disguise, one of the priests lowered himself into an enclosure and the other installed the cover over his colleague. He handed Dick their ID documents and the video camera, then scrambled into the second enclosure. Dick made quick work of securing the cover.

A few moments later, Dick Williams and Jim Conrad were proceeding up the pier in their priestly attire. Dick fought off the painful leg cramp, and they walked slowly. The pier was swarming with security personnel; all of them assumed these were the same two priests they had just cleared to get a camera from the Costa Rican cruiser.

The elderly Father Figueres sat in the backseat of the van with Dick and Jim. As they wound their way carefully through gathering throngs, he explained quietly in good English: "A fourth of Nicaragua's population lives in this city. President Ortega won't have a problem assembling a crowd for his inauguration. To make sure, he's scheduled it to coincide with the annual celebration for Managua's patron saint, San Sebastian." He chuckled. "The revelry is more for San Sebastian than it is for the prospect of continued government by the Sandinistas."

"Father Figueres," said Dick, "I thought the Sandinistas were having difficulties with the church; that the church was criticizing Ortega for drifting away from the ideals of the revolution. I'm surprised you guys got an invitation, and that you're being treated so royally."

"The church has been critical of the Sandinistas' slowness in land reforms," answered the old priest. "Ortega's making a gesture of friendship at this inauguration. Catholic delegations have been invited from every nation in the Western Hemisphere. The head of the church in Nicaragua, Bishop Vega, will be giving the invocation today. I'll be listening more to his speech than Mr. Ortega's."

They turned east on the Pan-American highway and picked up speed. The elderly priest pointed out the ruins from the '72 earthquake. Thousands of dilapidated shacks crowded the roadside. "As you can see, the economy's not improving. Most of the population still lives in poverty."

Jim Conrad nodded. "Most of the nation's income is spent fighting the Contras from Honduras."

"Yeah," agreed Dick, "my President dumped ten million dollars into arming them. I guess the U.S. corporations, which have been raping Central America since the early nineteen hundreds, must contribute a lot to Republican campaigns."

Father Figueres smiled. "Absolutely! How ironic--your military does a courageous job keeping the Russian bear at bay, while your political foxes raid the chicken coops in your own backyard."

The van slowed, they turned south on Resistance Highway. After a couple miles, they joined a line of cars waiting to pass through a guarded gate into a large field, where a soccer stadium was under construction.

Father Figueres bent forward to speak with the driver. Then he leaned back in his seat and said softly to Jim and Dick. "We're at a check point for vehicles carrying dignitaries to the ceremonies."

Jim said quietly to Figueres: "It's important that we know where the diplomatic corps limousines are parked. If possible, have the driver drop us in that area."

In a few minutes, their van was at the head of the line. Armed guards saluted the Costa Rican flag smartly, then motioned for them to roll down the windows. The priest seated alongside the driver presented their documents. Jim's artistry in disguises passed the test. The van pulled through the gate into a paved parking area.

Vehicles passing through the gate were separated into two lines. Diplomatic corps limousines were directed to the far end of the parking area, they unloaded near a section of partially completed bleachers. The dignitaries were then escorted into a large colorful tent. Other vehicles were directed to a secondary entrance to the soccer field.

Dick muttered to Jim: "Not many limousines in line, what time is it?"

Jim looked in his sleeve at his wristwatch, only inches from the Beretta. "One hour till showtime, Bear. I was told forty nations will be represented, at the ambassador-level or below. Castro and two others will be the only heads-of-state."

There were about twenty vehicles in front of them waiting to off-load at the secondary gate. Father Figueres leaned forward and spoke to the driver. He pulled out of the line and proceeded to the area where vans were being parked.

Figueres whispered to Jim: "You should be able to see the limousine parking area from here. I told the driver we wanted to stretch our legs before the ceremony. He's going to park in our assigned row, and we'll walk back to the entrance."

The sun was bearing down, the humidity was high. After they parked, their driver left to join others in the shade of the bleachers. Dick and the three Jesuits waited by the van, while Jim wandered alone down the row of limousines parked a few yards in front of them. They saw him pause by the Lincoln with the Canadian maple leaf flying from the front fender. None of the drivers paid him any attention, the guards at the tent's entrance were busy saluting dignitaries. In a few moments, he rejoined Dick and the Jesuits.

"Shall we walk to our entrance?" asked Father Figueres.

"Yeah," said Jim. "Guess we're not invited to the reception."

"No, but it's not a big deal." The old priest chuckled. "Our rum at the monastery is much better than theirs."

Jim spoke quietly in Dick's ear: "Our get-away vehicle is the Canadian Ambassador's Lincoln. The key's on the top of the left front tire."

"Will we have a driver?"

"No, we're on our own, Bear. If you're the last one standing when this is over, head up Resistance Street to the Pan-American, then east to Sandina Airport. You remember the plan. There'll be an Otter with Canadian markings that belongs to the embassy. All you have to do is fly it to Honduras."

The Jesuits walking in front of them halted abruptly. Two guards had signaled them to stop.

"Damn," swore Dick quietly. "What going on?"

Then they heard the siren approaching. The guards pushed them clear of the traffic lane, and the limousine rolled through the gate toward them. As it passed, Dick caught a glimpse of the bearded face in the back.

Jim looked out from under his hood at Dick. "There goes your old buddy. Think he recognized you?"

Dick laughed. "Not hardly. I'd have to be thirty years younger, and sitting in the old J-3 Piper Cub we used to fly for him."

The guards stood aside, and the group of priests crossed the traffic lane to the soccer field's entrance. There were two lines waiting to file by girls with metal-detector wands. The three Jesuits went into the right line, but Dick and Jim chose the left--the girl was shorter than her tall colleague.

Jim was first. The young girl smiled at him, and he said in Spanish: "Bless you, my child." He raised his hands high over his head. She ran the wand over his body. His left sleeve covered the Beretta, she didn't raise the wand high enough to detect it. Jim walked through the gate and turned to wait for Dick.

Dick repeated Jim's movements, but didn't risk a greeting. He kept his face hidden, so she couldn't see his blue eyes. As the girl was searching his lower body, Jim called to her in Spanish. She giggled, stepped aside, and motioned Dick through the gate.

As they waited for the last Jesuit to be searched, Dick whispered to Jim: "What the hell did you say to her?"

"I asked if her wand could detect lead in an old pencil."

Thirty minutes after the inauguration was scheduled to begin, the dignitaries were still in the reception tent. The invited guests, jammed inside the soccer field, were surrounded by a long single column of uniformed soldiers. Behind them, thousands of people spilled into dirt roads lined with hundreds of old buses. The street to the paved parking lot, and the exit to Resistance Street, were being kept clear. Armed soldiers were also maintaining open corridors from the reception tent to the shaded bleachers, and to the shaded elevated stage in the middle of the field.

After they entered the field, the Jesuit entourage had been escorted to the standing area in front of the bleachers. They were soon joined by scores of other priests. They had slowly maneuvered their way to a position alongside the corridor leading from the tent to the center of the bleachers.

Armed guards occupied the highest row in the bleachers and the seats at the end of each row. The center aisle led to a hundred or more plush seats reserved for the diplomatic corps. The remainder of the bleacher seats were already filled with well-dressed young people, most likely students. Dick recalled it was the enfranchised sixteen-year-olds who had given Ortega his 67 percent majority in the election.

They'd been standing in the hot sun for almost two hours, and the cramps were coming back to Dick's leg. He sagged against Jim for support.

The RCMP representative to *Purple* looked at his partner and muttered into his priestly hood: "Dick, we'd better plan right now for me to do this alone. You stay with the Jesuits and go back to the boat with them when this is over."

"It's my leg that's cramping, Mountie, not my trigger finger," growled Dick. "Too late anyhow. Here they come."

President-elect Ortega and Cuban President Fidel Castro led the file of dignitaries out of the tent and down the open corridor. The corridor split about ten yards short of Dick and Jim's position. Ortega and Castro continued up the corridor to the center stage.

"Know any of those guys behind them?" asked Dick quietly.

"Yeah," breathed Jim, "the stocky European's the President of Yugoslavia. The guy beside him is number two in the Kremlin. The one in uniform's the Vice President of Argentina. I'd guess the next four are Latin American foreign ministers, and the last guy's Bishop Vega."

The remainder of the dignitaries followed the corridor to the bleachers, passing in front of Jim and Dick before they turned to climb the steps to their reserved seats. Peering from under their hoods, Jim and Dick studied the faces. Together near the head of the line were the Ambassadors of the United States and Canada. It was a long procession. The bleacher seats were filling up.

Jim nudged Dick with his elbow. "Here he comes--white jacket, black trousers."

Dick edged forward to look down the corridor. "Yeah, I see him. I recognize him from the picture you gave me in Manila."

Dick studied the swarthy features of the tall slim Syrian. Bile rose in his throat, from the absolute hatred he felt for the monster who had tortured and killed Rita. He fought for control--then froze as his gaze shifted to the woman walking beside Ahmad Salah, and the big man next to her.

"Holy mackerel, Mountie! The girl's Carla, from Don Paolucci's family in Sicily. The big guy's Jerry, one of Paolucci's body-guards. He's the former SEAL I told you about."

They were approaching Jim and Dick's position. The fingers of Dick's right hand found the end of the tape holding the Beretta to his left forearm. Jim saw his arms move slightly and guessed what he was doing.

"Relax, Bear, we take him on the way out. Otherwise we're dead meat. Keep your head down, so Carla can't see your eyes."

Dick bowed slightly, but kept the curvaceous lower body of the woman in view. He remembered her soft-orange gown from their time together at Paolucci's villa. "What the hell is she doing with that bastard?" he groaned silently.

After they passed, Dick raised his head to watch them climb the steps to their seats.

Was Jerry now Salah's bodyguard? Could a former Navy SEAL be involved with such slime? Dick was relieved to see Jerry extending his arm to steady Carla as they climbed the steps, and then seat himself next to Carla and not Salah. He reassured himself that Don Paolucci had sent Jerry to take care of Carla, and not the Syrian. However, the fact remained: Carla was Salah's companion--and it could only be a sexual relationship.

It was hot and uncomfortable in the robe. Dick felt nauseous as memories of his night with Carla flashed through his mind.

The marital music blaring from the loud-speakers ended. The dignitaries rose from their seats. The Nicaraguan national anthem began. It ended with a roar from the huge crowd, which was pressing in from all sides of the soccer field.

Jim put his face close to Dick's ear. "With this open corridor, we'll have no problem getting to Salah, but our chances of escape are damned slim with all these soldiers. Remember, whoever is closest shoots the bodyguard. The other guy takes Salah."

"I don't believe Jerry's here to guard Salah. Give him the benefit of the doubt, . . . but he's damned quick," remembered Dick. "He's right-handed and carries a big-frame revolver in a shoulder-holster under his left arm."

"Okay, Bear. How's your leg?"

At that moment, the crowd quieted and Bishop Vega began his invocation. Dick was amazed that such a huge mass of people, now extending for at least fifty yards beyond all sides of the soccer field, could be so silent and attentive.

They'd been standing for over three hours. Dick's leg was not doing well. He focused his eyes on Salah's face and remembered the horrid things he and Enrico had done to Rita. The hatred blocked all feeling in his leg.

As the invocation ended, Father Figueres nodded his approval.

Apparently the Bishop had met his expectations. The ceremony proceeded quickly to the swearing in of Nicaragua's duly elected President. The crowd applauded politely, and Ortega began his inaugural address. Dick couldn't understand a word. Suddenly the crowd outside the field started a cheer that turned into a loud roar.

Jim translated for Dick: "He told the soldiers surrounding the field to let all the people in--said it's their ceremony."

The massive surge of people engulfed the soccer field. Dick looked over his shoulder, half expecting the stage to be toppled, but it wasn't. It was surrounded by a ring of soldiers at least four or five deep. Those guarding the corridors between the tent, the stage, and the bleachers were not able to hold their ground. The corridors closed as the soldiers were crushed into the crowd.

Dick and Jim embraced each other tightly to avoid being separated. Jim's brown eyes were smiling from under his hood. "That stupid bastard may have saved our lives. If we can get Salah when he comes down from the bleachers, this crowd will give us a chance to get away."

The roaring and surging of the crowd continued for at least ten minutes. Dick remembered the young children he'd seen entering the gate. Thankfully, there hadn't been many of them. They would not survive the crush of this mob.

Finally the loud-speakers were turned high enough that Ortega's voice could be heard. The crowd quieted. He launched into a forty minute speech that was interrupted by applause only a few times.

After the benediction, a police official took the microphone. Jim translated for Dick. He was urging the crowd to clear a path so the soldiers could escort the presidential party from the stage. He also asked the dignitaries in the bleachers to remain in their seats "for a few minutes" to allow the crowd to clear.

It was thirty minutes before the Ambassadors and Foreign Ministers rose to leave. There was still a crowd of people in front of the stands, but the soldiers that had been sitting on the perimeter of the bleachers formed a phalanx to push through the throng.

"Link your arm with mine, Bear," said Jim. "We don't want to separate until Salah's on the field."

They moved closer to Figueres. Jim addressed him in English: "Thanks for everything, Father. We'll take our leave now, to wreak God's vengeance upon a murderer."

"May He strengthen your right arm, Mr. Conrad," replied the priest, "and give our blessings to Mr. Nelson again--for his miraculous rescue of our brothers from El Salvador. They both say they could not have endured the torture for another day."

"They've more than repaid us by taking part in this mission," said Jim. "Go with God, Father."

Figueres replied by touching them both on their foreheads and making the sign of the cross. "Go with the angels, my sons." Then he drifted away through the crowd.

Dick recalled his own words, the night they rescued the battered and violated Rita from the white-slave auction. He had likened her to an angel--sent to them by God for only a short while--to be taken back to heaven where they would all meet again, someday.

Salah had risen from his seat and started for the middle aisle. Carla and Jerry were following. Dick and Jim were directly in line with that aisle, about ten yards from the bleachers.

They unlocked their arms and simultaneously reached into their left sleeves with their right hands, to free their Berettas from the tape.

Dick prayed quietly: "God, if You're here, we need help. This is Rita's show. Let her know what's happening. We may be seeing her soon, but please let us remove this scum bag from the face of Your earth before You take us."

Salah was halfway down the bleacher steps. Carla and Jerry were a couple steps behind.

"Okay, partner," said Jim. "It's showtime. Got your weapon free?"

Dick nodded. Rita's Beretta was nestled in his hand, ready to repeat the vengeance it had dealt Enrico three years earlier.

"Let's split," continued Jim. "You go left. I'll stay right. The one closest to Salah takes him out. The other has to watch Jerry."

"Roger that, Mountie. Let's lock and load. By the way, it's been a pleasure working with Canada's finest."

Jim grinned. "See you at the car--or the airport. That Canadian Otter's not an F-8 Crusader, but I may let you fly it to Honduras."

Dick pushed through the crowd and moved left. It was slow going, but he was in position when Salah reached the last step.

Salah paused momentarily, waiting for Carla and Jerry. She took hold of the Syrian's left hand, Jerry fell in behind them. Dick grinned and cocked the small pistol. Salah was his! After three years, Rita's Beretta would finally achieve her revenge.

The crowd was unyielding. Salah waited several minutes before leaving the bottom step and pushing his way into the throng.

Dick held his hands against his chest, with the pistol hidden in the robe's flowing sleeves.

He elbowed his way into a position where Salah would pass down his right side. Through the throng, he saw Jim maneuvering to put Salah and Jerry between them.

Peering from his hood, Dick studied the face of the swarthy thug-turned-diplomat. He was sweating profusely. His dark eyes were darting around the crowd. Was he expecting something? He pushed an elderly man to the side, and the lapels of his white jacket fell open to reveal a holster hanging from his left shoulder. Dick guessed the pearl-handled pistol was a 9mm Browning.

Now he was only two steps from Dick. An old woman was between them. Salah shoved her roughly aside, but Dick stepped forward to block his way.

With a toss of his head, Dick threw back his hood and glared at Ahmad Salah. "Still abusing women? You ugly piece of crap!"

Carla recognized Dick and screamed, "Captain!"

Dick was bringing his right hand forward, to press the Beretta's muzzle against Salah's heart, but the old woman grabbed Dick's arm to keep from falling.

In that split second, Salah drew his pistol and shot Dick in the chest. There was immediate chaos. The crowd panicked. Women screamed and men pushed violently to get away.

Salah was knocked off balance and went to his knees. Still screaming, Carla reached down to help him. Dick sagged slowly to the ground. Jerry drew his revolver, but froze as Jim's Beretta pushed against his spine. The Canadian Mountie growled: "Freeze, SEAL man, this is not your fight."

Dick was gasping for breath, but still holding the Beretta. It was in his right hand, clasped to his chest, covered by the robe's sleeve.

Salah was back on his feet, his pistol in his right hand. He gripped Carla's arm with his left. "You know that son-of-a-bitch?" he shouted at her.

He threw her aside and bent over to stare into Dick's face.

Dick was recovering his breath. He smiled into Salah's evil face and said: "Greetings from Rita, you bastard. Say hello to Enrico for me."

The .25 caliber flat-nosed bullet with the initial "S" tore into Salah's nose, and lodged somewhere in his brain.

Jim's kick sent him sprawling into the crowd. The Mountie turned back to Jerry, but the former SEAL holstered his revolver and raised his hands to his shoulders. "You're right, man. This isn't my fight, but Carla's my responsibility. Leave her alone!"

"Okay," said Jim, bending over Dick. "You know this guy--you met three years ago in Sicily." Dick began coughing and spitting blood.

"Yeah," said Jerry, "from Carla's reaction, that has to be Captain Orden."

Carla stopped screaming, but she was in shock. She bent over Salah, watching the blood spurt from his shattered face onto the green grass of the stadium.

Jerry took her arm. "Come on, Baby. He's dead. Let's get out of here."

Jim was feeling Dick's chest, where the vest and padding had stopped Salah's bullet. He called to Jerry, "If you want a ride home, give me some help with the Captain."

"Why not," said the big man. He knelt down and cradled Dick in his bearish arms. "I don't want to face all the questions those Kremlin guys will be asking. You bring Carla." With that, Jerry began bulldozing his way through the mass of panicked people.

They were halfway to the field boundary when Jim saw the body of Father Figueres huddled on the ground. "Give me a hand," he ordered Carla. She helped him lift the old priest's slight figure to his shoulder.

They maintained their position behind Jerry. He was using Dick's booted feet to clear a path by swinging his legs from side-to-side, like a club.

In a matter of minutes, they broke through to the guarded parking area. Carla flashed a VIP card at the guards, they stood aside. One asked if they needed assistance. Jim answered quickly, in Spanish, that the priests had been overcome by the heat. They would be okay once they got to their vehicle.

Jim took the lead, with the unconscious priest over his shoulder. They wove their way through the exiting autos to the Canadian

Ambassador's Mercury. Jim laid Figueres on the hood and found the key on the left front tire.

He opened the limousine's back door. Jerry laid Dick gently on the seat. Blood was running from the corners of his mouth. His breathing was choked and uneven. Jim jumped in to cradle his head, with Carla close behind. Jerry returned with Figueres and laid him on the seat next to Carla.

Jim handed the key to Jerry. "Take Resistance Street to the Pan-American, then east to Sandino Airport."

"Know the way," he replied. "Did a couple weeks down here for Uncle Sam in the '60s."

Jerry's big fingers deftly fastened the wet towel around the elderly priest's forehead. "Is the dizziness gone, Father?" he asked.

"Yes, thank you, but my ankle's really throbbing."

"Sorry about the pain. Hope it's only a bad sprain, but it may be broken. Unbuckle that seat belt, sit sideways, and rest your leg on my knee. You want another aspirin? Hang on, Father, we'll have you at the hospital in Choluteca very soon."

The tough old Jesuit's dark eyes regarded the former SEAL, who was twice his size. "You're very gentle for such a big man. Thanks for rescuing me. I became separated from the others and was trampled by the crowd. I'll pass on the aspirin, but how about another swallow of that Canadian whiskey--for medical purposes."

Jerry chuckled. "Certainly, Father. I imagine that's why the Ambassador carries it in his plane. Never know when this old crate might forget how to fly."

The priest took a stiff drink, closed his eyes, grimaced as he swallowed, and returned the bottle to Jerry. "I appreciate the ride to Choluteca. I was scheduled for transfer to our monastery there next month."

"Not a great place to be right now, Father," warned Jerry. "The Contras aren't treating priests much better than those thugs in El Salvador."

"That's why I'm needed there," explained the kindly old man. He drew a worn Bible from his robes. "The word of God will keep me safe." His wrinkled face broke into a grin. He looked at Jerry and continued: "But I'd sure like to have a man like you standing beside me, when I speak to those who are hard of hearing."

Dick and Carla were in the rear of the Otter. The droning of the big reciprocating engine made conversation difficult. He was lying on his back in the aisle, with his head elevated on Carla's lap. Her soft-orange satin gown was stained with his blood. She held a wet towel on his forehead, and occasionally dabbed at the blood oozing from the corners of his mouth.

Enroute to the airport, Jim had removed Dick's robe. The bullet had not penetrated the vest. From the discoloration and swelling near the center of his chest, it was apparent the force of the impact had at least broken a rib--or his breastbone. Jim was concerned about Dick's coughing, and the blood. Perhaps a sliver of broken bone had penetrated a lung. Fortunately the coughing and the flow of blood had lessened, after they got him settled in the Canadian Embassy's aircraft.

Dick's breathing was still labored. The movement of his chest created intense pain. He moved his mouth to speak. Carla lowered her ear to his lips. "How did you get mixed up with Ahmad?" he gasped.

She dabbed at the corners of his mouth and smiled. "I waited two years for Captain Orden to return, . . . guess there weren't any more NATO officers to ransom from the Mafia."

Dick tried to smile, and she continued: "Don Paolucci had a message to deliver to Moscow. Since I knew Ahmad, who was the Syrian liaison at the Kremlin, he sent me. I was overwhelmed by the Bolshoi and all those fine things. When I asked the Don if I could stay, he agreed--but only if Jerry stayed with me. With Ahmad's background, Paolucci wanted to make sure I wasn't being forced into something."

Dick gasped for breath and muttered: "Chivalry lives."

"Only in Sicily," she said. "When I later refused to go to Damascus with Ahmad, I was lucky to have Jerry. I'd have been part of his damned harem by now!"

She looked out the window and gave a start. "My God, Captain! There's a big helicopter flying alongside. Are they going to shoot us down?"

Dick shook his head slowly and gasped: "If they were going to shoot, they wouldn't be on our wing."

He struggled for breath and continued: "Put that seat cushion under my head and go ask our priest-pilot what's happening."

She laid his head gently on the cushion. Dick watched her sexy body twist forward to the cockpit.

She was back in a few minutes. "The priest says that's a King Cobra helicopter, sent to guide us to a Contra base. He said to tell you we're across the Coco River and in Honduras."

She lay next to Dick and cradled his head in the soft bosom that he remembered so well. "How can a priest fly an airplane? What's a Contra base?"

Dick grinned, fought the pain to move his arms around Carla, buried his face in her charms, and gasped quietly: "He's got his connections, . . . and I've got mine."

Four days later, Dick was back in Room 109 of Avery Hall on the University of Nebraska campus. The white sweater on the busty dark-haired senior in the second row brought a "Carla flashback" to his mind. His train of thought was interrupted for a nano-second. Then he was back on track with his lecture on the U.S. government's strained relationship with the Ortega regime.

His breathing was constrained by the heavy tape protecting his cracked sternum, but he forcefully encouraged his Poli Sci class: "Watch the inauguration proceedings this weekend. We'll have a quiz Monday. You'd better know the color of the dress Nancy wore to the ball."

The bell rang. The students rose hurriedly to rush around campus to their next classes. Dick erased the board and returned his lecture notes in his briefcase. He paused for a moment to check his watch. It was the 22nd of January. Four years ago today, Aura One had exploded, and Rita had rescued him from the Philippine Sea. Three years ago today, he had partially avenged Rita's death by killing Enrico in Sicily. Now Salah was dead, and that revenge was complete. In one month, Maria would be returning to Lincoln to finish the semester with him. They would leave for Vienna together in May.

4

MAY DAY IN WIEN

Sunlight streamed through the trees in the park. The fifteen-minute walk, from his apartment on the southern edge of Vienna to the U-Bahn station, was a springtime treat. Dick enjoyed the early morning lyrics of the birds. The occasional call of a Chinese ring-necked pheasant searching for a mate reminded him of May in western Nebraska.

Although the University of Vienna was located near the city's center, his commute was entirely painless. Seven minutes on the U-1 subway, ten minutes on Strassenbahn #43, and Dick would be at the door to the historic building housing his German Grammar classroom.

He smiled as he recalled his hectic commute to the Pentagon: about the same distance but more than an hour by bus or car. Small wonder the residents of the Austrian capital were more relaxed and friendly than their American counterparts.

Dick's classmates were a reflection of current world affairs. There were a dozen middle-aged Czech, Polish, and Yugoslav refugees--free of communism and eager to start a new life--and there was a Persian-speaking contingent of three young men and a girl. They claimed to be Iranian, the Meldezettel documents they presented to the instructor listed Tehran as their place of birth. The Austrian government was particularly accommodating to rich upper-class Iranians, who had fled the Ayatollah Khomeini. By the mid-80s, there were about 40,000 living in Vienna. A sizeable colony had settled in the 10th Bezirk, where Dick and Maria lived.

A few years earlier, Dick had encountered five of the Shah of Iran's junior naval officers at the University of Missouri. They were dedicated playboys, they failed every class during their first semester. Their primary goal was clearly the conquest of all *fair-haired maidens* who fell for their trick of lighting cigars with hundred-dollar bills.

The young men in Dick's German Grammar class were entirely different. In their early twenties, handsome and physically fit, they lived a comfortable life-style; but they were dedicated scholars. Abrahim was majoring in Chemical Engineering, Ali in Mathematics, and Musavi in Physics. All were on the Austrian equivalent of the Dean's List. During class breaks, they eagerly impressed Dick with their English-speaking skills. However, he sometimes drew a blank stare when he tactfully quizzed them about Tehran.

When the instructor left the class roster lie on her desk, Dick got a list of their names and Tehran addresses. In a few days, Jim Conrad had confirmed the boys were imposters.

Conrad had also cautioned him to conceal his own identity from the group. Dick assured him that it was retired U.S. Navy Captain *Edward Orden* who was enrolled in Frau Wilke's class. That alias had been developed by *Purple* earlier and had served him well.

The young Persian-speaking woman was quite another matter. Her former residence in Tehran had been confirmed by Jim's report from *Purple*. She had lived there before following her grandfather into exile in Vienna. Sabena was a modernized Muslem, mindful of her heritage but proud of her independence and education, and obviously acquainted with Vienna's fashion houses. She chose colors that complimented her startling white skin and flowing black hair. She did not dress provocatively, but there was ample evidence that her medium-height slim figure was fully developed. Her makeup accentuated the glamour of her wide dark-violet eyes, her full lips, and her altogether beautiful face.

During the first week of the language course, she and Dick had sought refuge from a sudden spring shower in a coffee house near the university. She seemed enthralled by the idea of making friends with an American military officer, and invited Dick to meet her grandfather.

They lived in an apartment that occupied the entire top floor of a new 21-story building in northern Vienna. The elderly man was frail, but sound of mind. His English was relaxed and accomplished. Dick suspected he'd been schooled in the States.

He was eager to know all about Dick, but succumbed to Dick's urging to discuss violent Middle East politics. Grandfather was quick to express his dislike for King Hussein of Jordan, attributing to him many of the problems in the region. Dick reasoned the basis for that criticism might be the differences between the Jordanian's Sunni and the grandfather's professed Shia muslim beliefs. The grandfather's hatred of Israel was absolute! The emotions he displayed during their discussions led Dick to an easy conclusion: this old man had a much closer association with the Palestinian-Israeli conflict than one who had only viewed the situation from Tehran.

Sabena took Dick on a tour of the luxurious apartment. In a room containing the grandfather's memorabilia, he noted a diploma on the wall from the University of Southern California. It was a Ph.D. granted to Fahed al-Benna in June, 1955. That was not the name by which Sabena had introduced her grandfather.

Dick later transmitted the diploma information to Jim Conrad. He was not too surprised when *Purple's* research revealed Fahed al-Benna was Palestinian by birth--and the uncle of the infamous terrorist leader, Mirhashem.

The al-Benna family had fled Palestine for Jordan during the '67 Arab-Israeli war. From there, Fahed and Mirhashem led Fatah attacks against Israel.

Three years before the war started, Fahed had sent his son Issam to school in France. There he met, married, and impregnated a French girl. Sabena was born in Marseilles. In '68, Fahed joined Issam in France to consolidate support for the Fatah. When Issam was summoned to Jordan for a Fatah briefing, he took along his French wife to meet his family. Five-year-old Sabena had a cold and was left with her grandfather in Marseilles. Her parents arrived in southern Jordan in September 1970--the day before King Hussein, at the urging of Israel and the U.S., turned his Bedouins loose upon the Palestinian refugee camps. Only Mirhashem and a handful of others survived the massacre. Issam and Sabena's mother, along with Mirhashem's father and the rest of the al-Benna family, had been put to the sword. Black September rose from the ashes of the burned camps.

Dick was advised by *Purple* to maintain a close, but cautious, contact with Sabena's grandfather. Sabena was eager to continue their friendship, and Dick (Captain Orden) was regularly invited to the apartment for lunch after class on Mondays. The grandfather's passionate descriptions of life and history in the Middle East were very informative.

On this particular Friday after the fourth week of class, Dick was climbing the stairs from the U-Bahn station when he spotted

Sabena waiting for the Strassenbahn. She was an eyeful, with sunlight glistening in her black hair and a flowing white silk blouse contrasting with her black formfitting slacks. Normally, one of the three boys would have been with her. They apparently took turns escorting her to and from the university. However, this morning she was alone and rather nervous--carefully averting her eyes from the people around her.

Dick walked quickly to her side and smiled. "Hello, Sabena, where's your bodyguard?"

"Good morning, Captain." She glanced shyly into his eyes. "I don't need them when you're here, do I?"

At that moment, they were joined by other members of the class. They all climbed aboard the #43 tram. During the short ride to the university, they conversed in German as they compared plans for the weekend.

At the university stop, Dick extended his hand to help Sabena down the steps. She squeezed his hand and whispered seriously: "Captain, I must speak with you after class. Could we meet for coffee?"

He nodded his head. "Certainly. The café next door okay?"

"No, the Aida by the Stephansdom would be better. We should not be seen walking together. You go first, I'll follow later."

As always, the Aida was packed; but Dick found a small table by the window on the second floor. He ordered two teas with milk and one of Sabena's favorite small cakes with Himbeere sauce.

In a few moments, he saw her walking out of a side street into the Kärtnerstrasse. She paused to light a cigarette, looked casually behind her, then crossed the street to enter the coffee house.

Obviously, she was worried about being followed. Dick continued to watch the entrance to the side street, but saw nothing unusual before she joined him at the table.

He rose to greet her. "I've ordered tea with milk. Is that okay?"

She smiled shyly and sat down. "Thank you for remembering."

The waitress brought their order, Sabena continued: ". . . and some raspberry cake. How nice of you, Captain."

Dick waited until the waitress left, then leaned across the table. "Sabena, is something wrong? You seem upset today. Is it because the boys aren't with you? This the first time they've missed class."

"Yes," she responded hesitantly. "They left last night and won't be back for three or four days. It's a bad time for them to be gone."

She raised her hand to the table and took hold of Dick's. She was trembling. Her eyes darted around the room.

"Is your grandfather ill?"

"No, but he's very worried about a situation that has come up. With Abrahim gone, he told me to ask if you might help us?"

"Why, certainly. How can I be of assistance?"

She squeezed his hand harder and fixed her deep violet eyes on his. "The situation's very unusual, Captain. If you choose not to get involved, we'll understand."

"Does it involve your personal security?"

"Yes, it does. We expect to be in a lot of danger, very soon."

"Why don't you go to the Austrian authorities?"

"Grandfather says they cannot be trusted in this situation."

"How is it that he chooses to trust me?"

She smiled, but her eyes continued to penetrate his. "Years ago, when Grandfather was studying in America, he met a navy officer. They were taking the same classes and became close friends. They stayed in touch until '67, when the officer was shot down and killed in Vietnam. Grandfather held him in high regard. From his conversations with you, he believes you're also a man of honor that can be trusted."

"I'm flattered to hear that, Sabena. Your grandfather's a wise and experienced man. I hope I'm worthy of his trust. What can you tell me about the situation that's placing you in danger?"

Without releasing his hand, she rose slightly and moved her chair closer to his. "If we look like lovers, we'll be able to speak more quietly."

She leaned against Dick's shoulder, while pressing a shapely leg against his under the table. He was aware of an exotic perfume, and the exceptional warmth of her upper body.

Dick glanced around the room. "Well, we fit better with this crowd when we sit closer together. However, don't forget you're a very sensual woman. I might have trouble concentrating."

She blushed slightly, but did not draw back. She whispered into his ear: "From the intense conversations you've had with Grandfather, I'm sure you realize he's made a lot of enemies. Now we've heard that someone is planning to kill him."

Dick again felt her hand trembling. "Here in Vienna?"

"Yes. They may try as early as this evening. With Abrahim gone, we're defenseless."

"Can't you leave town until he gets back?"

"Captain, we've been advised to stay in our top-floor apartment, rather than risk being caught in the open. Grandfather's not able to move very quickly."

"Are there others in town who might help us?"

He felt her hand relax. She leaned forward to kiss him softly on the cheek. "Thanks for saying *us*. Does that mean you'll help?"

He brushed her full lips lightly with his own. "Sabena, could any man refuse you?"

The slight blush returned, she whispered: "Please, this is only an act, so we can speak without others hearing."

She paused, then continued: "There's no one else in town that we can trust. We're trying to contact my uncle, but he's in a remote area. What should we do, Captain?"

"How reliable is the information that you'll be in danger this evening, and the advice that you should stay in the apartment?"

"Oh, that's from a very reliable source!"

"Can't that source help you?"

"No, they're not in this country. They are the ones trying to contact my uncle. They're sure they can get him here by Sunday."

"So," breathed Dick, he took the opportunity to caress her face with his fingertips, "we must find a way to keep Grandfather alive for forty-eight hours."

She turned her head and kissed his fingers with her moist lips. "Yes, that's the situation."

Dick rose from his chair. "Then we'd better get busy. Take a taxi home. I'm going to be busy for a few hours, but I'll be there before five. Keep your grandfather away from the windows."

He took a small paging device from his pocket and gave it to her. "If you need me, use this, and I'll call you as soon as I can."

She rose from her chair, turned to him, put her hands around his face, drew his head down, and kissed him passionately. She withdrew slowly and said: "To make sure people believe our lover act."

She smiled at his surprised look. "Am I the first Muslim girl to kiss you?"

Dick reflected momentarily on the death of Güla during ill-fated

Operation *Starlight* twenty years earlier, then replied cautiously: "No, but I hope you're the luckiest."

Dick walked Sabena to the taxi stand, then hurried to the city park. An orchestra was playing near the southeast corner, the tables of the outdoor café were all occupied. He walked farther into the park and found a vacant bench near a small pond, where a flock of ducks were busy with the rituals of spring. He took the satellite phone from his briefcase, selected the scramble mode, and actuated the switch to call Jim Conrad. He used his handkerchief to conceal the device from passers-by.

"Hello, Bear, Mountie here. What's keeping you busy today?"

"Hi, Mountie. You still in Lebanon?"

"No, I came out to Frankfurt last night. That hostage situation seems to be a no-win ball game, unless we can figure how to get inside. Nelson's here beside me, listening on the remote."

"Glad you're there, Mr. Nelson. I may be sitting on a golden opportunity, if we can make the right moves at the right time. Remember Jim's report on Sabena's grandfather a few weeks ago?"

"Yes, certainly, but that's a pretty big fish to catch with your thin line."

"Well, get set to jump in the water, because someone's trying to throw a net over him."

"What do you mean, Bear?" asked Jim.

"Sabena has asked for my help. Someone may try to assassinate him this evening. The bodyguards are out of town, and her famous terrorist of an uncle's in a remote area somewhere. He's supposed to be here Sunday. An outside source has advised her to hole up in their apartment. Can you help me with this?"

"We'll surely try," replied Jim. "Nelson just left to research the possible assassins, we have a good idea who that would be. Let's you and I work on keeping him alive. Give me the basics."

"The assassins may already be in town, and Grandpa doesn't get around very good. Don't believe there's any chance to make a run for it. We'll be in the top-floor of a 21-story building on the northern edge of Vienna. I've been there four or five times. The building's one of three that sit alone on adjoining five-acre lots. Car parking is on the surrounding streets. The roof top's used as a private sun deck for their apartment. It's about thirty meters across and its walls are one meter high. The chimneys in each corner are two feet higher than the walls, no antennas or other obstructions, only a red aircraft beacon on one chimney. There's easy access for Grandpa--if you've got another Whisper to come get us?"

Jim chuckled at Dick's reminder of the stealthy helicopter which they had used to fly from Manila's hotel roofs to Aura One's launch site in the volcanic crater.

"We don't have a Whisper here at HQ, Dick, but there is a helo we can use at the Wiener Neustadt airport, about thirty miles south of Vienna."

"Hey, don't forget, I'm only a fixed-wing type! Is there someone at Wiener Neustadt that we can trust to fly it for us?"

"I have a Saberliner sitting on the flight line at Rhein-Main. I can be at Wiener Neustadt in three or four hours."

"Fan-damn-tastic, Mountie! Have you still got the monitor for the chip in my shoulder, or should I find another homing device?"

"The chip will do fine, Bear. What's your weather like?"

"Clear and beautiful. We had a big moon last night, but it won't be up until nine-thirty."

"Okay, I'll bring my night-vision helmet. Wait a minute, here's Nelson again."

"Any info for me, Mr. Nelson?"

"Yes, Dick. Like I thought, it's the Mossad. Our informant is right up near the top, where we need him, and he's familiar with this operation."

"What should I expect, Sir?"

"Two men are scheduled to arrive at Schwechat Airport at five this evening on El Al Flight 34. Both are members of the Mossad's bomb squad. They're planning to blow the apartment."

"It won't take more than an hour for them to clear customs and drive to the apartment. Do they have support people here?"

"According to our informant, the explosives will be picked up at the Westbahnhof."

"Well, that's a break. That will give Jim a little more time to get overhead--but maybe I should try to get them out of there with my car, right now!"

"No, Dick. Not a good idea, for at least two reasons: First, the Mossad probably has the apartment under surveillance, and we don't want them to ID you or your car. Second, if we pull this off--

with some excitement and suspense involved--you may get in the good graces of the world's deadliest terrorist. The uncle's somewhere in the Bekaa Valley, in charge of all hostage-taking. This could be the break we've been waiting for. We want him to know you had some powerful connections when you saved his relatives."

"Don't worry, Bear," added Conrad. "I'll be there with the helo in plenty of time. I don't think those guys will try anything until after dark. What do you think, Mr. Nelson?"

"That's probably true. Mossad's pattern of residence bombings over the years shows they tend to strike between ten and midnight, depending on the access to the building. What's it like at that apartment, Dick?"

"It's a good system: video monitoring of the building entrance, intercom between the entrance and each apartment, and an electric lock opened by a signal from the apartment."

Jim interrupted, "Those locks are easily opened with a device the Mossad's sure to have. Best bet is to keep an eye on the video."

"The *best bet* is to make damned sure you pick us off the roof before they get there!" exclaimed Dick.

"You'd better plan some delaying tactics in the event Mountie's a little late," advised Nelson, "but don't make it too drastic. I promised our contact we'd avoid inflicting casualties."

Maria had left for Kirchberg before Dick returned to their apartment. She was visiting her mother for the weekend. They were planning on meeting Dick at the nearby Wiener Neustadt airport tomorrow morning. He had arranged to rent a Cessna from her brother's flying club to take them flying.

He took the equipment he needed from his locked storage bin in the cellar of their apartment building. The remote-controlled toy-car bomb was from *Purple*. It could be controlled from a distance of two kilometers and contained enough C-4 to destroy a vehicle. It could move silently across a moderately rough surface at speeds of 10mph, and would right itself if turned over. Two flares, normally used for highway emergencies, had been modified to ignite when dropped on a hard surface. Rita's Beretta, a flashlight, and a pair of wire-cutters completed the list.

Dick slipped the Beretta into his pocket holster. He packed the other items in the shopping bag that he had taken earlier from a grocery store near Sabena's apartment.

Descending the five flights of stairs from his apartment to the street, Dick felt the familiar ting in his right shoulder. That would be Sabena trying to signal him with the pager.

He opened the door to his BMW and placed the shopping bag behind the seat. Then he took the Skyfone out of his coat pocket, selected the local option, and manually entered Sabena's number.

"Hi, Sabena, were you trying to contact me?"

"Yes, Captain Orden. I've been on the sun deck with grandfather's binoculars. There's a man in a black Mercedes parked on the street south of our building, where he can watch the entrance."

"Was he there when you got home?"

"Yes, and he's still there. Whenever someone goes in or out, he checks them with binoculars."

"Did he see you on the roof?"

"No, I don't believe so. I've been very careful. Oh, Captain, I'm so frightened. What should I do?"

"Don't be worried. I was sure they would have someone watching the building. I'll be with you in less than an hour. I'll call before I come up. I'll be dressed differently. Look carefully at the video, make sure it's me before you open the door."

"Okay, Captain, please hurry. My uncle called. He's on his way, but he won't be here until after two in the morning."

Dick was five minutes from Sabena's apartment when he called her again. She went to the roof and verified that the man with the black Mercedes was still there. Dick told her to stay in the apartment with her grandfather, he would be with them shortly.

He approached from the north and parked on a street bordering the apartment building's lot. He checked the roof with his binoculars but couldn't see Sabena. He sat quietly for awhile, then opened the door and set the toy-car bomb under the BMW. He left his sport coat in the car, took the shopping bag with the equipment, and walked to the grocery store located east of the apartment.

He had to wait only a few minutes before the delivery boy returned from an errand on his bicycle. As Dick had noted during an earlier visit, the boy parked his bike behind the store and hung his uniform cap and coat on the handle bars before he went inside. Dick watched through the store window until the boy was occupied with customers. Then he hurried to the bike, put on the cap and coat, laid his shopping bag in the basket, pedaled down the alley, and turned into the street leading to the apartment building.

As soon as he pushed the buzzer for the top-floor apartment, Dick heard the door unlock. He wheeled the bicycle into the spacious lobby where he'd seen it parked before. He checked his watch, it was five o'clock. If El Al was on time, the Mossad assassins were landing at Schwechat.

The elevator door opened at the twenty-first floor. Sabena was there to greet him.

She grinned at the delivery boy's cap and coat, and embraced him warmly. "Thanks be to Allah you're here. I'm so frightened."

"How's Grandfather?"

"Nothing scares him, but he does wonder how you plan to protect us until my uncle gets here."

"Let's go speak with him."

Fahed al-Benna was sitting by the dining room table. An AK-47 was in his lap and several magazines of ammunition were on the table. He looked up as Dick and Sabena entered the room.

"I don't have much in the way of firepower, Captain. Were you able to bring anything?"

Dick set the shopping bag on a chair. "Yes Sir, I brought along a few items that might be useful. Do you have any idea who's trying to harm you?"

"You're in this with us now, Captain, so I must be completely honest with you. I'm not really Iranian. I'm Palestinian, and I suspect it's our ages-old enemy who's coming to kill me."

"Well, Sir, it will take a lot of killing to get both of us. We make a pretty good pair, and Sabena will certainly be able to help."

"She's a brave girl," nodded the old man, "but that won't make any difference to the Mossad. What should we do first? Sabena says a man has been watching our building most of the afternoon."

"That's correct. Otherwise, I would have taken you out of here hours ago in my private auto."

"Can we make a stand in this apartment, Captain?"

"Don't really think so. I could disable the elevator, and we could prevent them from coming up the emergency stairwell for awhile, but--depending on how many there are--it would only be a matter of time before they'd be in here. That's unless you would allow me to contact the Austrian police?"

"No, I'm afraid they would only make matters worse. Not only for me, but for the rest of my countrymen in this city."

"Then, Sir, our only option is to flee this building."

"If the man watching the building is Mossad, we wouldn't get five meters!" exclaimed the experienced old fighter.

"I agree we couldn't get very far out the front door, but what if we go out through the roof?"

In spite of the gravity of the situation, the old man chuckled. "If they plant a bomb below this apartment, that may happen."

Dick was glad to see him becoming more relaxed. He took the AK-47 from his lap and laid it on the table.

"Give me a few minutes. I'll see if I can find a taxi that makes roof calls."

Sabena exchanged a quizzical look with her grandfather, Dick left the apartment through the door to the roof.

It took a couple minutes for Jim to answer the Skyfone. He was in the Saberliner, about an hour from Wiener Neustadt. To avoid confrontation with Austrian authorities, he wanted to wait till dark to fly over Vienna with the helicopter. When Dick told him about the man in the black Mercedes, Jim cautioned him to be on watch for the two Mossad bombers. If Dick felt threatened, he should call immediately; otherwise they'd talk again at sundown.

Back in the apartment, Dick told Sabena and her grandfather there was a way out of their predicament. He advised them to get ready to leave: pack clothes, passports, and valuables in soft bags that would fit into the cramped cockpit of a small helicopter. There was no need to hurry, he was sure they wouldn't be attacked until after dark. He would watch the entrance video until Sabena was finished packing, then she could watch the door while he went to the roof.

The golden sun had descended softly into the greenery of the Wienerwald hills, lights were beginning to twinkle in the Heurigen wine cellars of northwestern Vienna. A southerly breeze caressed Dick's face, promising another warm spring day tomorrow.

Jim was on the Skyfone. "I'm topping off the chopper's fuel tanks, Dick. What's going on there?"

"I'm on the roof, Sabena's watching the door video. Wait while I check the black Mercedes again."

Dick crawled to the south side of the roof and peered cautiously over the wall. The man was leaning against the side of the car.

"Yeah, he's still there, Jim."

"Okay, it'll be dark in about forty-five minutes. I'll be in your area by then. Any clue as to when you're going to be hit?"

"Probably before ten. Sabena and her grandfather have been told Uncle Mirhashem will be here by two. I imagine the Mossad also know that and will want to be long gone before then."

"We'd better plan to make the pickup as soon as I get there; but let's try to follow Nelson's advice and make it a narrow escape."

"Yeah, I agree, Mountie. There's a five-knot wind from the south. Use the monitor to home on my chip and come in from the north. That will make it difficult for the Mercedes guy to see you. There are three tall buildings here, about five hundred yards apart. We're in the one to the east. I've disconnected the red beacon and removed all loose stuff from the sun deck. It's about thirty meters across, and strong enough to hold Austrian snow, but I don't know about your helicopter."

"I'll keep some weight off after touchdown, Bear. Bring your people in the starboard side. There's a jump seat in the back, with a little space behind it for luggage. Put that in first, then strap Grandpa in the jump seat. You and Sabena will have to share a front seat. Is there an open field in the area where I can set this thing down if we have a problem?"

"There's a helo pad at a big hospital, a couple klicks to the southeast. What's your cover tonight, Jim?"

"The Saberliner and helicopter are unmarked, they're registered to a phony Austrian firm. Let's speak German when I pick you up. Tell them I'm Armin, an Austrian friend. I'll keep my night-vision helmet on. Okay, partner, I'm on my way. Let's be safe, but make the timing as close as we can."

"Roger that." Dick returned the Skyfone to his pocket.

The light was beginning to fade. There was only occasional traffic on the parking street surrounding the building. It was time for his diversionary plan.

He crawled to the northeast corner of the roof, where he could see his BMW without being seen by the man at the Mercedes. He balanced Sabena's binoculars on the low wall, and took the remote control for his toy-car bomb from the shopping bag.

He maneuvered the toy from under his BMW. There was barely enough light to drive it around the corner and down the street to the south. It was hidden from the Mercedes until it approached the corner for the street heading west. Dick parked it under a car on the far side of the street.

Perhaps he could maneuver the quiet toy around the corner, down the street, and under the black Mercedes without it being seen; but it would be better to create a diversion.

He peered over the wall with the binoculars. The man was in the Mercedes, holding a radio transceiver to his ear, most likely talking to the Mossad bombers. It wouldn't be long till showtime.

Dick took a flare with a contact igniter cap from the shopping bag and cut it two inches long. He wanted it to burn for only a few minutes. He went to the west edge of the roof, checked that the concrete apron below was clear, and dropped the flare.

He was rewarded with a sharp pop and the flare's reddish light reflecting off windows of cars parked along the street. He moved quickly to the southeast corner to watch the man in the Mercedes. He was already out of his car, walking west on the sidewalk to see what was burning.

Dick raised the remote control. By the time the man reached the southwest corner of the sidewalk, the toy-car bomb was in position under the gas tank of his black Mercedes.

The man started up the sidewalk along the west side of the building. The flare flickered and went out. Dick breathed a sigh of relief, he certainly didn't need the Vienna fire department on the scene. Two boys on bicycles had seen the flare and stopped near it on the concrete apron. The man approached them. He apparently believed they had lit the flare. He began cursing and threatening them. They fled on their bikes. The man returned to his Mercedes.

It was getting dark. Dick went down to the apartment. Sabena and her grandfather were watching the security video monitor in the kitchen. Two travel bags were lying on the table.

"Our transportation will be here soon," he reassured them. "I'm sorry you can't take much luggage. Make sure you have your passports and valuables, your enemies will likely enter the apartment before your uncle arrives. Anything unusual on the video?"

"No," replied Sabena, "only people that live here. Some of them are going out for the evening."

She pointed to the monitor screen where a middle-aged couple in evening clothes were leaving the building.

"I intend to disable the elevator before we leave, but I'll wait till the last minute to do that."

"That is a good idea," agreed Grandfather. "It will make it more difficult for our enemies. I'd love to have them in this apartment when Mirhashem gets here." In the tenseness of the moment, Fahed al-Benna had used the code name for Sabena's uncle.

Dick suppressed a smile and said: "Sabena, go to the south wing and turn all the lights on bright. That will make it more difficult for the Mercedes guy to see the edge of the roof. Leave the curtains like you normally do, otherwise he may get suspicious. Then watch the monitor with your grandfather. I'm going to the roof to wait for our helicopter. It should be here before long. I'll leave the door open. Call me if you see someone coming."

The sun roof afforded a glorious panorama of Vienna by night. The Prater's ferris wheel near the Danube oriented Dick's gaze. To the southwest was the distinctive circle of the Burgring around St. Stephen's Cathedral, which had been restored after it was damaged during a W.W.II bombing raid. The southern edge of the Ring was outlined by the lighted dome of the Karlskirche and the glowing Opera House. The magnificent Hofburg houses of government highlighted the western Ring.

The wind had picked up to over ten knots, it was getting cool. Dick shivered, thought about his sport coat locked in the BMW, and put the remote control for the toy-car bomb in his shirt pocket.

It was seven-thirty. Jim had arrived fifteen minutes ago, approaching from the north until Dick heard the chopper, then backing off to establish an orbit out of earshot. With the wind, that was only a few hundred meters away. It was a lucky break that would help conceal their pickup.

"Brown Bear, Mountie, over."

Jim was on the Skyfone again. They had left the channel open, so they could converse immediately if things began to happen.

"Brown Bear here. Getting tired of making circles?"

"Not really. This is a sweet little flying machine. Unfortunately, it doesn't have much endurance. We'll have to make the pickup within the next forty-five minutes, if we're going to make it back to Wiener Neustadt."

"How about refueling at Schwechat? It's only ten minutes away. Could give you another half hour on station."

"We'd draw too much attention out there, Bear. Where do you intend to drop these people?"

"Subject never came up. They're pretty frightened. If they get the hell scared out of them before we leave, they'll go wherever we say. It would impress them if you volunteer to take them anywhere they want to go in the Saberliner. I'm certain they won't take you up on it. They'll want to stay around here, so the uncle can join them when he arrives."

"Got a place in mind?"

"Yeah, there's a short asphalt landing strip near Mariazell--the village with the golden church. It's about seventy klicks south-west. Was there last weekend with Maria."

"That would be in the mountains, wouldn't it?"

"Some fantastic scenery out there, Mountie. The strip is on the top of a hill, by a Gasthaus and some small hotels, about five klicks north of town. No runway lights, but the moon would be up by the time we got there."

"This little bug won't fly over those mountains with so much weight, Dick, and we'd have to stop at Wiener Neustadt for fuel."

"Understand. Let's take them to Wiener Neustadt and offer them a ride somewhere in the Saberliner. When they refuse, I'll offer to take them to Mariazell in a Cessna. I'm already on the flying club's schedule in the morning. The security guard will let me take it early--if the price is right."

At that moment, Dick saw the headlights of an auto entering the parking street from the east. "Hold on, Mountie, car approaching. Be ready! If it's our visitors, I'll give you a four-minute countdown for pickup."

"Okay, Bear, I'll be in position. Keep me informed."

Dick trained Sabena's binoculars on the new arrivals. They proceeded to the south side of the building and parked across the street from the black Mercedes. The observer in the Mercedes held a transceiver to his ear. The passenger in the second car was holding a similar apparatus. They sat quietly in their cars.

Dick called Jim: "Two men in the second car, one of them on a radio. The guy in the Mercedes is also on a radio."

"Mountie, roger that."

Time dragged by--five, then ten minutes--with no one moving. Dick glanced at his watch. Jim had only twenty minutes of fuel remaining before they'd have to make the pickup.

Then the Mossad assassins made their move. The two men went to the trunk of their car and removed two medium-sized suitcases. The observer stepped out of the Mercedes with a briefcase. Dick smiled. The man's feet were only one meter from the toy-car bomb, which could blow him into the next county.

The three men began to walk toward the apartment building. Dick checked his watch and spoke on the Skyfone: "Showtime, Mountie. Mark four minutes and counting for touchdown."

"Rog, Bear, let's do it."

Dick hurried down the stairs from the sun deck to the kitchen. Sabena and her grandfather were glued to the security monitor.

"Someone's coming," said Dick quickly. "Get a good look at them and wait for me here. I'm going to disable the elevator." He grabbed a chair and went out the door.

He held the call button until the lights indicated the elevator had left the first floor. He checked his watch, Jim would be on the roof in three minutes.

The elevator doors opened. He leaned inside, selected the 20th floor, and jammed the chair in the doors as they tried to close.

He stepped back into the apartment and secured the four locks on the door. Sabena was staring at the monitor. The old man was struggling to lift the canvas bags off the table.

"Oh, no!" she exclaimed. "Look, Captain, look!"

On the video display, a man holding two suitcases was standing in the background. Another was pressing an electronic box the size of a cigarette pack against the door lock. A third was removing a can of spray paint from his briefcase. A moment later, he sprayed the camera lens and the screen went blue.

"Recognize anyone?" asked Dick.

"No, no one." Sabena trembled. "Are they coming for us?"

"Yes, I'm sure that's the enemy you're expecting." Dick checked his watch. "Fortunately, someone else is also coming for us. He'll be here in two minutes, he's much more friendly than those goons.

Let's go! Sabena, take the bags. I'll bring Grandfather."

She responded quickly, and was on her way up the stairs with the luggage.

The old man had trouble moving. Dick hoisted him in a fireman's carry, locked the kitchen door behind them, and climbed the stairs to the roof.

They could hear the helicopter coming from the north. Dick raised the Skyfone to his lips. Remembering Jim Conrad's cover for the evening, he spoke in German: "*Hallo, Armin, wir sind oben. Die Feinden sind drinnen Haus.*"

Dick had warned Jim that the Mossad were in the building, but it wasn't necessary. The helo appeared out of the darkness and flared for a noisy landing on the spacious roof top. Dick huddled his small group together on the western edge, until its skis were resting on the sun deck.

"Wait here with Grandfather," shouted Dick. He took the luggage, picked up his shopping bag, bent low, and hurried to the helo's right door.

He leaned in behind the front seat and threw the bags into the rear of the cockpit.

"Where are they?" asked Jim.

"Climbing stairs," shouted Dick.

He glanced at his watch and hurried back for Grandfather. The Mossad would be climbing the ninth or tenth flight of stairs.

He cradled the old man in his arms and shouted at Sabena: "Stay low and follow me."

He strapped Grandpa in the backseat, then leapt into the front and held out his arms for Sabena. She turned to slide gracefully onto his lap.

Dick closed the door, and Jim applied full power to lift the heavily laden helicopter from the roof.

Rita had often joked that Jim could fly the box a helicopter came in--tonight was no exception. They cleared the southern wall and departed to the south. Jim signaled Dick with a twirling motion of his fingers and flashed his open hand twice.

Dick spoke in Sabena's ear: "We have fuel to stay around for ten minutes. Want to keep an eye on your apartment for that long?"

She turned carefully in his arms to put her lips by his ear. "Yes, please, if you think we're out of danger?"

Dick nodded to Jim and answered Sabena: "We're safe. It's dark enough for Armin to keep the helicopter out of sight, but we can still see the building."

Jim made a climbing turn to the east. A few moments later, they were doing a lazy figure-eight north of the apartment. Jim pointed toward the building. A light was visible on the southern edge of the sun deck. The Mossad had gained access.

Dick watched Sabena. She bit her lip, her dark eyes were moist.

"They're in there, aren't they, Captain."

"Yes. I'm sorry, but I'm glad you're here with me."

She turned to kiss him firmly on the cheek. "Thanks be to Allah for you, Captain."

Jim broke out of the figure-eight on a southerly heading. He pointed at the gas gauge, Dick nodded.

They were passing east of the building. Sabena leaned forward, twisted her body, and took one last look at her home of five years. Dick felt her shudder, then she screamed! A fiery blast blew out the windows and ruptured the roof. The upper floor was immediately engulfed in flames.

Sabena stopped screaming and began to cry. Jim maneuvered the helo so Grandfather could view the scene. He cursed loudly.

Dick took the toy-car bomb remote control from his shirt pocket and showed it to Jim, he nodded. His face was hidden by the night-vision goggles, but Dick knew he'd be smiling.

The RCMP representative to *Purple* turned west to parallel the southern edge of the apartment complex. Dick quieted Sabena's sobbing by speaking sharply to her: "It's payback time, Honey."

He raised the remote control with one hand and lifted her right hand to it with the other.

"Press the red button," he urged. "Press the red button!"

She turned her face, as if she didn't understand.

They were passing directly south of the apartment.

"Do it!" he shouted. "Press it now!"

Her finger came down on the red button, Jim tilted the nimble helo to the right. A huge orange fireball lifted the black Mercedes from its parking place and threw it forward on the lawn. They saw three men on the sidewalk, about halfway between the blazing car and the apartment building.

A brilliant moon cleared the eastern horizon, as Jim Conrad flared the helo to a soft landing alongside the Saberliner. The Wiener Neustadt field had changed since its W.W.II days. It had been a busy air facility for transporting German war material from the surrounding industrial complex. Most of the warehouses were now empty. The runways and taxiways were in bad repair.

After shutdown, Jim kept his helmet and night-vision goggles on, making it impossible to recognize him.

In spite of Dick's best efforts, Sabena had cried most of the flight. His shirt was wet from her tears. While Jim helped Grandfather from the backseat, she clung to Dick. He held her tenderly.

Jim supported the frail old man and addressed him respectfully in German: "Dr. al-Benna, we're in Wiener Neustadt." He gestured toward the Saberliner. "This aircraft is at your disposal. I'm ready to fly you and your granddaughter wherever you want to go."

Dick glanced at the old man's face, watching for a response to Jim's knowledge of his true name.

Perhaps there was a sharp glint in the elderly eyes, but his face was enveloped with a warm smile. He answered Jim in perfect German: "Young man, you're a very talented pilot--thank you for saving our lives. It won't be necessary for us to leave this country. In fact, we'd prefer to stay somewhere in the vicinity of Vienna."

"May I suggest a location that would be quite safe," said Dick. "It's not far from Vienna. I'm familiar with the local population and guarantee you'll enjoy the stay, for as long as you like. It's in the mountains, about sixty kilometers west of here."

"Captain Orden," sighed the old man, "you have performed a miracle to save our lives tonight. Certainly Allah intends for us to continue to follow your advice."

"Is there a car available?" asked Sabena.

Dick smiled. "We can do better than that. Help Armin get your things from the helicopter, and I'll be right back with your next mode of transportation."

They circled to the west of Wiener Neustadt. Dick nursed the Cessna to a higher altitude. He smiled at the old man in the right seat. "Doctor, care to take the controls for awhile?"

Fahed al-Benna placed his hands gently on the yoke. "I'm not exactly in my element, Captain. Don't let me get in trouble."

"Let's head west to St. Pölten while we're climbing. The apricot orchards are in bloom. They should be beautiful in this moonlight."

It was indeed a remarkable sight!

"The last time I touched the controls was in this same type aircraft. My dear friend and classmate, Lieutenant Reyes, took me up one weekend. We flew around Catalina Island, off the coast of California. Like you, he was an accomplished pilot. Unfortunately, he did not survive Vietnam."

"I was acquainted with Lenardo Reyes. You probably know he was the leader of an air wing, when he was shot down on a bombing run near Vinh."

"Did you know him well?"

"He flew A-4 Skyhawks, I was in the F-8 Crusader. We didn't fly together, but I attended some functions with him. He was much admired by his colleagues."

"When we were classmates, I knew he had a superior intellect. His mind was clear and sharp. He quickly solved the most difficult problems. Like you this evening, Captain, he had a magical sense of timing--coming up with the right answer at the right time."

"Doctor, it was by the grace of my God, and your Allah, that we escaped tonight. I'm sorry you lost so many things."

"Only a few minor materialistic items, none of which have any bearing upon my existence here on earth."

Dick banked the aircraft gently to the left and set a course for Mariazell.

The landing strip was deserted and unlit, but the moonlight was all that was required to land safely. Dick taxied the Cessna to the parking area.

After shutdown, he looked in the back. Sabena was sleeping. He touched her gently on the shoulder. "Wake up, Princess. Let's find you a more comfortable bed."

"Sorry, I must have dozed off. Can't imagine how I could fall asleep after the horrible events of this evening."

"It's a blessing from Allah, little one," consoled Grandfather. "In the worst of times, he prepares our bodies for the next challenge."

Dick pointed at three large houses bordering the landing strip. "All those establishments have fine rooms and good cooking, but I recommend the one on the south end. They're more modern--with telephone service in the rooms. I'm sure you have people to call."

He had an ulterior motive. He and Maria often stayed in the Gasthaus on the north end. He was acquainted with the owner, who would have his real name and address on file. It was a risk Dick dare not take.

He had a diversion planned to misdirect any attempt by Sabena, or her uncle, to inquire into his background. As they removed the baggage from the Cessna, he explained that he'd check them into the small hotel using his (Captain Orden) passport and credit card. Given the media publicity that might follow the bombing of the apartment, it would be a good idea for Sabena and her grandfather to disguise their identity and their whereabouts.

"But, Captain Orden," objected Sabena, "please understand we will repay you at the first opportunity."

"Don't worry about it," said Dick. "I'll tell the management to charge everything against my card for a week. Would that be sufficient time for you to make other arrangements?"

"More than enough," answered the grandfather. "I'll soon be in contact with people who will assist us."

It was about a hundred-meter walk to the hotel. "Would you like me to go for a taxi?" asked Dick.

"Not at all necessary. If you carry the bags, Sabena and I will manage; but we may be a little slow."

"To walk in this moonlight is a blessing," echoed Sabena.

Dick was halfway back to Wiener Neustadt when he felt the familiar ting in his shoulder. He took the Skyfone from his pocket. The red light for an incoming call was flashing.

"Hi, Mountie, where are you?"

"According to your monitor, I'm at your twelve o'clock."

Dick stared toward the brilliant moon. "Yeah, got a rotating red beacon at about ten kilometers."

"That's me."

"Sorry I didn't get back in time to help you refuel."

"That's okay, Bear. We have a contractor at Wiener Neustadt. How did it go?"

"I believe we pulled it off exactly as Nelson wanted. It's sad the Mossad blew their apartment, but the timing was great. Sabena and Dr. al-Benna have a very hairy story to tell Uncle Mirhashem.

What kind of reaction is Nelson expecting from him?"

"Well, Vienna may become a battlefield for awhile--as the hits go back and forth--but Nelson's hoping Mirhashem will choose to thank you personally for saving what little family he has left. If he does, the ball will be in your court, Dick."

"Does Nelson want me inside Mirhashem's organization?"

"You're not Palestinian, you're over twenty, and your family wasn't killed by Israelis. You flunk all three entrance exams. The best you can hope for is a relationship where he has reason to trust you. Tonight was a good start. Follow up very carefully--if you get the chance. Don't forget, Dick, this guy chops up Americans like you and eats them for lunch."

"Roger that, Mountie. Speaking of good food, when are you going to visit a Vienna Heurigen with me?"

"Before too long. How's it going with you and Maria?"

Dick chuckled. "I'm supposed to take her and her mother flying in the morning. I'd better get Sabena's perfume off before then, or you'll be calling Arlington for a plot for me."

"Take care, partner. We'll be waiting for your call."

"Why couldn't I go to your room?" Maria's bright blue eyes glistened when she was mad. They were lighting up the front seat of her small car as she glared at Dick.

"Oh please, Snookie, you know how that makes me feel. I only paid for a single room in the Gasthaus."

". . . and you paid for the breakfast I ate with you, and you gave him the biggest tip he ever got! He wouldn't have thought twice if you'd taken me to your room."

Maria directed her smoldering stare at the road and turned into the Wiener Neustadt airport.

"Sweetie, if we were only going to the room for a few minutes, I'd have asked you. But you didn't bring your mother along for the flight--and the way you were touching me during breakfast--we'd still be in that room!"

"Yes," she wet her lips and grinned sarcastically at him, "and you'd be a very happy man."

It was vintage jealous Maria! She had tried to call him last night at their apartment and received no answer. Her last attempt was after midnight.

Dick's excuse was that he had worked until eleven at his UNO office; and, since Maria would have her car to drive them back to Vienna, he'd taken the late train to Wiener Neustadt. He'd checked into the old Gasthaus and called her at seven in the morning, so she could pick him up on her way to the airport with her mother.

Dick thought her mother was really looking forward to her first flight, but Maria told him at breakfast that she'd changed her mind. Not likely!

He had advised Maria to wear slacks for the flight, but she had worn a mini-skirt that showed her slender legs to great advantage. Experience told him she was on another jealousy tangent.

She parked the little Autobianci by the flying club hangar. Dick smiled as she checked her makeup in the mirror--an incredibly beautiful female! Her tremulous lips were always sending the message they wanted to be kissed. Normally, her fine-spun golden hair would be flowing to her shoulders, but this morning it was pulled behind her head in a tight wrap.

The Cessna was ready. The attendant was waiting with the log book. As Dick signed for the plane, he noted the attendant had not logged last night's flight. That omission was part of the service for which Dick had paid him a rather large sum. It included pretending Dick had not been at the airport last night.

When the attendant helped Maria into the plane, he got a bonus. Knowing Dick was watching, she made some unnecessary bodily contact that would have the young man's head spinning for days.

Maria followed Dick through the takeoff. At five hundred feet, he smiled at her and removed his hands from the controls. She was doing great, very smooth for only her second try. Passing one thousand feet, he had finished calling in his clearance when the aircraft banked sharply. He glanced at Maria. She had let go of the controls and was unbuttoning her white shirt.

Dick righted the plane and frowned at her. "What are you doing, Snookie? If you're going to learn to fly, you have to keep your hands on the controls."

Her fingers had finished with the buttons and began to untie the knot holding the shirt tails together.

Her inviting blue eyes locked with his. "You're always bragging. Let's see how good a pilot you really are."

The shirt fell from her shoulders, revealing an alabaster-white, rounded bosom. Dick couldn't take his eyes away. She unbuckled her seat belt and draped the shirt over the yoke.

"Whoa, Sweetie. If we hit an air pocket, you may get hurt."

"Then make sure we don't!"

She arched her agile body, lifting the mini-skirt to pull off her white cotton panties.

She hung them on the yoke with the shirt. Then she rose and twisted herself onto Dick's lap. To prevent her from pushing the yoke forward, he had to pull her naked body tightly against him. Her firm warm breasts pressed into his chest.

"Is this okay, *Brummi Bär?*" She grinned mischievously. "You do want me to watch our six o'clock, don't you?"

5

THE MOUNTAIN OF TRUTH

Frau Wilke opened Monday's class session with a moment of silence for Sabena. Austrian newspapers had carried the story: she and her grandfather, political refugees from Iran, perished in an explosion and fire that destroyed their apartment. Police investigators blamed a gas leak. News photos showed the apartment had been totally demolished. Only prompt, courageous, and skillful actions by firemen limited the damage to the top floors of the 21-story luxurious apartment building.

Abrahim, Ali, and Musavi were not in the classroom. Later that evening, Jim explained why on the Skyfone. The photos Dick had taken of the three with his mini-camera had been circulated to *Purple* contacts, who worked as immigration officials at key airports. The contact at Tripoli had processed them into Libya last Friday. *Purple* learned they had leased a suite of expensive offices in Tripoli, paid a year's rent in advance, spent the weekend on the beach, and caught Monday's flight back to Schwechat.

"Mirhashem's unhappy in Damascus," said Jim. "Maybe he's going to team with the Libyan Colonel. That would be an unholy alliance if there ever was one."

"Did Mirhashem make it to Vienna Friday night?" asked Dick.

"He flew from Damascus to Munich, rented a car, and drove into Austria near Salzburg. Then we lost him. He probably made contact with Sabena through a third party and went to Mariazell."

"Mountie, if *Purple* can track that guy around, why don't they take him?"

"Come on, Dick! If he was locked up, can you imagine how many hostages would be grabbed to trade for him?"

"Then why don't we just hit him?"

"Same rationale! GP-7 won't give *Purple* permission, because they're afraid of retaliation against themselves personally. There is a line of reasoning that this guy's network's so deep and secure that taking him out wouldn't change anything. He's probably the only one who knows the entire system. As long as he's alive, there's always a chance to get next to him and unravel it."

"Not likely, Jim. Sounds like a CIA pipe dream."

"You're right, Bear. Let us know when the *Three Musketeers* are back in class."

The next day, Abrahim, Ali, and Musavi returned to the classroom. They graciously accepted Frau Wilke's condolences for the loss of Sabena.

During the break before the last class session, Abrahim quietly asked Dick: "Sir, could you join us after class for a *reunion*?"

Dick looked into the handsome Palestinian's stern countenance and replied: "Yes, I'd be interested in such an event."

"It would be necessary for you to come with us immediately after class, with no phone calls before then."

"Certainly. I understand."

Dick followed the three young men past the #43 Strassenbahn stop. They crossed the street and waited in the coffee shop until the rest of the class boarded the streetcar. Then they continued down the street to a green 700-series BMW.

Abrahim opened a back door for Dick, Musavi angrily snatched a parking ticket off the windshield, Ali got behind the wheel.

In a few moments, they were driving south past the Rathaus. Abrahim looked at Dick's briefcase. "Sir, would it be okay if I checked that for weapons?"

"Of course. Got some class notes in there that might help Ali improve his grade."

Ali laughed. "Gimme a break. I had the same answers as you on that last test--I know because I copied from your paper. Frau Wilke has an ulterior motive for giving you a higher grade."

They passed the museum, and Ali turned west on the Linke Weinzeile.

All Dick truly had in his briefcase were his class notes--and the Skyfone. It was cleverly disguised as a General Electric transistor radio. He grinned at Abrahim: "I listen to *Österreich Zwei* on the way to class. They have the news in English for us foreigners."

Abrahim put it back in the briefcase. "Their broadcaster's English is better than his German. Could we lock the briefcase in the car while we attend the reunion?"

"Certainly."

They passed the Theater an der Wien where preparations were underway for the opening of the new musical, *Cats*. Minutes later, they entered the parking area for Schloss Schönbrunn. The famous castle had served as the summer home for the Hapsburg royalty. It was beautifully maintained, and one of the prime tourist attractions in Vienna.

After they stepped from the car, Abrahim turned to Dick. "Sir, do you mind if we search you for a weapon?"

"No, certainly not." Dick casually raised his elbows shoulder-high and Musavi made quick work of it.

The park was not crowded. They entered through the main gate and walked the full length of the long garden of colorful flowers. They climbed the hill at the far end to the statues and pavilions. It provided a magnificent panorama of the castle's grounds, with the Wienerwald in the background.

They followed Abrahim to the pavilion on the east end of the hill. A few tourists were standing in the front, taking photographs. On the far side, Dick noticed two well-dressed Arabic men leaning against the pillars. Seated on a marble bench along the south side was a middle-aged man. A woman stood before him. Her hair and most of her face were covered with a scarf, but Dick recognized Sabena.

As they approached, the man rose from the bench. Impeccably dressed in an Italian-style business suit, he was about five-seven with a stocky build. His dark hairline was receding, his wide forehead was scarred, his stern features were adorned by thick tinted glasses. It was not the kind of face that smiled often. Dick knew this was the most feared man in the deadly world of international terrorism--Mirhashem.

"Sir," said Abrahim, "I have the honor to introduce Captain Orden."

"Good afternoon, Captain. I'm Sabena's uncle. Thank you for meeting with me. Let's sit here on the bench and converse."

His English was schooled and without accent. His forceful voice was deep and a little hoarse. No hand was extended in greeting, his face remained stern.

"My pleasure," said Dick.

- 78 -

As he stepped past Sabena to sit down, he smiled at her and said: "Good day, young lady. How are you?"

She didn't answer. She quickly lowered her eyes and went to Abrahim. In the presence of her uncle, Sabena apparently had an entirely different role than at the university.

"Captain," began Mirhashem, "I must first thank you for saving the lives of my uncle Fahed al-Benna and my niece Sabena. Without your timely actions, the newspaper reports of their death might have been correct."

"By chance, and perhaps with the grace of Allah," replied Dick, "I had resources available to be of service to Dr. al-Benna. I hold him in high regard and was pleased to assist him."

"I'm sorry he could not accompany me today. He's exhausted from his miraculous escape, but he sends his thanks and blessings."

The terrorist leader turned to look directly into Dick's eyes. Even through the heavy tinted lenses, his black eyes were cold as ice. "Please don't think we're any less grateful because it's taken a few days to thank you. You employed a wide range of assets while performing that miracle, we needed to find out as much as possible about you before risking a meeting."

Dick's eyes were steady under Mirhashem's cold stare. He grinned wryly and said: "It was simply a matter of a few friends being available to help me at the right time."

"Perhaps," the Palestinian paused for a moment, "but it's clear from your performance at NATO, which is a matter of record, that you are a man of action and courage."

Dick waited. He need not fear Mirhashem's ability to get information out of NATO, or anywhere else. *Purple* had gone to great lengths to ensure the credibility of his *Edward Orden* alias.

"Having recently been in Damascus," continued Mirhashem, "I know that regime was favorably impressed with your disposal of Ahmad Salah last January. Ahmad had been running wild for the last couple years, and offended many of the more traditional clerics. You also picked up a few votes when you killed his Mafia henchman Enrico in Sicily three years ago. He was another embarrassment to the Syrian government."

Dick felt the adrenaline surge through his system. Was it common knowledge in the terrorist world that *Captain Orden* had hit Salah in Nicaragua? How, and how much, did others know about that *Purple* operation?

He sought to change the conversation: "I'm sorry that Sabena and Dr. al-Benna lost their beautiful home last Friday. What are your plans for them? Can I be of help in their relocation? I know Austria quite well. There are mountain villages where they would be safe and comfortable."

Mirhashem shook his head. "Grandfather Fahed would like to stay in this pleasant country, but a mountain top's no place for a young woman. I promised my dying brother that his baby Sabena would grow up free. Unfortunately, our homeland may not be liberated in her lifetime. Her and Fahed's *deceased* status, that resulted from your miracle rescue, will buy some time. I'll create another identity for them, and hope it will endure longer than this last one. Fahed placed his total trust in you Friday and came out a winner. Could I trust you to find them safe haven in America?"

"Well," Dick thought for a moment. Could he make this powerful terrorist even more indebted to him? "It's been obvious in class that Sabena could do well at any university in the States. I have connections in the field of Political Science. Many universities are actively recruiting females--especially those from ethnic groups--to enroll in that course of study."

Mirhashem motioned for his niece to come closer. "Sabena, what do you think about studying Political Science in America?"

Dick could see her smile through the scarf, but her answer was quiet and reserved: "Uncle, it's for you to stay. What's important is that Grandfather has good medical care when his time comes."

"Many American universities have medical schools with good hospitals," assured Dick. "If your identity remains as an Iranian refugee, and if you provide transcripts through the undergraduate level, I could guarantee your acceptance at a major university."

Mirhashem and Sabena seemed interested. After Dick described the academic and visa application processes, Mirhashem decided Sabena and her grandfather would remain in hiding near Vienna until their new identity was established. In the meantime, Abrahim would coordinate with Dick and supply the necessary documents for the applications. Their agreed goal was to have Sabena in an American university by the start of the fall semester.

Mirhashem signaled Abrahim to take Sabena to the other side of the pavilion. The sun was shining on the bench, it was quite warm.

Mirhashem rose to remove his coat. As he did so, his comb fell to the floor under the bench. Dick immediately knelt to retrieve it. Rising from the floor, he shifted it from his left hand to his right, drawing the comb's teeth firmly between his left thumb and forefinger. After handing the comb to Mirhashem, he casually stuck his left hand in his trousers pocket and wiped his fingers on the lining as he sat down.

Mirhashem returned the comb to his coat, folded it on his lap, and again seated himself on the bench. "Captain Orden, a political confrontation of considerable international importance is taking place. Are you up to date on the hostage situation in Lebanon?"

"Only what I read in the papers," responded Dick.

Cold eyes glared at him over the top of the tinted spectacles. "Knowing your other connections, I'll take that as a *yes*. Let's not play games, Captain. I'm going to offer you a deal with fame if not fortune. I'm willing to let you see some of the hostages."

Dick returned the cold stare. "A wise old Italian told me there's no such thing as a free pizza. What do you expect from me?"

Mirhashem turned his stocky shoulders and stared at the castle. "Maybe you can convince your President to be as reasonable as the Hapsburgs were with Napoleon. He set a smart precedence during his first term, by paying the ransom for his NATO General, but now he seems willing to let hostages die without even an offer."

"Perhaps that has something to do with two hundred and forty-four Marines dying in their beds at the Beirut airport two years ago," said Dick harshly.

"In return for which fighter pilots like you killed Palestinian women and children in the Bekaa Valley," was the icy reply.

"So . . . , of what possible use could I be to you?" asked Dick. "I'm sure you have contact with the White House--on a frequent basis."

"That's correct," nodded Mirhashem. "They are sending the same arrogant Marine officer every week. He always demands to see the hostages, to prove they're alive. Of course, he really wants to find out where they are--so a stupid rescue could be attempted. You worked with this President before, Captain. He trusted you with a million dollars for General Thomas. Come to Lebanon with me, see the futility of any rescue attempt, then talk sense to him. While you're there, you'll have the opportunity to speak with many of my colleagues. They're eager for exposure to the American *mind-set*. In return for answering their questions, they'll answer yours. As a combat-experienced officer, you'll have no problem communicating with my talented fighters."

"If I could remove one grain of sand from the hourglass that will mark the end of the killing between the peoples of the Middle East, I'd be glad to cooperate," said Dick thoughtfully; "but I'm sure you know that I would have neither the backing nor the blessing of any government during my visit."

A slight pursing of the lips was the only change of expression Dick had noticed during the tense conversation. "The backing you demonstrated during the rescue of Sabena and her grandfather is enough proof that I have the right man. If you agree to come, the logistics are simple. Abrahim will tell you when we're ready. He'll make the arrangements and accompany you. This must be come-as-you-are. Even with the trust that's now between us, we cannot take the chance of our plans becoming known to anyone else."

In spite of the seriousness of the situation, Dick smiled at the terrorist's use of the old American party-time idiom.

At Dick's request, Ali dropped him at the McDonalds on Maria-hilferstrasse. The busy shopping street was one of the easiest areas in Vienna to ditch a tail, and he was sure the boys would once again attempt to follow him home. They'd been trying two or three times a week after class; but, with *Purple's* help, Dick always managed to elude them. *Purple* had developed computer programs to assist in escapes in those cities where the subways were extremely reliable and usually on time. That included Vienna and Munich. Dick had used the service many times. His individual specifications were already entered in the Vienna program. He need only enter the time and his location through the Skyfone, carry the instrument in his shirt pocket like a transistor radio, and place the earphone in his ear. He would receive continual advice on transit schedules, and two or more proposed routes from which to choose.

After eating a cheeseburger at an upstairs table, Dick waited fifteen minutes. Then he casually took the Skyfone from his brief-case, entered the criteria for evasion, selected the option for three pursuers with one auto, put the instrument in his shirt pocket, stuck the earphone in his ear, and walked down the stairs.

A few minutes later, he entered the U-4 subway. He walked briskly through the station, climbed the stairs on the far side, and grabbed the single taxi at the exit. That particular stand had room for only one taxi, and was the perfect place to peal off a pursuer on foot. As his taxi pulled away from the curb, he saw Abrahim climbing the stairs. Ali and Musavi were in the BMW, driving down the street from McDonalds. One down and two to go!

Dick had the taxi driver drop him at the Schwedenplatz U-Bahn station. There was no parking in the immediate area, and he'd lose Ali and the car with that maneuver. He paused at a Tabak stand for a newspaper, then proceeded to the ramp for the northbound train that terminated at the United Nations building. He stepped into a middle car just before the door closed, and noticed Musavi doing the same thing at the end car. Two down and one to go!

At the end of the line, Dick left the U-Bahn and walked to the guarded entrance for the UNO building. He flashed his ID card and proceeded to the second floor where his research office was located. Peering from the window, he saw Musavi sitting on a bench at the entrance to the U-Bahn. That was the same mistake Ali had made last week. Dick went quickly to a side entrance of the complex, and hurried to one of the many taxis waiting there. Minutes later, he was stepping into a streetcar that would take him to the next subway station south of the UNO stop. From there, it was a nine-minute ride to the Rheumanplatz and his apartment. Three down, game-set-match!

It was three-fifteen. Maria would be coming through Rheuman-platz station in about thirty minutes, on her way home from work.

Dick treated himself to a cup of delicious Tichy Eis, and found a bench near the back of the small park to wait for her. It was a perfect time to contact Jim at *Purple* HQ in Frankfurt. He hid the Skyfone behind his newspaper and initiated the scrambler-call.

"Hi, Bear," came the immediate response. "What's playing in the city of music?"

"A finely orchestrated symphony, Mountie. Would you like to hear the allegrettos?"

"Should I get Nelson on the line too?"

"Yeah, good idea."

It took Dick only a minute to update them on the reappearance of the *Three Musketeers* and his meeting with Mirhashem. Then he asked, "Mr. Nelson, do you think he'll really take me to Lebanon?"

"I'd bet on it," answered the *Purple* Field Supervisor. "He's done that with two British and two American agents in the past, but they never got close to a hostage. He enjoys taunting his opponents. His early-day aircraft hijackings bear that out."

"Assuming you want me to follow through with this, have you any idea what I should expect?"

Jim was quick to respond. "*Purple's* compiled a lot of information about his operations. We anticipated he might invite you, so we spent all weekend getting ready. This is hot info. Are you in a place where you can concentrate?"

Dick glanced around the small park and laughed. "Conrad, it's a warm day in Vienna. This place is full of liberated women catching some sun, but I'll do my best."

The RCMP officer gave Dick a summary of what others had experienced as guests of Mirhashem in Lebanon. All had been taken from Beirut to the eastern edge of the Bekaa Valley, near the Syrian border. The camp was a cluster of stone houses surrounded by rudimentary military training facilities. Southeast of the camp rose a sharp hill strewn with large boulders. It was about two kilometers across, with an elevation of 750 feet.

The programs for Mirhashem's guests had included intense, sometimes heated, conversations covering a broad range of Middle East political issues. Mirhashem and five or six senior members of his organization usually took part in the debates. There were nearly forty guards in the camp, but the same five guards were always present during the debates--which took the entire first day and the morning of the second. After that, all the guards would stage an impressive demonstration of their military prowess. The visits had terminated on the evening of the second day, with the return of the guests to Beirut. Mirhashem had always remained at the camp.

Jim paused to ask Dick if he had any questions.

"Yeah, Conrad, did all his guests come back alive?"

"No, Dick," answered Nelson, "they didn't, and that brings us to the plan we have for your visit."

Nelson began by explaining *Purple* had penetrated the camp. One of the guards who was always present at the debates had a sister illegally in America. In return for her citizenship, the promise of a comfortable life, and his eventual welcome to the States, the brother had been cooperating with *Purple*--though his contributions thus far were minimal. The camp was simply too confining a situation! However, *Purple* had slipped him a special weapon, in the form of a knife that looked like those carried by his fellow guards. The apparent difference was a small brass tip on its sheath.

Purple's motivation for establishing a contact in the camp was the killing of one of Mirhashem's two British guests. The story had been brought out by the survivor: During the first day of debate, the deceased had gotten into a heated argument with a Palestinian official. It resulted in a shouting match, during which the Englishman called the Palestinian a liar. Mirhashem had intervened by saying this was a matter for Allah to decide--who was telling the truth? At sundown, the discussions had ended and the two antagonists were taken to opposite sides of the rocky hill, known as the *Mountain of Truth*. When darkness fell, they were stripped to their shorts and shoes, given a knife, and sent up the mountain. The one who came down alive in the morning would be the one that Allah had decided was telling the truth. The Brit had not returned. The Palestinian had pointed proudly at the blood stains on his shoes.

"That could happen again, Dick," warned Jim. "It all depends on Mirhashem, and he's an unpredictable bastard!"

"Here is what we have done to give you the edge," continued Nelson. "Our messenger will be enroute to Vienna within the hour. He'll have satellite maps of the camp and a relief map of that hill, and he'll have a knife with instructions for its use."

"The maps are a great idea," said Dick.

"I've circled places on the hill that look like good ambush sites," said Jim.

"Okay, thanks, but don't bother with the knife. Not sure how much time I'll have before Mirhashem sends for me, but I know damned well I can't become a good knife-fighter by then."

Nelson intervened to explain the basics of the knife. It was identical to the one carried by the guard at the debates. When a certain part of the blade, and a portion of the handle, were warmed to body temperature and twisted in a certain way, the handle would come apart. Inside was the latest in the emerging technology of night-vision. The scope could detect live targets at ranges up to five hundred yards. Also enclosed were two mini-canisters: one functioned like a spray can, the other held a pressurized vial. Both contained a knockout gas that could incapacitate the inhaler in seconds. There was also a coil of fine wire with a tensile strength of over 500 pounds. The printed instructions enroute with the maps would show Dick how to employ the weapons.

The *Purple* contact in the camp had agreed to wear the knife they'd given him to the debating sessions--though he had no knowledge of its special capabilities. He'd also been instructed to lend it to any of Mirhashem's western guests that might ask for it.

"Between the map and the night-vision, we're betting our old fighter pilot could pull off a successful ambush," said Jim.

"My last ambush was *pulled off* eighteen years ago, when my vertebrae were in a straight line, and when I was with a squad of the free world's bravest and best," remembered Dick. "All I had to do was point an M-16 and pull the trigger."

"I hope it won't be necessary," said Nelson. "Try not to argue with any of those guys; but, if you do, choose the smallest one."

Dick chuckled, then asked: "What should I do with the maps and your knife? Don't want to leave them in the apartment while I'm gone. Oh, yeah, may have gotten a few strands of hair from the guy I met today. Can you check if it was the real Mirhashem?"

"Good work!" exclaimed Jim. "Burn the maps and instructions when you're through with them, then mail the hair and knife to us special delivery." He added reassuringly: "You won't be alone, Brown Bear. We'll be tracking you when you leave Vienna. When appropriate, we'll signal you through the chip in your shoulder. We are positioning a satellite to pick up your chip's voice transmitter while you're in the camp. That satellite also has the same video and audio surveillance capability we had in Aura One. Can't put up any TACAIR, it would be within range of Syrian surface-to-air missiles. If everything goes to hell, say *Purple* real loud three times. We have missiles targeted on the camp, and we're negotiating with the IDF for a rescue chopper to look for you when the smoke clears. If all else fails, hike south for the snow-capped peak you'll see in the distance. Mr. Hermon's about twenty miles from Israel. I'll join you there for some late-season skiing."

"Thanks, Jim. That is a hell of a plan; but I've always been a better talker than a hiker or fighter, and I'm a terrible skier. Let's hope I can stay in Mirhashem's good graces, so we can set him up for something really big later on."

"That's the main idea, Dick," echoed Nelson. "Let's also hope he calls for you in the next few days, while there's still no moon."

It was Friday noon, only three days after the Schönbrunn Castle introduction to Mirhashem, when Abrahim took Dick's arm as they left the classroom. Ali drove them to Schwechat, where Abrahim and Dick boarded Lufthansa for the five hour flight to Damascus. There they joined a group of twenty others, for the helicopter flight to the meeting site at the eastern edge of Lebanon's Bekaa Valley.

It was too dark in the helo for Dick to study the faces of his traveling companions. All were clothed in military-style uniforms. Eight of them were apparently senior officials. They were accorded special treatment. The remainder were in their late teens or early twenties. They sat in the back with Abrahim and Dick.

It was a dark night, with few reference lights on the ground, but they flew at a very low altitude--perhaps to avoid Israeli radar. When the pilot flared for landing, Dick saw only three small red lights marking the helicopter pad. They deplaned quickly and were blinded by dust from the rotor blades. The big Soviet-made helo rose from the pad and departed to the east.

Abrahim led him over rough ground through the darkened camp to a long, narrow, stone building. He left Dick at the door to one of the many rooms, with the advice to get some sleep. He'd come for him in the morning.

There were no chairs in the small room. Dick sat precariously on the old army cot and removed his shoes. He smiled as he recalled Maria had chosen them for him during a holiday in South Tyrol. They were made from buckskin leather, with nylon laces and medium-high tops. He had assumed that Abrahim would take him directly from the language class to the meeting in Lebanon. He had continued to wear his normal coat and tie to class, but reasoned wingtips would not do well on the Mountain of Truth--if his conference with Mirhashem and friends should go astray.

Dick set his shoes on the dusty floor and swung his legs on the cot. The single blanket would obviously not be enough to ward off the cold. He removed his coat, pulled the blanket over his body, and laid the coat over his feet. At that moment, he received a sharp--but welcome--shock in his right shoulder. Somewhere high overhead, the monitor for his chip was transmitting successfully through the *Purple* satellite. A few seconds later, he received two sharp jolts followed quickly by two more--the all-clear signal.

Dick sighed. "Yeah, Conrad, might be *all-clear* for you in Frankfurt, but I'm in for a cold night in Lebanon." His muffled comment was immediately rewarded with another jolt. Incredible! After five years, the chip's transmitter, which keyed off the vibrations of his vocal cords, was still working.

He tried to doze off, but his thoughts of Maria's warm body were shattered by the sounds of mice scurrying around the room. God, how he hated those little creatures--ever since he was a kid!

Between the mice, the uncomfortable cot, and the cold room, it was a sleepless night. When he heard the chanting outside, Dick went to the window and peered into the early morning light.

The adjacent training field was about the size of a soccer field. It was surrounded by a dusty running track. Its interior was a maze of obstacle course barriers. Forty-five dark figures were jogging in a three-abreast formation around the track. Two instructors ran alongside the formation. Their chants reminded Dick of his preflight days. The rhythm was the same, but the words were Arabic.

As the formation passed the barracks building, Dick saw the black hoods over the instructors' heads. One of them shouted an order. The first rank of three broke formation and raced to the nearest obstacle on the field. It was a scaling wall with three ropes suspended from the top. It appeared to be a typical military training exercise--individual competition scrambling up the ropes--but, when the first one reached the top, he turned to assist the others. The instructor shouted again. The second rank raced to the rows of parallel bars. The first one to reach the end turned back to encourage the other two. Dick noted this procedure over and over again. Obviously, the emphasis was on functioning as a group of three.

With the first rays of sunlight, Dick saw the Mountain of Truth, jutting into the sky southeast of the camp. As it grew lighter, he looked for the boulders and trails he had memorized from Jim's photographic map. Confidence whelmed inside him, as he began to recognize the mountain's features. He took off his shirt and washed himself in the basin of cold water.

Abrahim came by at seven and took him to breakfast at a stone hut in the middle of the camp. They sat alone at a big table, which occupied most of the dining room. The Turkish coffee was very bitter, but the food was great--ham, eggs, and English muffins with jam. Abrahim responded to Dick's surprised look by explaining European *exchange* students and instructors were in the camp.

They had finished eating before Mirhashem arrived with four guards. He greeted Dick warmly and explained they'd be starting late, some of the participants had been delayed in Beirut. He sat down to have coffee with Dick and Abrahim. The guards positioned themselves in the corners of the room. They carried sheath knives on the belts of their green uniforms--none had a brass tip.

Mirhashem told Dick that he would have academic transcripts for Sabena by the end of next week. Dick replied that he had alerted contacts at Nebraska, Colorado, and Florida State to expect an application from an exceptional candidate. He had also been in touch with the U.S. Consul in Vienna who confirmed student visas were usually automatic with university acceptance. Mirhashem seemed quite pleased. He directed Abrahim to give Dick a tour of the camp. He planned on starting the discussions at ten.

From Jim's photographs, Dick knew the camp was about a mile square. The camouflaged material that the photographs had shown in the northwest sector was covering six Soviet-made tanks. Their turrets were painted with Syria's red-white-black horizontal striped flag, with two green stars on the white stripe. Along the southern and western boundaries, Dick spotted three Soviet SA-6 mobile surface-to-air missile launchers. They were also camouflaged, but armed and apparently ready for operation. Soldiers in Syrian uniforms were lounging around the missile launchers.

The eastern half of the camp was devoted to terrorist training. Dick recognized the typical lay-out from photographs he'd viewed earlier, of the Colonel's camps in Libya. There was a live-firing exercise underway in the two-story frame house at the northern end of the complex. Dick recognized the staccato of AK-47's and the angry buzz of Uzi's. As they walked through the facility, Abrahim explained the current class was in its last week of a three-month course. The students would soon take their final exam in Beirut, and a new class would be flown in from Damascus.

They heard a large helicopter approaching from the southeast. Abrahim checked his watch. "It's almost ten, Captain Orden. That is probably the Iranian contingent arriving. Let's walk to that cypress grove. The discussion will be outside, under those trees."

There were no tables or chairs. They were seated in a circle on luxurious pillows, which were protected from the dusty ground by a large tarpaulin.

Mirhashem began by introducing Dick, who was seated at his right hand. "My friends, this is Captain Edward Orden. He is also my friend, having saved the lives of my uncle Fahed al-Benna and my niece Sabena. In doing so, he outwitted and outmaneuvered the Mossad in Vienna. He is a retired naval officer, who worked at NATO headquarters in Belgium. He delivered his President's ransom of General Thomas--an event familiar to all of you. Perhaps you recall that the Captain chose that opportunity to kill the Mafia operative Enrico, who had been embarrassing the Syrian government with a white-slave racket in the Philippines. He also disposed of Ahmad Salah, killing him under the very nose of Nicaragua's new communist regime. I have not satisfied myself why he's now living in Vienna instead of the United States, but I do believe he's an honorable man. His knowledge and experience could benefit both sides, as we struggle with our current hostage problems."

While Mirhashem introduced him, Dick's eyes scanned those seated around the circle. No one was looking at him or Mirhashem. All were either staring vacantly at the center of the circle or watching the birds playing in the cypress. The four uniformed men, who had accompanied Mirhashem at breakfast, stood guard around the outside of the circle. None of their knife sheaths had a brass tip.

Mirhashem glanced over his tinted spectacles at the uniformed middle-aged man seated on Dick's right. "Captain, the officer next to you is Abu Misra. We've been partners since our early days in Jordan, where we both recognized Arafat's betrayal of our cause and formed our own Fatah Revolutionary Council. He was a friend of Sabena's father before his murder by the traitor King Hussein. As my coordinator with Tehran and the Islamic Jihad groups here in Lebanon, Abu Misra's eager to hear your translation of the U.S. reaction to the hostage situation."

The Palestinian officer's dark eyes regarded Dick briefly, but courteously, from under his large uniform hat. Dick nodded a greeting, then looked again at Mirhashem as he continued: "Seated by Abu Misra is Lebanon's greatest military hero. Only six weeks ago, General Beyrri led his Amal Militia, and some of my fighters, to victory in west Beirut. Arafat's PLO traitors, and the Sunni's Mourabitoun, are no longer viable forces in this country."

The others greeted Mirhashem's proclamation with a solemn round of "Allah be praised." The General graciously touched the gold-trimmed brim of his hat in acknowledgment. Mirhashem continued: "The General now protects all American hostages in Lebanon, and is eager to converse with you." Beyrri smiled and waved his hand at Dick, who nodded his head politely in return.

Mirhashem gestured across the circle at the tall, slender figure dressed in the flowing robes and Kufiyah headdress of an Islamic cleric. "We're also honored today by Sheik Omman from Tehran. He distinguished himself six years ago, when he led his students in the seizure of your embassy. He's eager to hear your views of his influence on American politics."

Sheik Omman regarded Dick briefly with a cold stare, then returned his eyes to the tops of the cypress.

Seated next to the Sheik was a stout man in a Syrian major's uniform. He acknowledged Mirhashem's introduction as a representative of the government to which they owed many favors, including the use of the camp.

Mirhashem casually returned the Major's salute and moved on to the elderly man dressed in robes similar to Sheik Omman's. The man stroked his gray beard thoughtfully as Mirhashem introduced him: "Sheik Fidlah's home is Qom, but he's sacrificed his time and energy to assist our brothers in this ravaged land. His well-planned revenge on the Marine barracks a couple years ago led to the departure of your military--for which we're all grateful."

There was another solemn round of "Allah be praised," to which Mirhashem added forcefully: "and thanks be to Allah that Sheik Fidlah survived the cowardly car-bomb attack by your President's assassins three months ago today!"

Mirhashem turned to his left to introduce the last of the participants. "Sheik Odieb is another who has forgone the comforts of Tehran to take up the challenges in this country, which has been raped repeatedly by our common enemy, Israel."

While dressed like the other Sheiks, Odieb appeared more relaxed--if not personable. He had a slight smile on his face, and nodded graciously as his dark eyes met Dick's.

Mirhashem again glanced over his tinted spectacles at his old friend, Abu Misra began the discussion: "Captain, I've been told the details of your miraculous rescue of little Sabina and our dear Fahed al-Benna. I want to thank you personally." Abu extended his hand, which Dick shook warmly. That drew a subdued round of "Allah be praised."

Misra smiled and continued: "Your media's exaggerations often exceed our wildest expectations; therefore, I'll begin by reminding you which Americans we're currently protecting. Three employees of your university in Beirut are enjoying our hospitality. The first arrived in February last year, the third joined us only last week."

Misra paused for a moment, and Dick asked quickly: "Why do you take them away from the task of rebuilding Lebanon's defunct educational system, particularly at this time?"

Sheik Fidlah answered: "We reviewed their courses and methods of instruction and found them in conflict with the teachings and customs of Islam. There's also the question of why your President left American citizens here, after he withdrew his armed forces. Wasn't that a rather idiotic decision?" The mastermind of the Marine barracks massacre emphasized the word *idiotic*.

"Doesn't the American public recognize the fact that you're neither wanted nor needed in this part of the world?" asked Sheik Omman. His cold, hard eyes were fixed on Dick.

It was uncomfortable sitting on the ground, and his herniated vertebrae were beginning to ache; but Dick leaned forward to extend his hands and touch his fingertips together--as he'd seen Ambassador Mumfred do so often in Manila: "Gentlemen, to confirm your suspicions, the American public is indeed a fat, dumb, and happy gathering of disinterested people. Only occasionally does an unusual incident arouse them to action. The Japanese made that mistake at Pearl Harbor in December 1941. Now, over forty years later, babies born in Nagasaki still have two left feet."

"You're talking about an America that vanished into the dustbins of history, Captain," responded Sheik Omman sarcastically. "The Americans of today looked the other way, while I held the spies in your embassy hostage four hundred and forty-four days."

"Please let me identify the rest of our American *guests* for the Captain, before we get too deeply involved," interrupted Misra. He turned to Dick and continued: "We thought it might be productive to have your Cultural Attaché take a break from his embassy duties to learn more about Mideast culture firsthand."

"Yes, I know," said Dick. "He's been with you fifteen months. Haven't you proven your point by now?"

Omman's voice cut like a knife: "Imagine our surprise, when we discovered he was a spy--actually your CIA Chief of Station for this neutral country. The Lebanese were so offended that we had to move him to Tehran for his own protection."

"What makes you think he's involved with the CIA?" asked Dick.

"He told me so," grinned Omman evilly. "We had a private conversation in which he revealed his inner soul to me."

The taste of bile surged into Dick's throat, but his countenance remained calm.

Misra continued: "We're also educating some of your media. As you know, the Chief Correspondent for the Associated Press has been investigating our side of the issues for almost three months."

"I'm surprised you consider intimidation a tool for controlling the world press," replied Dick. "You kept that CNN guy around for almost a year, but he didn't have many good things to say about your hospitality after he escaped."

"You have been the victim of a press conspiracy, Captain," said General Beyrri. "No one leaves the umbrella of my protection without proper clearance. The dishonest CNN reporter discovered our side of the story was the truthful one. That wouldn't have sold many TV commercials in the States, so he falsely dramatized an escape adventure. Did it make him a hero in America? He was free to leave at any time."

"If I might take a moment," said Dick, "I'd like to clarify a point about the media and the American public. In order to sell more commercial time, and maximize profits, our media has continually increased the amount of violence it portrays. This saturation has resulted in a public that is not easily aroused--the slang word is *jaded*. As Sheik Omman noted, we sat quietly while our embassy was destroyed and our citizens imprisoned for more than a year. If you were watching American television during that time, you saw only *talking heads*. There's nothing exciting about uneducated news analysts discussing hostages sitting in cells."

Dick turned to stare at Omman and continued: "However, history shows that the learned Cleric was wise enough not to brutalize those hostages. If he had, babies born in what would have been left of Tehran would also have had two left feet."

"We have no fear of America!" snarled Omman. "You have the weapons--built by German scientists you took hostage after the war--but your decadent society lacks the will. Your defeats in Korea and Vietnam proved that conclusively."

Misra intervened: "Captain, we know we have much to learn about exploiting America's weaknesses. However, rest assured we are learning. Your greedy, immoral, media will soon be our strongest weapon--and ally."

General Beyrri withdrew a card from his pocket and passed it to Dick. "Don't underestimate our understanding of American ways." The card was a valid green card, authorizing Beyrri to work in the U.S. "My wife and children remain in Michigan. I returned here only to serve my homeland in its time of need."

The General launched into a long and boring tirade about the problems with Americans and their lack of knowledge of the Middle East. The others were apparently accustomed to his boasting and lounged quietly.

Finally Mirhashem clapped his hands twice, and veiled women appeared with baskets of fruit, bread, and cheese.

As they ate, the others conversed in Arabic. Dick sat quietly, enjoying the peaches. The tone of the conversation became heated, with a sharp exchange between Mirhashem and Sheik Omman. The others seemed to be siding with Mirhashem. Omman finally grew quiet, staring coldly at Dick as he finished his lunch.

It was almost three before the baskets were cleared away. The four guards had been joined by a fifth. Dick was relieved to see a knife sheath with a brass tip on his belt.

Misra began the discussion again: "I must identify two more of your countrymen who are spending time with us, Captain. There's a Catholic Priest, who came to us in January, and a Presbyterian Minister, who's been with us for over a year."

"I'm sure you have had enough time with them to realize their religious beliefs and teachings are not a threat to Islam," said Dick. "Doesn't Islam respect those who seek only peace and an end to the violence?"

"Your White House has little respect for the Islamic clergy," scoffed Sheik Fidlah. "They tried to kill me in the street, like a common criminal."

"Perhaps a case of mistaken identity," said Dick. "Our State Department identified you as the leader of the Hizballah group that killed two hundred and forty-four Marines, while they were asleep in their barracks, near the airport they were guarding for you."

"Captain, we didn't need your Marines to keep our airport open," said General Beyrri. "That was a ruse by your President. He finally realized we weren't intimidated by your warships and attempted to interfere more forcefully in our internal affairs by sending ashore--how do you say it--*a few brave men.* You can be comforted by the thought that, although obeying illegal orders, they did not die in vain. Their sacrifice convinced the White House to withdraw from our affairs."

"I share the General's opinion of your Marines, Captain," said Omman. "They were brave men obeying orders, although those orders were in violation of international law and threatened the Muslim population of this land. If you understand Islam, you know our religion and laws are bound together. It was the duty of Sheik Fidlah, as an Islamic Cleric, to act in defense of our true believers. It was also the will of Allah, because it took only two of our children to kill two hundred and forty-four of your best warriors."

"Those two youngsters were sent with a message from Allah, and with my blessings," confirmed Fidlah. "Unfortunately, after sacrificing their sons for Islam, the parents of the boys were among the eighty killed when your President tried to assassinate me."

Dick responded carefully: "A couple weeks ago, an American newspaper claimed the bombing directed at you was sponsored by a few rogue members of our National Security Agency. The next day, the paper reported the President had taken action to prevent another such occurrence. I don't believe Americans are ready to fight terror with terror."

Omman laughed. "I don't have to read newspapers to know about your administration's evil plots. Your *Cultural Attaché* told me all about the CIA's savage killers operating in Beirut."

The implication of torture was very clear. The bile again surged to Dick's throat. Mirhashem interceded: "You must admit your current national security team is a strange group. Some of those people are trying to make a deal with Tehran to trade arms for the Americans we're holding. This Marine, whom your President sends every week to see if they're still alive, has made it clear that his boss is willing to trade hi-tech parts and weapons for their return."

"Are you handling the negotiations?" asked Dick.

"Not directly," answered Mirhashem. "I gave the Marine some names, and your White House apparently went for it. They're dealing on anti-tank missiles, and replacement parts for the F-14's they sold the Shah years ago."

"Are you going to release some Americans?" asked Dick. "I saw a document the Israelis captured--the record of a conference in Tehran--where the Ayatollah appointed you commander of a brigade of special operatives here in Lebanon. I'm sure you have the power to release our people whenever you like."

"It's not that simple, Captain," sighed Mirhashem. "Those who handle the transactions are very greedy. There's also the problem of your President asking an exorbitant price for the weapons."

Dick was shocked. "I thought the price was the release of the Americans!"

Mirhashem nodded. "It started out that way, but the Marine showed up last week with a bill for what Tehran had ordered. That stopped any releases for now."

"Damn our defense contractors to hell!" swore Dick.

"No, I believe something else is going on," said Mirhashem. "The money paid by Tehran would not go to Washington, but to Swiss bank accounts."

"You were told that by an officer in the United States Marine Corps?" Dick was aghast.

"Not directly." Mirhashem explained his information came from intermediaries handling the sales. However, his conversations with the Marine convinced him the White House knew all about it.

"Will the hostage releases get back on track if Tehran pays the U.S. price?" asked Dick.

"The Ayatollahs were more amazed than you, Captain," said Mirhashem. "Now they're worried about where the money might go. Your President's been very vocal about supporting insurgents around the world, for which your Congress has often denied funding. A couple years ago, he was backing a terrorist group in Iran, led by one of the Shah's former naval officers. Perhaps you heard about it at NATO? That was Khomeini's first demand to the President in their *arms-for-hostages* negotiations. His Marine liaison apparently took care of the matter, and that group in the Talish Mountains has been all but eradicated."

Dick's blood ran cold! He recalled the sudden U.S. withdrawal from the first airdrop of arms for Admiral Toufani, and the leak of the mission that had almost cost Dick and Colonel McKenzie their lives. Obviously, that betrayal had taken place in the White House. He struggled for composure, forcing himself back to the issue at hand: "What's happening to the hostages in the meantime?"

"What hostages?" sneered Sheik Omman. "Abu Misra has told you the educators, the media, and the holy men are under General Beyrri's protection."

"Yeah," replied Dick sarcastically, "I saw your Islamic Jihad's tape on Visnews TV in London last January. Our Cultural Attaché, the Presbyterian Minister, and the CNN reporter were on the tape; along with your declaration that five U.S. hostages would be tried as CIA spies."

Dick paused to look sharply at Sheik Omman. "The people with whom I watched the Visnews tape were very concerned about the poor physical appearance of our Attaché. It was clear he'd been severely mistreated. Was that before or after your private conversation with him?"

The Cleric glared at Dick. "If the minister and the reporter were with him on the tape, then it had to be before he was taken to Tehran for his own protection."

"Why'd you wait ten months to *protect* him?" growled Dick. "Did it take that long to decide he was a CIA spy?"

Omman's features were again distorted by an evil sneer. "Of course not, Captain. Like I said this morning, he told me the story of his life shortly after I met him."

"Sheik Omman," Dick's words sliced the warm humid air, "if you have also tortured the two religious Americans in your custody, I'm sure you've been impressed by their honesty, and their loyalty to their faith. I thought the same about the holy men of Islam--until I met you."

The Sheik coiled on his pillow, pulling aside his robe to reveal a long curved knife. "Would you like to take this conversation to another level, Captain?" he hissed.

Mirhashem interceded in a strong voice: "The Captain has a right to his opinion, and I remind you that he's under my protection while he's here."

". . . and mine!" echoed General Beyrri.

"There are those who say the Cultural Attaché was transported to Tehran immediately after the Visnews tape was made--that he was tortured--and that he died last week." Dick's voice was colder than ice. "The arrogant comments I've heard from Sheik Omman today have convinced me, that he's an abuser and murderer of helpless prisoners, a liar, and a disgrace to Islam!"

With a cry of rage, Omman leapt to his feet and drew his knife. Mirhashem rose quickly and barked an order. The five guards jumped into the center of the circle with their AK-47's ready. The one with the brass-tipped knife sheath stood immediately in front of Dick, who was also on his feet. With one quick movement, Dick jerked the knife from its sheath.

Mirhashem grabbed his arm. "Wait, Captain," he demanded, "this is not the way!"

The other two Sheiks went quickly to Omman, speaking sharply to him in Persian. He held the long curved knife above his head, but did not attempt to go through the guards.

The Syrian Major went quickly to General Beyrri. They began a heated discussion in Arabic. Mirhashem released Dick's arm, he lowered the knife slowly.

Finally General Beyrri shouted in English: "Stop this nonsense! Everyone sit down, or I shall have the guards arrest you."

Still chattering and gesturing wildly, the three Sheiks returned to their pillows. The Major returned to his side of the circle. Dick sat down by Mirhashem, with the knife cradled in his lap.

Mirhashem raised his right arm and the circle fell silent. He glared at Dick through his tinted spectacles. "Captain, you have called Sheik Omman a liar. What is your specific charge? Of what do you accuse him of lying?"

Dick's face was chiseled from stone. His hard blue eyes were fixed on Omman as he spoke in a measured tone: "Sheik Omman has said the Cultural Attaché was taken to Tehran for his own protection. That's an absolute lie! He was taken there to be tortured and killed by Omman personally."

Instantly, Dick received three sharp jolts in his right shoulder. He'd been expecting it and didn't flinch. Jim was monitoring his conversation and had warned him with the emergency signal.

Mirhashem stared at the Iranian Cleric. "Sheik Omman, how do you answer the Captain? Does he speak the truth? Have you lied to us during this discussion?"

"By Allah I swear," snarled the Persian, "it is the Captain who has lied. He intends to provoke me. He's not here in the interest of his countrymen. He's been sent as a spy to kill me."

Mirhashem calmly addressed the group: "It has become necessary to explain one of our customs to my guest." He looked at Dick. "If anyone is proven to be lying during our discussions, he's dealt with harshly. He's stabbed by each of the other participants in turn, until he's dead. Do you understand me, Captain Orden?"

"Yes, I do," nodded Dick solemnly.

"Then let us search for the truth," continued Mirhashem. "General Beyrri, do you have specific knowledge whether the Cultural Attaché was taken to Tehran?"

"Indeed he was," replied the leader of the Amal Militia, "but I have no clear evidence of what happened to him there."

"Major?" Mirhashem looked at the Syrian officer. He shook his head.

"Sheik Fidlah?"

"No, honorable Mirhashem. I saw him taken through the Beirut airport, but I have no direct knowledge of the outcome in Tehran. However, I do support Cleric Omman's assertion that the Captain may be an assassin, sent to kill him."

"I must reject that notion," said Mirhashem. "Until three days ago, he had no idea that I would bring him to this place; and I cannot forget that he took on the Mossad to save my family."

Abu Misra concurred: "It's absurd to consider Captain Orden a spy. We have controlled the circumstances by which he is here."

"Sheik Odieb," asked Mirhashem, "what say you? Is Sheik Omman lying? Is the Cultural Attaché dead, or is the Captain falsely accusing our brother?"

"Honored Commander," answered the Islamic Jihad leader, "I can offer no proof for either. Only Allah knows. We must turn to the Mountain of Truth for the answer."

Dick lay flat on his back and stretched his body to absorb the heat from the huge boulder. The night air was cool but still. Clad only in shorts and shoes, the heat from the boulder was sufficient to keep him comfortable.

He had arranged the items from the knife carefully at his side. Alongside the knife and the night-vision scope were the spray canister and the glass vial, both containing the fast-acting gas which he hoped to use on his opponent.

Jim's package from Frankfurt had contained several canisters and vials, filled with inert contents. Dick had practiced using them. The spray canisters were highly pressurized. They could project their contents about ten feet. The trick was to aim precisely at the opponent's head for immediate results. Because of their fragility, the glass vials were not so highly pressurized. It would be necessary to break the vial within a few feet of the opponent's nose to insure rapid incapacitation.

It had clearly not been Mirhashem's intention that Dick should be on the Mountain of Truth. After the challenge developed between Dick and Omman, he had argued passionately against such a settlement. In the end, he was forced to follow the ancient custom.

Before sunset, Mirhashem had dispatched Abrahim in a helicopter to make certain no one was on the mountain. At nightfall, Dick and Omman were stripped to their shorts and shoes and taken to opposite sides of the rugged, boulder-strewn hill. Mirhashem had driven Dick in a jeep. Abrahim escorted Omman's party in another vehicle. At the agreed time, Dick and Omman had been allowed to start up the hill with their knives--Dick from the west, Omman from the east.

Apparently, Mirhashem did not believe Dick had much of a chance. Omman was at least twenty years his junior and appeared in better physical condition. Mirhashem had offered Dick the services of a Catholic Priest before the drive to the mountain. After learning the priest was not the one being held hostage, Dick had declined by saying he was a protestant. He assured Mirhashem that Allah would protect him this night.

As soon as he was out of sight of the jeep, Dick had paused to establish a simple communications system with Jim. Through the satellite overhead, he would respond to Dick's questions with a specified number of jolts from the chip's monitor.

With the satellite's superb surveillance capability--a follow-on to Aura One--they had quickly determined that two people were coming up the hill to oppose Dick, one from the east and one from the south. The paths they were taking indicated they would rendez-vous on the eastern side of the summit. Based on that information, Dick agreed with Jim to set the ambush at a previously identified site, about one-third of the way down the western side.

Dick had hurried to establish his ambush before his opponents arrived. The night-vision scope proved invaluable on the dark mountain. With his previous study of the terrain, he reached the ambush site quickly, without injury and with minimum effort. The site was a ninety-degree turn in a path coming down the hill from the east. Near the corner, the path was four-foot wide and bounded by crumbling stone walls about six-foot high. At the corner, was the huge boulder upon which Dick was perched. About ten-foot wide, it protruded above the top of the walls. The sloping backside of the boulder made it easy to get up and down.

Dick's first action was to string the high-tensile-strength wire across the path. He anchored it securely to stones on either side of the path, a few feet before the corner and ten inches above the ground. The trip wire was invisible in the dark. He set a second stone on top of each anchor stone to mark the wire's position.

Then he searched for a flat surface on the wall opposite his perch on the boulder, where he could smash the vial when his opponents were within range. He selected a smooth stone halfway up the wall, five feet before the trip wire. He set a marker stone on the top of the wall to help him find his aim point.

Dick rolled over to bring the warmth of the boulder to his chest. He asked, "Mountie, have they rendezvoused?" His response was two jolts in his right shoulder--a *yes* answer.

"Did that other guy bring Omman some dark clothes?" Again the affirmative answer. "Cheating bastard!" exclaimed Dick. He smiled as Jim gave him another *yes*.

Dick held the night-vision scope. It would negate his opponents' advantage of dark clothing.

"Have they reached the summit?" Two jolts in his shoulder told

Dick they had.

This was the deciding point. Would the ambush be difficult or easy? There were two paths from the summit leading down the western side of the hill. One was the path to Dick's ambush. The other wandered off to the southwest. There was a north-south path connecting the two about 100 yards up the hill from Dick. If his opponents took the southwestern path, he'd have to lure them over to the path leading to his ambush. That might be difficult.

Three jolts in his shoulder alerted Dick. He asked quickly, "Are they starting down the hill?" Jim's two affirmative jolts followed immediately. "Are they coming down my path?" Only one jolt in the shoulder, the negative reply. "Are they going down the path to the southwest?" An affirmative response. "Should I go up the hill to the connecting path and head south to intercept them?" The two-jolt signal sent Dick on his way.

Grasping the night-vision scope in one hand and the spray canister in the other, he slid down the back of the boulder. He hurried around the side, spotted the two stones, stepped carefully over the trip wire, then scrambled up the hill.

"What do you think, Conrad? Can I beat them to the connecting path?" He was rewarded with an affirmative answer.

Dick arrived at an intersection. "Am I at the connecting path?" With the affirmative reply, he began picking his way along the rough trail. The night-vision scope was now very important, but holding it steady and maneuvering around the stones was not easy.

"Jim," he panted, "my plan is to stop short of the intersection and make some noise when they approach. Do you agree?" Conrad's signal confirmed his thinking.

"Okay," said Dick. "I can throw a rock a hundred yards, and I don't want to get very close to them. I'll need a big head start to get back to the ambush point before they catch me." Conrad agreed.

"I'm a little lost on this path, Jim. Give me four jolts when I'm a hundred yards from the intersection."

Dick was tiring rapidly. He was relieved when he felt the four jolts stinging his cold shoulder. While the RCMP officer was thousands of miles away in Frankfurt, he was also at Dick's side.

He was now in position to lure his opponents. "I'm wondering how far they are from the intersection, Jim. Give me the emergency signal to start throwing rocks. Give me another when they start up this path, so I can get the hell out of here."

Dick selected a few rocks the size of golf balls. He leaned against a boulder to catch his breath. With the night-vision scope, he could see the intersection of the paths. "God help me if they have one of these things!" he thought to himself.

He held the scope and canister in his left hand and picked up a rock with his right. A few seconds later, he got Conrad's warning. Aligning his body, he lofted the rock toward the intersection. He heard its sharp impact in the still night air and took a quick look with the scope. The intersection was clear, but he saw the heads of two figures bobbing down the hill. Their bodies were hidden behind a wall of stones. When they were five yards short of the intersection, he tossed another rock about halfway to them. They paused when it hit the ground, then carefully picked their way to the intersection and turned up the path toward Dick.

Jim's emergency signal reminded him that he was in a race for his life. The noise he made scrambling over the rocky path could be heard by his opponents, but the time for stealth had passed. It was a foot race he had to win!

"I'm on my way, Mountie. Give me emergency beeps if those guys start to close."

It was dark--very dark! Without the scope, it was difficult to pick out objects more than a couple yards ahead. Having been down the path a few minutes earlier gave the advantage to Dick, but he soon got an emergency signal from Jim. His opponents were gaining ground.

Ten yards short of the intersection with the path to his ambush, Dick slipped on the side of a rock. His ankle twisted, and he went down. In that nano-second, he protected the scope and canister like a football and fell on his left shoulder. The side of his head struck a large rock, lights burst in his eyes.

He was stunned, his eyes wouldn't focus. The adrenaline was pumping, but he couldn't move. Jim's emergency signal in his shoulder energized his system, but lights were flashing in his head. Another series of sharp jolts--then more. He staggered to his feet and struggled to focus his eyes on the path ahead. With a few unsteady steps, he reached the path going down the hill.

His vision began to clear, but he could move no faster than an erratic stagger. He knew his opponents were closing, but he had no time to look. "I'm in trouble. How far back are they?" Realizing Jim couldn't answer that question, he said: "Give me a beep for each ten yards of separation."

Five measured jolts in his shoulder boosted his morale. He still had a fifty-yard lead, and his coordination had returned, but he began to have double vision.

He resumed a faster pace and was soon approaching the ambush. He paused to locate the trip wire. He could hear his pursuers stumbling down the rocky slope behind him. He stepped over the wire and hurried to the back of the boulder. Holding the scope in one hand, and the spray canister in the other, he scrambled up the smooth surface on his forearms and knees. Reaching the top, he located the gas vial. Then he looked up the path with the night-vision scope.

Omman was forty yards away, with his long curved knife in his hand. A giant of a man, carrying a baseball bat, was about ten yards behind. Dick wondered if they might have pistols, but then dismissed the thought. The sound of gunfire would be heard by the "referees" waiting at the foot of the mountain.

Dick studied the Islamic Jihad leader's grim features, Omman paused to listen. The giant behind him stood motionless. The mountain was deathly quiet. Omman turned to his partner and waved him forward. They conversed quietly for a moment. Then the large man slowly led the way down the treacherous path, staring at the ground in front of him.

Dick rose quietly to his knees to locate the stone in the wall that was his target for the glass vial. He held the vial gently in his right hand and balanced the scope in his left.

Pointing the scope up the path, Dick saw the big man twenty yards away. He was moving cautiously, his eyes concentrating on rocks in the path. Omman was about ten yards back. There would be no chance of getting them both with the gas in the glass vial.

Dick drew his right arm back slowly, hoping the approaching giant could not see him in the darkness. It would be a matter of timing. He had to throw the vial against the stone only a couple feet in front of his opponent.

Returning the scope to the lead man, Dick saw him stop and stare into the darkness--he had seen the corner. The man again looked at the ground, extended the bat in front of him, and picked his way slowly forward.

Dick laid the scope down and steadied himself with his left hand on the boulder. He saw the man emerging from the darkness, with the bat still extended before him. If he looked up now, he was sure to see Dick.

Absolutely motionless, Dick scarcely breathed as the man edged forward. When the end of the bat was directly below his target stone, he threw the vial with a smooth swift motion.

His aim was perfect. The giant heard the glass strike the stone and turned in that direction. His nose and mouth were engulfed in the knock-out gas.

Dick grabbed the knife in his left hand, the spray canister in his right, and slid down the back of the boulder. He rounded the corner and looked up the path.

His target was on his knees, grasping his throat with both hands. Omman was coming quickly from behind him. He attempted to grab his big partner, but he pitched forward on the rocks. Omman looked down at him, then he saw Dick.

Dick laughed loudly and shouted: "That guy's name better be Allah, you cheating son-of-a-bitch!"

Omman lifted the curved knife above his head and screamed: "I don't need his help to carve you for the crows!"

Dick's right index finger was poised on the canister's directional trigger. He held it behind him, extending the knife with his left hand. "I expected a dishonorable liar like you to bring at least an AK-47. If you want to use that butter-cutter, be my guest; but I'll be a tougher target than a hostage chained to a chair."

Omman screamed in Arabic and charged, with the knife slashing in front of him. It took him only four steps to reach Dick's trip wire. As he went down, his momentum carried him through the corner and headfirst into the stone wall. At that instant, double vision blurred Dick's eyes. He could only stagger to one side.

Omman screamed in pain, rolled on his side, and slashed at Dick with his knife. He stepped back, blinking as his vision returned to normal. Then he gave the Islamic Jihad Cleric a blast from the canister--directly in the face. Turning quickly to avoid the gas, Dick jumped clear. When he looked again, Omman was flat on his back, gasping for air. In a few seconds, he lay motionless.

Dick held his breath and went around the corner to check the giant. He was also motionless, face down on the rocks.

"Damn good stuff, Conrad!" he shouted. "I may be in command of this situation." Jim's two jolts in his shoulder were reassuring.

While the gas was reportedly good for an hour or two, Dick quickly set to work.

First, he stripped both men. It was getting damned cold, so he donned the giant's shirt and Omman's trousers. Then he cut the legs off the giant's trousers and took the laces out of Omman's shoes. He fashioned masks by tying a knot in the end of each leg and lacing a shoestring around the open end.

Omman had a gash on his head from hitting the wall. It was oozing blood. A nasty bruise on the giant's forehead was also bleeding. Dick slipped a mask over each man's head and tied the laces around their throats. He pulled the material away from their noses and cut breathing holes with Omman's razor-sharp knife.

Working methodically, Dick found the trip wire and bound the big man's hands behind his back. He left five feet of wire hanging from the giant's wrists and tied a snare loop in the end. He took the laces from the giant's boots and tied Omman's hands behind his back. Then he dragged the Iranian up the path and laid him next to the giant. He pulled the giant's hands back with the trip wire and placed the snare loop around Omman's neck, fitting it below the mask so the wire was in contact with his throat.

Impressed with the size of the giant's arms, Dick tied his elbows securely with the tough fabric of Omman's shirt. Then he removed his own shoelaces--the nylon ones Maria had given him. He used one to again bind the giant's wrists. He looped the other in a slip knot around the giant's throat, strung it down his back, and tied it to the bonds on his elbows.

Satisfied with his work, Dick gathered his belongings. He replaced the safety cap on the spray canister and put it in the pocket of his new trousers--for further use if necessary. He put the night scope in his other pocket and reinserted the canister that had contained the vial into the knife handle. He threw Omman's shoes, the giant's boots, and their socks and underwear over the stone wall.

He picked up Omman's knife and studied the cruel blade, shuddering as he visualized the torture of the Cultural Attaché. He went to the unconscious naked bodies lying in the path, raised Omman's head, and placed a rock under the back of his neck. His head fell back, exposing his throat and the wire snare around it. Dick placed the knife's razor-edge against Omman's jugular. A quick movement of his hand would rid the world of this monster. Double vision again disrupted his sight, and he pulled the knife away.

He blinked his eyes a couple times, his vision cleared. Why had he taken the time to bind these guys? Why hadn't he simply applied the "will of Allah" and slit their throats? He asked loudly: "Mountie, why am I not ridding the world of these two pieces of crap?" There was no answer.

He paused for a moment, then said: "It's going to be a long walk down the mountain with these two donkeys. Am I doing the right thing?" Two jolts reassured him. After this outing, Omman would lose all credibility in the terrorist world.

Dick rose to throw Omman's knife into the darkness, but had a sudden inspiration. He drew a light cut down each of Omman's inner thighs, not far below his scrotum. "Just gave the learned torturer something to remember us by," he grunted. Conrad acknowledged with two jolts.

Before throwing the knife away, he cut the giant's belt into three narrow strips. He needed something to lead his charges down the mountain. He tied the three strips together, fashioned a slip knot in one end, looped it around the big man's scrotum, and pulled it tight. He would have preferred a ring in the nose to lead this bull, but this would do the trick. He had the bat to enforce his orders.

It took an hour for his captives to regain consciousness. Omman was the first. Dick explained where the other end of the wire snare around his neck was fastened. Omman panicked, chattering rapidly that his partner spoke no English. Dick reassured him that he could make it down the mountain without being decapitated, if he translated correctly and obeyed Dick's orders promptly.

The giant regained consciousness slowly, with Omman jabbering constantly in Persian. When he finally sat up, Omman had to lean forward to loosen the pressure of the wire snare around his throat. Dick ordered them to stand up. Omman translated, but the man refused. Dick asked if the giant had understood the order. Omman said that he had. With one swift blow, Dick smashed his big toe with the bat. The giant screamed in pain. Omman screamed at him to obey. It became clear to him that he had no other choice.

When Dick tugged on the leather leash tied to his testicles, the giant limped meekly along, with Omman close behind. They proceeded slowly down the mountain, one small step at a time.

Dick stopped his prisoners behind the same bend in the path where he'd contacted Jim earlier. They were less than a hundred yards from the jeep. He reopened the knife handle and inserted the spray canister and the night-vision scope. He took off Omman's trousers and the giant's shirt and tossed them behind a boulder.

A bonfire was blazing behind the jeep. Mirhashem was sitting on a stool near the fire, beside him were General Beyrri and the Syrian Major.

Dick approached quietly with his charges. They were within the fire's glow when one of the guards saw them. He shouted and ran to meet them. Mirhashem ordered him back.

Dick tugged on the leather leash and continued the last few yards to the bottom of the Mountain of Truth.

Mirhashem rose to meet them. He extended his hand to Dick and proclaimed: "Allah be praised!"

General Beyrri uttered an Arabic expletive and handed a roll of dollar bills to Mirhashem.

Dick nodded at his hooded, bleeding, naked captives. "The will of Allah has been done."

6

PH.D. IN TERROR

Dick sank wearily on the marble bench and removed his shoes. "Damn," he muttered, "hope I get my laces back in the morning."

He was in a Turkish bath inside Mirhashem's villa, a fifteen-minute blindfolded jeep ride from the Mountain of Truth.

He set his shoes by the wall and hung his wrinkled sport coat and trousers on a hook with his dirty shirt and underwear. He was still cold from the five-hour ordeal on the mountain, the steam in the room felt super.

He returned to the marble bench and began to ladle hot water over his head. He had once visited a Turkish bath with Maria, and remembered it was proper to wash himself before entering the water. The two of them had barely fit in that ancient hot-tub in Vienna. Mirhashem's bath had a modern whirlpool Jacuzzi, which could seat at least a dozen.

The bruise on the left side of his head ached, he closed his eyes to visualize that night with Maria. She had insisted it would be too hot in the bath for sexual escapades, but he had proven her wrong. Of course, he had cheated by beginning his advances before the hot steam could take effect. Pouring hot water over their heads, and washing each other with sponges, had been the ultimate finale.

That's what was missing! He needed soap and sponges. He rose from the bench. The room began to spin and he sat down again. It was probably a concussion; but not as severe as the one the radar scope in the F-8 had given him when his shoulder harness failed during an arrested landing.

He rested his elbows on his knees, cradled his head in his hands, closed his eyes, and returned to his memories of Maria.

He heard a soft sound and opened his eyes to peer through his fingers. Was this a dream? He was looking down at the shapely back of a young girl, kneeling before him to kiss his feet. She remained in that position, with her lips pressed against the arch of his foot. Somewhat mesmerized, he studied the soft curves of her bare shoulders and slim neck and admired her creamy-brown skin.

Her dark hair was swept high on her head and held there with a golden band. Her costume was right out of the *Arabian Nights*.

Her pantaloons and strapless bra were a transparent material, that shimmered emerald green in the dim light of the bath. The pantaloons were worn very low, allowing Dick a sensual view of her curvaceous hips.

Finally he noticed that her arms were filled with towels and sponges. "*Na*, come little one, how long are you going to stay down there?"

She rose gracefully to her feet, but kept her head and eyes lowered. "Thank you, Master. I am here to help with your bath."

Raising his eyes from her small feet and slender legs, Dick was shocked to see the pantaloons were indeed transparent. Embarrassed, he fixed his gaze on the towels she clasped to her bosom.

Her head and eyes were still lowered. "Thank you," said Dick, "but I'm certainly not your *Master*. My name is Ed Orden."

He held out his hands. She remained motionless, with her eyes on the floor.

"May I please have a towel?" he asked.

She extended her arms and gave him the towels. Dick gasped. The bra was also transparent--Allah had really blessed this petite young girl!

He pushed the towels back to her and turned his head. "Please put them on the bench. May I have a sponge before you leave?"

Out of the corner of his eye, he watched her lay the towels on the bench beside him. He looked away and held out his hand, waiting for a sponge.

His fingers were enclosed by soft hands, his palm was caressed by moist lips. "Please, Mr. Orden, it is my duty to assist with your bath. My Master, Mirhashem, has requested that I do so." Her soft voice had a delightful lilt, her precise English had no trace of an accent. Perhaps this girl was not so young as she looked.

It had to be after one in the morning, Dick was totally fatigued, but who was he to argue with his host--especially when he was the king of the terrorists.

"Then let it be so," sighed Dick. He picked up the ladle, but she took it from his hand. "Allow me, Sire," she whispered in his ear.

He turned his head to see an adorable pixie face, with warm brown eyes. She cast them quickly to the floor, but not before he had discerned their mischievous look.

She raised the ladle and unceremoniously dumped warm water on his head. She continued to do so as he sputtered: "Is it allowed for you to tell me your name?"

She put the ladle down and started on him with a soapy sponge. "Yes, certainly. My name is Shreeba, the protected servant of Mirhashem and the sister of Ali. Abrahim says you have met my brother in Vienna."

Dick tried to reply, but was silenced with a mouthful of soapy water. She quickly washed the soap away, patted his mouth with a dry towel, and began to kiss him gently on the lips. She squeezed her eyes tightly closed and continued the kiss, until Dick gently placed his fingertips on her shoulders and pushed her away. She immediately lowered her eyes and continued washing him.

He chuckled. "I know I'm tough to look at, but didn't know I was that bad."

The color of pink roses flooded her smooth cheeks. "Please, Sire, I find you to be an attractive man, but that's not for me to say. It is forbidden to look in the eyes of any man--until I have been with him." A grin tugged at the corners of her delicious mouth.

Dick returned the grin. ". . . and how many men have you looked in the eye, little Shreeba?"

The pixie face flushed, she turned away momentarily. Then she haughtily replied: "Please, Mr. Orden, don't ask me such questions. Thanks to my brother and Mirhashem, I am an innocent girl."

"It's great to have an older brother," agreed Dick.

"Especially a brave one like Ali," she continued. "When I was only twelve, two Israeli soldiers with rifles caught me in the street outside our home in Hebron. They were tearing off my clothes when Ali came from the house and killed them with a knife."

Dick sat quietly. She gently sponged the bruise on the side of his head.

"He saved me from a terrible fate, but two days later the Israelis took a hideous revenge. Ali and I were hiding in the Mosque. They came to our house with a bulldozer and pushed it down. Mother and Father were crushed to death."

Her voice caught in her throat. Dick turned to her. He couldn't be sure if there were tears in those big brown eyes, but he took her in his arms.

She sat in his lap, her arms wrapped around him, her head resting on his shoulder. Dick became aware of the unusual warmth of her firm bosom. Then he apologized: "Oh, Shreeba, forgive me. I've gotten you all wet."

She kissed him tenderly on the cheek and rose to her feet. "It doesn't matter, Mr. Orden. I've finished with the sponge. It's time we go in the bath."

Without the slightest inhibition, she pushed the sheer pantaloons to the floor and pulled the filmy bra over her head. It became tangled with the golden band holding her hair, and he rose to help. As he untangled the veil material, she closed her fingers around his wrists. With her arms extended, she leaned against him. He felt a violent urge to crush her nakedness in his arms.

At last he freed the material from the band. "That thing is like a crown," he said. "Are you a princess?"

He lowered his arms to his sides. She continued to grasp his wrists. She stood on her tiptoes and thrust her slender body against him, kissing his chest as she did so.

"Yes, I am. My name Shreeba means *Princess of the Bath.*"

She descended the steps into the bubbling water. Dick followed. He sat on an underwater bench, near a powerful water jet. It was a deep tub. The water level was at her shoulders. She moved to the center, then turned to Dick. He glimpsed the glow in her hot brown eyes for a mere second, before she slipped and started to fall. He caught her delicate wrist, put his arm around her slim waist, and pulled her nakedness to him.

Dick was breathing heavily. He again seated himself on the bench, this time with Shreeba firmly on his lap. She averted his eyes, but her sensual lips were smiling. "Something wrong, Mr. Orden? Are you okay?"

"Nothing a cold shower wouldn't cure," growled Dick. He had to focus his mind on something else. This bundle of sex was also Ali's sister, and Mirhashem's protégée. "You're an incredibly beautiful woman, Shreeba, and your brother's a handsome young man."

Her eyes were downcast, but a mischievous smile lit her *Audrey Hepburn* face. "Sire, I am not yet a woman, but I will be soon."

She moved slightly on his lap. It was enough to excite him. "How did you and your brother meet Mirhashem?" he asked.

She laid her head on his shoulder, explaining in a matter-of-fact tone: "After our parents were killed, Ali and I went to a refugee camp in southern Lebanon. We had lived there two months before an associate of Mirhashem's came to talk with Ali--he had become a hero for killing the two Israeli soldiers with a knife. When the associate learned our parents had been killed by the Israelis, and discovered Ali was only seventeen, we were taken to Mirhashem. He was very nice. Ali took a serious pledge of personal allegiance to him. A few weeks later, we were enroute to Dallas, Texas. We stayed with friends and went to school for five years. Mirhashem brought us here last year. Ali trained at this camp, before he was teamed with Abrahim and Musavi. Mirhashem took me into his home. I now have a safe and comfortable life."

Dick bent his head to kiss her gently on her lowered eyelids. "That's a fabulous story, Shreeba, of two very brave children. I'm proud to know Ali and pleased to have met you."

He thought for a moment then asked: "Do you often have duties as the *Princess of the Bath?*"

The roses returned to her face. She replied firmly, "No, certainly not! Tonight is only the second time."

"May I ask who was the first?"

"It was a high-ranking official from Tehran, who was interested in taking me for his wife. He was very ugly, and I gave him only a bath. By custom, he could demand no more at that time."

"Are you going to marry him?"

"He made Mirhashem a generous offer--the ceremony had been scheduled for next week--then I came into good fortune for the second time in my life."

"Are you being sent back to the States?"

"No, nothing like that, Mr. Orden. You are the good fortune I'm talking about."

"Come on! I just met you. How could I possibly help you?"

"You already have, Sire. The Iranian Sheik you killed on the Mountain of Truth a few hours ago was the ugly man to whom Mirhashem had promised me."

"Whoa," thought Dick silently. "He was pretty much alive when I left him."

She turned in his lap and pressed her shapely body firmly against him. "How can I repay you, Mr. Orden?"

"Well," he grinned, "you can stop calling me *Sire* or *Mr. Orden.*

Ed will do fine. What makes you think Sheik Omman is dead?"

"Mirhashem told me, *Ed.* He said you killed Omman and his giant bodyguard with your bare hands, and left their bodies on the mountain for the buzzards. He said you're the greatest warrior he's ever met. That's when he asked if I'd like to be your *Princess of the Bath* this evening."

She tilted her face to kiss him softly on the lips, but her eyes were still downcast. "He told me you would be the perfect husband. He said we should make as many children as I possibly can."

Once again, Dick's body was dispelling the myth about the derogatory effects of hot water upon sex. It was time to find a cold shower.

He carried her from the bath to the marble bench. They wrapped themselves in large towels, and she led him to a side door. "Leave your clothes, Mr. Orden. Someone will care for them."

They entered a warm dimly lit room. The only furnishing was a low round bed in the center. Shreeba carefully locked the door behind them. She threw her towel aside and dove playfully into the pile of blue satin pillows on the bed.

Dick kept his towel wrapped tightly around his waist and seated himself on the edge of the bed. Her eyes were no longer lowered. They smoldered in the soft blue light. She lay back upon a pillow and challenged him: "Come to me, Mr. Orden. Let's begin our family with a son."

Dick wanted to be serious, but he couldn't suppress a tired grin as he replied: "Princess, I'm not a prophet, but it's easy to see that you'll be bringing many sons into this world. Unfortunately for me, none of them will be mine. You are worthy of a far mightier and braver man than I--and a much younger one."

A look of dismay clouded her pixie features. Dick continued quickly: "Mirhashem has access to the best of Palestinian manhood. He could certainly offer you far better matches, and not one of them would say *no* to making a son with you. You're a young, but very desirable, woman."

The cloud disappeared and her eyes shone brightly. "Then how is it that you are saying *no* to me, Mr. Orden?"

"I fear for my life, Shreeba."

"Are you concerned about my brother or Mirhashem? He has given me permission to be with you, and Ali would accept my wishes." A grin teased the corners of her precious lips.

Dick replied seriously: "Both of those warriors are worthy of my caution, Shreeba, but it's you that I fear. I'm much older than you, I doubt I'd survive the night." He laughed. "I have shoes older than you!"

Twice during the short night, he awoke to find Shreeba's supple body wrapped tightly around him. Maybe she was asleep, but he didn't think so. He focused on making a night carrier landing--in the rain--and maintained his composure, and perhaps her virginity.

The jeep bounced over the broken pavement on the road to the training camp. They were out of sight of Mirhashem's villa, Dick's blindfold had been removed. Off to his right, the Mountain of Truth rose sharply in the midday sun. A flock of buzzards circled near the summit.

Dick glanced at his host. "Shreeba told me those birds will be having a banquet today."

"Yes indeed!" Mirhashem nodded his balding head. "It was a magnanimous gesture to bring Omman down the mountain alive, but Allah had already ruled against him. The only acceptable outcome was his death."

"How did he die?"

"General Beyrri was outraged that he cheated with his bodyguard. He sent five of his soldiers back up the mountain with them and they killed them with bullets in the head."

They turned in the camp entrance. Mirhashem continued: "After Omman's shameful performance, the General is too embarrassed to meet with you again; so we've changed the schedule. I'm prepared to let you view one of the hostages, if you agree to speak with my graduating class about America's response to our struggle."

"I welcome the opportunity to converse with your students. If they are like Abrahim, Ali, or Musavi, it will be very stimulating."

"This class of fifteen includes three Ph.D.'s, five Master's in physics, and three Master's in mathematics--all from American or British universities."

"Sounds like a real challenge. Must I engage all of them at the same time?"

"No, not necessary," grunted the feared Palestinian leader. "We will split them into five groups of three. You'll have thirty minutes with each group. We must be enroute to Beirut by five o'clock."

The jeep stopped in front of a stone house. Dick climbed down slowly, grinning as he glimpsed Maria's nylon shoelaces back in his mountain-climbing shoes.

"Will I see the hostage in Beirut?" he asked.

"That's the plan," replied Mirhashem. "I also want you to see my graduates in action. Part of their final exam is to neutralize some members of the Mossad, who entered Beirut on a murderous rampage a couple days ago."

The convoy wound its way out of the farm land of the Bekaa Valley, through the narrow streets of Baalbeck, and into the urban battleground that was Beirut. A Syrian armored personnel carrier, bearing Mirhashem's graduating class, led the procession. It was followed by a Mercedes with General Beyrri, the Syrian Major, and Sheik Fidlah. Then came a Lincoln Continental with Dick and Mirhashem. Another APC with Syrian troops guarded the rear.

Mirhashem was eager to hear Dick's opinion of the fifteen graduates, with whom he had spent the afternoon in intense debate.

"They are very intelligent and well educated," observed Dick. "Compared to the Ph.D. candidates I've worked with at a major American university during the last few years, I'd rate them at the head of the class--or rather, way ahead of the class!"

"How would you rate their understanding of your political system?" asked the terrorist leader.

"On a par with the most experienced Professors under whom I studied," said Dick. "They demonstrate a unique understanding of how the American view of democracy fits into the current world situation. They have a sense of realism far in advance of our *classroom cradle-to-grave* educators."

Mirhashem's harsh countenance was broken by a rare smile. "I can assure you, those fifteen are identical to the hundreds I've sent to study at the graduate level in your top universities."

Dick responded thoughtfully: "After reading the captured report of your conference with the Ayatollah Khomeini, most western governments assumed the 2,500-man brigade you were asked to put together would be trained as suicide bombers."

"What a fatal mistake that will prove to be for those arrogant idiots!" declared Mirhashem hotly. "The ultimate goal of my volunteers may be to martyr themselves, while avenging the killing of their family by Jews and their American lackeys. However, after talking with the MIT Ph.D. you met this afternoon, I'm sure you realize she doesn't expect to martyr herself on an Israeli bus. She's quite capable of taking out an entire city with a chemical attack."

"What city are you talking about?" asked Dick quietly.

"If your government continues its blind support of the Jewish occupation of our homeland, the smoggy city of LA would be an ideal candidate." The deadly terrorist, feared by friend and foe alike, glared at Dick over the top of his tinted spectacles.

Dick's eyes were hard and unforgiving. "You really believe it could come to that? Are you talking about the end of the world?"

"We'll see how far down the slippery slope your current administration, and its successors, are content to slide. For the time being, we'll continue with isolated incidents that can be controlled and contained. I'm hopeful the American public will awaken and react strongly to the current round of hostage taking. If they do, if they question your leaders about the reckless policies that resulted in those hostages being seized, then maybe American democracy will act to save itself--by recognizing Palestinians have as much right to a homeland as your patriots did in 1776."

Dick shook his head. "You are underestimating the power of the Jewish voting bloc, and their influence on America's media."

A slight smile broke through Mirhashem's fierce features. "It seems I have more faith in democracy than you, Captain. The Jewish bloc is only a small minority in your country--to be cast aside by the majority when it awakens."

". . . and that brings us back to what it will take to awaken that majority," grimaced Dick. "I don't believe holding a correspondent hostage will make a significant contribution, nor will hijacking an occasional airliner--though you have pulled off some spectacular stunts in the past."

"Stay tuned!" warned Mirhashem. "In the meantime, share your impression of my graduates with others. One reason for inviting you here was to send the message, that my educated Palestinian patriots are capable of far more than hijackings and bombings."

"How much time does the American majority have to *awaken?*" asked Dick.

Mirhashem glanced coldly at him. "The incline of the slippery slope depends on world events, and they are unpredictable. Your leaders must be made to realize their all-powerful military has no capability against my 2,500 patriots, who will be positioned around the world in an impenetrable network. How will you fight us? We're not a target for your weapons of mass destruction--but your population is for ours! America's not prepared mentally or morally to defeat us. You cannot deter us like you have the Soviets."

"May I make a comparison?" asked Dick. "Within the nuclear balance between America and the USSR, stands the problem of aging weapons. How do you view your 2,500 *weapons*? Will they become obsolete?"

"On the contrary, Captain. The longer they are immersed in the society they plan to destroy, the more effective they will become."

"But won't you have an aging problem?"

Mirhashem's true character was reflected in his evil grin. "That brings us to the *use them or lose them* theory of weapon employment. Doesn't it, Captain?"

"A personal question, please," responded Dick. "I appreciated conversing with your students on a face-to-face basis. It provided a clearer evaluation of their character and personality, but did their lack of masks or hoods make me a condemned man? I'd have no problem recognizing them in the future."

"Perhaps you could for a few months, Captain, but memories of faces are hard to retain, even for a man of your intelligence. They will, of course, employ various disguises as they venture forth. I have fully considered that aspect of our relationship and am willing to take the risk, in exchange for your informing others of the capability of my Brigade."

The red flash of an RPG, launched from atop a building in front of them, ended the conversation. It detonated beside the lead APC, and all hell broke loose. Machine guns on both carriers raked the building, disintegrating the top floor. Muzzle flashes came from windows across the street. Small arms fire ricocheted off the doors and windows of the armor-plated Lincoln. Dick and Mirhashem dove for the floor board. The machine gunners on the APC's made quick work of the ambushers. The convoy sped down the street and out of the area.

As they rolled into west Beirut, the convoy separated. Dick and

Mirhashem followed the APC with the graduating class down a main avenue to the south. The rear guard APC detached to escort General Beyrri's Mercedes to the airport.

There was evidence of heavy fighting along the route south. Buildings had been gutted by fire, some were completely flattened by explosions. Peering through the ruins and darkness, Dick could see the lights of ships in the harbor. He sensed that he had driven through this district some twenty-four years earlier, during a Sixth Fleet visit by the USS *Intrepid.*

He glanced at Mirhashem. "Beirut's changed a lot since '61. My aircraft carrier was in port for a week. Somewhere around here was a great bar on top of a historic old hotel, believe it was called the King George."

Mirhashem reacted with a nod of his head. "How's that for coincidence? The King George is the location for our exercise this evening. It's ahead and to the right, on the water."

The Lincoln followed the APC into the littered parking lot of what had been a multi-story shopping center.

"The King George is on the other side of this building," said Mirhashem. "A Mossad unit has occupied the hotel for the last two days. They are holding an undetermined number of hostages, and have established a killing field in the open area surrounding the hotel. The mission of my graduating class is to take out the Mossad, without harming the hostages or destroying the hotel."

Dick chuckled. "Sounds like a terrorist situation in reverse."

"Exactly! To create the perfect hostage incident, you have to know how to take it apart as well as put it together."

"That's a hell of a training concept," agreed Dick.

Mirhashem stepped out of the Lincoln. "Come, Captain, we've been invited to attend the team's briefing in the basement of this shopping center, which the IDF bombed a couple months ago. More than two hundred innocents died here."

In the early '60s, Beirut had been the banking hub of the Middle East. Dick remembered market places and upscale stores, with everything from exotic fruits to golden treasures. It was all consumed in the fiery civil war that began in the mid '70s. Christian forces, supported by Syria, opposed the Muslim and Palestinian coalition in a bloody conflict. Israel invaded in the spring of '78.

When they withdrew, they left Christian militia groups in control. With the Israeli intervention, Syria switched sides to back the Muslems and Palestinians. Beirut was the focal point of continuous heavy fighting between several factions, with air strikes by the IDF adding to the chaos and destruction.

A couple months before Mirhashem invited Dick to the Bekaa Valley, General Beyrri's Shia Amal militia had kicked the Sunni Mourabitoun militia out of west Beirut. The General had established a command post in the King George Hotel.

Two nights ago, a Mossad team on a mission to rescue a captured IDF pilot attempted to penetrate Beirut from the sea. After landing near the King George, they encountered a reinforced Amal patrol. In the battle that followed, they had taken over the hotel.

Twenty-four years earlier, Dick had looked down from the hotel's roof bar at beautiful gardens surrounding the building on three sides. From the west, the Mediterranean's crystal blue waters had gently washed the hotel's massive stone walls.

Now he peered from across the street, through a crack in the shopping center's crumbled wall. The gardens had been replaced with concrete parking lots. Floodlights surrounded those lots, and a patrol boat's searchlight illuminated the west side of the hotel.

Only a few of the dozens of bodies scattered around the cluttered parking lots were in uniform. The remainder were apparently locals, caught in the murderous crossfire between the Mossad and the militia. Several women and children were among the victims.

There was still a low wall on the north side of the roof top where Dick had stood to view the gardens. Now there was a pile of broken bodies on the concrete below.

During the briefing, the Amal patrol commander explained the Israelis were trying to bargain for the release of the downed pilot they'd been sent to rescue. In an attempt to force their demands for the pilot and safe passage to the sea, they had been throwing a hostage off the roof every few hours.

It was an especially fierce confrontation. The Mossad had an unobstructed field-of-fire surrounding the hotel. They had killed everyone who ventured into the parking lots, and the patrol boat was forced to remain a safe distance away.

The brutality of the situation was evidenced by the plight of a young German mother, a resident of the hotel. She had been at the market when the Mossad took over. When she returned, she explained to the Amal commander that her week-old baby was in the hotel. It would starve unless she were allowed to feed it. The Amal commander had presented her case to the Israelis. They had agreed to let her enter the hotel, provided she stripped entirely naked before crossing the parking lot. The distraught mother had quickly complied. Still naked, she and her baby were the next to be thrown off the roof.

The Amal commander briefed Mirhashem that only two members of General Beyrri's staff were known to be in the hotel. They had not yet been thrown from the roof. He assumed they were being held for a final negotiation effort. The commander was more than happy to turn the entire mess over to Mirhashem's students.

The student team was expertly prepared and well equipped. Their mode of assault closely resembled the British SAS rescue of hostages from the Iranian Embassy in London five years earlier, which the world had witnessed on live television.

To create a diversion, the patrol boat commenced a run toward the hotel, firing tracers from its machine guns and shining its light in the windows.

Through a hail of Israeli small arms fire, the APC rumbled across the parking lot to the hotel's main entrance. Dick wondered if they were going to crash their way into the building, that would have been against the basic rule of minimizing collateral damage.

The APC halted with its nose against the front door. Team members spilled from the back. Hugging the sides of the building, they moved to strategic positions along the walls. Simultaneously with the APC backing away from the building and the patrol boat sounding its siren, the assault team fired grappling hooks into top floor windows and onto the roof. The APC and the patrol boat raked the top floor and roof with machine gun fire.

With the Mossad forced back, the students scrambled up their ropes. In a few moments, they were hanging beside windows on all five floors. When the patrol boat silenced its siren, it was the signal for the team to throw concussion and gas grenades through the windows. After the grenades exploded, the students swung back on their ropes and crashed into the building--exactly as Dick had seen during the SAS assault on the Iranian Embassy.

In a few seconds, various other types of grenades were lighting up the windows of the old hotel. Mirhashem and Abrahim were riveted on the loud and violent action. Dick drifted some distance away from them in the ruins of the shopping center. He put his handkerchief over his mouth.

"Mountie, are you listening through the satellite?"

After his second call, he felt two jolts in his right shoulder.

He quickly reviewed the situation for *Purple,* mixing a cough or two with the words spoken firmly into his handkerchief.

"Mountie, the Mossad team must be in contact with their HQ. They haven't got a snowball's chance in hell of getting out alive. They will probably call in an airstrike to end it. If you have a way of confirming that, give me the emergency signal and I'll try to get out of here. I'm in a very vulnerable position. After the emergency signal, give me a beep for every five minutes I have left."

Two sharp jolts in his shoulder acknowledged *Purple's* receipt of his request.

Dick edged his way back through the twisted steel and broken concrete to Mirhashem and Abrahim. With a final sneeze, he put away his handkerchief.

"An impressive show by some very brave and well-trained lads," said Dick.

Abrahim grinned. "Several of those who crashed the windows were female, Captain, not lads but ladies."

"So much for the weaker sex," grunted Dick. "Any casualties?"

Abrahim adjusted his headset. "I've heard of one cut forearm for our team, but they have two more rooms to go. It will take some time to see how the hostages fared. Five Mossad are dead."

Mirhashem put down his headset and turned to Dick. "In a few moments, I will fulfill my part of the deal. The hostage you are about to view is in the basement of the hotel. The Israelis didn't know he was there, but they couldn't have penetrated that area."

Dick flinched from three sharp jolts in his shoulder. The emergency signal was immediately followed by a two beeps.

"Don't you expect immediate retaliation from Tel Aviv?" he asked. "I doubt if they have any interest in preserving landmarks in Beirut, not even this beautiful old hotel."

Mirhashem glanced at him over his thick spectacles. "The IDF will launch an airstrike, as soon as they know their murderers are dead. Our communications network will tell us when that strike is airborne. Our radar will track them on their way north. We have planned to pull our team out quickly, and we'll be transporting our hostage to another location."

Dick stared into the terrorist's hard eyes. "Sir, in the interest of saving my own skin, I must inform you--you have less than ten minutes to get your people, the hostage, and myself, out of here!"

Mirhashem's head jerked perceptibly. "How can you say that? What the hell information do you have?"

"I'm sure you listened carefully to Fahed and Sabena's description of their rescue. Perhaps you recall the precise timing of that operation. Believe me when I say *nine minutes--and counting.*"

"We'd better believe him, Sir," echoed Abrahim.

It took Mirhashem only a split second to react. He picked up his headset, barked some orders in Arabic, then looked at Dick. "We'll have to pass on viewing the hostage. Maybe another time." He turned to Abrahim. "Take him to the airport in the Lincoln, arrange his transportation back to Vienna, and meet me at the camp."

Dick yawned and pushed back his seat in the first-class section of Egypt Air Flight 14. It was the midnight flight, the only one out of Beirut until ten the next morning. He would have to wait around the Cairo airport for several hours in the middle of the night, but the connection should get him to Vienna by 8:30 a.m.

Their departure from the King George Hotel had been with only a few minutes to spare. Bright flashes had lit up the western horizon as he and Abrahim reached the coastal highway to the airport. Dick had seen those flashes many times before, they were 5-inch naval guns.

Abrahim parked on the side of the highway, and they witnessed the death and destruction that rained on the hotel. The first rounds were air bursts, designed to kill unprotected living things. Those were followed by armor-piercing rounds that penetrated deep into the old stone building. It was all over in three minutes. The explosions and fire resembled the very pit of hell.

Dick reached in the backseat for the headset and handed it to Abrahim. "Did they get out?"

Abrahim's handsome face was blanched. He reacted slowly, but he was soon in contact with Mirhashem. After a brief exchange in Arabic, he removed the headset and turned to Dick. "The boss says to thank you, Captain. He and the team were in the APC, a few blocks from the hotel, when the air bursts hit. They took some shrapnel, but no one was seriously hurt."

"How about the hostages?" asked Dick quietly.

Abrahim sighed. "Our team has the American hostage. The Amal were bringing the Mossad's hostages out of the hotel when our team left. It's doubtful anyone survived." He paused for a moment, then continued: "Many foreigners were living there. One of our girls has the hotel's register. We'll know whom the Israelis killed in this mass murder."

Dick lowered his head and muttered: "Dear God, how does this ever end?"

Abrahim started the Lincoln and drove slowly down the highway. "I've been in this struggle all my life. My father was shot the day after I was born in Jerusalem. My two older brothers and I were orphaned five years later. Our mother was crushed when an Israeli tank plowed into the Palestinian café where she was a cleaning woman. The next day, my oldest brother stood in the street, throwing rocks at tanks. He kept throwing stones until a tank ran over him. A few years ago, my other brother went to Yemen for training, then Mirhashem invited me into his Brigade."

Dick sat silently, shaking his bowed head.

Abrahim continued: "Those of us who've been educated know our nation will not have a homeland--until American politicians end their naive support for Israel and consider our side of the issue. I met many fine Americans at the University of Kansas, Captain. Those God-fearing people would be protesting on the lawn of the White House right now, if they knew what's really going on over here. Unfortunately, there's absolutely no way your media will ever tell the true story. They'd lose their jobs if they tried!"

"I think I understand the tactics you're using in your struggle, Abrahim, but what can you tell me about your long-range strategy? How will you ever achieve victory? How could you ever have a homeland again?"

An ironic grin crossed the slim Palestinian's handsome features. In a way, Abrahim reminded Dick of Jim Conrad. "The easiest path for us lies through Moscow. If the Soviets defeat the U.S. in a nuclear war, our problems are solved. Jewish occupation would disappear in a wisp of smoke, and our flocks would once again graze peacefully in the hills east of Jerusalem."

"But what happens if there is no nuclear holocaust?" asked Dick. "What if détente goes on forever?"

Abrahim chuckled. "Not likely, Sir. The differences between the superpowers are too extreme for this unstable world system to continue."

"What's the strategy if the USA wins the confrontation, whether it's nuclear or economic? Or, maybe the USSR won't fight when the chips are down?"

"That may be true," sighed Abrahim. "The Russians already have a homeland, their situation is not so desperate as ours. But, I hope you realize, Captain, our weapons of mass destruction will prove much more effective than the Soviets'. You won't be able to deter us. You can't possibly make our lives more miserable. You will have no defense against our weapons, they will be intermingled within your population and your country."

He turned to smile at Dick. "I pray to Allah this will not happen. I pray that Americans will learn the truth, and see the light before so many of them die. Go back, read about your Revolutionary War again, Sir. You did not hesitate to take on a foreign superpower to win your freedom, and we shall not be found wanting when our time comes."

"Abrahim," asked Dick, "could you tell me who the hostage was that I hoped to see tonight?"

"You saved our lives, Captain. I guess I owe you that. It was a faculty member from the university."

7

THE RAGING WAR OF TERROR

He swam slowly, his thoughts on the first time he had followed Rita's shapely legs through the canals of the Philippine Plaza Hotel pool. To quiet his emotions, he decided to swim underwater for awhile. It was about thirty meters to the next wooden walkway over the canal. He set that as his goal.

He kept his forehead pointed down to remain submerged. When the canal narrowed, he knew he was approaching the bridge.

Suddenly, there were five sharp jolts in his shoulder--the signal to escape! He rolled on his back to look through the water at the walkway. A figure dressed in white was on the bridge. His eyes burned from the chlorine, but he could see the red hair.

His head burst above water. Rita was crouched on the bridge, laughing. She extended her hand to him. He took her hand and pulled her toward him.

"No, no, don't you dare!" she screamed. Then she was in the water. He pulled her to the bottom. He was holding her and kissing her. Her red hair swirled around their faces.

They surfaced. She was laughing and blowing water. She took his head in her hands and pulled him to her. Her tongue was deep in his mouth as they went again to the bottom. His hands caressed her firm bosom and became entangled in her long hair. He could feel the strands tugging at his fingers . . .

Dick awoke with a start. The fishing line wrapped around his finger was jerking his hand. A trout had grabbed the bait and was thrashing wildly in the cold water of the small pond.

Jim Conrad laughed. "Your namesakes would be ashamed of you, *Brown Bear.* You are the worst fisherman I've ever seen. If we're going to have *Forelle* for dinner, you'd better stay awake."

Dick pulled gently on the line, bringing the trout to the edge of the pond. "Hell of a time to get a bite. Rita and I were swimming at the Philippine Plaza. Her hair was tangled in my fingers."

Jim stared thoughtfully at the reflection of the sunset on the pond's glassy surface. "You dream of her often, Dick?"

"Not as often as I'd like."

"She loved you very much," reassured the Canadian Mountie. "She told me several times, but made me promise not to tell you."

Tears came to Dick's eyes. "She changed my life completely. For twenty years, I was the fighter pilot cast from steel--nothing inside but pure ice." He lifted the trout, gently removed the hook, and let it swim away. "I'll never forgive myself for not telling her how much I loved her, and for not taking her away from this crazy life. She should have been living on a Colorado mountain, instead of being blown to bits in a damned terrorist ambush."

Unabashed tears streamed down his face. "The ice is all gone now. I cry like a baby at the mere thought of her."

Jim Conrad wound his fishing line around a stick. "Maybe you are becoming human, Bear, but you couldn't have handled Enrico and Salah if you'd gone soft inside." He abruptly changed the subject: "We've lost our warm sun. Let's throw ourselves on the mercy of the kitchen and see what's for dinner."

"Yeah. We'd better drop by the rooms and ask Abood to eat with us. He's been working too hard on those sketches. He's certain to have a splitting headache by now."

"We have been pushing him. I'm amazed how you can remember the faces of that entire class of fifteen terrorists. Do you really have a photographic memory, like Abood says?"

They brushed the dried grass and twigs off their clothing, and began the short walk from the hotel's pond back to the lobby. The quaint hotel was located near Zweibrücken, West Germany. Along with a fabulous restaurant, it had ideal isolated facilities for their current task--recording the faces of the terrorists with whom Dick had spoken at Mirhashem's Bekaa Valley camp.

"Oh, I don't think I have a photographic memory," answered Dick; "but, when I was a kid, I developed a trick for remembering things." He grinned as he recalled: "My country school had twelve students in eight grades. There was only one room, and we all had to listen while the teacher conducted each class. If you didn't recite your lesson correctly, it could be very embarrassing. One day, I did poorly on an assignment of five pages of history. The little-old-lady school teacher really blasted me. I went home and completely memorized those five pages. The next day, when it was my turn, I recited it word for word--without a single mistake."

Jim smiled. "Pretty impressive, especially for a future fighter pilot. What was your magic? How did you do it?"

"My sister had a phonograph and a record of Gene Autry singing *Back in the Saddle*. I played it over and over while I studied the pages. Finally I realized, all I had to do was keep that music in my head, and I could recall exactly what was on those pages."

"Don't tell me you were humming *Back in the Saddle* while you were discussing the real world with Mirhashem's terrorists?"

They had reached the hotel entrance. Dick grinned and opened the door. "No, I needed a longer song; so I used *Stand up, Stand up, for Jesus*. We started Sunday School in the old school house with that hymn."

Jim Conrad paused in the doorway to regard his partner. "You are really one strange son-of-a-bitch. I thought I was going crazy when I heard you humming while you were working with Abood."

"Maybe I was taking the chance of offending him, but there can't be many Muslems who know that song."

"He probably doesn't either, but that rascal can draw Arab faces! Wonder what Mirhashem would say if he saw our finished products?"

They paused by the open fireplace and checked the spacious lobby. The talented Egyptian, who had served *Purple* for several years, was not there. He was probably still completing the details, bearding or unbearding boys' faces and changing girls' hair, on the basic images he'd drawn from Dick's memory over the preceding three days.

It was 7 p.m. The *ZDF* evening news was beginning on the lobby's big-screen TV. Jim and Dick paused to watch the headlines. "Damn, damn, damn," swore Dick softly. The TWA flight from Cairo to Rome had been hijacked after a refueling stop at Athens, and had been forced to land in Beirut. There were 104 Americans among the 153 passengers.

"Guess Mirhashem needed more than a half-dozen American hostages," said Jim quietly. They seated themselves on a sofa to watch the details.

"Doesn't make sense," observed Dick. "I had the feeling he was tiring of the hostage business. Things weren't happening fast enough for him."

A photo of an accomplice of the two hijackers appeared on the screen. The three of them had traveled together from Cairo to Athens, but there wasn't a seat available for him on the flight to Rome. He had foolishly waited around Athens; where he was arrested by Greek authorities after news of the hijacking broke.

"Did you see that guy in Lebanon last week?" asked Jim.

"No."

The television picture shifted to a gathering of officials inside the Beirut airport. Dick stared at the screen and exclaimed: "But I sure as hell saw him! Guy in uniform, with the big hat, on the left side of the screen. That's General Beyrri, commander of the Amal Militia and self-proclaimed *protector* of all hostages in Lebanon. Maybe he's increasing the number to make his chances of a prisoner exchange with the Israelis more favorable."

"Could be," agreed Conrad. "Almost a thousand of his fighters were captured by the IDF, many were moved to Israel." He looked down at the small electronic apparatus in his hand. "Got a call from Frankfurt. I'll take it outside. You find Abood, and I'll meet you guys in the restaurant. Order the *blau Florelle* for me."

Abood Nasser was a renowned artist of Arabic leaders. His gigantic mural portraits adorned palaces from Aden and Tehran to Tripoli and Morocco. He was in demand by arrogant rulers, who wanted their images constantly before the people they dominated.

Abood's works began with portrait sittings, which afforded him unusual access to important people in closely guarded places. He was quietly devoted to the concept of a peaceful world of freedom and democracy. *Purple* had enlisted his talents in the late '70s. Short of stature, his slim and fragile body belied his strength and stamina. Prematurely balding at forty-five, the bare crown of his head was ringed by meticulously styled black hair. His narrow nose was dwarfed by wide dark eyes and gold-framed spectacles. He was light-complexioned for an Egyptian. Perhaps English blood had crept into his family in the previous century. His most notable physical attributes were extremely long fingers, which magically produced God-like images of weak-faced characters.

Abood and Dick were on their second helping of *blau Forelle* before Jim Conrad joined them.

"I sent yours back to the kitchen," said Dick. "Didn't think even the Royal Canadian Mounted could handle cold poached trout."

Jim laughed and reached for the bottle in the ice bucket. "You're right about that, partner. Some French champagne, Abood?"

"No, thank you," answered the bespectacled artist. "I prefer this German beer."

"Didn't think you Muslim guys drank alcohol," said Dick.

Abood smiled. "I obey that rule when I'm in America--your beer isn't worth incurring the wrath of Allah. However, a professor in Munich told me that beer's the liquid bread of Germany. So, I'm accepting his definition; but only at dinner time."

"Well, you've certainly earned a *cold one* during these last three days," said Dick. "You've done wonders creating those photo-like images of Mirhashem's students."

". . . and just in time," added Jim. "Nelson wants us in Frankfurt with the pictures by noon tomorrow. People will be there to debrief you, Dick, but you should be able to catch the night train to *Wien*. Abood, he's got a job lined up for you in London."

"Then I better have another Löwenbrau," shrugged the talented Egyptian. "Their Stout is certain to be on Allah's accursed list."

Dick studied the driver's face in the rearview mirror. His black-rimmed glasses had a white nosepiece, like the taxi driver who had driven he and Maria around Stuttgart four years earlier.

"Driven anyone to the Landstuhl Army Hospital lately?" he asked.

The middle-aged German's broad face broke into a cold smile. "No one so cute as that blond *Fräulein* you had with you."

Fifteen minutes after leaving the train station, the Mercedes taxi pulled into the dimly lit parking basement of a shopping center.

"Watch your step, Gentlemen, but move quickly," advised Jim. "We're switching to a van."

The transfer was completed in seconds. Dick's head snapped back against the headrest as the van accelerated out of the basement and into traffic. He muttered, "Only thing more terrifying than driving in Frankfurt is riding with a German."

"Won't be long now, Bear," comforted Conrad.

Within ten minutes, the van came to a stop in another darkened basement garage. An attendant with a knit ski-mask over his head opened the van's doors. As they disembarked, he handed each of them a similar mask. "You know the way, Mr. Conrad," he said. "Please have your colleagues put these on before they step out of the elevator. Mr. Nelson's in the fifth-floor conference room. I'll bring your things after they've been screened."

"Thanks, Hans," replied Jim. "We'll need the sketches straight-away, so do them first. Follow me, Gentlemen." He led Dick and Abood toward the faint light marking the elevator door.

"This is the one I really like!" said Nelson. He turned the full-length sketch of Shreeba so the others could see it.

There were six of them at the table: Nelson, Jim Conrad, Dick, Abood, a *Purple* agent from the UK and another from West Germany. All except Nelson were masked.

"Yes!" agreed Dick. "Her face is identifiable, but she has other more distinguishing features. I thought it would be best if Abood drew her complete body."

". . . and that's a body!" echoed the German.

Conrad laughed. "Now I know why the monitor was overheating while you were in Mirhashem's steam bath."

"Do you think she could be useful to us?" asked Nelson.

Dick thought for a moment. "She has Mirhashem's trust, or she wouldn't be there. She said Mirhashem had promised her to that son-of-a-bitch Omman, but I doubt it. Unless he was being black-mailed, no man in his right mind would pass a piece of pastry like her to someone else."

The German asked. "Mirhashem also offered her to you, didn't he?"

"Maybe . . . ," pondered Dick, "but I believe it was just a fishing expedition."

"Some bait!" exclaimed Abood.

"I think we should regard her as one of Mirhashem's insiders, whom he will use however he wants," said Nelson. "Dick, if you get another chance in the future, get as close to her as you can. If that pearl chooses another oyster, we might get lucky."

The group laughed, and Nelson continued: "Only a manner of speaking, Gentlemen. We're in the process of reproducing Abood's expert productions. You'll all have copies before you leave. Hell of a job, Abood!"

The Egyptian smiled. "I'm only as good as Dick's memory."

Nelson pointed at a big-screen TV monitor. "Let's pause for a moment and review the footage from the TWA hijacking. As you know, the bastards have now killed an American sailor who was trying to protect others on the plane. These scenes are from the Beirut and Algiers airports. We'll run them slowly. Call out if you see anything familiar."

Dick stopped the video with the scene inside the Beirut airport. "That's General Beyrri, the commander of the Amal. Can you give us a blow-up of the guard standing by his left side?"

In a few seconds, an enlarged image of the guard filled the screen. "That's one of Mirhashem's guards from the Bekaa Valley camp. See his knife sheath with the brass tip? That has to be the knife I gave back to him, after I used it on the Mountain of Truth."

"That was a gutsy performance, Dick," said Nelson. "After this meeting, I'm inviting all of you to the bar, to listen to the recording from Brown Bear's monitor while he was on the mountain. From what I heard, that knife's no longer operational, is it?"

"Night vision's still intact, but the vial of knockout gas and the trip wire are gone, and the gas spray canister's about half empty."

"Maybe we can get a new knife to him, if he keeps showing up at the airport during this hijacking debacle," said Jim.

"Good idea," said Nelson. "Abood, would you give that a try through your Egyptian media friend?"

"Yes Sir."

After the available tapes of the hijacking had been reviewed, Nelson returned their attention to Dick's visit to Mirhashem's training camp. They listened carefully to that portion of the tape from Dick's monitor, where the discussion about trading hostages for weapons had taken place.

"Do you really think your President would authorize something like that?" asked the German agent.

"Based on experience during the ransom of General Thomas, I believe he might," answered Dick. "His reported attempt to communicate through a military officer would reinforce that belief. However, Mirhashem clearly stated the Iranians were being asked to sweeten the pot with contributions to Swiss bank accounts; and I don't think any American politician would take that kind of a risk."

Nelson sorted an envelope from the pile of papers in front of him. "Dick, this letter from Father Figueres may be the key to unraveling that dilemma."

Jim Conrad smiled fondly. "What's that cagey old Jesuit up to now? Last time I saw him was when we turned him over to a Honduran doctor in Choluteca, after Brown Bear took out Ahmad Salah at Danny's coronation."

"He's communicated with me over the last six months, through the Canadian Consulate in Tegucigalpa. He has sent photographic evidence of military arms and equipment--far in excess of that authorized by the U.S. Congress--being turned over to the Contras. He's also sent copies of shipping documents that show millions of dollars laid out by mystical third parties for non-U.S. equipment, which goes directly to the Contras."

Dick was taken aback by the thought of such shenanigans emanating from the White House he had served faithfully for thirty years. He could only mutter: "Sounds like the old priest could use a few prayers. If that information gets out, his life won't be worth a broken rosary."

"You're right," echoed the *Purple* Field Supervisor. He turned to Jim Conrad. "Mountie, get him out of Honduras. Stash him in one of our safe-houses till this thing plays itself out. Get it done in a hurry! We received a tall order from the GP-7 this morning, and we need time to do some detailed planning."

Five sets of eyes peering out of ski-masks were fixed on Nelson as he continued: "We have been directed to take out Mirhashem, and GP-7 Collective insists that it be accomplished immediately."

He paused to look around the table. "Normally I try to shield agents from the politics of a situation, but this is a special case. I disagree with the Collective. Killing Mirhashem now would make him a heroic martyr--forever enshrined in Muslim history. We must first discredit him in the eyes of those advocating radical Islamic terrorism--then we take him out."

"What politics are involved, Mr. Nelson?" asked Abood.

"The White House is looking for a scapegoat to pay for the Marine barracks in Beirut, the hostages in Lebanon, and now the TWA hijacking. They're also searching desperately for something to offset the scandal that's certain to erupt over the President's illegal support of the Contras. Reliable sources say the President wants to bomb Libya, but he's agreed to back-off if a terrorist of

Mirhashem's stature can be brought down."

"What's our first step?" asked the German. "Are we all involved in this? If so, why must we remain incognito?"

"I hope all of you will become involved," answered Nelson, "but remember--*Purple's* a volunteer organization. This may be the deadliest assignment any of you have come up against. Max, you are here because your work against the IRA, ETA, RAF, and others, proves you're the best when it comes to terrorist organization. Abood, you're here because you probably know the faces of more terrorists than Allah. Brown Bear, Mountie, you are here because that neat piece of work in Vienna--rescuing Mirhashem's uncle and niece from the Mossad--has made you indispensable to a successful operation. Mac, you know why you're here."

Nelson rose from the table and snapped his right hand to his forehead in a British-style salute. "Gentlemen, I have known all of you for several years, and I salute you. You have served *Purple* faithfully and flawlessly. If you choose not to involve yourself in this undertaking--which will be made extraordinarily dangerous by selfish politics--please adjourn to the bar without prejudice. The rest of us will join you there in a few minutes."

Nelson returned to his chair. "If you choose to remain, take off your masks and get acquainted."

Without hesitation, the five *Purple* agents removed their masks and tossed them in the middle of the table.

Dick began to laugh and moved quickly to embrace the ruddy faced Scotsman at the end of the table. "Special Air Service get too boring for you, Colonel?"

Mackenzie gave him a bear hug. "Not at all, Yank. Seems our Prime Minister has taken a shine to you. She sent me down here to baby-sit you."

"Baloney!" laughed Dick. "You're the one who puts the twinkle in her eye."

"Mac's on loan from the SAS," explained Nelson. Nodding at the six-foot fortyish German, he continued: "Colonel Maximilian Weber comes to us from the *Grenzegruppeneun* Commandos."

Dick shook the German officer's hand. Max was a solid man with a muscular body. The warmth of his grip belied the coldness of his icy blue eyes, pale lips, and neatly trimmed white hair. A slight smile creased his clean-shaven face. "I know of the bad experience you had with a few of our defectors, who were corrupted by *Herr* Strauss. I hope to correct your impression of us."

"I know about *Grenzegruppeneun*," replied Dick. "You guys are the best! I'm honored to be working with you."

Nelson pushed the intercom button on the arm of his chair. "Bring us some ice and a bottle of scotch," he ordered. He smiled at Abood and added: "We also need a couple pots of hot tea."

During the advanced planning session that followed, it was unanimously agreed Dick should re-establish communications with Sabena and her grandfather. They were considered primary sources of information on Mirhashem's activities; and, if necessary, could be blackmailed to force their cooperation--though that might prove deadly to Dick. Abood was currently in a position to keep track of Shreeba. She was placed high on the list of those who might become part of the *Purple* web--woven to first discredit, then eradicate, Mirhashem, the king of the terrorists.

The jostling of the train switching tracks, as it rolled south out of Munich, awoke Dick. He raised the curtain next to his berth and peered into the early morning sunlight. It was going to be another gorgeous spring day in Bavaria. He opened the window and looked forward along the side of the train. In the distance, he could see the snow-capped mountain that held Austria's glacier. The valley to the south, leading to Oberammergau, was shrouded in a low layer of thin mist. He remembered Mal Pierce now had a country house somewhere in that valley. Dick had fond memories of their time together in the Pentagon, and he was forever indebted to Mal for recommending him to the Aura consortium.

At that moment, Mal Pierce was actuating the switch that would allow him to exit the security system surrounding his home, without disturbing the serenity of the quiet country lane leading to the autobahn. The double garage door opened, and he backed his new BMW sports coupe down the driveway.

It promised to be a big day for the retired USAF Colonel. The Chancellor was on a campaign swing through Bavaria. He would visit Mal's office in Munich for an update on West Germany's participation in the American President's Space Wars program.

Mal's Pentagon and aerospace background, and his connection with the shelved Aura program, had allowed him to advance rapidly through the Munich-based electronic research firm. He was now vice president of the branch researching an ABM system utilizing Aura's technology.

His new German wife was returning from a walk with their golden retriever. He got out of the car and embraced her tenderly. They were expecting a child around Christmas time. She clung to Mal, while the retriever playfully nuzzled his ankles. He promised to call her immediately after his meeting with the Chancellor.

He drove slowly down the narrow lane, savoring the memorable picture of his wife and dog in the rearview mirror. The mist was clearing, the golden sun was breaking through. It glistened from the drops of dew adorning the branches of the huge hundred-year-old tannenbaums bordering the lane. He opened the BMW's windows to breathe the fresh spring air. Having survived a hundred missions in the F-100 over North Vietnam, he thanked God for sparing him for this special life.

Fifty meters from the intersection of Pierce's country lane and a feeder road to the autobahn, an Irishman and a Spaniard lay in wait. They were hiding in a thicket, but had a clear line-of-sight to the large tree where they had fastened the two Claymore mines. Foliage had been arranged to hide the powerful weapons, but a narrow gap allowed direct access for the beam from the terrorists' remote control trigger.

The Irishman was the IRA's expert with such weapons. His personal score in kills of British soldiers totaled twenty-three. He had chosen the trunk of a tree with a diameter of over four feet. To maximize the explosive force, the mines were hung on their sides with their bases firmly anchored to the tree. They were attached at the precise elevation to coincide with the windows of a BMW sports coupe. The tree protruded slightly into the country lane, which was only three meters wide at that point.

The young Spaniard was the whiz kid of electronics for the ETA Basque Separatist terrorist organization. His triggers were made from TV remote controls and had proven 100 percent effective in the 14 bombs he had already detonated. His personal score of opponents was 35 dead and over 300 injure. He was only nineteen.

In return for their services, a former sponsor of the Red Army Faction--disenchanted by its decline--had paid $50,000 to their *parent organizations. Traveling with French passports, they had rendezvoused in the West German university town of Freiburg and traveled by train to the small village of Ulm, west of Munich. There they picked up the Claymores, which had been stolen earlier during the RAF raid on a nearby U.S. Army depot.*

Eva, a hard-core RAF radical, had driven them to the Pierce residence. She had surveyed it for more than a month, and had been angered when her supervisor ordered her to break off the surveillance. She believed the RAF leadership was going soft and ignored the order. She was eager to finish this job and move on to other lucrative targets in the West German Space Wars Team.

The Irishman heard the whining engine of the approaching BMW and alerted the Spaniard. He focused the remote control through the brush. The blinking red light indicated contact with the triggers on the Claymores.

Dick finished combing his hair in the mirror above the sink, adjusted his tie, pulled on his coat, and left the compartment to have breakfast in the dining car. The next time he passed through Munich, he would take time to have lunch with Pierce.

Mal shifted down to second gear as he entered the narrow section of the country lane approaching the autobahn feeder. His eyes caught the unnatural protrusion of foliage from the trunk of the big tannenbaum, but it was too late.

The horrific explosion shattered the driver's side of the small BMW. U.S. Air Force Colonel, and Vietnam War hero, Mal Pierce died in a hail of shrapnel.

The IRA and ETA soldiers in the war of terror raging across Western Europe melted into the underbrush.

The debris stopped raining down. An eerie silence settled over the scene--then it was broken by the barking of a dog and the screaming of a woman running up the lane.

8

THE TERROR FROM WITHIN

While watching people board the train in Linz, Dick noticed the red light on his Skyfone. He stepped back into his compartment, locked the door, and returned Jim Conrad's call. The Canadian Mountie sadly gave him the news about Mal Pierce.

Last year, the RAF had publicly announced it was targeting the West German Space Wars Team. Jim Conrad's undercover work had enable *Purple* to place the terrorist leaders under surveillance. None of them had been involved in the hit on Mal. Jim's educated guess was that the Kremlin had recognized the internal collapse of the RAF, and had brought other terrorist groups into the battle against the U.S. President's initiative.

Dick was concerned for the safety of Helmut Angemann, their colleague in the Aura project and now a leader in West Germany's space program. Nelson had already acted. Helmut was enroute to *Purple's* safe-house in the crater of the old volcano in the Philippines. He would stop by Honduras and pick up Father Figueres.

Promptly at 9:02 a.m., the train pulled into Vienna's Westbahnhof. Dick strolled through the terminal hall and stood outside in the bright sunshine, debating what to do next. Maria would be at work in the Red Cross Hospital. He thought about Mal and waves of depression flowed over him. He did not want to return to an empty apartment. He glanced at his watch. He could still make the last half of his German Grammar class at the university. He had missed most of the last two weeks, but was sure Frau Wilke would go easy on him.

As he stepped off the Strassenbahn, he met the other class members coming from the historic old building. Among them were Abrahim, Ali, and Musavi--Mirhashem's staff in Vienna.

Abrahim called to him: "You're late, Captain Orden. With the weather getting warmer, the class is now meeting an hour earlier."

The three surrounded him and insisted that he join them for

breakfast in the city.

"Sounds good," said Dick. "Hop aboard! This streetcar stops at the *Oper*. That's only a block from the Sacher Hotel's sidewalk restaurant."

Without waiting for an answer, he stepped back into the tram. He wanted to separate them from their automobile, which was surely parked nearby. If he was successful, it wouldn't take so long to ditch the tail they would probably put on him later. The three young men scrambled into the streetcar behind Dick.

The early morning delivery vehicles were gone. The *pedestrians -only* Kärtnerstrasse was packed with window-shopping tourists. The sidewalk restaurants--their boundaries marked by boxes of flowers--were crowded, but they found a table in the corner of the Sacher Hotel's space.

"Frau Wilke missed you, Captain," began Abrahim, "but I guess you needed a rest after our *Ausflug* to Beirut."

"Yeah," said Dick. "If that's what you guys call a holiday, don't invite me along when you go to work."

"You impressed the hell out of our boss," said Musavi. "He told us that you're really a Muslim warrior, who was accidentally born an infidel."

Dick grinned. "I'll have to ask my mother about that."

Abrahim continued: "You saved our lives by insisting we leave the King George immediately. The boss is very interested in how you knew the shelling was about to start."

Dick replied carefully: "That's no mystery. I'm sure he now knows the ship was an old U.S. destroyer, given to the IDF several years ago. One of my first assignments in the Navy was at a target range off Cuba. For three years, I watched ships like that--maybe even that one--doing live-firing exercises. The IDF had moved the destroyer close to the harbor, probably to improve their accuracy. There are certain things ships have to do before shooting. When I heard, and saw, that destroyer going through the sequence, I knew when the shooting would commence."

The three terrorists exchanged glances. Dick could only hope they bought his story, which was not altogether true.

"It was pretty dark, Captain Orden," ventured Abrahim, "and there was a lot of noise."

"Not really," responded Dick. "Remember, you and Mirhashem were looking directly into the spotlights around the building, but I was in a position to watch the sea. The destroyer wasn't showing any external lights, but I could see her internal red lights reflecting off outside surfaces. Don't forget," he concluded, "things had quieted down around the hotel before I gave you the warning. I heard the whining of the wenches lifting the five-inch ammunition into the gun turrets."

From the way they looked at each other, Dick believed they had accepted his explanation.

Ali changed the subject. "I want to thank you for disposing of a man--a monster--who had become a disgrace to all Muslems. Sheik Omman was a torturer and a murderer. May Allah bless you, for your courage and skill on the Mountain of Truth. You are indeed a mighty warrior, whom Muslems would be proud to recognize as one of our own."

Dick smiled at the handsome young Palestinian. "I met your sister at the camp. She told me your story. I am proud to know someone who takes on armed soldiers with his bare hands."

He was uneasy about bringing Shreeba into the conversation, but Dick had to develop as many leads to Mirhashem as possible.

Ali's response put him at ease. "Shreeba called a few days ago, and said she had the pleasure of serving you dinner at Mirhashem's villa. She described you as a kind and considerate gentleman, whom she hopes to see again."

Dick suppressed a grin. Ali had clearly not been told about the bath--or the bed. He needed to put a classification on his relation-ship with Shreeba quickly: "Your sister's very cute. She reminds me of my niece in the States."

Ali smiled. "I don't think she regards you as an uncle. She will soon be part of Mirhashem's social entourage. She's looking for-ward to visiting Vienna."

"Great!" said Dick. "Maybe I could invite both of you to the *Oper. Fledermaus* is performed every night during the summer."

Abrahim leaned across the table and handed Dick an envelope. "Thanks to your efforts at the U.S. Consulate, Fahed al-Benna and his granddaughter are now settled in the States. Fahed's getting old. Sabena says his health is failing. He wants to see you again, and show you his new home in the Rocky Mountains. These are open tickets, which you can use anytime. The transatlantic flights are first-class. The last airline, Frontier, has only economy; but it's a short flight from Denver to Boulder. Sabena will be registering for summer school next week. She called to ask for your help."

"Maybe we can make a deal." Dick chuckled. "I've missed a lot of Frau Wilke's class. Ali, you take the final exam for me, and I'll go register Sabena."

Ali laughed. "Frau Wilke would give you an *examination* whenever you like." Then he added seriously, "Captain Orden, the class will soon be over. We would like to stay in contact, but we know you need privacy--so do we. Do you have any suggestions?"

Dick thought for a moment. "How about a post office box?"

The Frontier commuter pilot did a graceful turn over the Flat Irons before lining-up with the runway. The dark-colored flat rocks, topping the mountains above Boulder, contrasted sharply with the snow-capped peaks of the Rockies rising majestically in the west. It was an impressive view of one of America's most beautiful areas. Dick found himself humming another old Gene Autry tune, *When It's Spring Time in the Rockies.*

He had grown up on a prairie farm in Nebraska, about 150 miles to the northeast. His sister was a graduate of Colorado University's School of Medicine, and he had visited the campus several times during his younger days.

Strolling across the tarmac with his small suitcase, he checked the address in his notebook and debated whether he should rent a car or take a taxi. The decision was made for him when he heard someone calling his name from behind the chain-link fence.

Sabena was waving a large black and gold scarf. Dick walked quickly to the fence. She was obviously already acquainted with Denver's fashion houses. The lavender tennis skirt emphasized her trim bottom. He didn't remember her legs were so attractive. They had always been covered by the conservative fashions she wore in Vienna. The matching blouse was tight enough to notify wandering eyes there was a lot of woman inside. The late afternoon sun glistened in the black silky waves of her hair.

Her deep violet eyes were smiling at Dick. He set his bag on the tarmac and touched her fingertips through the steel mesh of the fence. She pursed her lips in a kiss.

"Wow!" exclaimed Dick. "Now I remember what I liked most about this campus. It was the knockout girls."

She laughed softly and leaned forward to kiss his fingers. "I bet your name's still in the sorority log books. How was your trip, Captain? You must be very tired."

"Thanks to the generosity of your uncle, it was very comfortable. How's Grandfather? Abrahim said he wasn't well."

"He's waiting anxiously to greet you, Captain."

Dick picked up his bag. "I'll only be a minute. Shall I rent a car or should we take a taxi?"

Sabena smiled and pointed at the black Porsche coupe parked behind her. "Your transportation awaits, *Sire*."

"Wow!" exclaimed Dick again. "You're the complete package, aren't you."

"Do you like the wrapping?" She giggled, held the black-and-gold scarf at arms length, and whirled quickly to show him her spring-time outfit.

"Outstanding!" Dick chuckled. "Wonder what they are wearing back at the Mosque?"

Her dark violet eyes caught his, and she said quietly: "Can't wait to show you how liberated I really am."

The Porsche accelerated on the narrow highway leading north from the college town. Dick remembered the country road. They were paralleling a noisy crystal-clear stream, tumbling over and around small boulders as it wound its way down the valley.

Sabina maneuvered through the curves like a professional. He had to speak loudly, over the rush of the wind and the whining of the engine: "Where in the world did you learn to drive?"

There was a sparkle in her violet eyes. "In the world of the Talish Mountains, north of Tehran. We vacationed there every summer. Grandfather had a car like this. I've been driving since I was thirteen."

"Didn't know Muslim women were allowed to drive. Do you have a license?"

She laughed. "My Iranian driver's license was printed on the back of a twenty-thousand rial note."

"How about in the sovereign state of Colorado?" asked Dick,

turning slightly to study the feminine form beside him.

She glanced at him, and caught his eyes moving up her body. "You should have seen the line at the police station." She laughed. "They all wanted to give me the test, so they could ride in my Porsche."

She braked abruptly and turned down a gravel road leading to the stream. "Unless you're very tired, Captain, I want to show you one of Allah's wonders. We're only a few minutes from the house."

She parked alongside the stream, behind a grove of pine trees. "Isn't this a page from paradise?" she asked. She stepped out of the Porsche, Dick followed.

A herd of red-and-white Hereford cows and their baby calves were grazing in luscious knee-high grass on the other side of the stream. The lyrics of the birds in the trees were competing with the songs of the larks in the meadow. The water tumbling over the rocks supplied the background music.

"Yeah," sighed Dick. "It's amazing that places like this still exist in our crazy world. Only three weeks ago, my friend and I snatched you off that apartment roof in Vienna."

She met him at the front of the Porsche and shyly put her arms around his waist. Her violet eyes found his, she whispered: "I've only seen you once since then, Captain--during your meeting with my uncle. The Schönbrunn Castle was hardly the place to say *thank you* for saving my life. May I do so now?"

Without waiting for an answer, she placed her hands behind his shoulders and pulled herself strongly against him. Her full lips were wet and moist. They parted slightly and her tongue touched his. Dick closed her in his arms and enjoyed the fullness of the bosom thrusting against his shirt.

She closed her eyes and twisted her body slowly against him, her kiss became even more passionate. Dick resisted the urge to lower his hands to the tennis skirt.

Finally he drew back and said: "What a miracle! You've been in the States two weeks, and you already kiss like a movie star."

She opened her eyes and sighed: "One doesn't have to be born in America to have seen romantic movies."

"Which was your favorite, *Suddenly Last Summer?*"

She smiled. "Good guess! Elisabeth Taylor is my heroine. The movies she made with Montgomery Clift are her best."

They were still locked tightly in each other's arms. Dick bent his head to brush her lips gently with his own, then asked: "Tell be again why we're standing here like this?"

"I wanted to thank you that I'm still alive." She again thrust herself against him, trying to touch him with every inch of her body. Her eager lips sought his. She opened her mouth and relentlessly drew him inside.

They continued embracing, kissing with ever-increasing passion, until the lowing of a cow interrupted the peace and quiet, and brought them back to reality.

Dick broke away with a laugh. "That poor creature must wonder what's going on. She never saw Colorado cowboys doing this."

The smile on Sabena's face belied the hunger in her violet eyes. She straighten her blouse and tucked it back inside the waistband of her tennis skirt. "I'd like to continue her education," she said breathlessly, "but we must go to the house. Grandfather's waiting." She paused, "Promise me you'll come here with me later, Captain."

They strolled hand-in-hand to the car. Dick responded: "Okay, Sabena, but you must promise me two things: that you'll use my first name instead of *Captain*, and that you'll make sure the people who own this property don't mind our trespassing."

She slid her trim bottom into the bucket seat and smiled. "Okay, *Ed*, don't worry about trespassing. This piece of paradise belongs to me. I bought it two days after we arrived in the States."

She eased the Porsche back to the pavement. Minutes later, they turned into a lane leading to a sprawling ranch house, sitting on a hill above the stream.

They stopped in the cul-de-sac, in front of the double doors. She turned in the seat, gesturing with an open hand. "Isn't it beautiful? We have 240 acres, extending down the creek to my paradise."

"How did you find this so quickly?" asked Dick.

"There's a very active Muslim support group at the university. I thought you knew about it."

They sat on the marble patio, facing a golden sunset that framed the magnificence of the mountains.

The physical condition of the elderly man had indeed declined sharply in the last few weeks. When they moved from the dinner table to the patio, he had gratefully accepted Dick's arm.

- 144 -

He slumped in the comfortable chair, sipping his orange juice with a trembling hand. "Captain Orden, would you care for something more substantial?" His speech remained surprisingly clear and concise. "We have a westernized bar for our guests, complete with anti-freeze to ward off the mountain's chill."

Dick chuckled. "No thank you, Sir. The juice is fine. Sabena showed me the bar when we toured the house. It would have been the envy of Errol Flynn in his Hollywood heydays."

A smile creased the old Palestinian's features. "While I was at USC, Lieutenant Reyes and I saw every movie he ever made. It was our weekend ritual for taking a break from classes." He paused for a moment, his smile faded. "I'd like to visit Leonardo's grave again. He's buried in Rosecrans, near the top of the hill."

"I know it well. I have a couple wingmen there. Maybe we could make the trip together."

"That would be very kind of you, Captain, but first we must get Sabena settled at the university."

"I'm amazed how quickly you've established yourselves here."

"We owe Sabena's acceptance by the Graduate School to you. Beyond that, it was all rather automatic. Mirhashem has an extensive program at more than thirty major American universities, including CU. I believe he's funding about forty students here, and this is one of his smaller groups."

"Must be incredibly expensive!"

The elderly man nodded his head. "He encourages his protégés to become citizens as soon as possible, and to establish residence near the school where they're being educated. The longer they are here, the less expensive it becomes."

"Yes, that would make a difference; but isn't Mirhashem eager for his graduates to return to the Middle East?"

"Oh, no!" replied Grandfather al-Benna. "He intends for them to become part of the American scene. He started his network program in 1974. It now includes bureaucrats at the state and federal levels, lawyers in prestigious law firms, medical doctors at important institutions, and educators in high positions."

"Fantastic," said Dick, "but isn't that counter-productive? Won't he lose control of those people when they become so successful?"

"You must understand his selection process," continued Fahed. "They come to America under a variety of passports--Kuwaiti,

Iranian, Saudi, Jordanian, Egyptian--but they are all Palestinians, personally selected by him while they were teenagers. The basic qualification is a close relative killed by Jews. You have been to a camp where he fans the flames of that hatred in their souls."

"Do they control each other while in foreign countries?"

"No, that hasn't proven necessary. In fact, his policy is for them to seek other nationalities for marital partners. In the eleven years of his network program, he's had only one defection."

Dick grinned. " . . . and that person is . . . ?"

" . . . no longer with us." Fahed chuckled.

Dick remembered his discussion with Abrahim on the way to the Beirut airport, when he learned of Mirhashem's strategic goal to attack America from within.

"How many graduates are there? I heard rumors the Ayatollah asked him to form a 2,500-man brigade."

"There are at least that many in his *Brigade,* Captain. Only half are the suicide bombers that Khomeini visualized. They remain in the Middle East. The *educated* half are now abroad, and more are going every month. When Khomeini found out what Mirhashem was doing, he stopped funding the program."

"We must be talking hundreds of millions of dollars," said Dick. "How has Mirhashem managed to keep it going?"

The elderly Palestinian grinned. "Gas-guzzling Americans give him all the money he needs. Of course, they send it via despots like the Saudi and Kuwaiti royal families. America's insatiable appetite for Arab oil ensures an unlimited expense account for Mirhashem."

"Guess I don't understand why the Saudis and those other folks would be passing the big bucks on to your nephew?"

"To use an old Al Capone term, it's called *protection.* You're a student of modern international terrorism, Captain. Ask yourself how many oil-rich Arab governments have been bothered by terrorist attacks since 1970. Mirhashem not only keeps them off his hit lists, he guarantees their personal safety at home and abroad."

Dick grinned. " . . . with the exception of Jordan."

"Yes indeed! Since his Bedouins massacred our family, King Hussein's been at the top of our lists."

Dick listened attentively. It was the first time the old man had included himself in Mirhashem's activities.

Fahed thought for a minute, then concluded: "Like Al Capone,

Mirhashem sometimes finds it necessary to remind certain govern-ments why his *protection* is necessary. There's a prince in Kuwait who's refusing to anti-up. I would hate to be in his family's shoes for the next few months."

The air had cooled. A young Hispanic girl appeared on the patio with two blankets. She tucked one around the grandfather. She turned to do the same for Dick, but Sabena came through the door-way to take the blanket from her. As she arranged the blanket around Dick's shoulders, she brushed his forehead with her lips and whispered: "This will have to do for now. I'll have something warmer for you later." She followed the girl into the house.

"You were lucky to find household help so quickly," said Dick.

Fahed shrugged. "All part of the package. They're from Central America. The Syrians have a deal with Nicaragua for domestic help, like the Saudis employ the Filipinos. Mirhashem uses his influence in Damascus to bring them to the States to work for his university groups. Ours speak English. I learned Spanish years ago in Madrid and practiced it during my three years at Southern Cal."

Dick wanted to steer the conversation toward the location and movements of Mirhashem, but it was risky business.

"I understand from Abrahim that Mirhashem's thinking of mov-ing from Syria to Libya." *Purple* had given that information to Dick, but he hoped the grandfather would believe Abrahim had spoken to him about it.

Fahed responded without hesitation: "Mirhashem started as a PLO representative in Iraq. When Arafat betrayed our cause, he stayed there to organize the fight against him. When Saddam attacked Iran, he asked for America's help. One of their conditions was that he kick my nephew out of Baghdad. He's been operating out of Syria for the last two years, but Assad's continually asking him to perform hits for him personally. Mirhashem's looking for a place with less strings attached. Colonel Qadhafi has promised to support his organizations across Europe. He is also interesting in contributing to this network in America."

"Would Mirhashem rather go back to Baghdad?" asked Dick.

"I believe he's more interested in Iran. He enjoyed Tehran when he visited us in the late '70s. Khomeini is disappointed Mirhashem misinterpreted his desire for a brigade of human-bombs--and Sheik Omman's Islamic Jihad has made things difficult--but I think

Mirhashem would rather be in Tehran than Tripoli."

Sabena appeared again on the patio. "Grandfather, haven't you had enough for today? The Captain must be tired from his travel."

Dick rose to his feet. "I look forward to talking with you tomorrow, when I pick up Sabena to register for classes." He laid the blanket on the chair and asked Sabena: "Would you have someone call a taxi for me? I have a reservation at the Sheraton."

Grandfather al-Benna immediately intervened. "Oh no, Captain. We have planned for you to be our first houseguest. Everything is ready in the guest quarters. Please spend the night with us."

Sabena glanced sharply at Dick. "Don't even think of leaving, Captain Orden. It would be a real disappointment for Grandfather, . . . and for me," she added.

Dick turned the shower hotter, but it wasn't working. Jet lag had him, he was wide awake. He dried himself and put on the guest robe from the closet.

The bedroom was positively elegant: deep carpets, a huge four-poster bed, a massive stone fireplace, walls adorned with paintings of mystical mountain scenes, a well-stocked bar, shelves of books, and an impressive home-entertainment system.

Dick found the remote and watched the news. The TWA hijacking to Beirut continued to unfold. There were no tapes of participants, so he turned off the set.

He checked the titles on the bookshelves. Amazing! Here was a copy of his all-time favorite, Zane Gray's *Spirit of the Border*. He selected background music on the remote control, poured himself a glass of cognac, and settled down on the sofa near the fire. The cracking and popping of the pine was perfectly suited to following the exploits of Lew Wetzel and Jonathan Zane, as they took on hordes of Indians to protect the pioneers--and Jonathan's sister Betty. The music was a Frank Sinatra tape, which did not contribute to the story, but was very quieting.

He heard the click of the lock opening. He snapped his eyes to the door and gathered himself to spring from the sofa. The door opened. Sabena stepped quickly inside and locked the door.

She was an absolute vision in white!

"Let me guess," called Dick across the room. "Elisabeth Taylor, in *Cat on a Hot Tin Roof?*"

The fire's glow accentuated the contrast between her dark hair and the white dress, with its fitted low-cut bodice and flared ball-room skirt. As she approached, Dick could see those violet eyes sparkling like the embers in the fireplace.

She smiled and turned gracefully, allowing the skirt to whirl above her knees. "You're magic, Captain. I gave the seamstress a video of that film, and she made this for me. Do you like it?"

"It's an exact duplicate--except for the girl inside."

She pursed her lips in disappointment. "Is something wrong with me?"

Dick laughed. "On the contrary, you have much better legs than that English wench."

He rose, tossed the book on the couch, and extended his arms. She folded herself into them, and lifted her lips to kiss his cheek.

" . . . and how about the rest of me?" she asked impetuously.

He placed a gentle hand on each of her shoulders and held her at arms length. His eyes caressed her body--from the smooth milky-white shoulders, to the tremulous bosom thrusting high against the low confines of the bodice, down to the narrow waist, and farther to her womanly hips. He ran his eyes slowly back up her body, to drink in the dark violet beauty of her eyes.

He cleared his throat and said huskily: "The rest of you is in a class by itself."

She seemed suddenly embarrassed and lowered her eyes. "I'm glad you're still awake. I wanted so much to talk with you."

He smiled and released her shoulders. "Yes, the jet-lag monster has me. I was hoping a book would make me sleepy, but I'm glad you're here. I would rather look at you than dream of Betty Zane."

"Thank you. May I sit down?"

"Oh, please." Dick sat discreetly in a corner of the large sofa, but she seated herself firmly against him.

"What a lovely dress!" he continued. "If you wear that around the campus, you'll have a long line of prospective boyfriends."

She gazed wistfully into his blue eyes. "Do you think of me as a friend, Captain?"

He paused, then answered carefully: "We've known each other for only a few weeks, but we've been through a lot together. I do want you to think of me as a friend."

She turned to face him, and took his hands in hers. Her violet eyes blazed. "I don't want to be your friend." She caught her breath and continued: "I want to be your lover, and I want you to be my teacher." A faint pink blush flooded her cheeks, but she held him with her eyes. "I want you to teach me about love, . . . and sex."

She was breathing heavily. Dick was keenly aware of the milk-white bosom straining against the low-cut bodice.

If he hesitated, it would be an awkward moment. He embraced her, drawing her tightly against him. He spoke softly, "Sabena, Sabena. What's this all about? You're a dream girl. You can pick and choose from hundreds of young men who'll be pursuing you. What could you possibly want from me?"

Her face was pressed into his shoulder. She turned to nuzzle his chest through the open robe. "Captain Orden, you're the only man who can help me with a very difficult problem. Only someone with your experience could understand what I've been through."

"You're trembling, Sabena. Are you cold? Would you like a cognac?"

"No, please," she whispered. "I'm just very excited. I think my heart may explode at any moment."

He lowered his lips to her forehead. She raised hers, and they exchanged a tender kiss. He embraced her. "Start at the beginning. Tell me everything."

"I'm only half Palestinian. I was born in Marseilles. My mother was French. She and my father were killed in Jordan in 1970. I moved to Tehran with Grandfather when I was only five."

She was trembling uncontrollably. Dick opened his robe and held her against his warmth. She snuggled against his chest and continued: "We had a nice life--until the Shah was deposed and we were exiled to Vienna. I was fifteen when I enrolled in my first Austrian school. I had a sheltered life in Tehran and was frightened by the aggressive behavior of the Austrian boys."

She paused to take a deep breath, but her trembling grew even stronger. Dick was completely aware of the hot bosom emerging from the top of the bodice and pressing against his chest.

"One day, Grandfather's driver picked me up at school. I had to wait in the backseat of the Mercedes while he delivered a note to the headmaster. He forgot to lock the doors. Suddenly, two boys jumped in the car with me, one from each side. I tried to fight them, but they were too strong. I had no chance."

Sabena's entire body was shuddering. She clung tightly to Dick. "They tore off my clothes. One of them held my arms, the other forced himself into me. I was a virgin, blood was everywhere. A group of boys gathered around the car to watch. The driver came running out of the school, but he was too late."

She buried her face in Dick's chest and sobbed hysterically. He smoothed the silky black waves of hair and kissed the tears streaming down her cheeks. When the crying eased, he lifted her delicate chin with his fingertips and kissed her full trembling lips. The salty taste brought her back to reality. She responded passionately.

They kissed wildly for several minutes before Dick drew slowly back. "Was that your first--and last--experience with sex?"

"Yes," she whispered through bruised lips. She took a breath, sat up on the sofa, and pulled up the bodice to cover her exposed breasts. Dick closed his robe.

She cleared her throat and spoke: "I'm trying to begin a whole new life in America, but I'm absolutely terrified! I'm 'hit on' by men whenever I go out of the house. I have no idea what to do."

"Would you say that you have no confidence in matters of a sexual nature?" asked Dick tenderly.

A smile crept into her fascinating eyes. "Exactly, dear Captain, and I want *you* to teach *me* how it should really be--what a man and a woman should do to please each other."

She paused. Frank Sinatra was singing about someone telling him that love was grand.

Sabena continued: "I want so much for you to show me how wonderful love--and sex--can be."

"Yes," agreed Dick, reflecting briefly to Rita, "especially when they come together--at the same time."

She smiled. "Dear teacher, is this sofa okay for a classroom, or should we drive to my paradise?"

Dick gently kissed her smiling mouth. "It would be a shame to trade that comfortable bed for a crowded car seat."

"I was thinking of the deep grass by the stream."

"That would be very cold. Let's do Love-and-Sex 101 here, and take a field trip tomorrow afternoon."

"Okay, Professor." She was breathing so hard her voice was husky. "You'll find me an eager, but totally uneducated, student."

"Sabena, with the horrible experience you had a few years ago, it might be better to use a *third person* approach. You play the role of Elisabeth Taylor. Think of your body as hers. It will be easier for you that way."

". . . and would you be thinking of my body or hers?"

Dick grinned. "From what I've seen so far, that won't be a problem."

"Please," she breathed, "let's begin. Are you going to undress me and carry me to bed?"

"No, lovely girl. Remember, *Maggie the Cat* was in complete control. That's your first lesson. If you let someone else remove your clothes, you don't have control. I'm going to wait on the bed. Think back to the movie--take off your dress like Maggie would. When you're ready, come to me." Dick rose, fastened his robe, and went to the bed.

She sat quietly on the sofa for a few moments, then put on her high-heeled shoes and stood erect. She walked slowly toward him, her hips swaying seductively.

She stopped near the foot of the bed and arched her back. Her proud bosom pushed high against the bodice. The faint pink blush returned to her cheeks, she cast her eyes to the floor.

"No, no, Sweetheart," prompted Dick. "Challenge your lover with your eyes, just like Maggie."

She raised her glowing violet eyes to engage his. The blush in her cheeks deepened. She reached behind her back to unzip the bodice. One hand was not enough. She bent forward and reached back with both hands. As she struggled with the zipper, her breasts began to emerge.

"Wow!" said Dick. "Maggie could learn a few things from you."

A smile blossomed across her blushing face. She walked to his side of the bed and turned her back. "Professor, would you be so kind?" Dick edged the zipper slowly downward.

She stepped away, clasping the bodice to her bosom. Then she pirouetted like a ballerina, with the skirt billowing high above her shapely thighs. She returned to the side of the bed, slowly peeling the bodice from her bosom.

He caught his breath. "Magnificent, Maggie, magnificent!"

She reached for the waistband snap, the white creation fell to the floor. She stepped out of it, turned slowly, and walked away from the bed. Her bottom was encased in white satin panties that tenderly held the perfect curves. She turned to face him. Her shining violet eyes held his, her fingers searched for the snaps on the white garter belt.

Dick groaned, "Ah, . . . unbelievably sexy, dear student. Please, always wear nylons, never panty hose."

"Yes Sir," she said meekly. The garters were unsnapped. She dropped the belt to the floor and returned to the side of the bed.

"Is this the way Maggie would do it?" She raised a foot to the bed and slowly rolled down one of the stockings.

Dick grinned. "If she had, I don't think Brick would have been interested in Skipper."

She laughed softly. The pink blush was disappearing from her face. "I'm glad you approve, Professor. Will there be many exams in this course?"

"It always begins with a snap quiz. You have a perfect score to this point."

She rolled the second stocking down a shapely calf, tossed it to the floor, and leaned against the edge of the bed with her thumbs in the waist of the satin panties.

"No, not yet." Dick shook his head slowly. "We must have a review before the first exam."

She lowered her hands and arched her back. The effect on her breasts was astounding. She bent to touch the knot on Dick's robe. "May I? Unlike Maggie, I've never seen the entire body of a man."

It took several minutes to satisfy her curiosity. She lay beside him and explored with slim exquisite fingers. Dick fought for control. She rolled carefully on top of him, crushing her bosom against his chest. She was breathing heavily and could only gasp: "Oh my! Dear teacher, something strange is happening to Maggie."

She raised her upper body, supporting herself on her elbows. Her fierce kiss bruised his lips. His fingers found the satin panties.

She moaned loudly, pushing herself up, raising her bosom to his face. Dick whispered, "Examination time, Maggie."

His mouth found her beauty, she began to shiver. Dick proceeded slowly and tenderly. Her shivering body began to tremble violently. She was panting for breath.

"Oh my! Oh my!" She was crying loudly. "Please, Captain, now. Please now."

Dick complied gently with her wishes. The floodgates within

her broke. Her body shuddered, again and again and again.

His wrist was on the pillow near his face. The glow from the fire was gone. He pushed the stem of his watch to light the dial. It was 03:00.

Those shapely legs were still locked around his groin. The sheet covering their bodies was wet. Dick threw it aside and pulled the comforter over them.

He brushed the dark hair from her face and tenderly kissed her swollen lips. His fingertips again found the perfection of her bosom. She stirred and gripped him tightly with her legs. She drew back her head and whispered: "Captain, Maggie needs you again, . . . please."

After the registration process was completed, they stopped at Tulagi's for a beer. Sabena's program would achieve a Master's in Political Science in eighteen months. She had committed herself to continue for a Ph.D.

In the booth, Dick glanced at her tight sweater and teased: "What a shame to waste all that on a career in politics."

"Politics is what Sabena wants to do in a few years," she giggled, "but Maggie wants to continue her studies immediately." She glanced at her watch. "If we leave now, we'll be on time for her *rolling-in-the-grass* class."

Dick laughed. "Wow! Maybe you should consider getting me a graduate assistant."

She reached across the table for his hand and smiled. "Thanks to you, Maggie will have no trouble continuing her education."

"Don't you let Maggie rush into things," cautioned Dick. "Good teachers are easy to find." He thought about Mirhashem, then continued: "Whatever you do, stay in political science--or go into law. Don't let your uncle talk you into studying chemistry."

Her violet eyes looked into his soul. "Thank you for that, *Ed.* I'm aware of my uncle's program. I also thank you for last night. You showed me that I have a life of my own. I intend to live it for a long time."

She rose quickly from the booth. ". . . and I'm very eager to live the next couple hours. Let's go!"

They lay side-by-side, naked in the tall grass. She chewed playfully on a stem of grass, took a deep breath, and glanced at him. "Will it always be so great?"

Dick smiled into her shining eyes. "If you take good care of yourself, it will. Always protect yourself. Anti-baby pills aren't enough. Make your lover protect you too."

They lay quietly for a moment, then Dick asked: "I'm wondering if that bad experience is now behind you?"

"Completely!" She smiled. "Maggie pushed the delete button for me." She turned and slid a shapely leg over his thighs.

He thought for a moment. "I'll be in Vienna soon. I could take revenge on those boys for you."

For a moment, a serious look invaded her glowing face. "Thank you, but that's not necessary. Right after it happened, my uncle and his friends came to Vienna. Mirhashem cut off their heads and threw them in the Danube."

"Sorry I asked," apologized Dick. "I didn't want you to think about that again. Let's get back to Maggie."

She took his hand and held it to her. "Back to class, Professor. I want to take the final, while the answers are fresh in my mind."

Maria was very unhappy with him. They had an argument the day he returned to Vienna.

The day after he had left for the States, to *visit his mother*, her "Binki" auto refused to start. She had tried to call, but couldn't reach him at his mother's home. He reminded her that he'd stopped at the Pentagon enroute, and that he had called her when he finally arrived in Nebraska.

Dick had, in fact, visited his mother after he left Boulder. He felt his alibi was intact, but Maria was very insistent. To soften her aggression, he took her to Vienna's 8th Bezirk and bought her a new German-made Ford Sierra. She was pleased, and immediately named it the *Doodlesach*. He understood that meant bagpipe, but the connection escaped him.

The next day, they left for a week's holiday on the Adriatic. While basting in the sunshine on the beaches south of Venice, the realization of what he'd learned on the trip to Colorado sank into Dick. America's foundations were being invaded by the deadly bacteria of terrorist cells. The very nature of her open democracy was the catalyst by which the infection was spreading, slowly but surely. Would America awaken in time? Even if she did, could she eradicate the poisonous cells without destroying her democratic foundations in the process--or would the terror from within finally end her 209-year experiment in "life, liberty, and the pursuit of happiness?"

9

FRÖHLICHE WEIHNACHTEN

Dick stepped carefully from the streetcar. The wet snow was accumulating and the Ringstrasse sidewalks were slippery. He walked to the pedestrian crossing and waited for the light.

It was one of those magical mid-December evenings in Vienna. Snowflakes the size of quarters drifted silently downward. They would swirl in gentle protest, if a slow-moving auto or Strassen-bahn disturbed their peaceful flight.

The light changed, he crossed the Ringstrasse to the entrance of the Christkindlmarkt. It was an annual affair during the weeks preceding Christmas. Gaily lighted booths were crowded together in the courtyard of the Rathaus. It was a shopping delight for adults and children alike. Even the wet snowfall could not discourage the holiday crowd.

Dick's quick eyes surveyed the benches bordering the northern edge of the courtyard. It was a game he and Jim Conrad often played: who would be the first to recognize the other's disguise? There were several possibilities--men seating by themselves, enjoying the silent maneuvering of the descending snowflakes. He walked along the sidewalk near the benches. Since the outcome of the game could not be left to chance, the rules required that they wear small Maltese crosses somewhere near their collars.

He scrutinized several candidates, finally choosing one in a black overcoat with a gray hat pulled low over his face. He seated himself at the other end of the bench and began to study the figure. Then he noticed the slim man in a brown overcoat, standing near a booth, examining the colorful nutcrackers. Gray hair protruded under his short-brimmed dark-brown hat. It was similar to the dis-guise the *Purple* operative had worn last month, when they met in cold and wintry Hamburg.

Dick approached the booth. He saw the Maltese Cross on the brown tie and said quietly: "Only the Royal Canadian Mounted would be out on a night like this."

"Yeah," came the muffled reply. "Who else would go looking

for a Nebraska farm boy in a blizzard."

Brown eyes smiled from under the hat's brim. "Let's try the *Zwölf Apostel Keller.* Better to have a hangover than pneumonia."

They crossed the Ringstrasse and walked slowly into the city's center.

"Are they in town yet?" asked Dick.

"No, but they have flight reservations for tomorrow that match reservations at the Marriott."

"That's kind of brazen, isn't it--or maybe they want to be in the same building as the U.S. Consulate?"

Jim chuckled. "Well, it probably removes your Consulate from their hit list."

"How many are coming?"

"We're sure of Mirhashem, Shreeba, Ali, and Abrahim. They've reserved two rooms and a suite at the Marriott, but that would only be for the higher echelon. It's Mirhashem's practice to place his *soldiers* around town in low-rent districts, where Arabs are not so noticeable."

"How are you able to keep such close track of Mirhashem?"

Jim explained through his bearded disguise: "It started in June, after you had lunch with his *Three Musketeers* at the Sacher Hotel. Since that meeting, *Purple's* been sticking with them like glue."

"Do we have enough people in Vienna? Is there a chance we can identify Mirhashem's soldiers?"

"Mackenzie and Maximilian will be at Schwechat Airport when those I've named arrive. If someone makes contact, they'll follow them. If we can tail just one soldier, we'll be okay. They usually stay together until the hit takes place. They might already be in town. After the last of Mirhashem's higher echelon arrives, we'll shift our watch to the Marriott. They have to meet the soldiers sometime, and we'll be waiting."

They strolled down the quiet street to the entrance of the Cellar of the Twelve Apostles, then descended the winding stairway. It was a long way down to the rooms that had provided shelter from Allied bombers in World War II, there were no elevators.

Dick grunted, "Always easier going down these steps."

"Yeah," agreed Conrad, "we usually weigh a liter of wine more when we climb them."

There was an open room at each level. The first was a small bar decorated in the holiday spirit. The second was a dance floor packed with holiday revelers. Continuing down to the fourth level, they hung their garments on the coat rack and found a corner table.

Dick leaned across the table and asked quietly: "The Marriott's my ball game?"

"Yes, but be careful with your disguise." The *Purple* operative scrutinized Dick and continued: "You did a good job tonight. That should do the trick, but stay as far away as you can. We think we know who's showing up, but we need positive ID's as soon as possible. Still got the mini-camera?"

"Yeah."

"We need a picture of Mirhashem without a disguise. Our last photos were taken nine years ago, when he was thirty-nine."

"There are bright lights over recessed phone cells in the lobby, near the elevators. Should make a perfect studio." Dick paused as the Kellnerin set the ceramic goblets and a pitcher of Rotwein on their table. She smiled politely and returned to the bar. He asked: "If they have rooms reserved, why don't we install video cameras?"

"Too risky. Mirhashem is probably staying at the Marriott because he has people working there. We do have one thing in our favor: the U.S. Consulate security team has video surveillance of the hotel's hallways. Abood will be monitoring and taping--from their moment of arrival until they check out."

"Any info on their intended target?"

"Nothing yet, but it's something big. Mirhashem's coming from Tehran with Shreeba. Ali's on a direct flight from Madrid."

"Understand he's now Mirhashem's number one *Toreador* in Spain."

"Yeah, but it was not an easy transition. Three of Mirhashem's cells had been there since '74. They called themselves *El Queda*. The leaders embezzled most of the five million Mirhashem got from Qadhafi last year. Ali was sent to straighten it out. He played it cool, dragged them into attacks on the Jordanian and British Airways offices in Madrid, then notified the authorities that it was going down. End result: two dead *El Queda* leaders. The third got the message and split with his entire cell. Ali caught up with them in Basque country, teamed with a couple of Mirhashem's old ETA buddies, and massacred them with knives. From Mackenzie's report, it wasn't pretty."

Dick took a long drink of the tasty wine, set the goblet carefully on the table, and shook his head sadly. "Ali seems to be such an intelligent, personable, young man."

"He's deadlier than a Nebraska rattlesnake, Brown Bear. Stay alert, or he'll be adding your name to his log book."

"May be," sighed Dick. "Is Abrahim coming from Kuwait?"

"No, from Geneva. He flew there yesterday, to make deposits in Mirhashem's Swiss bank accounts."

Dick chuckled. "Guess the Kuwaiti Royal Family finally got the message."

"Yes, but they're slow learners. Took fifteen dead and ninety wounded in Kuwaiti City restaurants before they paid Mirhashem's *protection* bill."

"Is Musavi still in Rome?"

"Yes. He's been a busy boy, working with one of Mirhashem's permanent cells. In September, they hit the *Cafe de Paris* with grenades and two weeks later the British Airways office with C-4."

"Are they concentrating on airlines?" asked Dick.

"Yes! If we consider Ali's work in Madrid and Abrahim's bomb in the Kuwaiti Airlines office in Beirut, I believe we can forecast what's going down. Musavi's still in Rome, and I have the feeling we're about to see one of Mirhashem's famous double-headers."

"Do you have a lottery ticket on the British Airways office on the Ringstrasse?" joked Dick.

"Would be a good place to keep your friends away from, but I'm betting on a hit against Jewish interests."

"Why's that?"

"One plus one always makes two," continued Jim. "Mirhashem went out of his way to let everyone know he was in Libya. Do you remember his September interview in *Der Spiegel?*"

"Sounded like he was happy as a pig in a poke."

"Yes, but he left Tripoli for Tehran the next day. Word is he's been smoking the peace pipe with the Ayatollah. However, the Ayatollah's demanding proof that he's ready to stop working his protection racket around the Middle East, and concentrate on what Khomeini sees as the overwhelming problem--Israel."

Dick interrupted, ". . . and warm-ups against airlines, plus Israeli interests, equals El Al."

"Here--and in Rome," confirmed Conrad solemnly.

"Then our job becomes easier; but why would Mirhashem set up those expensive offices in Tripoli if he was moving to Tehran?"

"Didn't Fahed tell you that Mirhashem preferred Tehran?"

"Yes, I remember him saying that."

"We've also heard Mirhashem has criticized Qadhafi as a *loose cannon,* who's daring the old American cowboy President to go for his gun. Nelson believes Mirhashem's too smart to stay in a place that the White House will bomb, sooner or later."

Jim filled their goblets with the last of the wine, set the pitcher on the table, and took a small package from his pocket. "You won't need a mike for this operation. We have a satellite overhead. Nelson will be monitoring the chip in your shoulder. I wired one of your monitors into the earphone system the rest of us will be using, so we'll all be able to hear you." He handed Dick the package. "Here's an earphone for you. The range covers Vienna. Each one lasts about three days. I'll give you more later."

Jim handed Dick a car key and a plastic card. "Courtesy of the U.S. Consulate. It's a brown BMW, parked in their garage, spot five, in case you have to tail someone. The card's for the gate."

The wet snow had continued sporadically throughout the night. Dick wrapped his scarf around his ears, pulled down the brim of his hat, and waited to cross the street from the park to the Marriott.

With the miniature apparatus in his right ear, he heard Max report Ali's arrival at Schwechat. Mirhashem and Shreeba were already enroute from the airport. Abrahim's flight from Geneva was due in another hour.

He crossed the Ringstrasse and walked along the south side of the Marriott. Across the street was the SAS Hotel, where Carlos had taken the OPEC Ministers hostage ten years earlier. "What secrets this old city could tell," he muttered to himself.

He paused in the Marriott's side entrance to brush the snow from his brown overcoat; then entered the lobby through the exquisite shopping area. He glanced at his watch, Mirhashem and Ali's sister would arrive in about fifteen minutes. Not enough time for coffee. He walked past the lobby café to find a seat in the lounge area. A smiling attendant took his hat and coat and hung them in the cloakroom. He kept his scarf draped loosely around his neck.

Dick sat for a few minutes in a comfortable chair before he

heard Jim's voice in the miniature earphone: "Limousine turning into the entrance, Brown Bear. Could be them."

He rose from the chair, crossed the lobby to the telephone area, and found an empty phone cell near the elevator door. He could see the reflection of the reception desk in a large mirror.

He dialed the number for Vienna's recorded weather report and leaned into the phone cell. "Can you hear me, Mountie?" he asked.

"Yes," came the immediate reply in his earphone. "Your chip's broadcasting loud and clear. They're getting out of the limousine. Looks like Mirhashem, . . . that dish with him has to be Shreeba."

"Does she look like Audrey Hepburn?"

"Yeah, but only the face. The rest of her is more like Marilyn Monroe."

"Must have put on some weight," replied Dick.

In a few moments, he saw them in the mirror. The smiling attendant was helping the woman with her coat.

Dick whistled softly. "Whew, did she put on some weight--in all the right places."

"You sure that's Shreeba?" asked Jim.

The short stocky man in the black silk Italian suit handed his coat to the attendant.

"Yeah, and that's Mirhashem," confirmed Dick. "Judging from the color of the passports he's giving the clerk, I'd say they're traveling as Tunisians."

The couple followed the bellboy to the elevators. Dick hung up the phone and moved farther into the telephone area, where he could still see their reflections in the mirror.

He spoke into his white scarf: "Abood, they're entering the lift. Standby to begin taping."

"Roger that," came the Egyptian's soft reply.

Within two hours, Ali and Abrahim had also checked into the Marriott. They were traveling alone. Neither Mackenzie nor Max had seen anyone make contact with them at the airport.

Dick maintained his vigil in the lobby. Abood's eyes were glued to the security cameras surveying the hallways of the Marriott's fifth floor. Jim Conrad remained in his parked Mercedes on the hotel's entrance street. Mackenzie waited at the Strassenbahn stop on the north-bound side of the Ringstrasse, while Maximilian covered the south-bound.

At three o'clock, Abood reported Ali and Abrahim had left their rooms and entered Mirhashem's suite.

A few minutes later, Jim was speaking: "Okay, . . . heads up, guys. We have a black Mercedes pulling into the Marriott with two men in the front seat. They've stopped in the no-parking zone. . . . One of them is getting out."

"Roger, Mountie," said Mackenzie. "I have him. He is heading for the north entrance."

"Brown Bear," said Jim, "get over there with your camera and watch where he goes. Mac, walk by that Mercedes. See if you can get a make on the driver."

Dick crossed the lobby and walked through the shopping area to the north foyer. A young man in a brown woolen sweater opened the glass entrance door. Dick was taking pictures with his mini-cam as the youth paused to check the elevator doors. One was a direct lift to the U.S. Consulate. He pressed the other button. Dick moved back. Several people entered the lift with the young man in the brown sweater.

Stepping quickly outside the hotel, Dick spoke sharply into his scarf. "Abood, he's on the way up. Don't know what floor. About twenty-five, Arab-descent, brown sweater."

"Okay, Bear, I'm ready."

A moment later, Abood reported the man in the fifth-floor hall-way. Seconds later, he entered Mirhashem's suite.

After Abood's report, Jim said: "Here's our chance to locate the soldiers. I'm parked two spaces behind their Mercedes. Mac, run for your car and get on the Ringstrasse in front of them. Max, get Dick's car and follow me. Abood and Brown Bear, stay put."

Dick met Max at the hotel's south entrance with the Consulate's car key and garage door opener.

When Abood reported the young man leaving Mirhashem's suite, Maximilian was parked on the street south of the hotel. Mac was waiting on a side street two blocks ahead, ready to pull into the Ringstrasse.

Dick watched the young Arab in the brown sweater step out of the elevator and leave the hotel, then he strolled casually to the lobby café. He ate a delicious Strudel, sipped a Melange, and listened to some of the world's greatest "tailing" experts at work.

When Mirhashem's soldiers drove away from the Marriott, Jim followed. As they passed Mac's position, he pulled out between the soldiers and Jim. Max fell in behind. A few blocks later, Max passed Jim and Mac. The game continued as the soldier's proceeded around the crowded Ringstrasse and turned southwest on Wiednerhauptstrasse.

Max turned off to parallel the route on a side street. Mac picked up the close tail position. Jim guessed they were heading for the tenth district where most of Vienna's Middle East population lived. He passed the convoy and turned up Favoritenstrasse. The soldiers followed him. A few minutes later, Jim pulled away. The soldiers turned right, drove two blocks, and parked in front of an apartment house. Mackenzie continued down the street and broadcast the address to Maximilian. They began a stake-out on the apartment.

Dick smiled and ordered another Melange. The problem of locating Mirhashem's soldiers had been solved.

For the next four nights and three days, the *Purple* team monitored Mirhashem's group closely. Apparently, only two soldiers were involved in the operation. They remained close to their apartment off Favoritenstrasse. Ali and Abrahim demonstrated the taste and assets of wealthy playboys. They plunged exuberantly into the seamier side of Vienna night-life. After the third night of debauchery, the older Mackenzie turned their surveillance over to the younger Maximilian. Dick and Jim alternated on Mirhashem and Shreeba. They spent their days shopping on Mariahilferstrasse and their nights in various theaters.

Nelson alerted law enforcement authorities and Jewish interests in Vienna. Security was increased at various restaurants and synagogues. The already intense security at the airport was tightened.

Mirhashem's rooms had been reserved for 19-26 December. On the morning of the twenty-third, Dick was on watch in the lobby café. He was startled by Abood's warning--bellboys were on the fifth floor, picking up Mirhashem's luggage! He went quickly to the restroom and called Jim Conrad on his Skyfone. He was in bed at the Kohlbeck Hotel, about fifteen minutes away by car. Abood contacted Mackenzie and Max, they were near the Favoriten apartment. It would take them at least twenty minutes in the rush hour traffic to get to the Marriott.

Dick strolled casually out the hotel's main entrance. Early morning sunshine was glistening from icy tree branches in the park. A hotel limousine was in the loading area, the driver was waiting by the open trunk. Dick asked him if transportation was available to the airport. The driver assured him it was, he was waiting for guests that had an 8 o'clock flight. Other limousines were available. Dick need only make arrangements with the concierge.

Returning to the lobby, Dick saw the bellboys with the luggage. Guessing Mirhashem would not be far behind, he retreated to the telephone area. The bellboys took the luggage directly to the waiting limousine. It was time to ask for some big-time help. He picked up a phone, dialed Vienna weather, and said: "Mr. Nelson, Brown Bear. Can you hear me on the monitor?"

The *Purple* supervisor responded quickly: "Yes, Dick, I've been picking up your conversation. What can I do for you?"

"Sir, we need to know what flights are leaving Schwechat at eight this morning."

"Okay, we're on it. Be right back."

Jim had been listening to the exchange and broke in: "Sir, if it's a flight to Rome, you'd better get seats for Abood and me."

At that moment, Mirhashem, Shreeba, and Abrahim stepped out of the elevator. Dick turned his back to them and said: "Mountie, they're in the lobby. You'd better head straight for the airport."

"Roger that! Abood, run for the nearest taxi and meet me in the departure area."

"Yes Sir," acknowledged Abood. "On my way."

"Nelson here. The 8 a.m. flight from Schwechat is Alitalia 75, a direct flight to Rome. Mountie, what identification do you have?"

"The Austrian passport, Sir."

"Are you carrying Egyptian, Abood?"

"Affirmative."

"Okay, we'll have your tickets waiting at Alitalia check-in."

"Thanks," said Jim. "Brown Bear, I'm turning off the *Gürtel* on the A-1 autobahn. Should be at the airport in twenty minutes. Give me a call when they leave the hotel."

"Okay, Jim. Mirhashem, Shreeba, and Abrahim are walking out the entrance now."

Dick hung up the phone and crossed the lobby to look out the large windows. He held his handkerchief to his mouth and spoke softly: "Wow! You're in for a treat this morning. Shreeba's wearing a tight knit dress. Abrahim's getting in the limo with them, . . . they're pulling away from the hotel. What can I do for you here?"

"Check me out of the Kohlbeck. Put my things in the suitcase and store it in a locker at the Westbahnhof. Keep an eye on Ali. He may be making a move this morning."

Dick turned to see the handsome young Palestinian at the front desk. A suitcase was at his feet. He was obviously checking out. Dick was in an open area. He could only turn his back and look out the window. It would be a real test of his disguise.

In a few minutes, the young man was outside. The doorman hailed a taxi for him. Dick brought his handkerchief to his mouth and called Mackenzie.

The Scotsman answered quickly: "I'm approaching Ringstrasse from the south, Dick, on Schwartzenberg."

"Great! Ali's getting in a green Mercedes taxi, . . . license number W-3779. They'll have to go south on Ringstrasse. Their first possible exit would be at the McDonalds, on Schwartzenberg."

"Okay, Bear, I'll wait at the intersection."

A few minutes later, Colonel Mackenzie was tailing the taxi. It proceeded directly to the apartment off Favoriten, and Ali moved in with Mirhashem's soldiers.

Later that night, Jim contacted Nelson and Dick on his Skyfone. The scene in Vienna was being repeated in Rome. Shortly after Mirhashem checked into the Grand Hotel Palatino with Shreeba and Abrahim, they were visited by Musavi. A *Purple* agent, who had followed Musavi to Rome five months earlier, was close on his heels. Musavi and his cell of three soldiers were holed up in an old villa near Leonardo da Vinci Airport.

After arriving in Rome, Abrahim ticketed Mirhashem, Shreeba, and himself on tomorrow's Iran Air flight to Tehran. Abood would also be on that flight, to monitor Mirhashem's movements in Iran. Jim would remain in Rome with the second *Purple* agent, to deal with Musavi and his cell. When Nelson asked if he needed more people, Jim said "no."

They discussed the most likely time for the action to begin. Tomorrow was Christmas Eve. Dick thought that was the logical time, but Nelson reminded him it was not a special day for Jews. It was also a time when people stayed home. Mirhashem would be looking for a big crowd. Nelson predicted the attack would come after Christmas, perhaps as late as New Year's Eve.

Jim reminded Dick of Operation *Mosquito* in Manila, and his suspicions about Maria's possible connection with the KGB. There was a direct line between Moscow and Mirhashem. Jim cautioned Dick not to give Maria a reason to think anything was happening. During the last few weeks, Dick had managed to confine his activities to the 12-hour shifts Maria worked at the Red Cross Hospital. He assured Jim everything was okay.

Dick thanked Nelson for setting up the *research* office for him in the UNO building. It was the perfect long-term alibi that he needed to pacify Maria. Actually, it wasn't far from the truth. During lulls in his *Purple* activities, Dick used UNO research facilities to write his Ph.D. dissertation on terrorism. Since his office was in the controlled area, Maria was not able to check on him.

With Mackenzie and Maximilian keeping tabs on Ali and his soldiers, Dick decided to fulfill an earlier promise to play St. Nikolaus for Maria's young niece and nephew. Her brother's family was in Grimmenstein, about 40 autobahn-minutes south of Vienna. Realizing he might have to change plans quickly, he encouraged Maria to leave early and spend the entire day with her mother and brother. He would drive down later.

About six, Dick made one more check with Mackenzie. Ali had picked up three Schlampies on the Gürtel, and a drunken party was underway in the Favoriten apartment. Obviously, the attack would not happen tonight, and probably not tomorrow. Wishing the Scotsman "Merry Christmas" and Max "*Fröhliche Weihnachten*," Dick donned the borrowed St. Nikolaus costume and drove to the small village of Grimmenstein.

It had been twenty years since he'd played Santa Claus for his own children in Jacksonville--this time he had to do it in German-- but with a car filled with gifts, how could he go wrong!

He arrived as the family was finishing the evening meal. Little Christina's brown eyes sparkled with happiness when St. Nicholas began to hand her presents. She immediately turned to give them to her little brother. Dick's heart almost broke when she suddenly fell to her knees before him, crying and praying. Maria came to the rescue. It was a very tender moment.

Driving back to Vienna, Dick reflected on Jim's continued concern about Maria. General Matos had identified as KGB the man she'd spoken with at the Baguio Hyatt Hotel in the Philippines, while Dick was airborne on a mission in Aura. Further, she had left Manila only a day before the KGB-designed bomb destroyed the room they'd shared in the Ramada Hotel. It was also possible that Maria had seen the letter Rita sent him at NATO, a few weeks before she was ambushed and killed in Manila. Those were the unanswered facts. However, that had all happened five years ago. When Dick considered Maria's dedicated work at Vienna's Red Cross Hospital, as a specialist in bone marrow transplants for children, and the tender love they shared in their small apartment in Vienna, it was impossible for him to equate her with the KGB.

It was 8:45 a.m., two days after Christmas. Dick was returning to the apartment after driving Maria to work. He noticed the Sky-fone's light blinking on the seat beside him. He answered quickly, "Brown Bear here."

Nelson came on the line from Frankfurt, then Jim Conrad was speaking from Rome: "Brown Bear, Mr. Nelson, this is Mountie. Listen close! Things are beginning to pop down here. Musavi and his cell are enroute to the airport. We are on their tail, estimate arrival at Leonardo da Vinci in about fifteen minutes. They don't have any luggage with them. This could be the hit."

"Roger," responded Nelson. "I'll alert the *Carabinieri*."

"Dick," said Jim, "have Mackenzie check on Ali and his team."

"Brown Bear, wilco."

They had been having trouble with the satellite monitor, which relayed Dick's voice through the chip in his shoulder to the earphone system *Purple* was using in Vienna. He laid the Skyfone on the seat, pulled to the side of the road, and spoke loudly: "Hello, Mac. Mountie says it's going down in Rome. He wants a check on Ali and his crowd."

Thankfully, the Scotsman heard him. "Roger that, Bear. They haven't left the apartment this morning."

"You been there all night?"

Max answered: "We've been here since they went in the door

about midnight, and there's only one way in or out of the building."

"We need to verify they're still there," said Dick. "Can you see anything through the windows?"

"Nothing showing this side," answered Mackenzie. "I'm on my way to check the back."

A minute later, Mac was on the air again: "Dammit, Dick, a fire-escape rope is hanging from their third-floor window."

Dick spun the Ford Sierra around and accelerated down the quiet residential street. "I'm enroute to the airport," he shouted.

Max responded, "Okay, Dick, I'm leaving for the airport. Mac, make sure the apartment's empty before you follow me."

"I'm halfway up the rope now," grunted the old Scotsman.

Dick entered the traffic circle at the south end of Favoriten and maneuvered quickly to the eastern exit. He again shouted: "Hope you guys are reading me. I'm taking a country road shortcut."

"Yeah," panted Mackenzie, "read you loud and clear. . . . I'm in the apartment. They're gone. I'll take a look around and follow you to Schwechat."

Dick was in the clear and accelerating. "Mr. Nelson, if you read me, you'd better alert the *Polizei*."

Nelson responded quickly: "I've already done that, Brown Bear. Be careful they don't mistake you for a terrorist."

Dick was out of the city. He turned into the gravel lane leading to the airport and gunned the Ford Sierra's powerful engine.

The Skyfone's red light was flashing again. Dick raised it to his lips. "Brown Bear here."

"Bear, this is it." Dick could hear the staccato of AK-47 fire over Jim's transmission. "They passed empty-handed through security at the main entrance, went to the luggage claim area, picked up three suitcases, took them into a restroom near the El Al counter, and came out shooting and throwing grenades. We have a hell of a fire-fight going right now. Dozens of people are down. Expect the same at Schwechat."

"Wilco, Mountie," replied Dick. "Keep your head down."

The connection was broken. Dick quickly notified Nelson, but he had also lost contact with the Canadian.

Dick saw a light plane lifting off the Schwechat runway. He relayed Jim's report to Mackenzie and Maximilian. Traffic was heavy in the city, they were both having trouble.

He turned north on the paved road that circled the airport. "Max, I'm one klick from the airport entrance. Not much traffic on the ramps. . . . Wait a minute, there's a black Mercedes on the entrance road. Could be our boys. Can't say for sure."

"Roger, Bear, I'm on the autobahn. Be there in ten minutes."

"Be careful!" cautioned Dick. "There's black ice out here."

Dick sped along the boundary fence. The sturdy Ford Sierra bounced over the potholes. Then he turned into the entrance road. The exit road ran parallel--a fifty-meter strip of grass separated the two. The blacktop was indeed icy. Dick fought to keep the light car under control.

"Watch the ice at the entrance, Max," he warned. "I'm going to check the arrival area first."

The departure and arrival ramps were on the same level. Dick surveyed the taxis and buses by the departure doors, where passengers were being screened by security. He continued to the arrival area. Taxis were waiting on a side street. Two buses were at the far end. Parked in front of the arrival entrance, with its doors ajar and engine running, was a black Mercedes. No police or security people were in sight. About a dozen people was gathered around the buses, loading their luggage.

As Dick stopped behind the Mercedes, he heard a series of loud explosions--like M-80 firecrackers. He jumped from his car and ran for the entrance. Suddenly, a flood of screaming people began streaming out the doors. There was another series of explosions, then another.

He entered the terminal through a side door. Another series of explosions added to the smoke billowing from the departure area. People were screaming, hiding behind shopping displays, or cringing on the floor. Above it all, Dick heard the angry buzz of Uzi's.

Twisting and turning like a Nebraska I-back, Dick plowed his way through the panicked crowd into the departure area. Rounding the corner of a display case, he came face-to-face with terror.

Ali's soldiers were on the balcony above the El Al check-in counter, tossing fragmentation grenades into the mass of bleeding humanity below. Ali was crouched at the bottom of the escalator, about twenty meters from Dick, his Uzi blazing at police and El Al security officials behind the adjacent TWA counter.

The soldiers abruptly ended their evil attack and started down the escalator. Unarmed, but without any other alternative, Dick shouted and charged Ali. The young Palestinian was shoving a new magazine into his Uzi. He sensed Dick coming and turned to meet him. At that moment, the first soldier arrived at the bottom of the escalator and swung a heavy briefcase at Dick. It hit him on the side of his head and knocked him down. He fell on his left side and slid on the blood-slickened tile.

The three terrorists ran for the arrival exit, with Ali's Uzi carving a path before them. Bouncing to his feet, Dick grabbed the briefcase from the floor and gave chase. Bullets from police and security guards whizzed around him, shattering the glass in display cases. He rounded the corner of the big display in time to see Ali's group going out the arrival doors.

The panicked crowd was clear of the area. Dick sprinted outside. The black Mercedes roared away from the entrance. He leapt into his car, throwing the briefcase into the backseat.

"What's happening, Dick?" asked Max. "I heard you scream."

Dick's tires were squealing as he hit the turn to the exit road. "Max, they're in a black Mercedes, leaving the terminal area. Block the exit drive."

"Wilco, Bear. I'm turning into the entrance now. Believe I can get across this grass medium. Where are they? I don't see 'em."

"They're clear of the terminal area and on the exit road. I'm a hundred meters back. This drive's about three klicks long. You'll see us when we round that small grove of trees."

"I see the trees."

"They're going like a bat out of hell, Max. I can't catch 'em."

"No sweat, Bear. I'm cutting across the grass now. I have an AK-47. When they clear the trees, I'll give 'em a surprise party."

The black Mercedes was approaching the grove. "Get ready, Max. They're almost to the trees."

"I'm blocking the drive, Bear, but I'd better take the driver out. Otherwise they might get around me."

As he rounded the grove of trees, Ali's handsome smiling face flew through Dick's memory. In the panorama before him, he saw Max's car blocking the two-lane exit drive. The German Commando was leaning across the hood with his AK-47. The black Mercedes was bearing down on him at a high rate of speed. Then flashes of flame were spouting from Max's weapon. The Mercedes weaved to one side, then the other. It flew through the air, turning end over end, finally landing on its crushed top in the middle of the grass medium.

Dick skidded to a stop and ran for the demolished car. He was on his knees, peering through the driver's side window, when Max joined him. Ali's body was hanging in the seat belt. His nose had been destroyed by the AK-47 round that blew off the back of his head. His blood was flowing on the Mercedes' roof lining. They heard groaning from the backseat. Then the eerie temporary silence was broken by the wailing of police sirens coming from the airport.

"We'd better clear out, Dick. Don't want to spend the rest of our lives explaining this to some Austrian police sergeant."

They were on the autobahn to Vienna when the police vehicles reached the crash site. With his window down, Dick heard the gunfire as they riddled the black Mercedes. "You have to be kidding," he growled to himself.

They had agreed to meet at the Rathaus Restaurant for lunch at two. Dick was late. He'd been trying to get the blood off the Ford Sierra's upholstery. When he was knocked to the floor near the escalator, the left side of his trousers and jacket had been smeared with the blood of the victims. Some of it had transferred to the door of Maria's new car.

"What the hell can I do, Mac? I have to pick her up at six."

The Scotsman thought for a moment. "You've tried cold water?"

"Yeah, lots of it, but the stain's still there."

"When you have so little time, maybe you should cover it with red wine," said Max. "I tried that once, and got away with it."

"What did you do with your clothes, Dick?" asked Mackenzie.

"In my trunk. I'll drop them at the cleaners before I pick her up."

"*Eine Minuten!*" cautioned Max. "If cleaners in this town get clothing with unexplained blood, they notify the *Polizei*. They might tie it with today's massacre. Give it to me, and I'll burn it."

"Thanks, Max," sighed Dick. "It's the first time I wore those trousers. Maria gave them to me for Christmas."

"Know where she bought them?" asked Mackenzie.

"Yes. She got them at *Fürnkranz,* on *Favoriten*."

"Then you'd better buy another pair, as soon as we finish these *schnitzels*." The Scotsman squeezed some lemon on his plate and asked: "Did you hear more from Nelson, about Jim Conrad?"

"Yes," answered Dick. "He's okay. His Skyfone was hit by a piece of shrapnel, Jim didn't get a scratch. Sounds like Musavi's cell handled their weapons the same way as Ali's. Conrad found a suitcase with a couple grenades inside. It had a luggage tag from the TWA flight that landed an hour earlier."

"Where did that flight originate?" asked Max.

"Madrid." Dick touched the bruise on the side of his head. "The briefcase that hit me was tagged for the early TWA flight from Athens."

Mackenzie shook his head. "Other terrorists were also involved today--the people who checked that luggage at Madrid and Athens, and later handed the claim checks to Ali and Musavi."

The U.K. Special Air Service representative to *Purple* continued: "Ali must have recognized you at the escalator, Dick, and he probably told the other two before Max killed him. It's a miracle they lived through that car crash, and the hail of gunfire from the police. If they made you, and if they get the word out, Mirhashem will make short work of you."

"You're right," agreed Dick. "Glad they're in Austrian custody! If this happened in America, they'd be back on the street already."

Max chuckled. "Too many lawyers! Don't worry, Bear, I have a friend at the jail where they're holding those guys. They won't be getting word to anyone."

"Any terrorists live through the Rome massacre?" asked Dick.

"Yes," replied Mackenzie. "Musavi and two others went down, but one of his soldiers was taken alive. Guess the crowd almost killed him before the *Carabinieri* got him out of there."

Max sipped his beer and said thoughtfully: "Wonder what's next for us. Abood's chasing Mirhashem around Iran. Hope we hear from that little guy soon. When's our meeting with Nelson?"

"He and Jim will arrive on the thirty-first," said Dick. "Hope we have an early meeting. I gave Maria tickets to the *Silversterabend* Ball at the *Staatsoper* for Christmas."

Max grinned. "You must be getting old, Bear. If I was living with that bundle of sex, she wouldn't be dancing! She would be in bed--barefoot and pregnant."

"Sounds like you guys have been watching more than terrorists in Vienna," said Dick.

"We do the best we can for you, Bear," said Mackenzie. "If Mirhashem's gang starts to put things together, your life won't be worth a bloody farthing."

They sat quietly at the small dining room table in their apartment, sharing a bottle of wine and listening to the late news. Coordinated terrorist attacks at El Al airport counters in Rome and Vienna had killed 18 and wounded 111.

"*Mein Gott,*" whispered Maria. "Why can't they keep their *verdammt* war in Palestine?"

"There are many strange agendas in this crazy world, Schatzie," answered Dick.

She leaned toward him, lips puckered. "When am I going to be on your agenda, *Bärlie?*"

He wet his lips and kissed her lightly. "You're always on mine."

Maria drew back. "It's so hard to believe--all that killing at our airport. I saw them bring in two of the children. They were soaked in blood, but they weren't hurt too bad. They should be okay in a few days. Were you at the office when it happened?"

"No. After I left you at the hospital, I drove to the *Naschmarkt* to order lobster for New Year's Day. Unfortunately, I also bought the Valpolicella that I dropped while opening the car door. I'm so sorry about your upholstery, Schatzie. Can you ever forgive me?"

She held up her wine glass and gazed at him over the rim with sparkling sky-blue eyes. "A mechanic told me a new car is like a young girl, they both have to be damaged a little to be enjoyed."

Dick grinned. "Shame on you. You've become a hussy since you've been living with me."

She rose from her chair and stood in front of him. "Let me show you how shameful I can really be."

She paused to run her fingers over the bruise on the side of his head. "Where did you get that?"

"From your car door, when I tried to catch that damned bottle."

She kissed the bruise gently, then her eager lips sought his. Her fingers began to unbuckle his belt. She hesitated. "Thought you were wearing your Christmas trousers when you took me to work."

"Yes, sexy girl, I was. Unfortunately, the red wine also splattered on them. I took 'em to the cleaners. They can get the stain out, but it will take a week." (That was how long the clerk at

Fürnkranz had said it would take to replace the trousers.)

"You don't take very good care of the things I give you," she teased. "Wait here a minute. I haven't thanked St. Nikolaus for the thrill he gave Christina."

She disappeared into the bedroom. Dick cleared the dishes from the table. He was waiting in his chair when she returned. He caught his breath.

Fine-spun golden hair framed her big blue eyes and tumbled to her shoulders. She wore a white teddy of thin lace that clearly revealed the roundness of her proud alabaster breasts, her slim waist, and the delightful curve of her hips. She pivoted slowly on high-heeled white shoes and smiled over her shoulder. "Like what you see, Santa Claus?"

Her slender back, curvaceous bottom, and perfectly formed slim legs were an exciting picture. Dick rose from his chair and held out his arms.

"What do you want, Santa?" she teased.

Dick grinned. "The next dance."

She crossed the room slowly. "Better take off those trousers. You can't afford to ruin two pairs in one day."

She folded herself in his arms. He crushed her petite demanding body against him. Their passion, born in the sweltering heat of a Philippines' summer, flared again in the mild caress of an Austrian winter.

They met in the classified section of the British Embassy. When Dick arrived, Mackenzie already had the coffee and semmels on the table.

"Swearing off tea, Mac?" asked Dick.

"Not at all," scoffed the Scotsman, "but when you're in paradise, you should taste the fruit. I may soon be addicted to the Austrian's breakfast."

"Yeah, know what you mean. No matter what you put on those crisp buns, they melt in your mouth; but they do need a cup of coffee to complete the experience."

They were joined by Max. The German Commando was nursing a cold. "When I need hot tea, you guys drink coffee!"

Mackenzie picked up the phone. "Won't be a minute. I'm not trying to spoil you, Colonel, I have to order some for Nelson."

The *Purple* Field Supervisor entered the room with Jim Conrad at his side. "Sorry to keep you waiting. Crappy weather around Frankfurt, we were an hour late getting into Schwechat."

Mackenzie gave the slender Canadian a bear hug. "Bloody glad you're still with us, Mountie. Close call at Leonardo da Vinci!"

Conrad grinned. "First time I carried the Skyfone in my shirt pocket, but it won't be the last."

Dick grasped his partner's hand firmly and looked hard into his brown eyes. "Thanks be to God, Jim."

"Amen!" added Max.

A British Sergeant entered with two pots of tea, another platter of semmels, and a jar of jam. He saluted Mackenzie smartly and quickly left the room.

They seated themselves at the table. Nelson began: "Gentlemen, our technicians spent two days studying the security videos from the Rome and Vienna airports. Let's review our tactics."

He paused to take a sip of tea. "Mountie, your disguise was perfect! When you knocked that fourth terrorist down and captured him, you became the star of the video; but it's impossible to form a valid description of you from the tape. You saved his life by staying on top of him. Those El Al guards were shooting at anyone darker than an albino."

"The media reported the crowd tried to lynch him before the police took him away," said Dick.

"That wasn't the crowd," replied Jim sarcastically. "It was those vicious El Al guards. They were trying to cut his throat, until the *Carabinieri* arrived to help me."

"Have they gotten any information from him?" asked Max.

"Had a paper in his pocket identifying him as Fatah." Nelson chuckled. "Mirhashem never misses a chance to pin something on his old enemy; but the Italians now say he belongs to Mirhashem."

"The two in Austrian custody claim they're Mirhashem's guys," said Max.

"Didn't take long," commented Dick. "Maybe the *Polizei* still have Hitler's experts on their interrogation teams."

"Not necessary," said Mackenzie. "Modern drugs make it quick and easy."

Nelson finished a semmel and leaned back in his chair. "Bear, we can not be sure what Ali told those two about you, while they were fleeing in the Mercedes. They may know who you are."

He regarded Dick carefully and continued: "Too bad you didn't have time for a disguise, but you did the right thing. The Austrians have decided the unidentified person, who charged the terrorist at the bottom of the escalator, probably saved the lives of the security guards trapped behind the TWA counter. They also believe his action saved the crowd from more grenades, because the two at the top ran down the escalator to help the shooter. Nicely done, Bear."

Jim chuckled. "Reminds me of an unarmed half-wit in Manila, who took on a sniper on a windy hotel balcony to save the Pope."

Mac smiled. "*Ja wohl!* Heard about that action. We Catholics will be forever grateful. Mr. Nelson, there's no need to worry about the two in Austrian custody. They're going to get a *cocktail* with dinner tonight that will push the delete buttons on their memory circuits for the next several years."

Nelson nodded. "Good work, Max. Because of camera location, and a few other lucky factors, the Vienna airport tapes don't have a clear shot of Dick's face--only his back. I don't believe Mirhashem could identify him from them."

"You think he'll get his hands on those tapes?" asked Dick.

"He probably got copies before we did," said Mackenzie. "Mr. Nelson, with all the advance warning you gave them, why didn't the Austrian and Italian police neutralize those chaps before they got into the airports?"

"Too much bureaucracy, Mac," replied the *Purple* supervisor. "*The inherent failure of all national security agencies is their inability to believe anyone but themselves.*" He paused for a moment and added: "May also be dirty politics involved. We'll talk about that later."

Dick swirled the tea leaves in the bottom of his cup and asked quietly: "Why didn't we take them out, when we saw what was going down?"

"Eighteen innocents would still be alive if we had," answered Nelson, "but we couldn't be certain what they were up to until they left for the airports--then it was too late. We did the best we could, Dick. Your and Jim's work inside the terminals saved many lives."

He cleared his throat and continued: "Let's not forget, we have to discredit Mirhashem before we kill him; otherwise he'll become the radical Islamists' *Joan of Arc*. When I first explained that to the GP-7, the White House was vehemently opposed. Now they're all for it."

"What changed their minds, Sir?" asked Dick.

"Your President's in political hot water, and it's getting hotter all the time. He failed to find an adequate response to the death of 244 Marines at the Beirut airport two years ago; and he failed to react effectively to the TWA hijacking last June. The hostages in Lebanon are a continuing embarrassment; and he hasn't been able to contain terrorist attacks on U.S. and NATO troops in Europe. Now the news Dick brought back from the Mountain of Truth last spring is proving correct. He's dealing with the Ayatollah--selling him spare parts and weapons--and using that money to fund his favorites, the old Somozan National Guard, which terrorizes Hondurans between attacks on Nicaragua and calls itself Contras."

Jim looked up sharply. "Didn't the U.S. Congress deny funding to the Contras?"

"Yes, Mountie," continued Nelson, "and they will soon find out they've been hoodwinked. In short, the President needs a big event to distract both the Congress and the media. He needs a hard target, and he needs it soon."

"Who's it going to be?" asked Mackenzie. "Qadhafi?"

"Exactly!" answered Nelson. "Since Mirhashem's September interview in Libya, the White House has been attributing every terrorist act to the Colonel. They're putting together a package to convince the media that the Vienna and Rome attacks trace back to Tripoli, via Mirhashem."

"So, . . . " ventured Dick. "Mirhashem gets a free pass, until the White House is ready to bomb Libya back to the stone age."

"That is correct. The U.S. airstrike will mark the end of the period of time GP-7 has given us to discredit Mirhashem."

Nelson rose from his chair. "That's all for today, Gentlemen. Understand most of you will be attending the ball at the *Staatsoper* this evening. I don't want to distract from a well-deserved rest, but be alert. That gathering is precisely the kind of target Mirhashem would love to deliver to the Ayatollah."

The young female aide-de-camp took a quick look at Dick's invitation and announced them to the Viennese Burgermeister: "Herr Professor Richard Williams of the United Nations and

Schwester Maria Tiala."

As Maria curtsied in front of him, the Mayor bent to kiss her hand--staring down his hawkish nose into the décolleté of her low-cut ball gown. She smiled up at him, but his eyes never left the alabaster bosom straining against the fitted black silk material.

Maria disengaged her hand and turned to the Mayor's wife, who was a singer at the Vienna Volksoper. She was more renown as a successful politician's wife than as a performer, but somehow she always had the lead in Volksoper productions. She hadn't missed the Mayor's interest and greeted Maria coldly. Maria returned her icy stare and waited for Dick.

The Mayor gripped his hand and whispered to him: "What was her name? Does she work in Vienna?"

Dick grinned confidently. "Maria Tiala, Mr. Mayor. She is on the staff of the *Rote Kreuz Krankenspital*."

Next in line were the West German Ambassador and his wife. The jovial diplomat was also smitten by Maria's porcelain-doll beauty and engaged her in conversation. "If you tire of working in *Wien,* I'm sure we could find an important position for you in one of our modern hospitals."

Maria rose from another revealing curtsey and regarded him with her amazingly blue eyes. "How nice of you, Mr. Ambassador. My uncle worked in your country during the war."

"Then you already appreciate the opportunities that exist in the Federal Republic."

"Not really, Sir. My uncle was a slave laborer in a munitions factory."

Oberst Maximilian Weber was a step behind the Ambassador. His cold Aryan face broke into a warm smile at the Ambassador's obvious discomfort.

The Ambassador's accomplished wife immediately intervened by complimenting Maria on her black silk ball gown. It was a beautiful creation. Dick and Maria had found it in Mons during his service at NATO.

As they were greeted by the U.K. Ambassador, Dick surmised the terrorist threat, which had concerned Nelson, was indeed imminent. Colonel Mackenzie was only one step from the Ambassador, looking resplendent in white tie and tails. Dick grinned at him. He was certain the Scotsman would have been more comfortable in his formal kilt.

Next in line was the U.S. Ambassador. Dick and Maria had wondered if she would attend the ball with her American husband, or her Austrian lover. Perhaps in an effort to throw the Viennese press off her trail, she appeared to be alone--although two gentlemen were standing close behind her.

The reception line ended at the edge of the dance floor. Dick whirled Maria away to the tunes of the *Wiener Waltz*.

She smiled up at him. "Why, *Herr* Professor, I do believe those dancing lessons did some good."

"Not really, but I did spend time watching the Lippanzaner horses. I may have picked up some of their moves."

She laughed. The radiance of her smile and the sparkle in her eyes seemed to light the huge ballroom. Dick had never seen her so absolutely beautiful.

"You may be getting a new job offer. The Mayor was enthralled by you, or at least your upper half."

Her eyes engaged his, like they always did before she tried to make him jealous. "He already made me an offer, last year, during a ski holiday in Badgastein."

"While I was in Nebraska?"

"Yes." Her smile was a promise of things to come.

"Well, what happened?"

"I turned him down, . . . but my friend accepted."

"Don't keep me guessing. Did she get a better job?"

"Oh, yes! Within a week, she was promoted to supervisor of a department she'd worked in for ten years." That sexy smile again flickered crossed Maria's face. "But it took two weeks for the rug burns on her back and knees to heal."

The waltz came to an end. They proceeded through the crowd to the table they shared with low-level UNO administrators. Dick knew none of them personally, but he'd seen them in the hallways.

It was after nine, the food service was light--caviar and other hors d'oeuvres. The white wine was exceptionally good. In the old Austrian custom, bottles of Sekt (champagne) cooled in silver ice buckets on the tables. There was one bottle for each couple, to be opened in unison at the stroke of midnight.

At ten, the dance floor cleared and the world famous Staatsoper Ballet appeared. Their half-hour performance was superb. As they closed with the incredibly beautiful *Blue Danube Waltz*, they invited the audience to join them. The entire ballroom was soon filled with couples whirling around the floor in a large circle. Dick maneuvered Maria toward the inside of the circle, where one was not required to move so quickly. He was surprised to see Jim Conrad following closely, with one of the ballerinas in his arms.

Dick whispered to Maria, "Check the couple behind us. That's a really beautiful girl."

Maria sighed, ". . . and that's a really handsome man. See how graceful he makes the turns."

"Yes Dear," said Dick. He caught Jim's eye and smiled.

Suddenly, Jim's eyes darted to the balcony over the entrance to the ballroom. His face froze. Dick's eyes followed.

A man was standing in the front row of seats, swinging a tablecloth like a slingshot. He was holding the cloth by its four corners. It was clear that a heavy object was inside.

Security guards were pushing their way down the long row of seats, but they would never get to him in time. Others on the ballroom floor had noticed the commotion and stopped dancing. Women began to scream.

Dick reached for the Beretta hidden in the rear waistband of his trousers. Jim's pistol was already in his hand. With the ballerina under his arm, he was maneuvering for a clear shot at the threat.

Dick instinctively gritted his teeth, expecting the muzzle blast of Jim's Walther in his ear. He focused his eyes on the forehead of the man swinging the tablecloth. Before he could bring his Beretta to bear, the man released two corners of the cloth.

A package sailed away from the balcony, high over their heads. Dick pulled Maria to the floor and covered her with his body.

The ballroom floor was total chaos. Women were screaming, men were shoving. The package burst open--hundreds of sheets of paper fluttered downward in a white cloud.

Before the papers touched the floor, Dick and Jim had concealed their weapons. The petite ballerina was wrapped tightly in Jim's arms, but he reached up to catch a couple of the sheets. He smiled grimly and handed one to Dick.

At the top of the notebook-sized page was the all-too-familiar swastika. The message was printed in four languages--German, Arabic, French, and English: "DEATH TO ALL FOREIGNERS!"

The screaming was fading--the *Wiener Philharmonic* hadn't missed a beat of the *Blue Danube*--Dick was lifting Maria to her feet--the petite ballerina's arms were wrapped tightly around Jim's neck--he was kissing her eager lips. The ball continued.

10

A SUN TO BURN THE SOUL

The British Ambassador's orderly had delivered the second round of semmels and tea before Nelson finally arrived. The tall man handed his gray hat and overcoat to the orderly, directed him to lock the door of the secure briefing tank on his way out, and tossed a copy of *Die Welt* on the table where the team was already seated.

"Get caught in traffic again, Sir?" asked Dick.

"No, I'm taking your advice and traveling around Vienna on the U-Bahn. I was waiting at *Karlsplatz* for the West German newspapers. Abood told me to get a copy of the 12 February *Die Welt*. Seems Mirhashem rose from the grave after the London *Sunday Times* declared him dead last month. Now the West German press reports he's in an East Berlin hospital with liver cancer."

"He may set a record for hypochondriacs," said Max. "Isn't this the third time he's contacted a fatal illness?"

"Don't forget the second open-heart surgery he had two years ago in East Germany," added Jim, "and remember the French media report that he died of heart failure in Baghdad."

Dick laughed. "Bet he has a hard time getting health insurance."

"Obviously his survival rate is much higher than his body-doubles," said Nelson. "A pattern has emerged from all this. The announcements of his incapacitation or death are always associated with a big event. Wonder what we have to look forward to now?"

"What's the latest from Abood?" asked Dick.

Nelson smiled. "Our Egyptian wonder-boy is still on his tail. Mirhashem's spending most of his time in Tehran at the feet of Ayatollah Khomeini, with an occasional side-trip to Damascus."

"What's he been doing in Syria?" asked Max.

"He's meeting with Muhammad Amri, one of his disciples and a specialist in miniaturizing plastic explosives. After every meeting, we pick up communications between Mirhashem and one of his cells in Athens and another in London. I'd bet on more attacks against airliners in the near future."

Nelson continued: "Let's move on to other business. Abood's Tehran informant reports Khomeini has asked Mirhashem to create a cache of terrorist weapons. Having expended the Shah's weapons stockpile on Iraq, the Ayatollah needs to re-supply his military; but his long-term program of implanting armed cells in the countries of his infidel enemies has top priority."

"Who better than Mirhashem to know what--and where--to buy," mused Jim. "How much is the Ayatollah willing to invest?"

"Not sure about the total program, but Mirhashem is authorized to obligate thirty million dollars in the next few months."

"Where's he going to spend it?" asked Max.

"Abood says the Ayatollah already tried to deal with the White House--attempted blackmail perhaps. With the extravagant prices he's paying for F-14 replacement parts, and other high-tech items, Khomeini felt he should also be allowed to buy some cheaper, less-sophisticated weaponry. When the White House objected, he hinted how disastrous it would be; if the American public found out where their President's getting the cash to fund his Contras."

"Filthy business," said Jim.

"Only in America," grunted Dick. "That will all come to a head soon. The Libyan Colonel better get the roof on his bomb shelter."

"Yes," agreed Nelson. "His is the only face your President can put on terrorism right now. He's certain to attack him. You already know about the ideology conflict between the Ayatollah and the Colonel. Abood says Khomeini has directed Mirhashem to launch a series of attacks against American targets, which the President will undoubtedly blame on Qadhafi. Those will start soon."

"Hence his preparations for bombs on airliners?" asked Jim.

"Correct," acknowledged Nelson. "The bottom line is that we have only a few weeks left to discredit Mirhashem." He looked around the table. "Who has a plan?"

After a brief pause, Dick took two envelopes from his coat pocket and tossed them on the table. "This may be out of line, Mr. Nelson, but hear me out. I told you last spring about establishing a post office box where the *Three Musketeers* could contact me. Our class at the university was ending, and they wanted a way to stay in touch. I rented a box at the Westbanhof."

"Yes, I remember."

Dick picked up one of the opened envelopes. "After the airport massacres, I checked the box and found this letter from Ali. It was postmarked in Vienna, the day before the attack."

He opened the envelope to remove a smaller one. "Inside was this sealed letter for his sister Shreeba, and a short note asking me to give it to her in the event of his death."

Dick folded a tissue around it and handed it to Nelson. "Would be better not to put your fingerprints on it, Sir."

The *Purple* supervisor cradled the envelope in the tissue and asked: "What does it say, Dick?"

"You think I opened it?"

"Of course! I assume it's very personal."

"Yes Sir. It's written in English, they were both very proud they had mastered the language." Dick paused to clear his throat, sadness clouded his eyes. "Ali explains that Mirhashem's sending him on a suicide mission. He objects to being assigned to that particular mission--feels it's not worthy of his life. He tells Shreeba to re-examine her relationship with Mirhashem, and not to trust him. He advises her to escape to America at the first opportunity."

"Hot damn!" exclaimed Mackenzie. "We've found our link."

Nelson fixed his steel-gray eyes on Mackenzie. "Does the SAS contribution to *Purple* have a solution to our problem?"

"It's all right there, waiting for us to mix it together." A smile creased Mackenzie's ruddy Scottish face. "An angry Shreeba could be the perfect catalyst."

"How does it work, Mac?" asked Dick.

"It's like a maze, so follow me through this carefully. When Mirhashem bought weapons on the open market in the past, he usually dealt with the North Koreans--and paid their extravagant prices. Maybe he can be convinced to save the Ayatollah some big money, by using Homboldt Trading in Macáu."

A smile crossed Dick's faced, as he recalled his last meeting with the fascinating Consuela in Hong Kong.

Mackenzie continued: "Dick has an extremely reliable contact inside Homboldt--who's been looking for a way out. Maybe he could convince her to set up a thirty million dollar package for Mirhashem. However, instead of Homboldt delivering the weapons to the Ayatollah in Tehran, we somehow re-direct them to Admiral Toufani's guerrillas in the Iranian mountains."

Dick's immediate concern reflected in his hard blue eyes. "How does Consuela get out alive?"

"Homboldt deals through Swiss bank accounts," answered Mackenzie. "She collects the thirty million from Mirhashem, takes it to Zurich, and disappears."

". . . and *Purple* guarantees her safety?" asked Dick cautiously. "Can we really do that?"

"Yes, Brown Bear, we can," assured Nelson. "We're probably the only agency in the world with enough special trust and confidence to keep people safe."

"Mac, how do we get control of the arms shipment, and redirect it to Toufani?" asked Jim.

"That's the whole ball game, isn't it," reflected Mackenzie. "We must have control before it enters Iran. Unfortunately, Homboldt's main supplier is North Korea, and you guys know how difficult it is to operate inside that country."

"Then we have to find a supplier in Europe," said Dick. "A Soviet satellite state with a stockpile of weapons, where Moscow's losing control and the locals are eager to make a profit."

A smile lit Maximilian's broad Aryan features. His ice-blue eyes twinkled. "You've described a situation in Czechoslovakia, Bear. A hundred kilometers north of here, outside Brno, is an arms depot the Soviets established after the '68 uprising. When they pulled their troops back, Moscow left a lot of stuff. Then they shipped in more sophisticated items--with the idea of arming terrorist groups in West Germany. Know what I'm talking about Mountie?"

"Yeah," nodded Jim. "The RAF's been able to pick up everything a modern terrorist needs from that depot. I've been inside. There are a few Russians around, but it's operated by the Czechs."

Nelson asked: "Could you somehow use your RAF connections to encourage the depot to communicate an offer to Homboldt?"

Dick chuckled. "Actually, Sir, a line of communication may already exist. Four years ago, I initiated a deal through Homboldt for a friend of mine--the Sematex came from Czechoslovakia."

Mackenzie's eyes narrowed. He glanced sharply at Dick, but a grin returned to his face as Dick continued: "That friend shall remain nameless. What's important is that my Homboldt contact, Consuela, was able to arrange a buy of Czech Sematex. I bet it came from the Brno depot."

"*Mein Gott!*" exclaimed Max. "We can do this! Dick persuades

Consuela to handle the order at Homboldt--RAF terrorist Jim Conrad gets next to the Czechs and accompanies the delivery--the weapons go to the guerrillas attacking the Ayatollah from the Talish Mountains--and Mirhashem loses thirty million of the Ayatollah's dollars."

Nelson interrupted, "But how do we encourage Mirhashem to deal through Homboldt?"

Dick grinned, tossed him the other envelope, and reached for another semmel. "This letter came today from Shreeba. Abrahim must have given her the box number. She'll be in Vienna next week. Mirhashem's dumping her for a few days while he does business in Paris. She's angry about not going with him, and has asked me to spend some time with her."

Jim Conrad chuckled and invoked an old saying from Air Marshal Frazier: "Sounds like fighter pilot time, Brown Bear."

They paused in the Marriott Hotel corridor, outside suite 505. Dick inserted the key in the lock and turned to Shreeba.

Her arms encircled him. She pressed her pixie face firmly against his chest. He held her gently, his hands buried in the luxurious full-length sable coat.

He bent his head and kissed the waves of dark hair piled high on her head. "It's almost midnight, Cinderella. Aren't you tired?"

She raised her head and stood on her tiptoes to reach his lips. Her tender kiss was soft and warm. She purred softly: "This night should never end. That wonderful dinner at the *Feuervogel*, dancing at the *Volksgarten*, . . . compared to Tehran, Vienna's a paradise."

His blue eyes smiled into her wide, warm, brown ones. "Then why don't you invite me in and tell me a story? All I really know about Middle Eastern girls is what I read in *Scheherazade*."

She laughed and lowered her arms. "Somehow, I don't believe you, Captain Orden; but maybe I could tell you a story you've never seen before."

He opened the door. "Don't you mean a story I've never *heard* before?"

She brushed her bosom firmly against him and entered the room. "No, I meant to say *seen*. Stay awhile, and I'll show you."

He locked the door and followed her into the spacious suite.

She shrugged the sable from her shoulders, it fell to the floor. The golden lamé gown sheathed her elegant figure. She turned to face him. It was difficult to move his eyes from her adorable *Audrey Hepburn* face, but her bare creamy-brown shoulders were too inviting. His gaze fixed on the curvaceous bosom straining against the tight confines of golden lamé.

Her eyes glistened. "Captain, do you really have shoes older than I?"

He laughed as he recalled the remark he'd made in the bath at Mirhashem's villa. "Shreeba, please forgive me for that night."

"Yes, certainly. I forgive you for what you said--you had just killed two horrible men on that mountain--but I'll never forgive you for not taking what I offered you." Her lips were pouting, but a smile tugged at the corners of her warm brown eyes. "Our son could have been born next month."

He drew her slowly into his arms. She melted against him. He whispered, "I must have been out of my mind."

She closed her eyes as their lips met. Her hands went inside his open tuxedo jacket. She pressed her body firmly against him. Her wet lips parted to receive his gentle kiss.

Dick's fingers slowly explored her smooth shoulders, enveloped her slim waist, discovered the sophistication of her hips, and came to rest where the golden lamé clung to her shapely bottom.

She thrust her warm bosom against his thin shirt and interrupted the kiss for a moment: "*No* is not an option for you this evening, Captain." She moved her hips against him.

Her eager mouth passionately sought his, then she drew back to whisper: "Take me to bed, . . . please."

With their lips locked tightly together, Dick lifted her into his arms, carried her across the room, and sat on the edge of the bed.

Seated in his lap, she leaned forward and put an arm behind her to point at the zipper of the lamé gown.

"Damn, it's hard to keep my mind on my work," he thought to himself.

He grasped her fingers gently. "Dear Shreeba," he began, "you do me great honor. You are a girl beyond my wildest dreams, but I have a sad duty to perform. It's a promise I made to a very brave young man."

She turned to him with a look of wonderment. A dark shadow

crossed her face and tears appeared in the corners of her warm eyes. "It's about Ali," she breathed. Then she could speak no more.

He nodded and took the small envelope from his jacket pocket. "This was in a letter Ali mailed to me the day before he was killed. I found it in the post box when I got your letter that you were coming to Vienna. There was a goodbye note for me, and he asked me to give you this."

Shreeba took the letter from his hand. Dick expected the tears to flow, but she remained calm. It was not possible for her girlish face to look stern; but her brows were knitted, her lips compressed.

She clasped the letter to her bosom. "How did you find out he was dead, Captain?"

"His passport picture was in the *Wiener Zeitung*."

"Do you know what's become of his body?"

"Yes, dear one. He's buried in the city cemetery on the east side of Vienna. I viewed the internment. An official from a Mosque was present." Dick sighed, "I said a prayer for him. I'm sure Allah could translate from my Christianity."

She looked at him with mournful eyes. "Could you take me to the grave?"

"Yes, I believe it's safe now. The police watched the cemetery for a few weeks, to see if anyone visited the grave, but I believe they've gone away. If you want, I'll take you there tomorrow."

"You think I could move his body to Palestine? We promised each other we'd be buried in the grave of our mother."

Dick took a sharp, painful breath. His thoughts returned to the gravesite he'd prepared for Rita, on that wintry hillside in western Canada. He looked into the teary eyes of the fair young Palestinian seated on his lap: "I'll do everything in my power to make sure that happens--one day--but it might be far in the future."

"Thank you, *Ed*." She rose and crossed the room to the dresser.

It was the first time she had called Dick by the name he'd been using in his contacts with Mirhashem's group. It was, perhaps, an indication that a higher level of familiarity and trust was being established between them.

She found a nail file and opened the letter. Seated on the vanity stool, with her face hidden from Dick, she focused on Ali's final words to her.

She remained in that position for several minutes. He expected her to begin sobbing, but she did not. Finally, she stood erect and turned to him.

Her pixie face had aged twenty years in that few minutes. The innocent warmth of childhood had been replaced by a cold mask. Her voice was strangely deep and controlled: "Before Allah, I swear revenge for the life of my brother."

She suddenly fell to her knees and raised her arms to the ceiling. "Before Allah, I swear to kill him who has sent my brother to an unworthy death." She clasped the letter to her bosom and bent forward to press her forehead to the carpet.

Dick sat motionless. She remained in that position for several minutes. Then she rose to her feet, found a book of matches on the vanity, and went into the bathroom. In the mirror, he saw her light the single-page letter and drop it in the sink. It burned quickly. With the envelope still in hand, she returned to Dick.

He stared at the floor as she approached. He hesitated to look again at the childish face that had become twisted with hatred.

She stood before him and said quietly: "In this envelope, will I bury the heart of Mirhashem."

He looked up quickly, and was amazed to see her pixie face returning to normal. Her brown eyes were somber, but they were warming. He paused. What was the best approach? Should he try now to enlist her in *Purple's* plan to discredit Mirhashem? Hatred had to be burning inside her--perhaps she'd react irrationally--but could he afford to wait for another opportunity?

Her soft voice solved his dilemma. "Ed Orden, you owe me."

She threw the envelope on the floor and turned her back to him. Her fingers again pointed at the zipper.

Her curvaceous bottom moved seductively, as she dropped a shoulder to look back at him. Her brown eyes were smoldering as they met his. "*Scheherazade* was only an Arabian fairy tale. *Shreeba* is a Palestinian sun that will burn your very soul."

His fingers found the zipper and moved it carefully downward. No bra, . . . no panties, . . . no stockings, . . . only high-heeled shoes that were soon immersed in shimmering gold lamé.

She stepped carefully from the folds of lamé and went to the nightstand. Dick caught his breath as the long-legged vision bent slowly to turn up the music. Then she straightened her body and proudly arched her back.

He sat quietly as she returned to him. He was hypnotized by the pointed bosom thrusting at him. She leaned forward, took his hand, and guided it around a slender hip to the small of her elegant back. "Would you care to dance, Captain?"

Dick rose and carefully took her nakedness in his arms. They glided slowly around the room.

She started to grin, then a smile blossomed on her precious face. "I was thinking of this while we were dancing at the Volksgarten."

Dick's mind was flooded with animal desire. Her sensuality was overwhelming.

"You're an extremely good dancer, little girl. Where did you learn all those steps?"

She pushed her proud bosom against his chest. "Who are you calling a *little* girl?"

Dick was becoming excited. He concentrated on the music. It was the meaningful *Chorus Line* ballad, *What I Did for Love.* The last time he'd danced to that song was with Rita. His emotions were in turmoil. His eternal love for Rita was overwhelmed by savage desire for the incredibly sexy naked female in his arms.

She stopped dancing and rocked back and forth in his arms. She removed his formal jacket, then his shirt and belt. He stepped out of his shoes and trousers, encircled her petite waist with his hands, and lifted her until their lips met.

She locked her legs fiercely around his waist. He fell back upon the bed. Dick tried to kiss her gently, but her demanding mouth closed on his lower lip and she bit him--hard. He turned his head to escape, but tasted the blood as it soiled the pillow.

Shreeba completely lost it, throwing herself violently against him, again and again. Her eyes were tightly closed. She seemed to be trying to kill herself by plunging him fiercely into her body.

Dick tried to hold her--to slow her wild movements--but she had the strength of a cornered tiger. Finally, he rolled on top of her and used his weight to subdue her.

Her aggressiveness abated. She began sobbing hysterically. He eased his weight from her chest, but kept her pinned beneath him. After four or five minutes of intense sobbing, she began to hyperventilate. Dick turned her on her side, held her tenderly until the sobbing eased, then took a corner of the sheet and dried her tears.

"Shreeba, dear little Shreeba." He kissed her forehead and her tightly closed eyes. The salt from her tears penetrated his senses and quieted his desire.

They lay together, without moving, for at least fifteen minutes. Then she opened her eyes and peered around the room, as if looking for some threatening monster.

Finally she focused on Dick's face. He spoke softly to her: "Dear, dear, Shreeba. You must have suffered a severe shock in your life. It's not supposed to be like that, little one. Sex is supposed to come with love, or at least tenderness."

She took a deep breath, and lay quietly in the protective circle of his arms. "You are a perceptive man, Captain. It is something I hate, but am unable to deny."

"Did it start with the Israeli soldiers--when you were twelve?" guessed Dick, remembering the story she had told him in the bath.

"Yes," she sighed. "They tore more than my clothes before Ali killed them."

" . . . and then?"

"I hid behind my Abaya during the years Ali and I were in school in America. Mirhashem protected me when he brought us back to Lebanon."

A shiver went through her body as she spoke Mirhashem's name. Then she continued vehemently: "Now he has betrayed Ali, and also me, and I shall kill him!"

She continued to shiver. Dick pulled the bedspread over them and held her against him.

"Were you also raped by Sheik Omman?"

"Yes, . . . ," she replied hesitantly. "I also lied about that. Mirhashem had asked me to bathe him as a courtesy to an important guest--and a prospective husband. The Sheik was forbidden by custom to have sex with me at that time, . . . but he did."

Her body trembled against Dick. "It was horrible! He forced me to do awful things. Afterwards, he showed me his long knife and said he'd cut out my tongue if I told Mirhashem."

He rubbed her back with his hands in an attempt to warm her, but she trembled uncontrollably.

"I'm sorry I'm not so slim as when we shared the bath."

He pushed back the strands of hair that had been moistened by tears and kissed her on the temples. "That extra kilo looks good."

Her teeth were chattering. "Mirhashem makes me eat to gain

weight. He wants me to have bigger breasts and a more round bottom."

"What's been going on between you two?"

She tried to answer, but her voice caught in her throat. She choked slightly, then said: "He began taking me on his travels last summer. He bought me expensive clothes but never tried to take advantage of me. He only wanted to show me off to his western friends. A few nights after Ali died, when we were back in Tehran, he became very drunk and forced me to have sex with him. When he discovered I wasn't a virgin, he became violent." Her voice trailed off, and she fell silent.

". . . and since then?" asked Dick.

"Every time he gets drunk, which thankfully isn't often. Maybe he's getting tired of me. I haven't been very satisfying to him, because I have no experience. Abrahim told me he has a girl friend in Paris, an older western woman."

Dick grinned. "Guess that's why you're here with me."

Her trembling subsided. The trace of a smile lit her girlish face. She tilted her head to look at him. "Don't you wish you had taken me in the bath when you had the chance? I was younger then, before Mirhashem used me."

He kissed her softly on her parted lips, then said: "Well, let's see. You told me you were twelve when you went to school in Dallas for five years, and you've been back here for two years. My gosh! You're already nineteen!"

She finally smiled and rolled her body on top of his. "Am I now older than your shoes?"

He laughed. "Not all of them."

Holding her soft brown eyes with his intense blue ones, he spoke firmly: "You're certainly not old enough to think about taking revenge on a powerful man like Mirhashem--even if he did send your brother to his death."

Her eyes began to smolder. "One night, after he has had his drunken way with me, I shall kill him with his own knife."

". . . and those around him will kill you, in a terrible way."

"It is something I must do for my brother."

"Surely you're aware there are those who would kill Mirhashem for you?"

Dick winced from two jolts in his right shoulder. Listening to

Dick's monitor in the U.S. Consulate's security office, Nelson was cheering him on!

"Are you okay, Captain? Am I hurting you?"

"No, no. It's only an old war wound that exerts itself now and then." His hands caressed her firm bottom. Her full breasts warmed his chest.

"Perhaps you could betray Mirhashem the way he betrayed Ali, and send him to his death without ending your own life."

She opened her legs and straddled his groin with her warmness. "Captain, you overrate me. I don't even know how to satisfy a man. How could I convince someone to kill Mirhashem for me?"

He grinned. "If you don't lie still, you may find out how easy it is to satisfy a man."

She giggled and he continued: "No single person could ever kill Mirhashem, but organizations exist that could use your closeness to him to avenge Ali. They could also protect and provide for you, for the rest of your life."

She wet her lips and sought his, . . . gently. They kissed tenderly for several minutes, while she moved slowly on top of him. "Ah, Captain," she breathed, "perhaps I could satisfy you--and finally myself. How many times would I have to do that, before you would help me find such an organization?"

"Sex could not be a bargaining tool between us, Shreeba. As for an organization, the Mossad would pay you well for betraying Mirhashem, but I wouldn't trust them."

She shuddered, then whispered: "Allah would never forgive me if I helped them."

"The American CIA, or perhaps a German or British intelligence service, would be eager to work with you; but I have doubts about their capabilities. None are on a par with Mirhashem."

Their intimate contact was having an urgent effect on Shreeba. A dark blush was rushing to her pixie face, her hot eyes were glistening, her heaving bosom was getting warmer, she pressed it tightly against his chest. She gasped as Dick drew her to him. "Oh, Captain, please help me. I must avenge Ali. Oh, yes! Oh, please, . . . please!"

They stopped at the flower shop near the cemetery gate. Shreeba selected a bouquet of marigolds. They continued up the rise into the heart of the city's centuries-old burial grounds.

"We have some distance to walk," said Dick. "Ali's grave is a couple hundred yards beyond this hill."

"Are you certain you can find it?" asked Shreeba, from behind her black veil.

Dick squeezed her hand. "Of course, I wouldn't forget something like that."

"I hope I can remember everything you told me about catching Mirhashem in our trap."

"We'll take it one small step at a time. Call me whenever you like. The number I gave you is a phone in the UNO building. If I don't answer, leave a message when you'll call back and I'll be there. I check the answering service twice a day. Of course, you could also write me at the box number Ali gave you."

"Ali didn't give that to me, Captain. It was Abrahim."

"That was nice of him. You can also share the phone number with him if you like."

"He encouraged Mirhashem to leave me here with you."

"It's great to keep up old friendships."

"I don't believe Mirhashem regards anyone as his friend, but he has twice told me the story of how you saved his niece and uncle."

"Have you met them?"

"No, but I've seen pictures of Sabena. She is *very* pretty!"

"So are you, dear one."

"Did you also show her how tender sex can be?"

Dick laughed. "You really think I'm a bad one, don't you." He quickly changed the subject. "Now, tell me again what you're supposed to say to Abrahim--about why I couldn't spend this whole week with you."

"You had to go to Macáu, something about business with an export company named Homboldt."

"Super! . . . and what do you say if Abrahim, or Mirhashem, asks if you remember anything more?"

"You were expecting to make a lot of money, and you wanted to show me Brno if I visited Vienna again."

"Absolutely perfect!" exclaimed Dick. He stopped and pointed down the slope to a small barren area. "Down there, Shreeba. Ali's down there, in the new part."

She squeezed his fingers hard. "No, Ed Orden. Ali's with Allah,

- 195 -

in paradise, with my father and mother."

"Yes, he is. Be careful you don't join him too soon!" cautioned Dick. "You must be a greater actress than *Scheherazade*. No matter how much you hate Mirhashem, you must make him continue to trust you."

". . . and when he rapes me again?"

Dick stopped, turned to her, took her in his arms, and hugged the young girl gently. "Block everything from your mind. Tell yourself that you can live through it--that you're doing it for Ali."

11

BAITING THE TRAP

Nelson leaned across the desk and handed Dick the Lufthansa tickets to Hong Kong. "What does Maria know about your travels, and where you've been for the last week?"

"I told her on the phone that I'm at NATO for some unfinished business. Mackenzie's made arrangements with his secretaries to back me up."

"How about that swollen lip?"

"Hope it heals before I return next week. Were you able to modify my phone at UNO, to forward calls to my Skyfone?"

"Yes, the caller won't know the difference. For your protection, I'll also monitor those calls here at headquarters."

"Thank you, Sir. I left the key to the Westbanhof mail box with Max. He'll let you know if anything comes from Shreeba."

Nelson rose from his desk, strolled to the window, and looked at the deepening haze over Frankfurt. "This place is as bad as LA."

"What have you heard from Mountie?"

The *Purple* Field Supervisor stroked his chin thoughtfully. "I pray every night that I'm not pushing him in over his head. During the last four years, he's done a miraculous undercover job of bringing down the Red Army Faction. He has fooled them completely, actually becoming a leader in that *world's-most-educated* terrorist organization. Now I'm asking him to use that position to spring the trap on Mirhashem, the *world's-most-dangerous* terrorist."

"He's going inside the Czech terrorist-weapons distribution system as a representative of the RAF?"

"Yes. You remember the Czech General who defected a couple years ago--the boss of that depot at Brno?"

"Yes Sir. NATO learned a lot from him."

"Jim's using that defection to work himself into the depot. His RAF friends are pressuring the Kremlin to appoint one of their members supervisor of depot security--they're claiming their operations are being compromised by leaks from the depot."

". . . and that supervisor would be Mountie. Is RAF influence in

Moscow strong enough to pull that off?"

"Correct on both counts, Brown Bear. To make sure, Mountie's arranged for the spy in the West German *BfV* to make the same recommendation to the Kremlin."

"The woman who betrayed Rita during our white-slave sting in Manila?"

"Yes."

"Jim told me she was connected with the Mafia, not the KGB."

"That was four years ago. He's since found out she's been cooperating with the Kremlin. Now she's in the perfect position to support the RAF's security initiative at the depot."

"Holy mackerel!" exclaimed Dick. "He's going to trust that bitch not to sell him out to the KGB?"

"She only knows him as an RAF operative, who's spent a lot of time in Moscow. There's nothing for her to betray, and she has a lot to fear from him."

"Damn!" Dick shook his head. "He really is in over his head."

Their conversation was interrupted by a soft knock on the door.

"That's your transportation to Rhein-Main. Remember, Brown Bear, this whole operation--and Jim's life--depends on the trustworthiness of your friend Consuela. Don't let emotions cloud your judgement, . . . and make sure she can control the timing of the weapons shipment, right down to the last minute."

"Understand, Sir. Say again how much of the money I can promise her?"

"Most of it, Dick, but tell her we'd like to use some of it to provide security in whatever new life she chooses. We'll also set aside one million for Shreeba."

Dick put the Lufthansa tickets in his jacket pocket and went to the door.

After stepping off the cable car, Dick paused to look down the steep incline of Victoria Peak at the harbor below. No aircraft carriers were anchored there, but it was still an awesome view. New skyscrapers seemed to be sprouting from the crowded chaos of busy streets.

He turned to walk up the circuitous dirt path, which led around the hill and eventually to the grassy rise that marked the top of the peak. Her note had been waiting last night when he checked into the Peninsula Hotel: "Meet me tomorrow, at the same time and place you left me."

Consuela was an incurable romantic. When they parted four years ago, she had insisted they say goodbye on the peak--like Bill Holden and Jennifer Jones in that unforgettable movie. There truly was a small weathered tree on that grassy rise. Dick and Consuela had exchanged several tender kisses, a few tears, and a promise of a many-splendored love, before he left to walk down to the cable car station. When he looked back, she was sitting under the tree, waving to him. A pair of hawks soared high above, in a cloudless blue sky warmed by a brilliant noontime sun. It was a scene that occupied a place in his heart--next to the memories of Rita on the beach at Palawan.

As he proceeded up the path today, there was no sun to tell him the time. Darkening clouds in the west warned of an approaching storm. He zipped his jacket to ward off the freshening breeze and glanced at his watch. It was already after twelve. He quickened his pace. He passed the observation buildings and continued on the well-trodden path through the brush and small trees.

Rounding the last turn before the grassy rise, he smelled cigarette smoke coming from a large bush. He casually rested his right hand on his hip, near the Beretta in its pocket holster. His quick eyes picked up a slight movement in the bush. His fingers found the grip of the Beretta. He kept walking, with an occasional glance over his shoulder.

Then he was past the turn, and there she was--standing by the tree on the top of the rise--her full white skirt billowing around her long slender legs. She raised her hand to wave, then began blowing him kisses as he ran the last fifty meters up the slope. She leapt into his arms, they were laughing for joy, he spun them around and around.

When they stopped, he lowered her toes to the ground and began kissing the beautiful dusky face and pouting lips that no man could ever forget.

She breathed softly, "Thank you, God, for bringing my White Knight safely back from his Crusade."

He drew back to admire her beauty. "Why do I have this feeling I'm starting on another?"

Her lilting laughter was music to his ears. "We're doing this one together, right?"

"Yes, Connie, there are so many things I want to do *together,* with you."

His hands moved down the warmth of her black wool sweater, then he stopped. "Is that your army in the bush by the corner?"

She tilted her head to smile at him. "Very good, Richard. Yes, they're two Chinese boys from Homboldt, who accompany me on all business trips."

"Damn," breathed Dick. "I was hoping we could start with a little pleasure, then get down to business."

Connie's smile adorned her classic Latino features. "Not this time, Captain. We, and the boys, are on our way to Macáu. My bosses are eager to meet the man who can put them in contact with a very lucrative market named *Mirhashem.* By the way, what's your name for this operation?"

He took a moment to steal another kiss from her full, soft, wet lips; then replied, "Ed Orden, Sweetie."

"Still a Navy fighter pilot?"

"Same life history as before, but with no family, and now a retired Captain."

She batted her long dark eyelashes at him. "Congratulations, my dear Captain, but I do hope you're not too *retired.* When you return to the Peninsula tonight, you're certain to have another visit from your favorite bellboy."

The suspension system of the old Hungarian passenger car had problems. It exaggerated the roughness of the rails. However, including the thirty-minute inspection by surly border guards, it was only a three-hour train ride from Vienna to Budapest. Dick's vertebrae were in no condition to make the trip by auto. The long trip to Hong Kong had taken its toll. His aching body needed rest.

Nelson's phone relay system had worked as advertised. Dick received the call from Abrahim through his Skyfone, while his Lufthansa flight was refueling in Bahrain. Abrahim had requested a face-to-face meeting. It was a tense moment. Mirhashem's aide would naturally assume Dick was on the phone in his UNO office in Vienna--but he was at least five hours from Schwechat. If Abrahim wanted to meet immediately, it would be a problem.

Thankfully, Abrahim had called from Damascus. He wanted to

meet Dick in Budapest instead of Vienna. Dick didn't ask why, but said it would take at least a day to get a visa from the Hungarian Consulate. It was the perfect excuse for the extra time he needed.

Nelson had monitored Abrahim's call. He later called Dick from Frankfurt with a support plan. Max would meet Dick at Vienna's Sudbahnhof, with a Federal Republic of Germany passport bearing the appropriate visa clearance.

Dick's flight had landed at Schwechat after midnight. Rather than start a new cover story for Maria, he spent a lonely night at the Kohlbeck Hotel near the train station.

The tracks nearing Budapest's Déli station were especially rough. The passengers were tossed about in the unsteady car. Finally they jerked to a stop.

Dick took his bag and walked down the lengthy concrete platform. He spotted at least four plain-clothes communist security agents before he entered the terminal building.

He stopped to change the Deutsche Marks Max had given him to Hungarian Forints, then entered Budapest's modern transportation system. It was the evening rush hour. Fortunately, the German Commando's briefing proved accurate and invaluable. In fifteen minutes, Dick was standing outside the Astoria Hotel on Rákóczi Street in downtown Budapest.

The air was bad--heavy with carbon monoxide--but there were not many autos on the streets. Unfortunately, the majority of them were little two-cylinder "Trabies," the East German invention that answered the need for taxis but left a dense cloud of smoke.

Dick could only shrug when the hotel clerks addressed him in Magyar. They immediately switched and began speaking German, perhaps better than he! After all, German had been the business language of Budapest since the 1920's. He took a small sleeping room, close to the bath, with the toilet farther down the hall.

At eight, he went down to the restaurant. Abrahim waved from a table in the back. Crossing the room, Dick reminded himself that he'd seen Abrahim during the Christmas airport massacres; but the last time Abrahim knew they'd been together was their June lunch at the Sacher Hotel.

The tall, handsome Palestinian was elegantly dressed in a charcoal-colored silk Italian suit. He rose and extended his hand to Dick. "Thanks for making the trip, Captain Orden."

Dick shook his hand vigorously. "Sorry I'm so poorly dressed, Abrahim. You look like a million dollars. Who's your tailor?"

"I found a great place in Paris."

"Yeah. Shreeba told me you and Mirhashem were there two weeks ago."

"Thanks for taking care of her during that time. She's a sweet little girl, but sometimes overwhelmed by the pace of our business. She apparently enjoyed her holiday with you."

The terrorist grinned and continued: "Please don't be offended, but she told me about a conversation with you that's of particular interest to us."

Dick looked in Abrahim's black eyes: "Hope I'm not in trouble."

Abrahim's eyes darted to the left side of the room, where two leather-jacketed men stood at the bar, then his face broadened into a smile. "No, of course not. Shreeba's one of your greatest fans, as am I. Mirhashem and I will not soon forget you saved us from that shelling in Beirut."

"What could I have said to Shreeba that interests you guys?"

"She mentioned you cut short your holiday to go to Macáu, and that you had interests in Czechoslovakia. Are you familiar with Homboldt Trading in Macáu, Captain?"

"Why, yes, . . . to a certain extent. I've done limited business with them over the past few years."

Abrahim's eyes were fixed on Dick's face. "Did that business involve Soviet armaments stored in Czechoslovakia?"

Dick's countenance remained cool and aloof. "It might have, but there were no big deals involved."

Abrahim's serious expression changed suddenly. He smiled and continued: "Please don't let my prying offend you. There's a distinct possibility we could both reap great benefits, by associating our businesses together."

Dick chuckled. "Associating my business with yours would be like pouring a cup of sand on the beach at Cannes."

Abrahim laughed. "That may be, but it sometimes takes only one drop of oil to keep a powerful machine running."

". . . and where would that drop of oil fall?"

"On the connection between Homboldt Trading and the Czech arms depot outside Brno." Abrahim's intense eyes were again focused on Dick's face.

"Is there such a connection?"

"If there is, and if you can apply a little oil, we'll make it worth your while--say fifty thousand dollars."

The young Palestinian glanced at his Rolex. "No need to give me an answer now. Whether you're interested or not, you have an invitation to dinner with my boss."

Dick glanced around the room. The somber leather-jacketed men by the bar were watching closely. "Is Mirhashem here?"

"No. The men you've noticed will take us to him. Shall we go?"

They sat in the back of the Mercedes, with the leather-jacketed men in front. Dick said quietly to Abrahim: "Those fellows don't look, or act, like Palestinians."

"They are Chechen. Their mafia is very powerful in Budapest. Mirhashem has a security arrangement with them."

The Mercedes darted to a stop in front of an elaborate building in the old Jewish commercial sector, near the center of the city.

A pleasant mid-March snowstorm was blanketing Bavaria south of Munich. Fortunately, the autobahns were clear. Dick and Maria made the drive from Vienna in three and a half hours.

They had left early, to ensure they'd be on time for Maria's dental appointment. Now they had time for a coffee break before continuing into the city. Dick noticed the sign to Dusendorf.

Maria had been dozing. She woke up when he braked to exit the autobahn. "Why are you going off here, *Bärlie*? We're still fifteen minutes from the dentist's office."

He smiled at her sleepy blue eyes. "We have time for a coffee, Sweetie. There's a great *Konditorei* near the train station here."

The confectionery was also near a house where Dick had visited the family of his former German fighter pilot colleague five years earlier. Klaus had tried to quit the Aura Project, but had been murdered by commandos working for the traitorous Herr Strauss. Dick had shared the salary he received from the project with Klaus's parents, telling them the $100,000 were proceeds from a life insurance policy. He had no intention of risking another visit to the kindly old people, or explaining the situation to Maria, but he wanted to show her this paradise nestled in the trees of Bavaria.

He saw the Jagerstrasse sign and turned into the narrow street.

Up the hill, around the corner, and there was the two-story house with the stone fence. It was covered with snow; exactly like the photo Klaus had kept in the pilot's locker room in Aura's volcanic crater hideaway.

Dick stopped in front of the driveway, and--like a dream--there was the golden retriever, Duchess. He opened his door. "Isn't this a beautiful spot? Give me a moment."

He stepped from the car. Duchess wolfed a quiet greeting and walked slowly up the cobblestones to his side.

Dick went to his knees and hugged the aging dog. "*Na, du bist eine Liebling,*" he whispered in her ear.

He released her and got back in the car. Maria was looking at him in amazement. "What is there about you and dogs?"

Dick grinned. "I know that one. She belonged to a friend."

"I've never been here before," he lied, "but I remembered the address and wanted to drive by on the chance of seeing the dog." He pulled away from the house and continued: "My friend was killed several years ago. *Na ja*, let's have a coffee and strudel."

"I can't eat before I go to the dentist," objected Maria.

Dick looked at the delicate features and brilliant blue eyes, framed by shimmering golden hair. "Schatzie, if I was a dentist, you could sit in my chair and eat garlic."

She slowly wet her pink lips with the tip of her tongue. "Now that's a place we've never tried." The radiance of her smile brightened the snowy morning.

He laughed. "Be sure you don't try it today--without me!"

The clerk at McGraw Kaserne billeting had Dick's reservation. He was assigned a suite reserved for senior NATO officers. The clerk informed him other NATO officers attending the conference were billeted on the same floor, and Colonel Mackenzie had requested that Captain Williams contact him upon arrival.

Dick borrowed the desk telephone. A few minutes later, he was knocking on the door next to his suite.

The stocky, red-haired, SAS Colonel opened the door. "Top of the morning, Brown Bear," he boomed. "Come in."

"Sorry I'm late," began Dick.

"You're damned lucky to be here at all, with this bloody snow."

"Jim Conrad get here okay?"

"Yes indeed, late last night from Berlin. He's sleeping in, but told me to wake him when you got here. Do you have the plans with you?"

"Yes Sir. I worked it out for the airfields Nelson specified."

"Grab a cup of coffee and lay your stuff on that table. I'll wake Mountie."

"How secure is this place, Mac?"

"My boys de-bugged it earlier this morning."

"Did they find anything?"

"Is this Munich?" The Scotsman's blue eyes twinkled. "Only two bugs--in each of the seven rooms my secretary reserved."

"You must have quite a collection by now."

"Enough to start my own business when I retire."

Dick chuckled. "Which will be never."

The interconnecting door opened. An unshaven Jim Conrad entered in his pajamas. "Damn, you guys are noisy."

He crossed the room and grasped Dick's shoulders. "Glad to have you back in one piece, partner. Guess you know *Purple* is having trouble with your satellite monitoring system. We lost track of you in Hong Kong and again in Budapest."

"Yeah, Nelson mentioned that. He was probably disappointed he couldn't monitor Consuela and me."

Mackenzie laughed. "If he wasn't disappointed, I surely was. How is that luscious lassie?"

"Just like you left her, Mac."

"How's Maria?" asked Jim.

"She'll be at the dentist for at least four hours. She has another appointment tomorrow morning, which will probably take all day."

"Glad I don't have to pay her dental bills," said Jim, "but that fits perfectly with our schedule."

"Yeah," echoed Mackenzie, "we have an AWACS coordinator, a Turkish Mirage pilot, an SAS helo pilot, and the Air Wing Commander from the USS *Kitty Hawk* reporting here tomorrow morning at nine."

"Sorry to task you with working out the entire air-order-of-battle, Dick," apologized Jim.

"No problem. Nelson arranged for the secure briefing tank at the U.S. Embassy in Vienna. The Air Force Attaché had everything I needed. You look tired, Mountie. How's it going at Brno?"

"Piece-of-cake. I've been inside that depot many times for the RAF. I'm one of the few Czech-speakers in that *highly educated* terrorist group. Their complaint to Moscow about security problems has worked. I've been named to replace the security officer in the depot's dispatch department."

"Does that mean you'll accompany the shipment of arms to Iran, if Mirhashem buys from them?" asked Dick.

The RCMP representative to *Purple* smiled. "Yes indeed, I can arrange that! There's only one other Persian-speaker at the depot, and his chances of being sick when the shipment goes are assured."

Mackenzie chuckled. "Glad I'm on your side, Mountie. Let's take a look at Brown Bear's air plan."

Dick cleared the table and spread the maps of the delivery route: from Czechoslovakia through Eastern Europe, over the Black Sea and eastern Turkey, and into northwestern Iran.

"Nelson said you expect the Czechs to have a Soviet VTA aircraft available to transport the weapons."

"Affirmative," replied Jim. "Moscow wants to demonstrate support for their Warsaw Pact satellites, their favorite terrorists, and Iran. Since this delivery involves all three, they have agreed to provide a new Il-76 Candid. They have a range of almost three thousand miles. How many air miles from Brno to Tehran, Dick?"

"Two thousand, but they won't make it to Tehran." Dick pointed at three locations on his satellite-photography map, northwest of Tabriz. "These are the airfields that *Purple's* intelligence says are the least defended. They could probably be taken and held by Admiral Toufani's guerrillas for a short period of time."

Mackenzie examined the map closely. "Yes. Those are the ones Toufani considered."

"Will we know his choice before takeoff?"

"Certainly!" Mac placed his finger on a satellite photo. "He has already chosen this deserted six thousand-foot strip near the northeast corner of Lake Urmia. Only minimal repair's required to make the north side of the runway useable. He will start deploying his forces when we're sure Mirhashem's taking the bait."

"It's practically a *done-deal*," said Jim Conrad. "Homboldt's been in contact with both parties. Mirhashem's weapons experts showed up at Brno three days after Dick left Budapest. Mirhashem is scheduled to visit the depot at noon on 25 March. The Czechs have reserved a resort villa outside town to celebrate the occasion later that evening. We'll do our final coordination in Vienna with Nelson, two days earlier."

"Will you be there, Mac?" asked Dick.

"No, I'm leaving tomorrow afternoon to join Toufani in the mountains. I'll be arriving by parachute--with new Iranian military uniforms--so his boys can look nice when the Czechs hand them Mirhashem's weapons."

"Say hello to Iris for me," said Dick.

Mackenzie grinned. "I'm sure that spirited lass will be waiting at the airfield when you chaps land."

"You think Toufani will agree to let the Czechs and Russians continue on to Tehran in the Il-76?"

"No chance, . . . but don't say that to Nelson. Sometimes he's too bloody honorable for this job. We have to blow that damned Candid after it's off-loaded, and we have to kill the crew." The SAS Colonel looked hard at his *Purple* partners. "You know that as well as I do."

Jim replied thoughtfully: "If we did blow the aircraft, Moscow would have reason to be angry with Mirhashem. However, our mission is to discredit him within the terrorist world. We need surviving witnesses--to tell the Ayatollah who stole his money and his weapons."

"Those witnesses could identify us for Mirhashem, Khomeini, and the KGB!" warned Mackenzie hotly.

"You'll be able to blend with Toufani's fighters," replied Jim. "As for Brown Bear and me, . . . it will be a costly operation. His life in Vienna will be finished, and I'll be through in the RAF. We'll both be marked targets--for vengeful fanatics."

"That's a hell of a price for *Purple* to pay," muttered Mackenzie.

"Nelson has his marching orders from the GP-7. They are more than willing to expend a couple agents--to make the king of international terrorism a target in his own empire."

Dick introduced himself to the Commander of the *Kitty Hawk's* Air Wing. "CAG, I'm Dick Williams. Are you the Ben Bender from VF-92 on the Connie back in 1980?"

"Yes Sir," acknowledged the startled Navy fighter pilot. "How did you know that?"

"Saw it in the paperwork we received. The Silverkites were my squadron, during my last Vietnam deployment."

"Oh, sure," smiled Bender, "in '73. I remember your name from the squadron history book."

Dick hoped that was the only way the CAG remembered his name. His wife, Mindy, had been Dick's guest at the embassy's VIP quarters in Manila. She had never quite faded from his mind.

As NATO coordinator, Mackenzie took the lead for the briefing. He informed them the mission was classified NATO Cosmic Top Secret. It was also strictly compartmentalized. Mechanics painting Iraqi markings on a Turkish Mirage at Ankara, and those painting Iranian markings on an F-14 aboard the *Kitty Hawk,* had no idea why they were doing it--and they must *never* know why!

The Special Air Service Colonel began with the big picture: The Soviet's predicted mid-day takeoff time for the arms delivery run, from Brno to Tehran, was uncertain. The NATO AWACS aircraft at Ankara, call sign Big Brother, would be placed in alert-five status at 11 a.m. They would be launched when covert sources reported the Soviet Candid, code name Santa, airborne from Brno. Big Brother would anchor over eastern Turkey. When the Candid approached the middle of the Black Sea, they would scramble the Mirage, call sign Nail, from Ankara. Simultaneously, the *Kitty Hawk* would launch the CAG's Iranian-disguised F-14, call sign Sledge, and two EA-6B electronic jammers, call sign Pouncer.

Big Brother would control Nail's intercept of Santa to occur 100 miles northwest of Tabriz. Nail would join on the IL-76, so the Soviet aircrew could see his Iraqi markings and the missiles loaded on his aircraft. Then he'd drift aft and fire an unguided missile, which would pass in clear view of the Soviets.

While the attack was being staged, Big Brother would vector Sledge into a position where the Soviet pilots could observe him engaging Nail. Nail would flee the area and return to base. Sledge would join on Santa, to be clearly identified as the Iranian F-14 that saved the Soviets.

Absolute control of communications would be the key to mission success. Two minutes before Nail's attack on Santa, a *Purple* satellite would commence jamming all communication frequencies in the northwest quadrant of Iran, with the notable exception of the secure AWACS frequency, and the long-range frequency which the Soviets used to maintain contact with their airborne transports.

The Pouncers would provide SAM protection for Sledge, while trailing him into the Tabriz area. They would also scan for other unjammed frequencies and immediately dispose of them.

Unbeknownst to the Soviets, NATO intelligence had compromised their transport-control frequency months earlier. After Sledge joined on the IL-76, a *Purple* agent would broadcast on that frequency in Russian, notifying the Candid that major airfields in Tehran were closed due to a massive Iraqi air attack. Simultaneously, Sledge would be signaling the Candid's crew to follow him down for landing at the airfield northeast of Lake Urmia.

Commander Bender interrupted, "What if they won't do that, Colonel? What if they ignore me?"

Mackenzie looked coolly at the CAG. "In that case, fire a few tracer rounds across their nose." He paused to look at Dick and Jim. "If that doesn't work, shoot Santa down. That transport must *not* get through to Tehran! Do you agree, Brown Bear? Mountie?"

Dick nodded grimly. Jim replied: "Yeah, CAG, if you have to, shoot it down."

"What would I be shooting down?" asked Bender.

"Under compartmentalized security, I can not tell you *what*, Commander," answered Mackenzie; "but to impress upon you the importance of this mission, I will tell you *who*." He gestured at Jim and Dick. "These two gentleman will be on board the Candid to witness your Oscar-winning performance."

The CAG glanced at Dick. "Don't worry, Brown Bear, I'll get you on deck."

Dick chuckled. "Be sure it's the right airfield."

To complete the general overview of the mission, Mackenzie addressed the young British Special Air Service helicopter pilot: "Jimmy, Big Brother will be in contact with us while we're unloading Santa. If everything goes as planned, he'll scramble you from your forward-staging base on the eastern Turkish border when it gets dark. Big Brother will vector you to our airfield. When you are close, attempt contact with us on his frequency. I'm Moon River. You're Night Rider. Don't fail us, son. I don't want to ride a damned donkey all the way home."

The SAS Lieutenant grinned: "I wouldn't wish that on any ass, Sir--yours or the donkey's. Will communications over the area be jammed during our flight?"

"Not possible, Jimmy. We're using super-secret gear and we're not allowed to expose it for more than thirty minutes. I have every confidence you can make it through the hills and valleys north of Lake Urmia without being seen by Tabriz radar."

"Yes, certainly, Sir; but if the jamming only lasts half an hour, how are Sledge and the Pouncers getting back to the Gulf?"

The CAG chuckled. "No sweat, Lieutenant. After six years of firing continuous salvoes, Iran and Iraq are almost out of air defense weapons. What they have left has been pulled back to their major cities. It should be a walk-in-the-park for us, if we stay close to the border, coming and going."

"Roger that," nodded the AWACS coordinator. "Sounds like you guys have been sticking your noses in interesting places."

"Only unarmed reconnaissance," responded the CAG quickly.

"Better keep your head on a swivel," cautioned the coordinator. "The F-14's that Tehran is putting in the air these days have working radars, and we have evidence they're carrying Phoenix."

"Damn!" swore Dick disgustedly. "That technology was too secret to include them in the F-14 sale to the Shah, but this White House uses them to bargain for hostages."

"None of which have been returned to date," reminded Jim Conrad. "Freeing hostages is what got your President elected. Now the Ayatollahs are playing him for a fool."

Dick picked up Maria at the dentist's shortly after four. The winter storm had passed. They made a long but pleasant drive back to Vienna. He had only six days to make his peace with her, and develop an alibi for what was certain to be a life-altering mission.

Nelson began the 23 March meeting in the British Embassy with a discussion of Mac's recommendation for blowing the Il-76 and killing its crew: "Mac's concern is for the future security of Dick and Jim. He is correct that it might make some difference, if it appears they also died in the explosion. However, we should consider that Mirhashem doesn't know Jim. He'll be seeing him for the first time at Brno, and there's no reason for him to think Jim is anything but an RAF terrorist. We could even consider letting Jim continue to Tehran with the empty aircraft and crew."

"Not a good idea, Sir!" interrupted Max. "The KGB's certain to be involved in the Soviet's investigation. Given enough time, they would eventually break Mountie's cover."

"I agree," nodded Nelson. "If it's okay with you, Mountie, you will join Mac and Dick in the SAS escape to Turkey. This mission probably spells the end of your effectiveness in this arena. However, there's another challenge coming your way. The GP-7 has named you to develop a second field office."

Dick laughed. "With age, comes responsibility."

"Don't forget you're my partner," responded Jim. "If I end up behind a desk, I might ask for you to bring me coffee."

"Here's another view of how to further discredit Mirhashem in the eyes of the Soviets," continued Nelson. "It will take Toufani's boys a couple hours to off-load the weapons. Mountie, would that be enough time for you to rig a Czech Sematex altitude-differential bomb in the Candid?"

"Certainly. There are two prototypes at the Brno depot. They have been added to Mirhashem's order to make it more expensive."

"Could you set one for a scenario where we free the crew to fly the Il-76 to Tehran, and the bomb explodes while they are making a descent during the following flight--probably to a Soviet base."

"Yes. The prototypes have the capability of two ascents and two descents, as long as the altitude differential is at least three thousand meters. That would fit the profile they would fly from the field near Lake Urmia to Tehran and back home."

Max interrupted, "If you free those guys, why should they want to continue to Tehran? It's about the same distance from Lake Urmia to the MiG base at Baku, as it is to Tehran. What's to keep them from considering their mission complete after the weapons are off-loaded?"

"A *big* wad of cash waiting in Tehran," said Dick. "Consuela told me Homboldt requires a final payment-on-delivery of ten percent. That payment is made directly from buyer to seller."

"Super!" exclaimed Max. "There's no telling what a Soviet pilot would do for three million dollars."

"Better explain to everyone how Consuela will be handling the money, Brown Bear," said Nelson.

"Yes Sir. Homboldt has become one of the world's largest corporations by serving as an *honest broker* in illicit arms trading.

They ensure reasonable prices and timely deliveries, and handle all the money except for the ten percent on delivery. They deal strictly through Swiss banks, preferring to transfer the money electronically. However, with their hard-currency crisis, the Soviets are insisting on U.S. dollars delivered to their Swiss bank accounts."

Jim asked: "Does Homboldt *guarantee* the twenty-seven million dollars Mirhashem gives Consuela at Brno will end up in a Soviet account in Switzerland?" When Dick nodded, he continued: "How is that accomplished?"

"Consuela will be accompanied by two Homboldt Chinese employees. We don't want to mess with those guys, but I'm certain Mirhashem will insist a couple of his boys escort them to Zurich."

"How do they cross borders with that amount of cash?"

"Homboldt has *greased* border crossings in all key countries, where Consuela and her escorts get special treatment."

Nelson interrupted: "We expect Consuela to depart Brno with the money before Mountie and Brown Bear are airborne with the weapons. Maximilian will be waiting in Zurich. Leap in here and tell us how that goes, Max."

"Certainly. We couldn't guarantee Consuela's safety if we took her escorts down enroute, so we're employing a more conservative approach. Brown Bear got us great mini-cam photos of Consuela's Chinese bodyguards. He also got some good shots of Mirhashem's Chechens in Hungary. Along with Abood's other work, we're sure we can provide photos of whoever escorts Consuela to Zurich."

"Provide to whom?" asked Jim.

Max grinned. "Swiss police and bank guards, through Interpol. When we're sure which photos to provide, they'll be accompanied by an Interpol warning of previous bank robberies by those individuals. Of course, we'll specifically identify the Zurich bank, and the time we expect them to strike again."

Max continued, "Consuela has explained the procedure she follows for cash deposits: Her escorts remain in the outer lobby, so they don't have to pass through metal detectors. She goes into a VP's office with the money, . . . and that is when our Swiss police and bank security will take down the escorts. They won't know anything about Consuela. She'll be just another customer, who happened to go in the bank ahead of those guys."

"How do you get her out of there with the cash?" asked Jim.

"The money stays, in an account Mac set up for Consuela years ago. As chief of the Interpol intercept force, I'll take her directly from the VP's office to a helicopter waiting on the roof. I'll tell the Swiss that we need her immediately, as a witness who might have observed the criminals before they entered the bank."

"Treat her like precious crystal, Max," advised Dick. "She's one special lady!"

"She is indeed," echoed Nelson. "Max will be escorting her all the way to our safe-haven in the Philippines."

"To the crater?" asked Jim.

"Yes. She has agreed to wait there, until everything is worked out to guarantee her future. If things go as planned, that will also be Shreeba's new beginning."

"How will she get there?" asked Dick.

"Abood reports it's uncertain whether or not she'll accompany Mirhashem to Brno. If she doesn't, he'll get her out of Iran before Mirhashem returns. If she goes to Brno, Abood has told her to ask Mirhashem if she can ride back to Tehran in the Candid. If that happens, you guys add her to the SAS escape group, and Mac will see that she gets to the crater. If Mirhashem forces her to return to Tehran with him, Abood has a plan to snatch her later."

"Sounds like the safest way is to get her on the IL-76 with us," said Dick.

"Absolutely!" agreed Nelson. "If she shows up at Brno, work hard on that angle."

"Dick, what makes you so sure you'll be on the IL-76?" asked Max.

"I believe Mirhashem regards me as insurance--that the delivery won't be shot down enroute. He has also promised me a $50,000 commission, upon arrival of the weapons in Tehran."

"With all the body checks you'll be going through, we can't risk your carrying a Skyfone," said Nelson. "Jim should be able to get his aboard the delivery aircraft. We can use the chip in your shoulder to signal you through the satellite. Has Maria agreed to a holiday when you return? You know how dangerous this town will be for you, when Mirhashem finds out he's been duped."

"Maria's tired of her job at the *Rote Kreuz Krankenspital.* She's looking forward to a three-month holiday to study for the RN exam in English in Geneva. I hope to convince her to return to the States with me after that."

"Be careful!" warned Jim. "Don't forget Operation *Mosquito*. I still believe she had something to do with that. We have more than your life at stake now, so stay the hell out of Vienna when this is over! Find a deep hole in Nebraska and crawl into it. The world will no longer be a safe place for you, my friend."

They were interrupted by a knock on the tank's steel door. Nelson opened it, and an orderly handed him a message. He read it quickly and turned to address the group: "Gentlemen, our mission will be very timely, and it *must* succeed. The U.S. Sixth Fleet has attacked missile sites in Libya."

12

THE STING

The pre-dawn air chilled Schwechat's observation deck. Dick watched as Consuela descended the ladder from the Lauder Air 737. The two Chinese bodyguards, whom Dick had met in Macáu, followed her closely.

She looked very professional in her black suit. Her smooth dark hair was cut at collar length and crowned by a narrow-brimmed black hat. Even at a distance, and in the dim light, she was a striking figure of womanhood. They boarded the terminal bus for customs and immigration.

Why did Dick feel such a strong bond with her? Their time together totaled less than two weeks, scattered over twenty years: one week in '67, when the USS *Oriskany* was in Hong Kong; one night in '81, before he fled for his life from the ill-fated Aura party where Joe Tashki was killed; two days in '82, when he made Mac's deal for the Czech Sematex to destroy the Argentine Etendards; and two days earlier this month, when he'd met with her Homboldt bosses to encourage them to deal with Mirhashem.

It was during this last meeting that he fully realized the danger involved with her job at Homboldt. Now he felt the same loyalty for her that he'd shared with his wingmen over Vietnam--only one of those four had survived. Looking over the edge of the observation platform as she stepped off the bus, Dick made a solemn vow that Consuela *would* survive! He would do whatever it took to make sure she escaped Homboldt and lived to enjoy the new life she was choosing.

He was waiting when she emerged from customs. A shy smile lit her dusky face as she recognized him. He wondered how much the presence of the Chinese bodyguards would dampen her ardor. His question was soon answered. She turned to give her bag to one of the boys, then stepped quickly into Dick's arms. She embraced him strongly. Her kiss was more than enthusiastic.

"Am I worth getting up early for?" she teased.

"Much more than that, Honey," he assured her. "Is everything in order?"

"Certainly," she breathed, still holding him tightly.

"Like you told me, I didn't arrange any transportation."

"We'll be taken care of." She released him and turned to the two boys: "Kondo, Kondu, you remember Captain Orden?"

Nattily attired in black cashmere suits, the two could have been identical twins. Dick offered his hand slowly, the muscles bulging from their collars indicated they could easily crush him. They both smiled, bowed slightly, and gripped his hand politely while offering a crisp "How do you do, Captain."

Kondu led the way through the terminal. Passing the shops, Dick reflected momentarily on his wild dash through the area last Christmas--dodging police bullets while in pursuit of Ali and his grenade-throwers.

The rising sun greeted them as they exited the terminal. Kondu hurried to open the back door of the waiting black limousine. The flag of the Czechoslovak Socialist Republic fluttered from a short staff on its left front bumper.

When they were alongside the car, Kondo tapped Dick politely on the shoulder. "Please don't be offended, Captain Orden, Kondu and I are pledged to protect the lady. If we can make a quick search, it makes our job less stressful."

"Certainly," agreed Dick. He unzipped his flight bag, handed it to Kondu, and raised his elbows above his shoulders.

Kondo's efficient fingers detected objects in the breast pocket of Dick's coat and in his trousers' pocket. He asked to see them.

Dick showed him the golden cigarette case Nelson had given him for the trip. He opened it and offered American cigarettes to the boys--being careful to keep his fingers on the four cigarettes on the right side.

Kondu and Kondo accepted gratefully. Dick removed the large cigarette lighter from his pocket--made sure he used it as Nelson had instructed--and offered the boys a light. The golden lighter was also capable of delivering a spray of knockout gas, similar to that Dick had used to subdue Sheik Omman on the Mountain of Truth. However, the effects of this particular gas were good for about five hours.

As they left the terminal, the driver lowered the window separating him from his passengers and said: "Madam, Sir, the Consul

General has invited you to breakfast and freshen-up at his residence, before we start our drive to Brno."

"How long will the drive take?" asked Consuela.

"Not more than two hours."

"With a three-hour wait at the border," reminded Dick.

The driver smiled coldly. "Not today, Sir, not in this auto."

Consuela responded with a soft throaty chuckle. "Then we have time for breakfast, and heaven knows I need a shower; but we must be in Brno by noon."

The business meeting was held in a magnificent old castle on the depot grounds. The participants sat around a huge antique table in a spacious room under the dome. The walls were adorned with paintings and flags from another time in history, but the two flags hanging in the dome depicted current reality. The long red banner with the hammer-and-cycle dwarfed the white-blue-red standard of the Czechoslovak Socialist Republic.

The depot commander's party was the last to enter the room. The Czech Army General was accompanied by his Soviet counterpart. They walked through a cordon of twelve soldiers to the head of the table, and occupied two identical chairs placed side-by-side.

At the General's order, his aide introduced the seated participants. Mirhashem was recognized as representing the Ayatollah Khomeini. His assistant, Abrahim, was by his side. Two Iranian weapons experts were next. Across the table were the adjutant of the depot and Jim Conrad, who was introduced as Mr. Winkleman of the RAF and the German Democratic Republic.

Dick suppressed a grin--how incredibly complete was Mountie's penetration of the Kremlin's German-based terrorist organization!

Seated by Jim was the Soviet pilot of the Il-76, Colonel Izatov. His aircraft was already positioned at the airport.

Connie was introduced as Vice President of Marketing at Homboldt Trading. It was the first time Dick had heard her professional name, Ms. Consuela Ramierez. It brought back memories of another Ramierez family, who would be waiting to greet her at *Purple's* safe-house in the volcanic crater in the Philippines.

Dick nodded politely to acknowledge his introduction as Captain Edward Orden, a facilitator for Homboldt Trading.

As if to remind Consuela that she was *only* a woman, the

chauvinistic General complimented her beauty before turning the meeting over to her.

Consuela's command of the situation became immediately clear. Her strong, yet even, voice penetrated every corner of the large room as she demanded verification of every point of the contract she held before her: Had the representatives of the Ayatollah inspected all the weapons offered for sale? Were all the inspected weapons listed in the contract's inventory appendices? Did both parties agree to all provisions of the weapons-operability guarantee attached to the contract? Was the specified method of delivery agreeable to both parties?

Dick scanned the delivery section of his copy of the contract, while Consuela discussed it point-by-point. The Il-76 was capable of transporting all the purchased weapons on one flight (it's capacity was almost double that of a C-130). The flight route would be non-stop direct to Tehran. In addition to Colonel Izatov's four-man crew, each party would be allowed two unarmed representatives on the flight. The depot commander stated that Mr. Winkleman would be his only representative. Mirhashem responded that Abrahim and Captain Orden would be his representatives. Consuela respectfully informed Mirhashem that Captain Orden would indeed be on the flight, but he would be representing Homboldt.

Mirhashem and Abrahim conversed quietly for a moment. Then Mirhashem announced he reserved the right to add a second representative to be named later. The depot commander and Mirhashem verbally agreed with Consuela's ruling--the representative had to be named before ten the next morning, two hours before Colonel Izatov's planned takeoff.

Concluding her discussion of the contract, Consuela confirmed she had indeed received the advance payment of $27 million from Mirhashem. The currency was being jointly examined and counted by her two assistants, two of Mirhashem's assistants, and two depot accountants. She anticipated the task would be completed before midnight. The containers would be sealed and remain under guard at the depot, until her 6 a.m. departure for Zurich.

She invited the General and Mirhashem to assign representatives to accompany her and the two Homboldt security guards to the bank in Zurich. She explained, however, that it was important to limit the size of her group to facilitate border crossings. She further directed their attention to a paragraph in the contract, where Homboldt assumed full responsibility for the deposit of the money in the specified Swiss bank account.

That was good enough for the Czechs, who had dealt previously with Homboldt; but Mirhashem wanted a little added insurance. It was agreed that he would provide two armed guards to escort Ms. Ramierez. Dick wondered if that would be the Chechens? They needed to get that information as soon as possible, so Jim could pass it to Nelson on his Skyfone.

Dick got his opportunity after the meeting adjourned. Consuela excused herself to check on the money. Dick accepted the depot commander's invitation for a tour of the castle grounds. It couldn't have worked better. The tour group was composed of a guide, Dick, Jim, Abrahim, and Colonel Izatov. Jim conversed with the pilot about the capabilities of the Il-76, that allowed Dick to ask Abrahim the important questions.

"Did Shreeba come with you?"

"Yes, she seemed perhaps a little too eager to see you again," Abrahim grinned, "but that may be a good thing. Mirhashem's losing interest in her. She may soon become another of his suicide soldiers. As her dead brother's closest friend, I'm concerned about her welfare. A friendship with you might stabilize her situation."

"We live in two different worlds, but I'll do everything I can to help her. I know it's important for her to take Ali's body back to Palestine. Soon as this delivery is finished, I'll start work on that. Can you help me with the Middle East end?"

"Of course, if your connections take care of Israeli customs, I can arrange everything in the West Bank."

Dick thought briefly to his friendship with the IDF's General Meled. "There's a good chance I can do that. Where and when can we talk about this with Shreeba?"

"Would be a good topic for our six-hour flight tomorrow," said Abrahim. "I recommended to Mirhashem that Shreeba fly with us. He wanted to send one of his Chechens, but I think they should both accompany the money to Zurich."

"Do you think that's what Mirhashem will do?"

Abrahim smiled. "He told me to ask for your opinion."

"Well," Dick paused thoughtfully, "it would give Ms. Ramierez considerably more firepower. They'll be driving through Austria's nine-mile Voralberg Tunnel on the way to Zurich. It's a perfect place for an ambush."

Abrahim glanced darkly at Dick. "Allah be with us! You think that could happen?"

"Last year, it would have been a distinct possibility. This depot had bad security problems. However, the word now is that their new security supervisor, Mr. Winkleman, has plugged the leaks." Dick smiled at Abrahim. "That's another reason for you guys to deal through Homboldt. Their money guarantee is a good one. The Czechs believe it's worth the three-percent commission they pay."

They had finished the tour of the castle's gardens, where hundreds of rose bushes were budding in the warm spring sunshine. As they waited for transportation to the resort villa, Dick quietly informed Jim of his conversation with Abrahim. Within the hour, Max was showing Dick's photos of the Chechens and Consuela's bodyguards to Swiss officials in Zurich.

The depot commander had invited a dozen local officials to the villa to celebrate the occasion. The dinner was excellent, but it was obviously only a pretense to have a drunken party. After the dessert of apricots in chocolate, a troop of showgirls appeared to entertain the guests. Mirhashem whispered to Abrahim, who departed with Shreeba on his arm. Dick and Consuela paid their compliments to the depot commander and Mirhashem--there was work to do with the money and she required Dick's assistance. As they left the ballroom, Jim caught his *Purple* partner's eye and flashed him a casual smile.

They returned to the depot. Under the Chechens' watchful eyes, Consuela's bodyguards were bundling and packing the $100 bills in two suitcase-style fireproof cases marked "diplomatic pouch." The Counsel General's armored black limousine was driven into the space where they were working. They completed their task by locking the cases in special compartments built into the vehicle.

Consuela briefed them on arrival procedures for the Zurich bank. They would survey the area in the limousine, then the driver would let them out near the bank. Kondu and Kondo would walk two meters in front of Consuela, with the Chechens two meters behind. The roller-equipped cases would be chained to Consuela's wrists. The Chinese would enter the outer lobby and ignore her as she continued through to the inner lobby. The Chechens would remain outside the bank's entrance.

Consuela reminded her bodyguards not to enter the bank's inner lobby--hidden metal detectors were certain to detect their personal weapons. She instructed the Chechens to carefully monitor every-one entering the bank after her. They should not hesitate to delay any suspicious individuals, politely of course.

Her business in the bank would take about an hour. Once the money was deposited, and Consuela had returned to the limo, the Chechens would be free to continue with other tasks Mirhashem may have assigned them.

Consuela concluded by explaining it was Homboldt's custom to tip additional security guards $10,000 each for their services. She would have their money with her when she came out of the bank. That brought a hint of a cold smile to the Chechens' hard faces.

It was after eleven when Consuela and Dick returned to the villa. The sounds of a boisterous party echoed through the grounds.

"May I walk you to your room, *Ms. Ramierez?*" asked Dick.

"Actually, *Captain Orden,* I took the privilege of having my things moved to your room while we were working. I've had bad experiences with buyers and sellers who mistakenly considered me to be part of the deal. With Kondu and Kondo guarding the money, I need to call up the retired reserves. You're available, aren't you?"

"For you, . . . forever," murmured Dick.

She gripped his hand tightly. They strolled down the garden walkway to Dick's room. In a darkened area, where trees sheltered them from the lights, she stopped. "Does that *forever* mean this is the last time for Lady Consuela and her White Knight?"

He took her trembling body in his arms. Tears began to erase the stern professional look that had encased her face all day.

"One day at a time, Connie." Dick paused and tried to hold back his own tears, but failed.

They lay on the bed, side-by-side, immersed in deep thought. Their sorrow in the garden had turned to white-hot passion in the room, as they re-lived precious moments of their friendship.

During a brief rest, Dick had described Max's appearance and explained *Purple's* plan for whisking her away from Zurich and on to the Philippines.

When she asked if they would see each other again, he had whispered: "There are drugs now that could make anyone tell their most precious secrets. If *anybody* knows your new identity, or location, it would be subject to compromise. Tomorrow you'll be taking a hell of a risk--for a world that is not deserving of you. Your courage will bring down the worst of the terrorists. Don't take any more chances, Sweetheart. Enjoy the life you've earned. You'll have the money to make things happen. The new Consuela can go wherever she wants and meet whomever she desires--that includes old fighter pilots. Go slow. Think it through carefully."

"One day at a time," she echoed.

"One kiss at a time," he replied, tenderly drawing her body to his--perhaps for the last time.

Dick checked his watch again. By his rough calculations, they should be over the northwestern border of Iran. The interception by the Mirage should occur during the next half hour.

He was seated with Abrahim and Shreeba in the galley area of the Il-76, behind a bulkhead that screened the flight deck. To their right was a comfortable sleeping room built into the side of the fuselage. To their left were two airliner-style toilets. Patterned after the C-141, the Candid had been designed to carry troops. However, it was adaptable to hauling large quantities of military hardware.

They had spent the first hour of the flight discussing the movement of Ali's body from Vienna to Palestine. Then they talked about the possibility of separating Shreeba from Mirhashem, without endangering her. As evidenced by the dark bruise on the side of her face, he had abused her after last night's bout of heavy drinking. When Dick voiced the thought of Abrahim also leaving Mirhashem, the Palestinian passionately informed him that his devotion was to the Palestinian cause, not to Mirhashem. However, at this time, service with Mirhashem was the best opportunity he had to inflict serious damage on his Zionist enemies.

The conversation had run its course. The three of them were now resting quietly in the comfortable seats.

Dick was toying with the idea of putting Abrahim to sleep with one of Nelson's special cigarettes. If something went wrong, it would reduce the odds against he and Jim. As he reached for the case in his jacket pocket, he received three sharp jolts from the chip in his right shoulder. The emergency signal could only have been relayed via satellite from Nelson in Frankfurt. It prompted Dick's immediate decision to give Abrahim a rest.

He opened the case and placed his fingers over the cigarettes so Abrahim would have to choose one of the four *specials*. He leaned across the dozing Shreeba and offered him a smoke.

Abrahim took a cigarette, as he had already done a couple times earlier in the flight. Dick returned the case to his pocket and leaned over to light Abrahim's cigarette, carefully holding the lighter so the knockout gas would not be expelled.

Abrahim smiled his thanks, took a deep drag, and leaned back in his seat. A few seconds later, his head sagged to his chest. Dick locked Abrahim's shoulder harness, extinguished the cigarette, and went into one of the toilets. Shreeba was still sleeping.

In the toilet, Dick spoke into a towel, transmitting through the chip in his shoulder to the monitor-relay in the satellite high over-head: "Nelson, if you read me, give me a single beep." He was answered with a sharp jolt in his shoulder. Dick's next transmission was: "Do you want Jim to call you?" The affirmative signal came immediately through the chip.

Dick left the toilet, crossed in front of the sleeping Abrahim and Shreeba, and strolled casually forward to the spacious flight deck. Jim was in a jump seat, centered behind the pilot and copilot seats.

The communicator and navigator stations were located in the protruding nose-bubble below the flight deck. Dick glanced down the ladder. They were busy with electronic equipment, neither looked up.

Dick stood behind Jim, slowly stretched his body, and leaned forward to ask: "Are we there yet?"

The copilot glanced over his shoulder and returned Dick's smile. "Another couple hours, Sir," he answered in perfect English. "Will that be enough time for you and the young lady?"

Dick laughed. "Guess I'm not her type. She only has eyes for the Colonel."

The Russian pilot looked over his shoulder. His eyes were bloodshot, he was still feeling the effects of last night. The copilot had been at the controls for takeoff and most of the mission.

The Colonel responded in broken English: "This hero of Soviet Union would gladly honor her with membership in our club."

Dick chuckled. "I'll tell her about your offer, Colonel Izatov."

As he turned away, Dick whispered to Jim: "Call home."

The Canadian Mountie responded with a quick glance.

Dick returned to the galley and checked Abrahim's pulse. It was almost back to normal.

Jim walked past and entered one of the toilets. Dick sat by the sleeping Shreeba and waited for Jim to complete his call to Nelson. It didn't take long.

They stood by the coffee pot and discussed the situation. "The satellite's jamming equipment and communications relay have failed," whispered Jim. "Nelson won't be able to broadcast the warning about an air raid over Tehran, and the Mirage is only a couple minutes from intercept." He glanced at Abrahim. "What's wrong with him? Why's his head hanging down like that?"

"Too many cigarettes," said Dick. "What should we do now?"

"We have to act fast. Our only option is to take the plane."

"Can you fly this thing?"

"Of course. It's almost identical to the C-141, and I've spent the last four hours studying the controls. Good job on Abrahim. Got a plan for the crew?"

Shreeba woke up, rose from her seat, and joined them at the coffee pot.

Dick grinned. "Here's the answer to getting Izatov out of his seat. I'll take care of him while he's in the sleeping room with Shreeba. You offer the rest of the boys a cigarette."

"Copilot doesn't smoke," said Jim.

"Then you'll have to take him with the knockout gas. Got your lighter?"

"Certainly. Let's get moving. I'm going back to my seat. Instruct Shreeba and send her forward as soon as possible."

Jim took two cups of coffee and left for the flight deck.

Shreeba noticed Abrahim's hanging head and went quickly to him. She tried to wake him.

Dick gently took her wrist. "Trust me, Shreeba, he's okay. He's going to sleep for the next five hours. By the time he wakes, you'll be free--but you need to help us now."

She looked apprehensively at Dick. He explained: "I want you to go to the flight deck and whisper to Colonel Izatov that you're ready to join his club."

"What does that mean?"

"It means you want to have sex with him."

Shreeba was startled. "Here? Now?"

"Over there, in the sleeping compartment," said Dick. "Don't worry, there's no lock on the door. Keep him busy for thirty seconds, and I'll take care of everything."

He showed her the lighter. "When you see me bending over him with this, scream! Then cover your nose, close your eyes, and hold your breath."

Dick impulsively took her in his arms. "You'll be okay, Sweetie. I promise."

She was trembling. "How far must I go with him?"

He held her at arms length. "Not far! Lie on the bed and open your blouse. Your beautiful bosom will be the last thing he sees for about five hours, . . . and he'll never forget it."

Shreeba returned Dick's grin. "When do I start?"

"Right now. He's sitting in the right seat. Lean over his shoulder so your breast touches him, tell him you want to join his club, wait for him to get up, then go to the sleeping room. He'll be right behind you."

Shreeba took a deep breath and left for the flight deck. Dick positioned himself in the seat next to Abrahim, leaning forward to hide the Palestinian's hanging head.

It wasn't necessary. In less than a minute, Shreeba was walking from the cockpit to the sleeping compartment. The Colonel's hands were on her hips, his eyes were fixed on her curvy bottom.

Izatov closed the door behind them. Dick checked his watch and waited thirty seconds. Then he rose quickly, checked the lighter for proper positioning in his hand, stepped to the door, and paused to take a deep breath.

In the cockpit, Jim had received permission to sit in the pilot's seat. Conversing in Russian, he was asking the friendly copilot about landing procedures.

He leaned back and casually offered him a cigarette. When he declined, Jim rose and descended the short ladder into the nose-bubble. He offered his cigarette case to the navigator. There were only four cigarettes in the case.

The navigator accepted eagerly. He and the communicator were lighting up when they heard the scream from the sleeping compartment.

The communicator laughed and said in Russian. "Sounds like the Colonel's coming through again."

"Yeah," smiled the navigator, "save a cigarette for him. He'll need it."

A second later, the navigator fell out of his seat. The communicator tried to catch him, but he also fell to the floor.

Jim climbed the ladder back to the flight deck. He slid into the right seat, and the copilot turned to speak with him. The blast of knockout gas from Jim's lighter caught him directly in the face. He gasped and clutched his throat with both hands, then his body slumped forward against the shoulder harness.

Fortunately, the Il-76 was on autopilot.

Dick appeared behind the copilot, unstrapped him, lifted him out of the seat, and laid him on the floor of the flight deck.

Jim turned to the disheveled Shreeba. She was standing behind Dick, buttoning her blouse. "Honey, two cigarettes are burning on the floor near the bottom of that ladder. Would you go down there and step on them, but don't pick them up."

Jim made an adjustment to the autopilot. Then he moved to the left seat and put on the communications headset. "Care to join me, Brown Bear. We're about to become members of the hero of the Soviet Union's flying club."

Shreeba had stomped out the last of Nelson's special cigarettes and heard Jim's remark as she was coming up the ladder. "I've had enough of Soviet Union clubs!"

Dick laughed. "Not to worry, pretty girl. May I introduce you to my partner, Jim Conrad of the Royal Canadian Mounted Police and former exchange pilot with England's Royal Air Force. Colonel Conrad, may I present Shreeba--born of the hot Palestinian sun and the Princess of the Bath."

Shreeba's laugh lit her pixie face and her brown eyes shone. "Thank you, Sir. I am pleased to meet you, Colonel." Then she frowned. "Shouldn't we do something with those guys? They are not going to be happy when they wake up."

Jim grinned at her enthusiasm. "That won't be soon, Princess, but maybe you'd like to bind their wrists. There's a couple rolls of tape under the seat where Dick was sitting."

"Dick?" she asked.

"Yes," replied Jim. "May I introduce Captain Dick Williams, U.S. Navy fighter pilot extraordinaire."

Shreeba put her arms around Dick and kissed him hotly on the lips. She drew back and said coyly: "Pleased to meet you, Sir."

In that instant, a missile flashed by the left side of the Il-76. Shreeba screamed. Jim spoke sharply: "Get us on Big Brother frequency, Bear! Let's hope that was the Mirage."

"Give me your Skyfone. I'll have to get an unscrambled frequency from Nelson."

Dick went to the communicator's seat, made the Skyfone call to Nelson, and a few seconds later was transmitting: "Big Brother, this is Brown Bear. How do you read? Over."

The AWACS' response was immediate: "Loud and clear, Brown Bear. What are you doing on this frequency?"

"Mountie and I are in control of Santa, but we don't have a scrambler. Was that Nail who fired at us?"

"Affirmative, Santa. Wait one while I get the others up on this frequency. Use caution, this is a non-secure frequency."

"Santa, wilco."

The radio was silent for a few seconds, then: "Santa, this is Nail. Only a half-hearted attempt, Brown Bear, otherwise you'd be minus a tail. Check your nine o'clock, about three thousand feet."

Jim peered out the left side of the Il-76. "Roger, Nail. Santa has a visual. Welcome aboard."

"Santa, this is Sledge. We're at your three o'clock, about four miles. Can we join the party?"

"Sledge, this is Big Brother. Roger your last. You are cleared to join."

Dick returned to the flight deck and took the copilot's seat. He watched as the F-14 and two EA-6B's completed their rendezvous.

"Santa, this is Big Brother. Understand you have been notified that primary jamming is not available."

"Santa, roger. What does it look like to you, Pouncer."

"This is Pouncer One. We are making it difficult for them, but primary threat radio indicates they've been tracking our flight for the last five minutes. They'll be painting us as we proceed south."

"Big Brother concurs. Standby for a change of plan from higher authority."

Jim turned to Dick and gave him a thumbs-up signal. He was confident Nelson would have the magic answers for them.

"Nail, this is Big Brother. Stay on Santa's wing until we confirm primary threat radar has you on their gadget, then Big Brother will vector you to Mosul."

"Nail, wilco."

Jim looked at Dick. "He's talking about Tabriz radar, right?"

"Yeah, they're trying to make the Iranians believe we're Iraqis."

The radio was crackling again: "Sledge, Big Brother. Keep the Pouncers with you and vector one-seven-zero for the primary threat. When you're within range, the Pouncers are cleared to fire. Radar has priority. Save one missile for your RTB. Use the others to shut down radio communications."

"Sledge, wilco."

"Pouncers, wilco."

The USS *Kitty Hawk's* Iranian-painted F-14 waggled its wings and pealed away from the Il-76, with the EA-6B's in close trail.

"Thanks, Sledge," transmitted Dick.

"See you at happy hour, Brown Bear," replied CAG Bender.

"Santa, Big Brother, your vector is one-eight-five."

Jim glanced at Dick. "They have to knock out Tabriz radar before we land, or the Ayatollah will know exactly where to look for Toufani."

Dick nodded. "Pouncer One, Santa. How soon can you take out that radar."

"Pouncer One, estimate firing range in eighteen minutes."

"Santa, rog. That's cutting it kind of close. Could you make it fifteen?"

"Sledge here. That's affirmative. Let's push it up, Pouncers."

"Nail, Big Brother. You are cleared to detach. Vector two-four-zero."

"Nail, wilco. Got a couple missiles left. Anything around here to shoot at?"

"Negative, Nail. You're the only flight activity we've had in the area since noon."

The Iraqi-painted Mirage did a victory roll in front of the Il-76 and broke away toward the southwest.

"Thanks, Nail," acknowledge Jim, then he turned again to Dick:

"Tell Nelson to have an expert on this aircraft standing by. We may need help."

Dick nodded and picked up the Skyfone.

The cockpit switches and instruments were labeled in Russian, but that was no challenge to Jim Conrad. He had also observed all the procedures since the copilot started the aircraft at the airport near Brno. The weather at Lake Urmia was reported clear, and he was confident he could safely stop on the six thousand-foot strip.

They were descending through 5,000 meters when the radio came alive.

"Heads up, Sledge. Pouncer Two has rays hot at twelve o'clock!"

"Not supposed to be any damned missiles here," swore the CAG. "Cleared to fire, Pouncer Two. Take 'em out!"

"Missiles airborne, dead ahead!" shouted Pouncer One.

"Sledge, tallyho on a salvo of three. Breaking right. I'll lead 'em away. You guys hammer that site."

"Pouncer Two, locked on the SAM radar. Firing number one!"

"Pouncer One, roger. Locked on air control radar and firing number one."

In the excitement, the F-14 RIO keyed the mike instead of the intercom and broadcast: "Break left, Sledge. The first SAM has us locked up."

"Pouncer Two concurs!" screamed the Electronic Countermeasures Officer in the EA-6B. "Take him hard down and to the left, Sledge. . . . Ah damn! Look at that fireball!"

"Pouncer One. Locked on early warning radar and firing number two. . . . Get your nose up, Sledge. If you read me, get your nose up. Pull up! Pull up!"

It was a long couple seconds before Dick and Mountie heard the next transmission: "Did you shut 'em down, Pouncer?"

"Affirmative, Sledge. All radar's quiet. Should we use our last weapon on their communications?"

"No, save it for the flight home. Come up here and see how many holes I have."

"Pouncer One, wilco. You're not streaming anything. Be right there."

Jim pointed at the windscreen and gave Dick a thumbs-up.

Dick nodded: "Big Brother, this is Santa. We are through two thousand meters and have the field in sight. Do you have contact with Moon River?"

"Big Brother, affirmative. He's on a scrambled frequency. Stay with us on this frequency. We'll relay."

"Santa, concur. Ask him if the runway's okay, and tell him to give us a green flare or smoke when we're cleared to land."

"Big Brother, wilco."

Jim called over his shoulder: "Okay, Dick, standby to give me a hand. Keep your eyes open. We'll make a circle to check for vehicles in the area."

Dick stared intently through the windscreen. The western edge of the airfield bordered Lake Urmia. The lake was low, two or three miles of dry bed were exposed. Only two roads led to the field. The southern road reached into an expanse of barren hills that appeared deserted. The road to the east went into a small village about five miles away. Dick saw two trucks in its center.

Jim banked the Il-76 into a leisurely turn around the airstrip. Trucks and trailers were parked at the east end of the runway. They were soon rewarded with a green flare soaring into the sky.

"Santa, Big Brother. Moon River reports the wind calm. Use the northern half of the runway."

"Santa, roger. Tell Moon River there are a couple trucks in a village eight klicks to the east."

Jim flew over the lake. "We'll make our approach from the west, Dick. It will save a few minutes when we don't have to taxi back down the runway."

"Okay, Mountie. Can you stop this thing in six thousand feet?"

"I did it in the C-141, and this is the Soviet's copy of that bird. Would you believe those brazen bastards made engineering plans from a U.S. Air Force display at the Paris Air Show? Even stole pieces of the skin to duplicate the material."

"Santa, this is Big Brother. Moon River reports the vehicles in the village are friendly. I'll remain on this frequency, and monitor Moon River, until we vector Night Rider."

"Santa, roger. Thanks. Looks like sundown in about an hour."

"Big Brother, concur. We'll be here for you."

Admiral Toufani hadn't aged a day since their meeting near Mt.

Ararat four years earlier. He was in superb physical condition. His *Omar Sharif* face was handsome and clean shaven.

He greeted Dick with a hearty handshake. "Thanks for dropping by, Captain."

Dick grinned. "Once every four years, whether you're home or not. Admiral, I'd like you to meet my partner, Jim Conrad. He's the guy who stopped that forty metric tons of hardware in only six thousand feet."

"A pleasure to meet you, Mr. Conrad. It was indeed a beautiful landing. I'm sorry we didn't have the runway in such great shape."

"I imagine the nearest bulldozer's over a hundred kilometers from here, Admiral," replied Jim. "Your people must have worked long hours to repair the Iraqi bomb damage with their hands. Please thank them for us."

Toufani gestured at the off-loading activity, which was in full swing. "They're being amply rewarded. With all that technology, we'll take our battle against the Ayatollahs to a higher level."

Mackenzie stepped into the tent. "Hello Wilbur and Orville! Seems you guys can fly everything."

Dick grinned. "If you have the box that thing came in, Jim will fly it home."

"If we had the box, maybe that's where we could hide it," said Mackenzie. "The Admiral's not too eager to blow it where it sits. The Iranian's run a photo-recce flight by here on a regular basis, looking for Iraqi patrols. If they see wreckage on this deserted strip, they'll investigate. That could turn into pure hell for the villages along the road to the east."

Jim nodded his head. "We understand and agree, Admiral. The Il-76 must be flown out of here."

"What are your options, Sir?" asked Toufani.

"Rather limited," said Dick. "Only three persons could get it back in the air: those two Russians sleeping it off in the plane, or this former RAF-exchange pilot."

"How soon could the Russians be fit to fly?" asked Mackenzie.

Jim glanced at his watch. "They swore-off smoking one hour and thirty minutes ago. They should wake up in another three and a half hours."

". . . but they'll be a little hung-over," added Dick.

Toufani chuckled. "Like you were the morning you had to brief the Shah, after we'd been out-on-the-town in Tehran."

"Yes Sir," nodded Dick, "somewhat out of focus, but capable of keeping the wings level."

"Could they make a night takeoff," asked Mackenzie, "with truck lights marking the edge of the runway?"

"They would need more time to sober up," said Jim. "Probably have to wait until first-light."

". . . and they would be able to mark this field for Khomeini later!" added Mackenzie.

"Yeah," agreed Dick. "The Russians don't seem to be a viable option. If they crashed on takeoff, we'd have visible wreckage for Iranian aerial reconnaissance. If we waited long enough for them to be safe, they'd have Iranian paratroopers raining down around here before the Admiral could make it back to the mountains."

"So, what's the answer?" asked the SAS mission coordinator. "What are our options with Mountie--other than a one-way trip to Tehran?"

Jim walked to the door of the tent and stared into the setting sun. "If we get the Soviets out of here before they wake up, they'll have no idea where they were; and, if the Il-76 crashes somewhere other than here, it would disguise the Admiral's location."

Dick looked at his partner. "Are you suggesting we take off while they're asleep, then bail out? That would solve the Admiral's problem, but it wouldn't do much to discredit Mirhashem. It would only look like another aircraft accident; unless the crash occurred where investigators could discover the weapons were missing."

"Here's what I'm thinking," said Jim. "About an hour before they regain consciousness, I take off with Abrahim and the Soviets. I circle around and bail out over the field--with the autopilot set for a steady climb toward Tehran. The aircraft has enough fuel for three hours. The pilots will wake up before they're over Tehran."

"There's no way to close the para-drop door after *we* jump," reminded Dick. "Without cabin pressurization, you'd have to set the autopilot to level off around twelve thousand feet. Otherwise they would never wake up."

"Yeah, you're right," nodded Jim, "but they'd still have enough fuel to make Tehran with an hour remaining."

"What kind of silk would you daredevils be using for this air show?" asked Mackenzie. "The Admiral doesn't have parachutes.

You can't use the one I came here with, I tore the canopy in a tree when I landed."

"I saw five or six on a rack in the Candid," said Dick. "They looked like the old backpacks we used in our T-28's."

"I'll only need one good one," said Jim.

Dick laughed. "No way! A takeoff on a blacked-out runway--in a plane loaded with Russians that may wake up at any time--and a terrorist who will be mad as hell when he does--that's too much for one man to handle, even if he is a Royal Canadian Mountie."

"Bear's right," agreed Mackenzie. "As mission commander, I'm taking the decision to launch both of you." He looked at his watch. "Let's shoot for takeoff at twenty-thirty hours. Admiral, can your people have the weapons off-loaded by then?"

"Without doubt!" confirmed the anti-Khomeini guerrilla leader.

"Great! Jim and Dick, check your passengers and concentrate on putting your air show together. I'll coordinate Night Rider's flight with Big Brother. Let's meet back here in one hour."

"Dinner will be waiting," said Toufani.

"Not necessary, Sir," answered Dick quickly.

"The person preparing it might do me bodily harm if you don't eat. The last time she cooked for you, it was only a rib of lamb over an open fire. She has promised to do better this time."

It was a tasty meal of *kebbe* (lamb and wheat). They sat on weapons crates in the spacious tent. Admiral Toufani's lovely wife wore a fatigue uniform like her husband's. Lieutenant Hakeem took a moment from the weapons off-load to present his and Iris's three-year-old son. The bright young lad had the fine chiseled features of his mother and the engaging smile of his father.

Shreeba had eagerly assisted with the preparation of the meal. She and Iris became immediate friends. It was Iris's first opportunity in four years to speak English, and she was enjoying Shreeba's company. They were bonding quickly.

However, there was precious little time for socializing. Except for the small child, whose loving ways were stealing Shreeba's heart, everyone understood it was necessary to discuss business during the meal.

Jim asked Mackenzie, "Do you have an ETA on Night Rider?"

"Yes. Big Brother didn't hold any airborne traffic between his launch point and our location. He should be here in about an hour. The weather is forecast to remain clear, but the wind may pick up. Admiral, will you have the weapons out of sight before sunrise?"

"With our ten trucks and five trailers, we'll have most of the equipment hidden in the village. We have some large camouflage tarps, from your '82 drop, to cover the rest."

"We'll be leap-frogging back into the mountains," explained Hakeem. "Moving only at night, from village to village."

"I'm surprised you have so much freedom-of-action in this area," said Dick.

Hakeem smiled. "Our fighters are very popular throughout these northern mountains. The Ayatollahs have deployed most of their soldiers to the Iraqi front, and have left this section open. If their reconnaissance detects some perceived threat, they send para-troopers in a C-130. We have lured them into ambushes, and their deployments are now few and far between. We've protected thousands of the inhabitants in this area from the Ayatollahs' cruelty, and they love us."

"Four years ago you had fifty fighters," remembered Dick. "Has that number grown?"

"Mightily," answered Toufani, his steel-gray eyes blazing. "We have over twenty-five hundred men under arms. Your project to disinherit Mirhashem will allow us to send a selected few into the heavily populated areas. These weapons will be put to good use. We will take our struggle for freedom to Khomeini's doorstep."

"Sir," began Shreeba, "may I speak?"

"At any time," smiled Toufani's wife. "We are an army of lib-erated Muslims, who value the contribution of women, whether with rifles or sewing needles. Our view of equality has been a strong point for winning people to our side."

"Thank you," said Shreeba. "I would like to speak for one of the captives being held in the aircraft."

Mackenzie looked sharply at her, but the brave girl continued: "Abrahim, the friend of my dead brother Ali, is one of the most courageous and well-trained soldiers in the world--to do the work in the cities as you described."

"He's also Mirhashem's right hand," growled Mackenzie.

"I know Abrahim's heart," continued Shreeba defiantly. "His loyalty is to his dead family, not to Mirhashem. If you leave him on the plane to Tehran, he will again fall under the spell of Mirhashem--and be sent on a suicide mission to atone for the loss of the weapons. Give him a chance to fight here, Admiral. He will not disappoint you."

"Our fight is not against the Jewish state," cautioned Toufani. "It's against the tyranny of the Ayatollahs. What assurance would I have that he would not turn against me?"

"You would have me, Sir." Shreeba stood in front of the guerrilla leader with lowered eyes. "I will stay here with Abrahim. If he betrays you, I shall kill him and then you may kill me, . . . or do as you like with me."

Toufani's wife gripped his hand. He replied: "Child, such drastic measures would never apply in our dream of an Iran free of radical Islamists. Captain Williams, do you vouch for this young lady?"

Dick met Shreeba's eyes for a moment, then shifted to Iris. "Four years ago, I tried to force a young woman to turn from your life to that of the western world. I realize now I was mistaken. Shreeba's loyalty to her friends is beyond question. Her courageous desire for a life away from Mirhashem is why his weapons are now in your hands. I know Abrahim to be an educated and honorable man, deserving of a better life than as an assassin for Mirhashem. He has trained to fight against a state propped-up by the White House. Your fight is also against a state now supported militarily by the White House. It seems to be a similar situation. What do you say, Mac? You're the mission commander."

"Bear, in six years I've never known you to misjudge a person. Of course, you're the one that will have to explain it to Nelson."

Dick smiled and rubbed his right shoulder. "I think I already have." He glanced at his watch. "It's eight o'clock. We had better off-load Abrahim and check our parachutes."

Hakeem asked Jim, "How many lights do you want by the runway, Sir?"

"Only a few. Put a truck on each side near the middle. Same setup at the west end. Parking lights only. Leave them off until we turn the aircraft around for takeoff. After we're airborne, leave on the lights at the end. We'll use them as a reference for bailout."

Hakeem and Shreeba removed the unconscious Abrahim from the aircraft. Dick peeled the tape from the wrists of the navigator and the communicator and strapped them in their seats. He dragged the pilot from the sleeping compartment, laid him on the cockpit floor beside the copilot, and removed the tape from their wrists. He checked the pulse of each member of the crew. All were as close to normal as could be expected while under the influence of Nelson's drugs.

Jim appeared on the flight deck with two of the backpack parachutes. "These seem to be in fairly good condition, Dick. The tags say they were repacked last month."

"Let's hope it was done correctly. Did you set the altitude-differential bomb?"

"Yeah. While I was going through the pilot's flight bag, I saw the orders for their return flight from Tehran. They're to transport one of the Ayatollahs and ten members of his staff to Moscow. Based on that information, I've set it to explode the second time this bird descends through three thousand meters."

"You think Izatov will wake up in time to land at Tehran?"

"Not sure. He's not in good physical condition. The drug will last longer on him, but I'm certain the copilot will be wide awake before they're over the city. Watch him carefully while I'm getting this thing in the air."

Jim continued: "You'll have to be in the right seat to help me with switches for start and takeoff. We'll leave the para-drop door open, so it will be noisier than hell in here. I'll turn north after takeoff. When I give you the signal, strap the pilot in your seat, put a headset on him, set the radio on Tehran tower frequency, and turn up the volume. We'll reverse course in two minutes, to fly back over the field. I'll set the autopilot and get out of the seat. We'll strap the copilot in and put his headset on. Then we'll put on our chutes and head for the door. Make sure your flashlight's in your pocket before you jump. Blink your light on the way down."

Dick checked the flashlight and .38 Special revolver he had borrowed from Hakeem.

"When's the last time you jumped, Bear?"

"I've never been stupid enough to jump out of a perfectly good aircraft. My last bailout drill was thirty years ago at Whiting Field, but it's only been five years since I drifted down from Aura."

Jim glanced at his watch. "It's eight-thirty. Let's get this thing in the air and turn it over to our sleeping beauties."

It was extremely dark. Jim pointed the nose of the Il-76 between the truck lights at mid-field and the lights at the far end. He aligned the compass and spoke to Dick on the intercom: "Will be an instrument takeoff, Bear. Give me half-flaps. With this westerly wind and cool air, we should be airborne a thousand feet past mid-field."

"Roger, we have half-flaps."

"Okay, going full power. Check the gauges for me."

"Roger. Temp, RPM, fuel flow look good."

Jim released the brakes, the powerful Il-76 thundered forward. The roar of the engines was incredibly loud. Dick remembered the last time he'd heard that roar. The critically injured Rita was being flown out of Manila in a C-141. He fought his emotions and focused on the takeoff.

Jim rotated the big transport's nose as they passed the truck lights at mid-field, and they were airborne.

"Gear up. Give me one-quarter flaps, Bear."

They continued on course for thirty seconds, then Jim reduced power and began an easy right turn.

"Okay, Bear, start strapping in the heroes of Soviet aviation."

When Jim rolled out on a heading of north, Dick already had Colonel Izatov strapped in the right seat; with his headset on and tuned to Tehran tower.

Climbing through 700 meters, Jim began the right turn back to the field. Dick made one last check around the cockpit. After Jim rolled wings level, it took him a few seconds to engage the autopilot for a gradual climb to 3,500 meters.

Dick had a headset on the copilot. They quickly strapped him in the left seat. The cockpit noise was deafening. They donned their chutes and checked each other in the red light of the cockpit. Jim leaned over to actuate the switch for the troop compartment red lights. Dick followed him closely as they made their way aft.

Jim paused in front of the open door and reminded Dick of the proper position for arms and legs during free-fall. He flashed a boyish smile, turned, and dove gracefully out the door. Dick followed without hesitation, but not very gracefully!

It was a relief to be away from the roar of the engines. They had jumped at about five thousand feet. There was only time to stabilize the free-fall, take a quick but unsuccessful look for the truck lights, and pull the rip cord.

Dick's chute opened quickly. The shooting pain in his neck reminded him of the bone spurs growing in his cervical vertebra.

There was no moon, but the stars in the clear heavens helped him get oriented. He peered intently at the ground, but could not see the truck lights. He pulled out his flashlight and began blinking its red beam downwards.

Thankfully, there was a visible horizon. Then he realized he was coming down on the dry lake bed.

He put the flashlight in his pocket and bent his knees to soften the landing. The ground rushed up to meet him. He didn't pick up the drift from the rising breeze, and was slammed backwards onto the hard surface. The pain from the ruptured disc in his lower back was paralyzing. He quickly opened the chest and leg buckles. The billowing canopy pulled the harness from his body.

He lay on his back, gasping for breath in the eerie silence. Then his ears picked up the sound of the Il-76 fading in the distance. The intense pain in his vertebrae was making him nauseous. He heard the engine of a truck, rolled on his side, and waved his flashlight in that direction. The truck stopped, the doors slammed. He continued to wave the flashlight. The truck engine started again. It was coming his way. He tried to stand up but passed out from the pain.

He blinked his eyes and focused on Shreeba's pixie face. "Welcome back, Captain."

He rose on his elbows and stared at his feet. Thankfully, they moved. He was lying on a stretcher in the big tent.

"Everything still connected, Yank?" asked Mackenzie.

"Yeah, I guess so. Did Night Rider show?"

"That is affirmative. We're ready to load you in his Sea King. Unless you can make it on your own?"

Dick twisted his body painfully and sat up. "I can do that."

The stocky Mackenzie helped him to his feet.

"Give me a moment alone with Shreeba," said Dick.

"Make it quick, Bear. I'll wait outside with the others."

Dick unbuttoned his breast pocket and took out the golden cigarette case. "I have a special present for the Princess of the Bath."

Shreeba smiled. "You know I don't smoke, Captain, but I am delighted to have a gift from you."

He turned the case over and pointed at the engraving on the

back. "These are the numbers of your account in the National Bank of Switzerland, on Schlüsselstrasse in Zurich. The account was opened earlier today with a deposit of one million U.S. dollars. I took the liberty of lifting your fingerprints from a glass in a Vienna hotel room. They are on file at the bank. You need only show up there with this number, let them compare your fingerprints, and do whatever you will with the money. Oh yeah, if you ever want to change your identity, or need help, dial the numbers of your account backwards into any telephone in Frankfurt, use the code name *Princess,* and someone will meet you."

Tears were streaming down her cheeks. She clasped the case to her bosom. "May Allah be with you, Captain. I praise the day you came into my life."

He smiled. "It wasn't a day, Shreeba. It was a night in a Turkish bath, and you were the sexiest girl I'd ever seen."

A grin broke through her tears. ". . . and all I wanted was to have your son."

"Big Brother, this is Night Rider. We are airborne. Climbing through three hundred feet over Lake Urmia."

"Big Brother, roger. Hold you on my gadget. Your steer is two-seven-two degrees, one hundred and seventy kilometers to home plate. Higher authority requests your number of souls on board."

"Roger, Big Brother," replied Jimmie. "I have a crew of three; plus Moon River, Mountie, and Brown Bear--but there's not a bloody soul amongst us."

The AWACS controller laughed. "Roger that."

The Sea King had been modified for combat rescue missions. In addition to pilot and copilot, the crew included a passive ECM operator. There were 20mm M-61 Gatling guns, equipped with night vision, mounted in bubbles on the sides of the forward fuselage. Jim Conrad and Colonel Mackenzie were manning those positions. Dick was on a canvas rack in the troop compartment, with a flight helmet and lip mike to monitor communications.

"Moon River, this is Big Brother with a flight advisory. We are monitoring Tehran control. They have launched a C-130 to repair the damage at Tabriz. They have also put up two F-14 escorts."

"Moon River, roger," answered Mackenzie. "Do you hold Santa on your gadget?"

"Big Brother, affirmative. He is two hundred kilometers north-west of Tehran, at angels eleven, but they haven't seen him yet."

"Has Santa made any course deviations?" asked Dick.

"Big Brother, negative. With his present course, and current wind conditions, he will pass twenty miles west of Tehran airport."

"Nice work, Mountie," said Dick on the intercom. "If Colonel Izatov doesn't sleep in, they will be in time for a night cap with Khomeini and Mirhashem."

"Moon River, Big Brother. The F-14's have Santa on their radars. Tehran control has detached one to investigate. The other's sticking with the C-130."

"Moon River, roger. Keep us advised."

It was very noisy in the Sea King's troop compartment. Dick tightened his helmet strap to shut out some of the engines' roar. The dim red glow reminded him of his rescue from the Philippine Sea, after Aura One was shot down. He and Rita had been hoisted, dripping wet, into the Wessex by Joe Tashki. His mind wanted desperately to cling to that moment, but the radio traffic forced him to focus on the present.

"Moon River, Big Brother. Be advised the lead F-14 has you on his radar. He is requesting permission to detach from the C-130 and investigate."

"What's his range?" asked Mackenzie.

"He is two hundred and ten kilometers southwest of you."

The ECM officer spoke on the intercom: "Jimmie, I'm picking up his radar signature. They really have their blooming sets tuned these days."

"Yeah," grunted Dick. "Wonder if Mr. President sent a factory rep to do that for them."

"Could be," replied the ECM officer. "I'm picking up evidence that he has a bloody Phoenix on board."

"Damn!" roared Mackenzie on the intercom. "How far can he shoot that thing, Dick?"

"Our guys like to get within a hundred klicks. If he has a bright target, it's good farther than that."

"This is Big Brother. The F-14 is at two hundred kilometers. Tehran has directed him to investigate. Be advised there have been heated transmissions during the last hour. They are mad as hell that someone shot up Tabriz radar. I'm sure they will give that yo-yo clearance to fire, if he can acquire you."

"Night Rider, understand. I'm going to dim our return. We are heading for the deck." Jimmie switched to intercom. "Colonel, do you concur?"

"Certainly," replied Mackenzie.

"If you want to lose that bastard completely," interrupted Dick, "land this bird and shut it down. The F-14's pulse doppler radar can only see motion."

"What do you say, Jimmie?" asked Mackenzie.

"Sir, I barely got this thing started back at the lake, and we're at bingo fuel."

"Okay," said Mackenzie, "take it lower. See if we can lose him. Keep your eyes peeled for a hill to hide behind."

"Roger that! Lots of hills here, with tall trees that eat rotor blades, especially in the dark."

"Send the copilot down to this gun," directed Mackenzie. "I'll join you with these night vision goggles."

"On the way, Sir!" replied the copilot.

"This is Big Brother. Maximum confusion at Tehran Control. The other F-14 has identified Santa as the Il-76 that's been missing for three hours. They are trying to figure that out, . . . and ignoring the lead F-14's requests to fire at you."

"God bless the bloody bureaucracies," said Mackenzie, "wherever they may be."

"Big Brother, Night Rider is descending through three hundred feet. You still hold me?"

"You are fading, Night Rider. The F-14 is now at one hundred and fifty kilometers."

"What's he saying about us?"

"He is requesting clearance to fire. Tehran control is telling him to report acquisition."

The ECM officer interrupted on the intercom: "Jimmie, he is locked on. His signal is very strong."

"Come a little left, Jimmie," advised Mackenzie calmly. "Let's get over that ridge and find a swale to hide in."

At that moment, as if decreed by the evil gods of war, the Kurdish uncle of Iris was crouching on the ridge. An hour earlier, he had heard a helicopter pass high overhead. Fearing another gas attack by the Iraqis, he carried the heavy .50 caliber machine gun Toufani had given him to the top of the ridge. His small tribe and their flocks were huddled in the swale below.

The large man nestled the powerful weapon in his arms. He had only twelve rounds of ammunition. It was not his intention to start a fight with the helicopter approaching low from the south. If he missed, they would see his firing position. He would fire only if it became clear that his people's hiding place had been discovered.

"Heads up, Night Rider! Big Brother has a missile in the air from the F-14, at one hundred klicks and closing."

"He's bloody right!" shouted the ECM officer over the intercom. "I have a Phoenix signal, loud and clear."

"How much time do we have, Dick?" asked Mackenzie.

"Less than two minutes."

"Okay, Jimmie," said Mackenzie calmly. "Clear the ridge and set us down in the swale."

Iris's uncle heard the noisy helicopter approaching, but it was difficult to see in the pitch-black darkness. Then he saw the dim red reflections of the interior lights on the windshield. It was well within range of his .50 caliber gun, but he held his fire. If he could not see the Iraqi helicopter, they could not see his people.

"Damn!" swore Mackenzie. "There are a lot of small trees in the swale. We'll have to hover above them."

"With your permission, I'm going to illuminate, Sir. Be a lot safer that way."

"You're right, Jimmie. Got my finger on the rescue floodlamp switch. Tell me when you're ready."

"Okay, wind is from the west, I'm going to swing the nose around and go into a hover. Light it up, Colonel!"

Iris's uncle was blinded by the brilliant light. He squinted his eyes and focused in time to see the big helicopter level with him, less than fifty meters away, with its nose swinging toward him. He raised the weapon and fired all twelve rounds into the windshield. Seconds later, he was startled by a sharp explosion on the other side of the ridge. He caught only a glimpse of the red flash, but the smell of the Phoenix warhead's detonation was carried to him on the wind.

The horrific implosion of the Sea King's windscreen was followed by the rush of downwash from the rotor blades. Dick heard the screaming, leapt from his rack, and ran for the flight deck. Jim was there ahead of him. The copilot was close behind.

The big helo was yawing wildly. Mackenzie was screaming: "I can't see! Give me a hand!"

Jim leaned over him. "I have the stick!" he shouted. "Keep your feet on the pedals."

Dick unsnapped Jimmie's seat belt and pulled his headless body from the left seat. The copilot jumped over them and into the seat. He grabbed the controls, steadied the Sea King, and began a climb out of the swale.

Dick slipped on the blood-covered floor and fell into the gun bubble. The rescue light was still on. He looked down to see sheep and goats running everywhere. He pulled himself back to the flight deck, grabbed Jimmie's feet, and dragged his body into the troop compartment. The ECM operator found blankets and covered the SAS Lieutenant's lifeless form, but blood was running everywhere.

Jim's arms were locked around Mackenzie's chest. He dragged him backwards into the troop compartment. Dick and the ECM operator helped lay him on the canvas rack behind the flight deck. The Colonel's face was a mass of pulverized flesh, his left eye was hanging from its socket, blood was spurting from a deep wound in his upper left arm.

The ECM operator ran to the back and returned with towels, blankets, and the emergency medical kit. The three of them fought to stabilize the Scotsman. Dick reconnected his flight helmet's radio cord to monitor transmissions.

"Big Brother roger. Understand you have no compass?"

"Night Rider, affirmative. Most of the instruments are shot away, along with the windscreen and the top of the cockpit. I have no altitude or airspeed indicators. It's windy and cold as hell. I'm flying visual, with night goggles."

"Big Brother roger. You are heading about three-zero-zero degrees. Can you bring it a little port?"

"Night Rider, affirmative. How far am I from home plate?"

"Home plate bears two-six-five degrees at ninety kilometers."

"Hello, Big Brother, this is Nail. You guys got a problem?"

"Big Brother, affirmative! What are you doing on this freq?"

"Up getting some night time. Thought I'd see how things are going."

"Nail, we need an escort for Night Rider. It's an emergency. He has been hit. Can you help?"

"Nail, affirmative. If you have me on your gadget, give me a vector."

"Wilco, Nail. We hold you fifty kilometers northwest. Vector one-one-zero degrees, two hundred and forty klicks for Night Rider. Expedite, please!"

"Nail, wilco. Accelerating."

"Big Brother, this is Night Rider. We have one dead and one critical. Dispatch an emergency team to home plate. We're going to need a lot of blood for Moon River."

"Big Brother, roger. A team of medics is launching in your other SAR Sea King. Will pass them the info on Moon River."

Dick adjusted the tourniquet on Mackenzie's arm. The .50 cal. bullet had passed cleanly through the upper arm, without hitting the bone, but had obviously torn out big arteries. Jim was carefully picking plexiglass shards out of the Colonel's head, neck, and shoulders. The ECM operator had already bandaged his seriously injured left eye.

"Nail, Big Brother. Night Rider is on your nose at one hundred kilometers."

"Roger that. I'm at V max for this old Phantom--waking up a lot of goats."

"Nail, Night Rider. Estimate my altitude somewhere around angels one. I'm at max range power, but my front end's all shot to hell. I'm probably doing less than a hundred knots."

"Nail, roger. See you shortly, Jimmie."

"Jimmie's dead," choked the copilot.

"Sorry," echoed the Turkish pilot. "You're on my scope now. I'm locking you up. I'll come in high and ease down to your altitude."

Dick checked Mackenzie's pulse and shouted at Jim above the roar of engines and the hurricane wind: "He's going into shock. We're still a half hour from recovery."

"Night Rider, Nail. I have a good lock. You are at angels point five and about a hundred knots. Can you go Christmas tree?"

"Rather not," replied the copilot. "People around here have this thing about lights."

"Nail, roger. It's not necessary. I have a good velocity lock. As we approach the field, I'll work you down to recovery altitude."

Jim and Dick laid the weakening SAS Colonel on the blood-soaked deck and began CPR. Between breaths, Dick gasped: "Don't know any of the hostages, . . . doubt if any of them . . . are worth the lives . . . of these two brave men."

Jim rocked back and forth over Mackenzie's bleeding chest. "The loyalty of politicians . . . stops at the ballot box. . . . Soldiers are expendable tools, . . . to be betrayed . . . and cast away. . . . You learned that in Vietnam."

"Yeah, . . . nothing's changed!"

13

AIN'T LOVE GRAND

The shivering gray wolf emerged from his lair in the pine grove. The late moon rising in the east cast an unearthly silver sheen over the landscape. A gusty north breeze swirled loose snow into the air. Moonbeams transformed the fine snowflakes into a heavenly veil of silver fog.

The wolf stared curiously at the figure huddled over the flickering light. The human had been there since sundown. He had not moved when the temperature dropped and the wind came up. It was now one o'clock in the morning.

The night belonged to the wolf--the human was invading his realm--he raised his voice in a plaintive howl. Over the whistling of the wind through the pines, he heard a faint reply from one of his own kind.

At the sound of the wolf, Dick slowly raised his head and stared down the valley. His eyebrows and the scarf around his face were coated with frost.

His body was numb, but his mind was filled with a heavenly vision. There, in the silver veil of swirling snow, Rita was pirouetting around and around. A shimmering white gown sheathed her slender body. Dick tried to call to her, but his lips wouldn't move.

She smiled and waved at him as she danced through the silver fog toward him. She stopped beyond the glow of the flickering gaslight.

Dick tried to stand--to go to her--but he couldn't move. She motioned for him to stay and began to sing: "I remember . . ."

Rita's vision drew closer, she bent over him. Her shimmering white gown brushed his cheek. "I remember you . . ." Her long red hair caressed his forehead.

Dick's head sagged to his chest. His body slumped in the snow by the flickering light. Rita knelt over him . . .

"*Reechard, Reechard,* wake up, you'll freeze to death."
He looked up into Maria's big blue eyes. She was shaking him

- 246 -

gently. He had rolled off his blanket into the snow.

They were sun tanning on a snow-covered meadow nestled high in the Austrian Alps south of Badgastein. Long ski lifts extended up the sharp slope to the northeast. The flat meadow was criss-crossed with miles of wondrous ski trails.

Dick's injured vertebrae had limited their cross-country skiing efforts to a few kilometers. They had joined the couples enjoying the brilliant sun on blankets in the snow. It was one of those magical places on earth, where wearing a bikini beneath a ski suit was entirely normal.

Dick crawled onto his blanket. Maria dried his wet back with a fluffy towel. "You were tossing in your sleep. I thought the cold snow would wake you, but it didn't. Were you dreaming?"

"Of a much colder place," he answered.

She stretched her trim shapely body on top of him. "Maybe I'd better warm you a little," she teased. She reached behind her and untied the top of her bikini. She shifted her weight, and he felt her bare bosom warming his back.

"If you're going to do that, give me a chance to sell tickets first."

"You're a half-hour late at the box office," she giggled, snuggling her bosom against him. "The breast-baring began after you dozed off."

"Let me guess who was first: the big blonde three blankets to our left."

Maria buried her face in the side of his neck and nibbled. "Yes, of course. She heard a cow-bell and dropped her top."

Dick laughed. "With her build she could feed all the babies in Badgastein."

She bit him more firmly. "Including the one I'm lying on."

He shrugged his shoulders and felt her warmth on his back. "I prefer quality to quantity, Snookie."

"Liar!" She reached for the ends of the bikini-top string and retied it. "Can I trust you while I go to the restroom?"

He rolled on his side and pulled her to him, for a warm hug and a long kiss. "It's about a half mile. Sure you can't wait? We need to leave within the hour."

She reached down and pulled on her ski suit. "Lie still and give your vertebrae some rest, I'll be right back."

She rose and fasten the *langlauf* skis to her shoes. "Keep your eyes off the heifers, cowboy."

"I can wait till we get back to the apartment."

"Be sure you do!"

Maria sailed gracefully down the slope and followed the trail to the restrooms. She was a gifted skier. Dick pulled on his ski suit and found the Skyfone in the pocket. He put the earphone in his ear, covered the instrument with his scarf, and selected Nelson's scrambled number in Frankfurt.

"Hello, Brown Bear," answered the *Purple* Field Supervisor. "I was about to call you."

"How did Mac's operation go?"

"They . . . they couldn't save his eye." Nelson cleared his throat and continued: "Did everything they could. Jim Conrad and Chief Air Marshal Frazier are with him at London's finest hospital. The Prime Minister's personal physician is attending. Thank God, they have him stabilized. He should recover full use of his arm, and they are already beginning plastic surgery."

"I pray for him every day. Wish there was something more I could do."

"You and Mountie saved his life in that damaged helicopter."

"It was that gutsy copilot who saved us all. The SAS can really be proud of that kid!"

"Yes indeed, I hope the U.K. will reward him in some way. Jim Conrad told Mac it was your blood that saved him during the MEDEVAC."

Dick chuckled. "What did the royal Scotsman have to say about that?"

"Jim said he just growled, *Bloody hell!*"

"How long is Mountie going to be in London?"

"He's chosen an office in MI-5 as his headquarters for cracking the code we've been picking up from Damascus with our new satellite communication-monitoring system. You remember him talking about the Sematex order list he smuggled out of Brno?"

"Yeah. Said he had all the orders for the last three years, but that it would be difficult to match names with faces."

"He's off to a good start. Our guard at the Bekaa Valley camp smuggled out rosters of the last twelve classes--genuine family names, not aliases. Jim's already been able to cross-check Abood's info on Muhammad Amri, Mirhashem's Sematex bomb-maker."

"Was it one of Amri's bombs that blew the hole in TWA 840 yesterday, and killed four Americans?"

"Most certainly! Unfortunately, the White House is muddling the investigation by trying to blame Qadhafi. A few days ago, we intercepted a communication from Muhammad Amri in Damascus to a Mirhashem cell in Rome. Jim was able to partially decode the message. Amri was reminding them that his Sematex bomb would not show on x-ray, but could be detected by a dog."

Dick grunted. "Last time a dog was allowed in Rome's airport, it was probably chasing a gladiator."

"We are fast-forwarding a warning to key airports, but it's going to take time to get them up to speed. Our immediate concern is Tegel, in West Berlin. Jim and Abood tracked a fifty-pound purchase of Sematex to the Syrian Embassy in East Berlin; and we've learned that one of Mirhashem's students--Ahmad Hazi--left his Damur camp in Syria for East Berlin yesterday. Max and his partner are enroute to Berlin to find out what's going down."

"What does Abood know about Mirhashem's current frame of mind?"

Nelson laughed softly. "Well, imagine yourself with a million-dollar price on your head, issued by Khomeini personally."

"Has Mirhashem, or Khomeini, figured out what happened?"

"Almost, but they still haven't identified the airfield we used."

"Toufani probably has the weapons in the mountains by now."

"That's what our satellite reconnaissance shows."

"How did Mirhashem get out of Tehran?"

Nelson chuckled. "Barely! A Syrian aircraft had flown him from Brno and was waiting to take him to Damascus after the weapons arrived. When he heard the Soviet copilot had radioed the tower that the IL-76 was empty, he re-boarded the Syrian plane and was airborne before the Ayatollah could get to the airport."

"Into every life, some rain must fall."

"Be careful you don't get caught in the downpour, Brown Bear! Abood's contact reported Mirhashem refused to believe Abrahim had betrayed him. He was focusing on you, Shreeba, and Jim Conrad. An RAF leader guaranteed him that *Herr Winkleman* was one of their most trusted agents--so Mirhashem painted a bullseye on you and the girl. Our guard in Bekaa Valley says the entire next graduating class is being sent to Vienna after Shreeba and you. They are studying maps and everything else they can get their hands on. He has a photo of you and Shreeba dancing at the *Volksgarten.* Every one in his organization will soon have a copy. Better sign a long-term lease and stay in the mountains!"

Maria was climbing the slope on her cross-country skis.

"Roger that, Mr. Nelson. Got to sign off. Give my best to Mac."

"Goodbye, Dick. Be careful! Mirhashem will be launching a barrage of terror, to show the Arab world he's still boss. He will try to pick you off along the way. I asked GP-7 for permission to hit him, but the White House vetoed it for six months."

The natural hot waters in Austria's Gasteiner Valley were a blessing for Dick's injured back. His favorite place was the City Health Club in Badgastein. They had a large indoor pool, with small canals leading under the walls to three outdoor pools--each with an increasing temperature of warm water. During the winter, deep snow accumulated around the outdoor pools. It was the custom to climb out of the comfortable water, roll in the snow, and jump back in the pool. The difference in temperatures induced a foggy mist that reduced visibility in the pools in less than a meter: an interesting scenario!

Inside the main hall were restaurants, cafés, shops, and rental *Kabinen*--large enough for couples to change their clothing, or whatever activity came to mind. It was one of Maria's favorite places to demonstrate her lithe sexuality.

This was one of those mornings when she had been particularly insatiable. Dick was relieved to finally enter the hot waters. He paddled slowly under the plastic air shield to the warmest of the outer pools. The mist was very thick, visibility no more than a foot. He found a seat along the pool wall, where a strong jet of hot water massaged his aching back. He was relaxing when he got the sharp signal through the chip in his right shoulder--call Nelson.

Trusting to fate that he wouldn't bump into Maria, Dick edged his way back to the indoor pool. He climbed out and thanked the attendant, who wrapped him in a large towel.

In the Kabine, he took the Skyfone from the pocket of his trousers and selected the scrambled circuit for Nelson.

"Heard the news this morning, Brown Bear?" asked the *Purple* supervisor.

"No, Sir. Just got up."

Nelson laughed. "Baloney! Since you've become Number One on Mirhashem's hit parade, we are constantly recording your chip's monitor."

"*Na,* what can I say?" sighed Dick.

"Nothing, just listen. I'll keep your personal activities as confidential as I can. Need to brief you on the La Belle Café bombing in West Berlin last night."

"Damn! The Sematex from the Syrian Embassy in East Berlin?"

"Yes. More than two hundred injured, with one American GI and one Turkish woman killed."

"Max and his partner okay?"

"Yes. They were almost able to stop it. His partner had staked out the embassy, while Max waited on the West Berlin side of the *Brandenburger Tor.* They figured the Sematex would be moved in a diplomatic pouch, and all diplomatic material has to pass through Brandenburg. His partner followed the vehicle from the embassy. Max picked it up at Brandenburg. His partner was held up by a gate-guard inspection, and Max had to tail the vehicle into West Berlin alone. He called ahead to alert security at Tegel, but the Syrian Embassy vehicle went straight to the La Belle. Max saw a woman and two men with briefcases exit the vehicle and go in the front door of the club. He drove around back to check for another exit, then parked and went in the front door. The woman and two men were coming out empty-handed. Max tried to warn club security but was caught in the blast."

"Oh my God!" groaned Dick. "How is he?"

"He's okay, Bear. Few minor cuts from flying glass. He's on his way to London to meet with Jim and Abood, to come up with images of the bombers."

"Was one of them Ahmad Hazi?"

"Absolutely! A few weeks ago, our guard at the Bekaa Valley camp heard him bragging about a big assignment in Germany. This hit is definitely Mirhashem's. West Berlin *Polizei* got a call before the bomb went off. They claimed to be an Arab Revolutionary Council group. That's the ID normally used by a Mirhashem cell."

"Looks like you were right, when you said he'd blast his way back to the top."

"For better or worse, the White House is laying this one on

Qadhafi's doorstep. CIA was on the scene within an hour, planting the seeds in everyone's mind. They have even turned the phone call on its head, saying it was an attempt to direct blame away from the Colonel. Now the CIA has named some of the Libyan Embassy staff as the bombers. Ridiculous! Max's partner followed the three perpetrators back into East Berlin. Ahmad Hazi had teamed with a hardcore woman from the old 2 June Movement and a young guy out of Yemen. I made the request through channels to send a *Purple* team into East Germany after them. It was--of course-- vetoed by your President."

"I bet those American aircraft carriers off Tripoli are turning into the wind; but why did you say, *for better or worse?*"

Nelson laughed. "They will definitely be launching soon. That will be the *better* part, and we have nothing to do with it. Unfortunately, the *worse* part will be when Mirhashem makes an even more spectacular hit to direct attention back to himself, and that *is* our business."

"What do you expect? Is there something I should be doing?"

"Glad you asked. We won't be sending you on any flights, Mirhashem has too many friends working at airports. However, there is a thing coming up that you could work on with Jim."

"With the train and hovercraft, I can be in London in about ten hours."

"Here's the situation. Jim had MI-5 run Hazi's family name. They found it in civil housing files in London. A couple months ago, an Irish girl registered *Nazer* Hazi as living with her. They hold El Al tickets from London to Tel Aviv, at the end of this month."

"Does Jim think these two Hazi's are related?"

"The list of Mirhashem's Bekaa Valley grads, which our guard smuggled to Abood, shows a Nazer Hazi graduated on 9 June '85."

"How about that! He has to be from the class that I interviewed for Mirhashem. Mountie wants me in London to identify him?"

"Right on, Brown Bear! We don't know exactly when, but certainly before Nazer's El Al flight on 30 April. Jim Conrad, Max, and Abood are turning over a lot of rocks, searching for something that connects. Be ready to go on a moment's notice. They'll wait till the last minute to call you. We don't want you exposed any longer than absolutely necessary."

If Colonel Qadhafi had been tried in an American court for the bombing of the La Belle Café, he would have walked. It would have been a slam-dunk for any defense lawyer worthy of the name. Absolutely no material evidence could have been produced to link the Libyan dictator with the attack. However, he was a much softer and politically-correct target than Syria, so the White House fabricated a case against him and took it to the court of world opinion.

At the core of White House motivation was the impeding disclosure of illegal support for the Contras. They were being funded by traitorous dealings with an Iranian government that had seized the U.S. Embassy in Tehran six years earlier and continued to hold Americans hostage in Lebanon. The White House needed a flash-bang event to misdirect media interest--something like the attack on hapless Grenada, which had followed the terrorist massacre of 244 U.S. Marines at the Beirut airport.

Eleven days after La Belle, the President had been able to enlist the support of only the U.K. The British already had a viable case against the Colonel for his funding of the IRA, an attempt on the life of the Queen, and the assassination of their most prominent military hero of W.W.II.

Pentagon strike planning was plagued by inter-service rivalry, with the Navy and Air Force jousting for position. The Air Force succeeded in getting a slice of the pie by launching F-111's from England. They flew an incredible circuitous route around France and Italy, who refused to participate. The four-hour trip gave the Colonel adequate warning. The end result was an ineffective attack upon Tripoli and Benghazi, with a hundred Libyans killed and two of Qadhafi's children reportedly injured. The same result could have been obtained with a far-less expensive terrorist-style attack, which might have gotten the Colonel himself.

The clear message received by the Arab world was that dictators who ruled oil-producing countries need not fear the White House. The very presence of that oil generated a sense of competition amongst the world's oil-dependent powers that would deny the unity necessary to de-throne even the worst of dictators.

In the meantime, the principal base of terror in the Middle East, Syria, remained immune from a White House cowed by their own blunders.

The dust had barely settled over Tripoli when Dick received the call on the Skyfone. It was early morning. Maria had left the apartment to get fresh, warm, semmel rolls for breakfast.

"Got your bag packed, Bear?"

"Yes Sir! What's happening, Mr. Nelson?"

"Mountie needs you in London, as soon as you can get there. He has spent the last couple weeks trying to find Nazer Hazi and his Irish girl friend, but he's always been one jump behind them. Now it's coming to an end. Their airline reservations to Tel Aviv have been changed. The girl, Ann Clancy, is booked on the El Al flight that leaves day after tomorrow. Nazer's booked on a British Airways flight, which leaves three days later and stops at Rome enroute to Tel Aviv."

"Son-of-a-bitch!" cursed Dick. "Mirhashem's going to answer the White House with a double-header."

"Looks that way. Get your rear end to England and give Jim a hand. He's hoping to grab Nazer at Heathrow, and needs your help to identify him."

A late spring storm was rocking the Channel. The hovercraft was tossed about like a cork. The forty-minute run from Oostende to Dover took two hours. Dick was late arriving at Victoria Station in the heart of London, but Max was there to meet him.

A bandage covered most of the muscular white-haired German's throat. Dick gripped his hand. "Souvenir from La Belle?"

"*Ja wohl, mein Herr.* Was my lucky night. Missed the jugular by less than a centimeter."

The Grenzegruppeneun Commando signaled one of London's famous old-style cabs, and directed the driver to the Elisabeth Hotel across from Hyde Park.

Max had already checked Dick into the comfortable family hotel. "Jim and Abood are holding dinner for us across the street. I'll wait here in the lobby while you freshen up."

Jim and Abood had a table in the back. The Canadian embraced Dick carefully. "How's your back, Bear? Last time I saw you, you were almost paralyzed--lying alongside Mackenzie in that helo with a transfusion tube connecting your arms."

"I'm doing fine, Mountie. What's the latest on the Colonel?"

Abood pulled out a chair for Dick. "Sit down, we'll bring you up to date over roast beef and Yorkshire pudding."

Dick shook the Egyptian's hand and glanced at the beer glasses on the table. "I thought Stout was on Allah's accursed list?"

Abood laughed. "It is, but I think he goes easy on those who choose Guinness--when it's on tap. May I order one for you? How about you, Maximilian?"

Their immediate concern was Mackenzie's condition. Three weeks after the disastrous flight out of Iran, the seriously injured Colonel was still battling infections.

"How's his morale?" asked Dick.

"Never a question about that," said Jim. "That tough old Scotsman attributes all his problems to the *bear* blood now coursing through his veins."

"What's in his future?" asked Max.

Jim shook his head. "He won't pass another SAS physical. MI-5 is ready to snatch him up. I hope Nelson will offer him that new Field Supervisor's position." He smiled at Dick. "I would rather stay active with my partner; unless he's retiring to family life?"

"Fat chance," grunted Dick. "Maria was mad as hell when I left this morning. Not sure how much longer I can use the old *NATO-business* alibi."

"Is she waiting in Badgastein?" asked Max.

"No. She dropped me at the train station in Salzburg, then went to Kirchberg to visit her mother."

"Will she stay away from Vienna?"

"You think she's in danger?" asked Dick quickly.

"No, not right now. All the time I was staked out on your apartment, I never saw any of Mirhashem's people; but that Tenth District of Vienna's a hotbed of displaced Arabs. If his Bekaa Valley class digs deep enough, they may get lucky--especially with that clear photo of you at the *Volksgarten*."

Dick drained the glass of Guinness. "We have more pressing things to discuss. What's the plan, Jim? How do we take down the Hazi brothers?"

They parted at the entrance to the Piccadilly Underground. Max and Abood took a taxi to Heathrow, while Jim and Dick used the Tube. Their separate routes allowed for London's unpredictable traffic problems.

At noon, they rendezvoused at the El Al ticket counter. They were greeted by two MI-5 agents and escorted to a security office where they met Harvey, the German Shepherd dog. Jim distributed the miniature earplugs and microphones for use by both *Purple* and MI-5. The senior MI-5 agent gave them photographs of Ms. Clancy. Abood furnished the fifteen images of Mirhashem's 9 June '85 Bekaa Valley class, as Dick had remembered them.

"Sorry we can't say which one is Nazer Hazi," apologized the bespectacled Egyptian artist.

"We hope the bloody bastard will be with his girl friend," replied the senior agent. "She should be easy to recognize. Your images may provide confirmation."

"Captain Williams and I will be at the street entrance to the departure area," explained Jim. "We'll have a reasonable chance to identify them. It would be a big help if the airport police could make traffic move slowly."

"That's a twist!" laughed the other MI-5 agent. "Normally those chaps have trouble moving it at all. We will ask them to set a pace that will afford you a good look in every auto. What time do you want to start the surveillance?"

"The Captain and I will be in position on our Vespas at fifteen hundred, three hours before Ms. Clancy's scheduled departure."

"Splendid," replied the agent. "Our men will sweep the terminal at fourteen hundred, in case she's already here."

"We must use caution not to spook Hazi," warned Max. "Once we've spotted Ms. Clancy, it would be best to allow her to continue to the point of boarding the aircraft."

"Totally agree," said the senior agent. "We intend to take her after she has walked down the boarding ramp to the door of the aircraft. That would be out of sight from Hazi."

"Her baggage will be delivered to this room immediately after she checks it," continued the other agent. "Harvey and our bomb squad will have a go at it before it's opened."

"I am sure the Sematex will be cleverly hidden," said Abood. "An expert has made the bomb for them." He reached down to scratch Harvey on the head, ". . . but this young fellow will find it."

"If we identify them while they're still in a cab or car, Colonel Conrad and I will follow them on our Vespas," said Dick, "but once they're in the terminal it's your ball game."

"Sounds *cricket* to me," agreed the senior agent. He turned to Abood. "The public's well aware of the bomb-detection assets we employ in the tubes, and at rail stations, to thwart the IRA. I don't believe they'll risk using the underground or the rails. However, I will have agents on the arrival platforms to assist you."

Jim spoke to Max. "If Hazi doesn't go into the terminal, Dick and I will stay on him. We must make sure he's out of Ms. Clancy's sight before we take him. Help us with the timing if you can."

"Gentlemen," said the senior MI-5 agent. "We have a request from the Prime Minister. She is interesting in giving the Syrians credit for this attempt on El Al. No matter how, when, or where we take Hazi, we're going to give the media the impression that he got away. We'll expose the Syrian connection, then have Hazi *turn himself in* a few days later."

Jim smiled. "Qadhafi may invite her to lunch for that favor."

"Indeed," replied the senior agent, "and we want to invite you. Let us adjourn to the kitchen. We can discuss further details there."

"Please go ahead," said Jim. "I'm going to do Captain Williams' disguise first, so you'll be able to recognize him--but Hazi won't."

The senior agent's eyes narrowed. "Have you dealt with this bloke before, Captain?"

Dick laughed. "We went to summer camp together."

Dick adjusted his helmet and the scarf around his neck. In spite of the stiff breeze, visibility was decreasing in late afternoon smog. Airport police had set construction signs to block all but two lanes of incoming traffic. Jim's Vespa was parked where he could view the left lane. Dick was positioned several meters farther on, with a clear look at traffic in the right lane.

His back was aching from straddling the scooter for an hour when he heard Jim in his earphone: "Small blue sports car in your lane, Brown Bear--two people--check it close."

"Bear wilco."

Dick saw the auto approaching. He focused his eyes on the driver. "Praise be to Allah," he transmitted. "That's Hazi. He was the student more interested in Las Vegas than American politics."

"Okay," said Jim. "I'm going to ease into the left lane and try to stay near him. Wait a few cars, then do the same in the right."

"Brown Bear wilco."

"Brown Bear, this is Witch Hazel. Understand you have the suspects in sight?"

Dick smiled at the MI-5 agent's strange call sign. "Affirmative, Witch Hazel. Small blue Aston, license GB76553."

"Witch Hazel, Mountie. Two hundred meters from the drop off point for El Al."

"Roger, Mountie. Agents are waiting inside. Keep us advised."

Traffic began to accelerate after the entrance choke point. Jim's Vespa was wedged in the left lane behind an old Volvo, occupied by two young Brits with their hair dyed red and green. The blue Aston was three cars ahead of him, in the right lane. Dick was also in the right lane, five cars back. Jim swerved abruptly onto the center line and sped past the old Volvo. The driver honked at him and the passenger flashed him the finger. Jim darted into the right lane, then to the curb at the first unloading island. Dick joined him.

"Witch Hazel, Mountie. The blue Aston's approaching the El Al unloading area. We are holding short at the first island."

"Witch Hazel, roger. We have the vehicle in sight."

Dick and Jim dismounted and stepped on the curb for a better view. The Aston braked to a stop. The young muscular driver leapt out and hurried to the trunk. He removed two suitcases, and was joined by his female passenger.

"The Aston's engine is still running, Witch Hazel," said Jim. "Don't believe he's going inside. Bear, confirm that is Hazi."

"Identity confirmed!" replied Dick.

The Palestinian set the suitcases on the curb, signaled for a sky-cap, took the female in his arms, and gave her a resounding kiss.

"Ain't love grand," muttered Dick.

A skycap arrived and loaded the luggage on a cart. Nazer Hazi released his Irish girl friend and tipped the skycap. Then he kissed his beloved again and returned quickly to the sports car.

"Heads up, Max," warned Jim. "He is leaving in a hurry."

"Roger that. I'm parked at the end of the off-loading zone. Tail in behind and give me a call so I can pull in front of him."

A baton-twirling traffic-control Bobbie was approaching their Vespas. Dick and Jim mounted quickly and zoomed into traffic.

"Witch Hazel, Mountie, call us when the girl friend's in the terminal."

The blue Aston moved away from the curb and accelerated down the off-loading ramp. Jim and Dick tried to accelerate also, but they were again blocked by the old Volvo. Jim pulled out to pass him on the left side. Dick was a few meters back.

"Here he comes, Max. He's in the left lane. Get out here quick."

At that moment, whether out of sheer lunacy or drug-induced hatred, the punk-rocker driver of the Volvo opened his door and knocked Jim's Vespa into the curb. The front wheel collapsed, the Vespa flew end-over-end, and Conrad was thrown into the grassed area bordering the street.

Dick had seen the event unfolding and veered around the right side of the Volvo. "Max and Witch Hazel, Mountie's down! Brown Bear's in pursuit."

"Witch Hazel roger. The woman is in the terminal. Take Hazi now!"

Dick was a hundred yards back when Max's black Mercedes darted in front of the blue Aston. The Mercedes' brake lights glowed as the Commando slammed on the brakes. Hazi swerved to the right, but Max cut him off. Hazi skidded the little Aston around, but was met by several autos leaving the off-loading area.

There was only one way out. Dick anticipated the situation. He eased his Vespa over the curb and into the grassed area. When Hazi's blue Aston bounced over the curb into the grass, Dick was in position to cut him off. Max was fifty yards behind Hazi, they were coming directly at him. Dick slowed the Vespa, but his closing speed with Hazi's sports car was at least 60 mph. At the last second, he dove off the right side of the Vespa--with the same practiced move he had used so many times when he was a kid, bull-dogging steers from his horse.

Hazi jerked the steering wheel hard right, but the Aston's left front wheel and fender smashed the Vespa. The small car rolled on its left side and catapulted into the air.

The grumpy Scotsman had finished his breakfast and was glaring with his one good eye at the group ringing his bed. Conrad's left arm was in a sling, the bandage still covered Max's throat, Dick leaned heavily on Abood's shoulder and supported himself with his cane.

"If you bloody fools are the winners, what the blooming hell do the losers look like!"

Jim Conrad laughed. "You would have enjoyed this one, Mac. We tore the front end out of an MI-5 Mercedes and totaled two of their Vespas in a matter of seconds."

"A real bunch of debutantes," growled Mackenzie. Dick knew he was trying to smile under the bandages which covered his face.

"It was for a good cause, Colonel," assured Max, in his imitation of a Scottish brogue. "The poor lassie was devastated when they found thirteen pounds of Sematex in the portable radio the loving husband-to-be had given her, as a going-away present."

"Would have been a hell of a send-off," grunted Mackenzie. His bloodshot blue eye had traces of a twinkle.

"It was set to blow El Al Flight 703 out of the sky, when they descended through nine thousand feet approaching Tel Aviv," said Dick.

"Has anyone advised the poor lass to break the engagement?" asked Mackenzie.

Max laughed. "I think she got the message."

Jim excused himself and stepped to a corner of the room to take a Skyfone call from Nelson.

"Nasty business," continued Abood. "They found another of Muhammad Amri's bombs in Nazer's apartment. It was designed to fit inside an electric razor case. It would have blown the second time the British Airways Airbus descended through nine thousand, approaching Tel Aviv. Hazi would have left the plane in Rome."

"Sounds like Mirhashem is blowing off a lot of steam," said Mackenzie quietly. "Is this still an attempt to re-crown himself the king of terrorism?"

Jim Conrad stepped back into the circle. "Certainly that, and more. He is also sending us a message. When MI-5 hustled Nazer out of his Aston, they were tending to Dick. Unfortunately, some-one had removed his helmet and disguise. Nazer saw him and started shouting: *Allah will have his revenge, Captain Orden!*"

The Canadian Mountie paused to look at Dick. "MI-5 must leak worse than SHAPE. Two hours ago, Nelson's satellite intercepted a communication between London and Damascus. Mirhashem knows you were one of those who rained out his double-header yesterday. A few minutes after Mirhashem got the message, he called Beirut with orders to execute one of the hostages."

Dick's face blanched. "Let me guess--the faculty member?"

"Yeah," sighed Jim. "The one he promised to let you see at the King George Hotel."

Tears came to Dick's hard blue eyes. He bowed his head on Abood's shoulder. "My God, I've killed him. His blood is on my hands."

14

FOR GOD, FOR LOYALTY

The rainbow circled lazily, enjoying his new-found freedom after being released from the hatchery two days earlier. A late-summer hatch of May flies had descended upon the Willows resort on the Colorado River, ten miles south of Hoover Dam. It was a feeding paradise for trout, and the little rainbow was eating his fill.

He had almost decided to return to the deeper cooler water, when another May fly hit the water, a few inches above his nose. It was too tempting. His enthusiastic lunge carried him out of the water and into the air, with the fly gripped firmly in his mouth. Unfortunately, he hadn't seen the fine leader tied to the fly.

Dick Williams set the hook, then was faced with the dilemma he always felt. Should he reel the beautiful little fish in quickly, inflicting sharp pain in his hooked mouth but returning him immediately to the water; or should he work him gently, easing the pain from the hook but fatiguing the game little fighter?

He chose the latter. If the trout showed the character attributed to his species, and fought with skill and vigor, he might throw the hook and escape to rejoin his brethren--with an education that would improve his chances of survival if he ever attacked the wrong May fly again.

The little guy was true to his billing. Thrashing and throwing himself into the air, he fought a gallant fight. Alas, it was not to be. Dick knelt on one knee and carefully gripped the hook with a needle-nosed pliers. Without raising the trout from the water, he removed the hook with a practiced touch.

The courageous rainbow lay on his side, near exhaustion. Dick stroked his nose gently until the small one righted himself, wiggled his tail, and began his journey back to deep water. He was only a few meters from shore, when Dick saw the silver flash in the water. There was nothing he could do. The meter-long striped bass crushed the trout in its massive jaws. The rainbow died a quick but painful death.

Dick sighed, picked up his fly rod, and retreated to the bench on the sandy shore behind him. He sat down to watch the last golden slice of sun slide behind the rocky hills on the Nevada side of the river. His situation was not much different than the rainbow's. He was tired and adrift in a world of predators waiting to tear him to shreds. How--and when--would Mirhashem find him? Would he finally be betrayed by those who thought they were helping him?

He heard a delightfully feminine squeal and looked up to see Maria's spinning rod bowing sharply. She had hooked something big, perhaps the murderous striper. Maria didn't regard fishing as a sport. She said she enjoyed it, but it reminded her of a hungry childhood. Injured in the war, her father had died when she was fourteen. Her mother's seamstress job could not supply the table. Maria and her younger brother became experts at hauling carp out of the local creek and finding mushrooms in the woods.

A month after they had taken the apartment in Badgastein, Maria became very worried about those woods and that creek. Instruments in Sweden had picked up indications of heavy radio-activity. The Soviets finally admitted to the Chernobyl meltdown. A spring storm carried the deadly clouds over Austria. The rain missed Maria's home but fell in Austria's southeastern corner, contaminating the grass and poisoning the milk.

The Chernobyl disaster pushed Mirhashem's Syrian-sponsored terrorist strikes off the front pages for a month. During the lull, Syrian President Assad offended Mirhashem by holding out the olive branch to Saddam Hussein, who had kicked Mirhashem out of Iraq a few years earlier; and to Jordan's King Hussein, who had massacred Mirhashem's family sixteen years earlier.

Mirhashem shifted his headquarters to Libya. When he closed the camps in the Bekaa Valley, some of his staff revolted and attempted to desert. Scores were killed in a violent realignment of loyalties--including the Bekaa Valley guard who saved Dick's life by providing the knife for the Mountain of Truth and later smuggled out the names of the graduates.

Mirhashem's operations suffered a temporary setback. He was professionally humiliated when one of his soldiers botched an assignment to martyr himself with an Amri-made bomb on El Al. The soldier lost his nerve, convinced a petty thief it was a suitcase of drugs, and paid him to smuggle it on board. A rank amateur, the

Spanish thief was the last one in line at the Madrid check-in counter when the suitcase started burning. Prompt action by El Al security prevented a major disaster.

Recognizing the opportunity presented by Mirhashem's temporary disorganization, Nelson approved Dick's request for an auto trip to Geneva, to be followed with a flight from Frankfurt to Omaha. Maria had finished her three months of study at the apartment in Badgastein. She was prepared to take the English-language Registered Nurse examination, which would qualify her for employment in the States. The test was given annually in western Europe, this year in Geneva.

Nelson made reservations for Dick and Maria outside the city, at a small hotel sometimes used by *Purple* as a safe-house. The fifth round of U.S.-Soviet disarmament talks was underway. A translator for the U.S. team would also be staying at the hotel-- George, Dick's Ph.D. advisor from the University of Nebraska. Dick would have another chance at the suspected spy.

Maria spent two days with the grueling examination, and scored high. Dick spent one evening with the boastful George, and further confirmed White House suspicions.

George was a braggart who, for some unknown reason, was envious of Dick's fighter pilot career. After the second bottle of vodka, the arrogant and profane professor began bragging about his importance as a member of the disarmament team. He disclosed to Dick, confidentially of course, that the Soviets were ready to trade a sizeable number of nuke warheads and missiles, if the U.S. dropped Space Wars. He launched into an apparently well-informed discussion about Space Wars, referring vaguely to some super-weapon that depended on the cooperation of Japan, the U.K. and West Germany. George cited recent Secretary of Defense success in bringing those three nations on board. That accomplishment had panicked the Soviets. Moments before he passed out, he confided to Dick that the super-weapon had the capability to intercept and destroy missiles used in air-to-air combat.

Nelson had been at Rhein-Main to clear Dick's "tail" for the flight to Omaha. Dick passed him the tape of George's conversation. He informed the *Purple* supervisor that only the Aura team and the Soviets knew about the destruction of the Foxbat-fired Acrid by the Viper missile, which Dick had launched from Aura

One. George could have that information only from the Soviets.

Dick had purchased a motor home in Omaha and began a leisurely journey westward with Maria. They arrived at the Willows fishing resort in August.

Dick wrapped aluminum foil around the buttered trout and the slice of lemon, then laid it in the hot coals. Maria joined him at the fire with two glasses of Chablis.

"I would have been glad to cook the *Florella, Bärlie.* I'm not so sure about your Sioux-Indian recipe."

Dick smiled at her brilliant blue eyes, which were reflecting the glowing embers. "Have to trust me, Snookie. Unfortunately, I don't have wet leaves and mud to wrap around it. If you don't like it, I'll go catch you another one."

She laughed softly. "From what I've seen, the only thing you keep after you catch it is a cold." She shivered and sipped the wine. "There's a chill in the air tonight."

Dick rose and embraced her. Then he pushed her gently away and glanced at the bra-less bosom under the shirt's thin material. "Mother Nature does wondrous things when you're cold."

A smile turned the corners of her delicious mouth. She rubbed against him. "If you don't want me to catch cold, you had better provide some body heat."

He scooped her diminutive beauty into his arms. As he opened the RV's door, she whispered: "What about our *Florella?*"

"It will take a long time to cook."

She giggled. "What did the Sioux Indians do while they were waiting for it to get done?"

He stepped into the RV, laid her gently on the bed, reached for the light, and answered: "Made little Sioux Indians."

Her slender body trembled as his hands found her. She caught her breath. "Show me how they did that, . . . please."

The sharp jolt in his shoulder woke Dick sometime after midnight. Maria's warm curves lay on top of him.

She stirred and reached for him. "*Mein Gott, Liebling. Noch ein mal?*"

He covered her with the blankets. "Sorry, Snookie, I have to go behind the barn."

She giggled sleepily. "Did Sioux Indians have barns?"

"No, guess not, but I'll find one." He pulled on his trousers and reached for his jacket with the Skyfone in the pocket.

Moonlight was streaming through the RV windows. She pushed back the covers to reveal her everything. "Don't be long, Chief, or Minnie Ha-Ha will start without you."

"*Ka masa kowie.*" He kissed the bikini sun-tan line on her lower stomach and left for the restrooms.

Dick picked his way carefully down the narrow rocky gorge. He found a boulder to sit on and quietly returned the Skyfone call from Frankfurt. A baby wild burro edged its way into the gorge. At the sound of Dick's voice, it bounced back into the brush.

"Hi, Mr. Nelson. What have you got for me?"

"Sorry to interrupt your holiday, but Mac and I have an update; and we need your help."

"So, you put that Scottish bagpipe back to work at last."

"Careful, Brown Bear," responded the SAS Colonel. "At least I have a musical hobby to fall back on in my old age. Judging from the activity on your monitor for the last five hours, your hobby requires a much younger man."

Dick laughed. "Yes indeed! I'm living proof that old Greek did not know what the hell he was talking about, when he lined up seventy-year-old males with twenty-year-old gals."

"You'll be glad to hear your monitor's going off-line tomorrow noon, your time," said Nelson.

"Roger that, but I've always slept more soundly knowing you guys are right here with me. Why the change?"

"Finances and politics, Bear," answered Mackenzie. "Some of *Purple's* early satellites, which were put up by French Arianes, are beginning to fail. The long-range plan was for them to be replaced by the U.S., but your President's trying a little blackmail. He wants to trade satellites for a *Purple* cover-up of his Contra funding."

"In true Hollywood style," grunted Dick. "What's the *Purple* response?"

"It's simply impossible!" said Nelson sharply. "Too many cats coming out of too many bags in the White House. We gave them an accurate--and respectful--evaluation of the situation, but it's hopeless. In their inimitable fashion, the French are delighted with the turn of events. They have scheduled another Ariane for us, but our coverage will be restricted for the next couple months. That's why we must reposition the satellite that's been covering you."

"The timing is bloody inconvenient," continued Mackenzie. "If you read a newspaper--while catching your breath--you know wide cracks are appearing in the Iron Curtain. Opportunistic defectors are flowing our way."

"How does that involve me?"

"What if I told you we have in our possession a former GRU Officer, who was assigned to the Eastern Mediterranean from '63 to '70, transferred to the KGB and served in the Philippines from '72 to '82, then returned to Moscow and was promoted to the West European desk?"

"I'd say you have your hands on the *Mother Lode,* Mac. How in hell did you bring that off?"

"All thanks to Mountie," answered Nelson. "He's kept that spy in the *BfV* at Bonn on a short leash for the last six years, and it really paid off. Last Friday, she was ordered by the Kremlin to watch the Frankfurt airport for a suspected defector. It was a KGB officer that she and Conrad knew. She asked Jim to back her up at Frankfurt. He arranged for Max to do that, while he played a hunch and staked out Heathrow."

"Did he get lucky?"

"Won the damned lottery!" exclaimed Mackenzie. "Took him down all by himself, while the guy was waiting for a flight to Washington. Jim's negotiated a deal with MI-6. They'll make some timely communiqués to McLean, in exchange for custody of the guy in about a month's time."

"What's Conrad's game? *Na,* I know, . . . he's going to flush a mole out of the CIA!"

"Yeah, Bear," acknowledged Mackenzie; "and, with *Purple's* help, you'll be fulfilling a promise you made to Iris. What we need from you is a face-to-face identification."

"When do you want me where?"

"MI-6 communiqués on the defector's history were sent to McLean yesterday. Jim wants to give the mole a couple weeks to sweat before we set him up. Be prepared for a flight to Europe within a month."

"How will you get word to me?"

"Without the satellite, we'll have to rely on your good old Pony

Express." Mackenzie chuckled. "It is still operating isn't it?"

At that moment, the mama burro appeared in the gorge and brayed loudly for her baby.

"What the hell was that?" asked Nelson.

Dick laughed. "One of their descendants is here with me. She'd probably be more reliable than our present postal system."

"Perhaps," said Mackenzie, "but Conrad wants an address. He's preparing a letter that any fighter pilot could de-code."

"I'll call you back in the morning with a zip code. What should I plan on doing with Maria?"

Mackenzie answered quietly: "Send her back to mama, Dick. Jim figures this defector will know the truth about Operation *Mosquito*. It would be better if she's at home when we find out."

"Nothing goes down in that direction, without my okay!" said Dick sharply.

"Don't worry, Brown Bear," answered Nelson firmly. "Your service to *Purple* has earned you at least that much."

Sitting in a window seat on the Air France 747, Dick had a panoramic view of the silvery harvest moon. It reflected off the waters of the North Atlantic far below and illuminated towering thunderstorms to the south. Streaks of lightning blazed through those distant clouds, but the pilot had forecast a smooth flight.

Dick needed the rest. The last week had been pure hell. He had arranged to receive Jim's letter at his mother's post office box in Nebraska. It was a two-page love letter in the German language, on perfumed stationery, in Jim's handwriting. It was addressed to *Mein Liebhaber Dick* and signed by *Deine Liebling Gisela.*

Gisela had been Rita's cover-name during the Manila sting on the white slavers. Dick immediately recognized the letter, and the two photographs, as materials for another sting--if he chose to do it. One of the photos was a Polaroid of an extremely well-built brunette taking a shower. The other was a color photograph, similar to the one Dick had sent Jim a couple years ago when he requested a photo of Maria. Obviously, the clever Abood had been at work. It was no longer Maria sitting on the sofa between Dick and his mother, it was the super-brunette, Gisela!

Jim was giving him what he needed to test Maria. If she saw the letter and the photos, she would certainly react. Naturally, Dick would safeguard those materials in the same way that he always safeguarded important documents. If Maria gained access, there would be reason to believe she had also done that in the past.

Dick had picked up Jim's letter at the local post office, driven to a nearby fishing lake, and deciphered the code. It was easy--if you were a kid in America during the forties. One of the *Shadow's* favorites was to use the second letter of each word to form a message. In a matter of minutes, Dick had extracted his orders from the love letter. His Air France ticket to Paris would be waiting for him at the check-in counter in Minneapolis on 23 September. Upon arrival, he would have to clear his own tail before meeting Jim at the Bradford Hotel off the Champs-Élysées.

Dick had debated for several minutes before locking the letter and photos in his briefcase. He had been in love with Maria for six years. While she sometimes displayed a flaring temper, it was her fierce passion for life that drew him so strongly to her.

His immediate reaction had been to burn Jim's sting materials. He had driven to the nearest barbecue grill; but, as he lit the match, the glow of the flame reminded him of the gas light burning over Rita's gravestone in western Canada.

Rita had been betrayed and killed four years earlier, during a fateful mission from Berlin to Manila. Her perfumed letter to Dick, explaining the mission, had been locked in his briefcase. The briefcase had been momentarily available to Maria, when she ran his BMW through the SHAPE car wash. Dick had found the case on the back floorboard, instead of on the seat where he had left it. Both combinations were still locked, but the contents were not in the order he normally used. He had dismissed that as his own error.

His loyalty to Rita now forced him to make Jim's test. He changed the combinations and locked the letter and photos in his briefcase, with other paper work. Then he stored the briefcase in its usual location in the RV.

Later that day, Dick returned unexpectedly from an errand to find Maria re-packing closet where the briefcase was stored. She hadn't seen him approaching, and he stayed out of sight until she finished. She was startled to see him at the door, but immediately flashed a big smile and commented on her ability as a housekeeper.

Hell-week began that evening. She didn't eat much dinner and drank far too much wine. She got up during the night to sit by the table. Pretending to be asleep, Dick heard her crying softly. They left the next morning for Omaha. Maria avoided all contact with him and sat quietly in the back of the motor home.

They had planned to store the RV at his aunt's farm and spend a week in Lincoln evaluating the Registered Nurse employment situation. However, Maria said she was too ill to continue. Time was running out for Dick. He faked a phone call from SHAPE, then told Maria he was being recalled and had to leave immediately. She agreed to remain with his aunt until their originally scheduled return flight next week.

When they said goodbye, the anger--which had been building in Maria--exploded in a tirade of screaming. While her outburst was directed at Dick's leaving early for SHAPE, he knew it was for another reason.

He made the one hour bus ride to the Omaha airport with a breaking heart.

Arriving at Charles de Gaulle/Roissy Airport, Dick cleared customs and immigration, then caught the Air France bus to Porte Maillot. He stood in the front, holding his travel bag. He was first off the bus and turned to view the faces of the dismounting passengers. Then he rode the Métro to the North Train Station, where he took the Roissy-Rail back to Charles de Gaulle. There he prepared to board the #351 bus to Vincennes, carefully watching the faces of those getting on the bus, and stepping aboard at the last second. At Vincennes, he went into the Métro and got off at the station closest to his destination on Phillipe Du Roule. He stopped at a sidewalk café on the quiet street across from the Bradford Hotel. Carefully surveying the area while drinking a coffee, he was satisfied he had successfully shaken any tail.

He took a quick shower and was shaving when he heard the quiet knock on his door. Peering through the view finder, he saw a casually dressed middle-aged man carrying a suitcase. He had long brown hair, a full beard, and tinted glasses. When he saw the Maltese Cross on the gold chain around the man's neck, he opened the door for Jim Conrad.

"If you have lost your razor, I got one you can borrow."

Conrad gripped Dick's hand. "Could have saved you some time, if I had told you what your disguise will be for this mission."

Dick laughed. "You look like a lost pebble from the *Rolling Stones*. Can I offer you some instant coffee?"

"That's what I hate about the Bradford," said Jim. "They are too Americanized."

"Are you staying here?"

"Yeah, I'm next door. Can't really talk here. It will take me fifteen minutes to give you a make-over, then we'll go for a stroll by the Seine."

Jim found a parking place for the blue Citroen along the Quai d'Orsay. "You'll never make it as a hippie, Brown Bear. You're too stiff. Loosen up a bit. You look good with long hair and a beard. Goes great with those brown eyes. You'll get used to the contacts."

"At least the loose shirt and torn jeans are comfortable. Too damned hot in this town. Were you here last month?"

"Yeah, August was a scorcher. I was glad to commute back and forth to White Hall. Many things to brief you on, Bear. Let's walk by the river."

Dick got out of the car and stretched his six-foot frame. "Was a long hard trip from Nebraska, Mountie."

They descended the concrete steps to the river's edge, then they strolled eastward.

"Wish I had a written program for you, Dick. This has become complicated, and extremely dangerous. There's a lot to consider, and to remember."

"Start me out with something simple."

"Okay. Think you can recognize the CIA agent you worked with in Sicily during Operation *Starlight?*"

"Yeah, I'm reasonably sure. Since the phone call from Nelson and Mackenzie, I've been thinking about him a lot. It has been twenty-two years, but he had a very distinctive, sarcastic voice. That should really help."

"We'll make it as easy as we can. Our defector, Yuri, has been very cooperative, and Nelson's contact in the CIA hierarchy has come through with some old and new photos. Yuri was closely associated with the Soviet SA-2 shootdown of the Neptune aircraft. He claims to have personally selected the site for the missiles."

"What did he say about my airstrike to avenge the Neptune?"

"They knew you were coming, Bear. That information was personally delivered by a CIA agent known as *Ralph*."

"What was the price tag for an F-8 Crusader and one Navy fighter pilot?"

"For sucking you into that SAM trap, Ralphie got $150,000 in cash." Conrad paused to clear his throat, ". . . and some time with Güla, before the Soviets took her."

A wave of revulsion swept over Dick. He stopped walking and took a deep breath to clear the nausea. "He's mine, Mountie!"

"Yes, he is Dick. Max will be your backup, and Toufani has asked for a part of the action."

"Is the Admiral in town?"

"Yeah, and he brought along a dark-haired pixie who's starting a new life."

"Shreeba's here too? It does get complicated, doesn't it!"

"We'll take it one step at a time, Dick. Nelson's CIA contact made sure that Ralph's section heard about Yuri's defection. They have also been told that MI-6 will deliver him to D.C. next week. Yuri has cooperated by blackmailing Ralph with a few phone calls. We expect Ralph to arrive tomorrow morning, with the $150,000 Yuri has requested to forget the whole Neptune incident."

"I imagine Ralphie would rather seal Yuri's lips with a 9mm than throw away a hundred and fifty grand."

"Of course he would, Bear. We have tried to visualize all his options. He's certain to have told the KGB where he's meeting Yuri tomorrow night. Several of those guys will be around. Abood and Max will be on Ralphie's tail from the second he steps off TWA. If he's hooking up with someone, we'll know it. Since the info on Yuri was circulated around CIA headquarters, there might be other rogue agents who also fear him. They may try to hit him over here."

"How and where is it going down, Mountie?"

Jim paused and pointed toward the Seine. "Right out there, in the middle of the river. Ralphie has never met Yuri face-to-face. Max speaks Moscow-Russian perfectly. He will be posing as Yuri. In their phone call yesterday, Yuri told Ralph to rendezvous at the entrance to the *Petit Palais*. Abood will be there to direct him to the dock below the *Tulleries* Gardens. He'll also tell Ralph to rent an outboard and proceed to the Franklin Street Bridge. You and

Max will be waiting and watching from that dark-blue cruiser tied up at the dock below us."

Dick scanned the sporty boat, then his eyes narrowed. "If Ralph has backup, what's to stop them from grabbing Abood at the *Palais?*"

Conrad smiled. "When he finishes his conversation with Ralph, a dozen Gendarmes will arrest him for drug smuggling. Three of MI-6's best will be in close, to make sure they do the job safely."

". . . and what's to stop them from targeting our cruiser with an RPG-7 from the Franklin Street Bridge?"

"You won't be at the bridge. Wait till Ralph gets tired and heads back for the *Tulleries* dock, then intercept him halfway. You'll be out of range."

"His backup will no doubt follow him to the *Tulleries* dock. They could have us bracketed between the dock and the bridge."

"Could be, Bear, but MI-6 will be on the bridge and Toufani's boys will take care of the dock. More questions?"

"Would be a walk-in-the-park, or rather a float-down-the-river, if we had some air cover."

"Once a fighter pilot, always a fighter pilot. Yes, there will be air cover. An improved version of the Whisper helicopter from our Aura days is waiting for me atop the British Embassy--outfitted with night-vision and a silencer-equipped three-barreled 7.2mm gun. I'll be overhead: intercepting, locating, monitoring, and jamming Ralph's communication system, which the KGB's certain to supply. I'll also be monitoring the *Purple* system you'll be using."

Conrad led him down the steps to the dock where the cruiser was tied. The RCMP Colonel smiled. "Yeah, Dick, we've tried to make your first couple days easy. You and I'll eat an early dinner tonight, so you can get some rest. After tomorrow night's activities, Toufani's inviting us to the restaurant in the Carillon Hotel."

"President Wilson's old haunt. Have I got a date?"

"Indeed!" Conrad smiled. "When I invited Shreeba for a drink last night, she took a gold cigarette case from her purse, kissed it, and said she was saving *all* her other kisses. I took that as a *no*. On their way here from Iran, she and Toufani stopped by Zurich. She left the original case you gave her in a bank box. Abrahim converted the one she now carries into an incendiary device."

"Did Abrahim come with them?"

"Toufani swears he wouldn't cross the street without him. Really loves the guy! Maybe you read about the hit at Qom a few weeks ago--shook-up the rest of the Ayatollahs. That was a solo effort by Abrahim."

Wakes from small craft on the river rocked the sleek thirty-foot cruiser. Dick and Max sat quietly, monitoring Abood's conversation with Ralph at the Petit Palais. He instructed Ralph to rent a boat at the dock below the Tulleries Gardens, proceed alone to the Franklin Street Bridge, and wait for Yuri's dark-blue cruiser. When they heard Abood surrendering to French police, Max and Dick smiled. The gutsy little Egyptian was safe!

Overhead in the quiet Whisper helicopter, Jim intercepted and located numerous transmissions from the KGB. At least two were positioned in the middle of the Franklin Street Bridge, two more were on the Concorde Bridge. Four others had surrounded the entrance to the Petit Palais. After Abood issued his instructions to Ralph, those on the Concorde Bridge apparently began moving to the dock below the Tulleries, those at the Petit Palais trailed Ralph.

Max smiled at Dick. "Going to be a little crowded on the dock. Business should be good for Shreeba."

Dick grinned as he remembered the street-walker disguise the impish girl was wearing. "Those KGB studs will have a difficult time concentrating. Hope she heard Abood's description of Ralph before he went off the air."

"I heard Toufani respond," said Max, "but they are going to be outnumbered. Counting Ralph, there'll be at least seven bad guys."

"That's hardly enough to be interesting for Abrahim. I imagine most of those guys will rent boats and follow Ralph."

"Moon River, this is Mountie. The boys from Concorde Bridge are nearing the dock."

"Moon River roger. I see two men coming down the steps."

Then they heard Shreeba: "Scheherazade sees Ralph, ten meters behind those two."

Toufani responded quickly, "I see him too. Stay where you are. Wait for whoever's following him, then do your act. Keep them at the top of the stairs. Mountie, Ralph's at the boat rental stand."

"Mountie, roger. I heard him tell the KGB guys to stay off the dock until he's underway."

"Scheherazade here. The first two are coming back up the steps, . . . and there's a group of four approaching."

"Moon River, understand. Wait to see what they're going to do before you distract them."

"This is Mountie. The KGB have told Ralph they'll wait until he's on the river, then they'll rent two boats."

Dick glanced at Max. "Six KGB with Shreeba at the top of the stairs. Not good!" He immediately began to transmit: "Be careful, Scheherazade."

Her lilting laughter came over the air: "Relax, Brown Bear, Abrahim's only two meters away."

Max grinned and said to Dick: "God only knows where she's hiding that wire, but it's working loud and clear."

"I'd bet in the cleavage."

"She could lose a whole radio in there. I'd like to adjust the volume for her."

Dick laughed. "Down, Max, down boy!"

"Mountie from Moon River. Ralph's in an outboard. A boy is helping him start the motor. He will be underway shortly."

"Mountie concurs. He just told the kid to get out."

"There he goes, Mountie. Heading downstream for the Franklin Street Bridge."

"Roger that Moon River. Have him locked up on my night-vision gadget. Heads up, Scheherazade! Sounds like four of the KGB are heading for the boat rental stand."

"Yes Sir, they are. Now, don't get jealous, Dick. I'm only doing my job."

Max laughed and slapped Dick on the back, then they listened as Shreeba did a very good job indeed.

She engaged the four as they started down the steps. The first two brushed by her, but the third and fourth were definitely interested. While the others rented boats, those two urged her to go for a ride. She played the role effectively, delaying the whole process by at least ten minutes. At the last second, she refused to get in the boat. The one who was bargaining with her grabbed the gold cigarette case from her hand. He told her to be waiting when he returned, if she wanted it back. She cursed at him, then took a seat where he could see her long slender legs. The boats moved slowly away from the dock.

"Mountie, Moon River, they are underway."

"Mountie roger. Scheherazade, which boat has your cigarette case?"

"The last one, Sir."

"Good work! Don't trigger that thing till I tell you, okay?"

"This is Moon River, I have the trigger and understand. Are you locked on the first boat."

"Mountie, affirmative. They're talking about holding under the Concorde Bridge. Ralph has agreed with them. He's waiting under the Franklin Street Bridge for *Yuri*."

"Mountie, this is Abrahim. Apparently no one's joining the two guys still at the top of the stairs. What have you heard?"

"Believe you're right, Abrahim. Haven't heard transmissions from any other source. Can you take them out without creating a disturbance?"

"If they're smokers, I have a *Brown Bear special* for them."

"Hey, come on, Abrahim," interrupted Dick. "You still carrying a grudge?"

They heard Abrahim's soft chuckle. "No, but keep your hand over your drink when you sit next to me."

"Better leave them alone until things start to happen out here," said Dick.

"Mountie concurs. Wait for Bear's call to take them out."

It was a long fifteen minutes before Mountie was again on the air. "Ralphie's got more patience than I thought. I have only forty-five minutes of fuel remaining. Wait one, . . . he's speaking with the boys under the Concorde Bridge. He's starting back upstream toward them. Brown Bear, get away from the dock. I'll vector you to him."

"Brown Bear, wilco."

Dick engaged the gears and eased the throttles of the idling engines forward. They moved smoothly away from the dock.

"Brown Bear underway."

"Steer two-nine-zero degrees. I'll give you a correction when you're out in the current. There's a fast mover at your two o'clock. Should pass well in front of you."

"Bear, roger. That's a cruiser like ours, only white-colored."

"No other traffic between you and Ralphie. Turn right to three-three-zero. That should put him at your ten-thirty position."

"Bear, wilco. Max, give me a call when you see him."

"Max has a shadow with one white light in that position."

"Has to be Ralphie. I hold no other traffic."

"Okay, Max, I have him now," said Dick. "Stand in the back where he can see you."

Dick executed a perfect rendezvous on the slow-moving outboard. He had his engines at idle as they pulled alongside.

As briefed by Yuri, Max shouted one word in Russian. Ralph's response was immediate. Max caught the bow rope that Ralph tossed him and fastened it to the cruiser. Dick held the cruiser's nose steady into the current, the smaller boat drifted against the side of the cruiser.

"Heads up, Bear," transmitted Jim Conrad. "He told his backup to come get him. Estimate you have three minutes before they're within range. Abrahim, give those guys on the dock a smoke."

Ralph grabbed Max's hand and stepped aboard the cruiser. The tall, thin, pale Caucasian carried a black briefcase.

"Got the cash?" asked Max.

"Yeah," replied Ralph sarcastically. "Somehow I pictured you as an older man."

"Open the briefcase. Dump the money on the deck," said Max.

Ralph unlocked the case and complied.

Watching and listening from the driver's seat, Dick whispered: "Positive ID, it's Ralph."

In their earphones, Max and Dick heard Mountie's call: "Okay, I'm jamming his frequency. Take him out."

Max grinned at Ralph. "Looks about right. You can go. Take your bomb-rigged briefcase with you."

Ralph twisted his narrow face and sneered at Max. "No honor among thieves?"

"Nor among traitors," replied Max. "Before you go, I'd like you to meet someone your own age--someone you know."

Ralph went for the pistol in his waistband, but Max's quick hand took it away.

Dick growled from behind him: "Greetings from Güla, you cowardly piece of crap." Ralph pivoted toward him. Dick's viscous right cross knocked him backwards into Max. Max rendered him unconscious with a blow from the handle of the pistol.

"Moon River, Mountie, light up those guys in the second boat."

"Moon River, wilco."

Dick and Max were lifting Ralph into his outboard when they saw the reddish flash upriver. It was followed by the orange explosion of a gas can.

"Nice work, Abrahim!" called Jim. "Expedite, Brown Bear. The lead boat's closing fast."

Max slapped the C-4 on the side of Ralph's gas can and jumped back aboard the cruiser. He threw Ralph's briefcase into the outboard. "Let's get out of here, Bear."

Dick freed the line holding the boats together and leapt into the driver's seat. He gunned the engines and sent the cruiser hurtling toward the shoreline.

"We're clear, Mountie," called Max. "Tell us when to send him to hell."

"Mountie," shouted Dick, "we're picking up small arms fire from the lead boat."

"I'm in my run, Bear. Watch what this British BB gun can do."

Dick swerved the cruiser to parallel the southern shore line and cut the engines. He looked up river to see a silent ripple of white muzzle flashes, resembling a small fireworks display. The gas tank explosion in the lead boat illuminated two figures falling into the water.

"Well done, Mountie," transmitted Max. "We're in the shadows on the south side of the river. We've lost sight of Ralph."

"Rog, Max. He's beyond the Franklin Street Bridge. Flame him now, before he gets out of range."

Dick lifted the trigger mechanism and pointed it toward the bridge. "For God, for loyalty, for the boys in the Neptune, and for Güla." He pressed the button. A ten-foot ball of fire illuminated the shores of the Seine.

15

KNIFE FIGHTING 101

Beams of early morning sunshine streamed into the room. Dick rolled on his side and focused his eyes on the naked figure by the window. Tousled black hair piled high on her head, long slim neck, elegant shoulders, softly curving back, firm shapely bottom, long tapered legs--he groaned quietly, "If only I were an artist."

Shreeba stretched her arms over her head, stood on her tiptoes, and pirouetted slowly to face him. The high pointed bosom accentuated the sensual figure that could fulfill any man's fantasy.

She batted her long eye lashes at him. He responded: "Sweetie, it would be a crime to hide all that in a ballerina costume."

A smile blossomed on her pixie face and revealed perfect teeth. Delicate wide cheek bones framed her enormous brown eyes. "Maybe I should take up dancing and narrow everything a bit."

"Don't you dare."

"So, . . . you like me the way I am?"

"After last night, how can you ask?"

She tiptoed to the bed and blinked her brown eyes at him. "Is there something more I can do for you this morning?"

He laughed and threw a pillow at her. "Yes, you can put on a robe and bring in the newspaper."

"How romantic." She puckered her lips at him, tiptoed to the door, peered through the view finder, and slid the bolt back.

"Don't even think about it!" cautioned Dick.

"Maybe there's someone who would enjoy looking at me more than you do."

She opened the door, stepped into the hall, and bent over to pick up the paper. Then she came back in, closed the door, and brought the paper to the bed--where Dick sat shaking his head.

"Tell me no one was out there," he said.

She giggled. "Only grandfather, and he is probably making grandmother very happy right now."

She turned and looked over her shoulder with that pixie smile. She began to bend forward. "Would you like to see it again?"

He threw the other pillow at her sexy bottom. "You crazy vixen! Settle down. You know the busy day we're going to have. Stop teasing me."

She threw the paper on the floor and flew into his arms. He crushed her nakedness to him. They kissed with wild abandon. It was impossible to deny her. Their bodies entwined, and they renewed the sometimes fierce, sometimes gentle, but always white-hot, passion they had discovered during the night.

The boy set the silver tray of croissants, jam, orange juice, and coffee on the table. Dick gave him a generous tip and closed the door behind him.

He picked the *Le Monde* off the floor and bent to kiss the tousled black hair protruding from under the sheet. "Come on, hot stuff, time to earn your keep."

She rolled over and tossed the sheet aside. "Did you ever stop to think you made a big mistake, giving me that million dollars in advance? You would have enjoyed it more at a thousand a night."

Dick chuckled. "I wouldn't have lived through the first fifty thousand. Now, prop yourself up on that pillow and read me the news. My French is limited to *faire le cour, Amoureux*."

". . . and you do that very well, Captain Williams." Shreeba opened the newspaper. She found it on the third page. "Here it is. The headline reads *Drug War Explodes on the Seine.* You want me to translate it word-for-word?"

"Not necessary. Sort out the main points for me."

"Okay. The first paragraph explains that an Egyptian drug lord was arrested near the *Petit Palais*."

Dick laughed. "Does it also say he was released in time for dinner at the Carillon?"

"No, it says he's still in custody." Shreeba smiled. "There's a lot to be said for control of the media."

"Yeah," he agreed. "Certainly helps protect Abood. He will be enroute to the Philippines shortly, for a well-deserved holiday."

Shreeba continued reading: "It says three boats were taken from the *Tulleries* dock by five men. One of the boats blew up near the Franklin Street Bridge. Only small pieces of it were recovered, along with some body parts. Apparently the gas tank exploded on another of the boats under the *Concorde* Bridge. It was only slightly damaged. The two men who swam ashore were arrested by police. The third boat was also recovered near the Franklin Street Bridge, riddled with bullet holes. Police are looking for the two men who rented that boat, but they are feared dead. They suspect a gunfight broke out between the occupants of the three boats."

Shreeba scanned through the article and began to laugh. "Two Russians were found near the boat dock, unconscious from a drug overdose. Police are beginning the investigation with their questioning. They are predicting it was another demonstration of the lawlessness of the Russian Mafia drug lords in Paris."

Replete in their hippie disguises, Jim and Dick met Yuri in the tank at the British Embassy where he was being held by MI-6. The stocky Russian's pale complexion, white hair, and icy-blue eyes were similar to Maximilian's.

Jim had cautioned Dick to avoid reference to the Aura Project, or displays of emotion, during the questioning.

Dick began with the KGB attempt to assassinate him in Manila: "Yuri, I'm familiar with Operation *Mosquito.* Could you enlighten me about your choice of targets, namely Captain Williams?"

Without hesitation, in good English, and in a clear strong voice, the KGB defector explained: "Ah, yes, the Ramada Hotel bombing. My mission in Manila included discrediting the U.S. military, making them appear vulnerable. Williams was an embassy official, a decorated fighter pilot, a member of the ambassador's counter-terrorism team, and active on the U.S./Philippines Mutual Defense Board--seldom have I been provided with so perfect a target."

"Why bomb him? Why not simply shoot him on the street?"

"It almost happened that way, before I got the situation under control." Yuri's cold chuckle sent a chill through Dick's veins. "Without thinking, I put a $500 price on his head. An NPA boy-girl machete team on a Vespa almost collected it, before the ink was dry on my offer. Fortunately for me, the Captain was guarded by an amazingly talented woman who took the team down. Incredible! I had been tailing Williams and watched the incident from a shopping center."

Memories of Rita surged through Dick's mind, but his face remained calm. "Why would a machete slaying have been unfortunate? It would have been a good demonstration of the vulnerability of individual Americans."

"*Da*," agreed Yuri, "but that team had performed the same hit a week earlier on a Filipino Policeman. It would have reduced the importance of the Captain's assassination to the same level. I retracted the price on his head and searched for ways to elevate his importance and increase the media coverage of the event."

"That led to the bomb in the Ramada Hotel?"

"*Da.* It took a few weeks for things to fall into place, but I was finally presented with the perfect situation. It guaranteed maximum international television coverage."

"Philippine Constabulary files show you spoke with an Austrian woman at the Hyatt Hotel in Baguio shortly before the bombing. Who was she? Was she part of the operation?"

An icy grin flashed briefly across Yuri's hard face. "Ah, yes, Maria the nurse. She had become romantically involved with the Captain, while he was under my surveillance, and was living with him in the Ramada. We did a routine background check. She had a childhood chum, Irina, who was married to an Austrian security agent that had come over to our side. When Maria went to Baguio with a tour group, I made her acquaintance in the Hyatt Hotel. She agreed to smuggle the bomb into the Ramada for me."

Dick was shocked, but his voice remained calm and even. "That is a far stretch, Yuri--from a chance meeting to participating in a bombing."

"Certainly," agreed the KGB defector. "Let me explain. She had entered the bar alone for a drink. A typhoon was blowing outside, and we were the only ones there. I engaged her in conversation. Within thirty minutes, I had informed her that the husband of her childhood friend was a traitor to Austria. When she asked why he was spying for us, I said he had fallen in love with one of our agents--a sexy bundle who had turned that trick for us several times before. Maria was concerned about Irina's three children: what would happen to them if she found out about the affair? That was the reaction I had hoped for! I promised Maria our spy's illicit affair would end quickly and quietly--if she agreed to do a small favor for me."

Dick interrupted: "Carrying a bomb through hotel security is hardly a small favor."

"She didn't know it was a bomb," said Yuri. "I told her it was a listening device--a backup for other systems we already had eaves-dropping on Captain Williams."

"Was that the only favor you tried to blackmail from her?" asked Dick, with his heart in his throat.

Yuri raised his albino eyebrows slightly. "If you have seen this woman, you already know the answer." He sighed. "Unfortunately, she refused to cooperate at such a personal level, at the Hyatt or at the Ramada--when I installed the bomb a few days later."

Dick quietly breathed a sigh of relief and tried to summarize: "So, to protect a friend, Maria agreed to smuggle into the Ramada what she thought was a listening device. Did you have contact or try to use her again?"

"I gave her a phone number, but it was over a year before she called me."

"What was that all about?" asked Jim Conrad.

"She seemed quite distraught. I volunteered to meet her in person, but she was in Belgium and I was in Moscow. We talked at length on the phone. She wanted revenge on some woman and asked for my help. She told me this person would be escorting a female terrorist from Berlin to Manila. She was unable to identify the prisoner, but thought it had something to do with Williams' tour in the Philippines. I told her I would research the matter and get back to her. I asked for her number, but she suddenly became very nervous and hung up on me."

"Did you hear from her again?" asked Dick.

"No, that was the last time," replied the KGB officer. "I kept track of her. She is living in Vienna with Captain Williams, who has left the Navy."

Jim asked, "What did you do with the information she gave you?"

"I recalled from my tour in Manila that Captain Williams was involved with rescuing some people after a bombing at the Philippine Plaza Hotel. I also knew the bombing was performed by renegade commandos, who were taking orders from a senior West German official. The commandos were later killed, but the female who planted the bomb disappeared. I tied one-and-one together, and contacted our KGB informant in the West German Office for Defense of the Constitution, the *BfV*."

"Was that informant the same woman you and I discussed last

week?" asked Jim.

"Yes," smiled Yuri coldly, "that was Janine. She confirmed my theory. She had contacts in Manila and knew the female prisoner was scheduled to be tried in Philippine courts for the Plaza bombing. She was certain the woman escorting the bomber would be Captain Williams' former bodyguard."

Dick's heart was pounding, but he asked quietly: "Do you know what Janine did with that information?"

"Oh, yes! She told me Captain Williams and his bodyguard had destroyed a business operated by her close friend--I believe she meant lover--and killed him. She told me other members of the *business* would dispose of the bodyguard when she arrived in Manila. She said they were professionals from Syria, who had done things for the KGB in the past. She asked me to provide a CCCP charter flight out of Manila for them."

"Did you do that?" asked Jim.

Yuri paused to think. "*Da.* I first checked the name she gave me, Ahmad Salah, through our Middle East files. He was indeed one of our *friends.* I asked our Middle East desk to contact him and arrange the CCCP charter. Salah was in Libya at the time, but the charter was scheduled for him out of Manila. Salah was also given authorization for a couple RPG's from the NPA in Manila."

Dick fell silent, his mind raged with thoughts of the horrific ambush of Rita on the Manila airport boundary road--they had used RPG's with phosphorous warheads.

Jim sensed Dick was in trouble and sought to change the subject. "Are you packed, Yuri? I'll be taking you off the roof tonight in a helicopter. We're non-stop to Mildenhall, where a special U.S. military aircraft will be waiting. You'll be at Andrews Air Force Base outside Washington D.C. in time for breakfast."

"I am thankful for that," answered Yuri. "I was looking out a window this morning and saw a familiar face outside the gate." He glanced at Dick. "Did you know Captain Williams' bodyguard?"

Jim Conrad immediately intervened. "We are asking the questions, Yuri! I warned you about that before."

"Yes Sir, but don't play me for an idiot. The Dick Williams in Operation *Starlight* in '65 was the same Dick Williams at the U.S. Embassy in Manila in '80, and at NATO in '81, and is now in Vienna with Maria. It's easy to connect the dots. I had at least ten photos of him at various stages in his career in my Moscow files."

Dick and Jim sat quietly. Yuri continued: "I read *El Monde* this morning. Your people did a hell of a job taking out Ralph last night--and at least two of my former colleagues who are in town looking for me. I imagine that evened the score for Operation *Starlight,* and I'm grateful for the $150,000 from Ralph."

"As promised," replied Jim.

"You'll need it if you live in the States," said Dick. "Surviving in America will require all your skills. The primary threat won't be the KGB, it'll be your next door neighbors. They could very likely be axe murderers. You can also rest assured there are more moles in the CIA, who will set you up for those guys waiting outside. Better consider the MI-6 offer to stay in the U.K. or go to Canada."

"Thanks for the advice," said Yuri. "You are correct. There is a much deeper mole in the CIA, and I plan to trade him for enough dollars to buy my own island somewhere."

Jim reacted quickly as the KGB defector suddenly opened his coat. Yuri smiled and withdrew an old-fashioned watch and chain.

Jim returned his Walther to its holster.

Yuri handed the watch to Dick and explained: "If you run across Captain Williams, please give him this. He had a friend named Paula at the U.S. Embassy in Manila. She, her husband Ray, and their son Jimmie, were aboard KAL 007 on its last flight, 1 September 1983. When it crossed into Soviet territory, I was summoned to the Kremlin, along with other KGB officers with Southeast Asia experience. Chairman Andropov was concerned that it might have something to do with an exceptionally dangerous threat, which we referred to as *Phantom.* We advised him there was no apparent connection, but it had him very agitated. He took this watch out of his pocket, laid it on his desk, and gave the order: *If they don't turn around in ten minutes, shoot them down!*"

Yuri paused and looked into Dick's penetrating blue eyes. "You know the rest of the story. It was not a high point in our history. Chairman Andropov left the watch lay on the table when he left the room, so I liberated it."

There was a fierce look of defiance in the hard brown eyes of the middle-aged German woman. She was seated on an uncomfortable wooden chair at the long table. Her faded brown hair was pulled tightly back and fell in a straggly pony tail below her shirt collar. High, sharp, cheek bones framed her narrow face. Her thin body sometimes trembled, and she frequently shifted her tightly closed legs from side-to-side. Her long bony fingers were gripped tightly in her lap. Twisted lips and tightly knit brows reflected the hatred Janine felt toward her interrogators.

Jim Conrad sat casually on a corner of the table across from the *BfV* clerk. In his hand was the remote control for the TV and electronic equipment on the far side of the room. An undisguised Dick stood at the end of the table. Shreeba was by the window. The interrogation was being videotaped, but Jim had insisted upon the presence of another female in the room.

He raised the remote control and stopped the audio tape of Yuri's description of Janine's involvement with the ambush of Rita.

"Would you care to dispute any of Yuri's observations?"

She took a sharp breath and screamed shrilly at him. "You filthy *Schwein!* When I told you he was coming to Rhein-Main, you promised me immunity in Switzerland. You had better release me immediately, or the wrath of the German government will once again fall upon London."

Jim responded calmly: "Are you talking about the government you betrayed in the FRG, or your communist cohorts in the DDR?"

"*You* are the communist traitor, *Herr* Winkleman." She glared at him. You wouldn't dare bring charges against me! I'll expose you as the *Rote Armee Fraktion* terrorist you have been for six years."

"Perhaps we are both traitors, Janine. You betrayed the Constitution that you swore to protect, and I betrayed the RAF that I swore to destroy."

Janine's hard face blanched, Jim continued: "The list of your betrayals is long, and the evidence is deep. Even if you escape the death penalty in West Germany, there are those countries, whose citizens you helped kidnap and murder, that will surely hang you."

Dick spoke softly and evenly. "In my country, there are scores of parents seeking revenge for the rape, enslavement, and murder of their innocent daughters by your *friend,* Luther Steinwald. Yuri's testimony of your involvement will make you one of America's most wanted. Your days on this earth are numbered."

Janine's voice trembled: "Luther was not a murderer or a rapist. He was an admired leader of our *Bundestag* and a gentle man. He made business arrangements with foreigners to care for unwanted girls from corrupt countries."

"We have concrete evidence to the contrary," said Jim. "What qualifications do you have to judge his character?"

Janine continued in a shaky voice: "I knew him all his life. We were *Kinder* together in *München.* We attended the same schools. Luther was brilliant! He seized the opportunity to advance through the universities. When it was necessary for him to leave *München,* he promised to return and marry me." Janine's voice failed. She paused for a moment.

"Would you like a drink of water, Madam?" asked Shreeba.

She snapped at the Palestinian. "Not from a whore like you! I'm sure it would give me an infectious disease."

Shreeba only smiled. Jim continued: "There are no records that Luther Steinwald married you."

"*Gar nichts!*" exclaimed Janine hotly. "When people recognized his intellectual brilliance and leadership qualities, he was pressured to run for office. That took money. I sacrificed everything, and stepped aside so he could marry a wealthy heiress."

". . . and he repaid you with one of the most trusted positions in the government, at the *BfV?*" inquired Dick.

"*Ja wohl.*" Janine regained her composure. "Luther wanted me near him in Bonn. I was his mistress until the end."

"He had three children with his wife," said Jim.

"That was only for political purposes! I was his true love."

Jim pointed the remote control at the TV. "You saw this before, in the office of the Chancellor, but I thought I'd remind you."

A segment of the videotaped *Purple* sting of Luther Steinwald in the Philippine Plaza Hotel appeared on the big screen:

Steinwald puffed out his chest and sat on the edge of the bed in his baggy underwear. "Ja, Schatzie, I am indeed the one with the power in the Bundestag. That's why the Syrians will do anything I say. It was my power that got them the sixty-five million Deutsche Mark loan. It was my connection in the BfV that informed them of the Muslim Brotherhood meeting in Karlsruhe, and the plot to assassinate the Syrian President and his brother."

"Assad owes me his life," crowed Steinwald. "He will give me whatever I want."

"Then ask him to give me some protection," begged Rita. "The

Mafia will kill me if they think I had anything to do with your idea."

Steinwald rose from the bed and dropped his boxer shorts to the floor. He pulled off his undershirt and stood naked before her. "Ja, suisse Gisela," he leered, "you do something for me, and I'll do something for you."

Jim pressed the pause button and commented: "Your gentleman lover in action."

Janine began to respond, "That was business . . ." The video re-appeared on the screen:

Steinwald grabbed a handful of Rita's hair and pulled her face to his groin. She reached forward and took hold of him with both hands. He groaned as she pushed him back.

"Luther, you'll get more satisfaction if you relax," she said, "and I'll treat you much better if you guarantee to keep the Mafia away from me. Isn't there something you can do to convince them I don't have anything to do with your Syrian dealings?"

Steinwald moaned and pulled her hair back, tilting her face upwards. "How soon can you have some girls ready?"

She kissed his bulging stomach and smiled at him. "How much time do I have?" She moved her hands slowly.

"Three weeks," he growled. "Now get busy!" He pulled her face against him.

Rita gripped the German's private parts and forced him away from her again. "Would you take my girls directly to Damascus?"

"Mein Gott," he snarled, "don't be so damned stupid! Get some girls ready for the Mafia's next auction. Give them a bargain, and the greedy bastards will have no reason to think you're involved with me or Salah."

He jerked Rita to her feet. Before she could resist, he peeled the fitted bodice of the dress down to her waist.

Jim stopped the video. "The kindly businessman at work." Before Janine could respond, the video re-appeared.

The German Congressman paused to admire Rita's charms. He grasped her crudely with his hands. "Na, ja, Australian girls are the biggest and best."

"Is that why you bought so many for your villa in Damascus?" she asked pointedly.

"Ja, ja," came the evil laugh, "it takes at least a dozen to satisfy

an Aryan like me."

Rita stood quietly as the pudgy fingers and drooling mouth explored her bosom.

Jim interrupted the video: "The faithful lover at the office."

Janine's shrill voice cut the air: "I'm so glad I had a part in blowing that bitch to hell."

The tape began again:

Steinwald cruelly hit Rita in the solar plexus. She was gasping for breath, he tore off her panties and forced her legs open.

Dick opened the hotel room door. Steinwald was trying to force himself into a twisting Rita. The German's back was to Dick. He was oblivious to everything in the room, except the squirming body beneath him.

Dick crossed the room quickly and jammed the barrel of the thirty-eight against Steinwald's rectum. "Say your prayers, Kraut," he shouted, "I'm going to blow your ass to hell!"

Steinwald froze. The fat hanging around his belly started to quiver. "Nein," he croaked, "nicht schiessen, nicht schiessen!"

He attempted to raise himself off Rita. Dick gave him a power-ful kick. He fell off the bed and rolled against the table. It tipped over and the bottle of bourbon spilled in his face.

He lay sputtering on the floor. Dick kicked him in the groin. He doubled in pain. Stepping on his ear and pressing his head on the carpet, Dick leaned down to thrust the revolver's barrel against Steinwald's nose. "Give me a reason not to splatter your brains all over the floor," he growled.

Jim pointed the remote control and the screen went dark.

Janine glared at Dick. "You cowardly bully!" she screamed. "Is that when you killed the helpless Congressman?"

Dick answered coldly, "You know better. You've seen the entire video. Your unfaithful *Liebhaber* was killed by the Mafia, when he tried to double-cross them."

Janine seemed suddenly calm and controlled. She rose from the chair and smiled coolly at Dick. "I took care of your red-haired whore, Captain Williams, and it now gives me great pleasure to avenge Luther. If you will look out the window, you'll see that I have also arranged your demise."

She moved purposely past Dick to the window and pointed with a long bony finger at two men leaning against a lamp post. "The

KGB will know how to deal with you. Your death will be slow and painful. I hope they abuse you like you abused Luther."

She raised her hands to the knot above her pony tail, as if signaling the men below.

Shreeba turned to look down at the street. With a swift fluid motion, Janine pulled a scalpel knife out of her pony tail, grabbed Shreeba by the hair with her left hand, and positioned the knife against her throat with the right.

Shreeba seemed to freeze. Dick gave a start, but Jim's strong voice rang throughout the room: "Don't move, Dick!"

Dick looked over his shoulder to see the Walther in Conrad's hand.

The Canadian Mountie spoke quietly: "Relax, Janine, no reason for anyone to get hurt."

The German woman's face was twisted with rage. She pulled Shreeba's head back to expose her throat. The knife was poised by her jugular. "You may shoot me, but I'll live long enough to slash your whore's throat."

"I have no desire to shoot you, Janine," replied Jim softly.

"Both of you move to the door," ordered Janine harshly. "You will escort me out of this embassy and deliver me to the men on the sidewalk, . . . or I will cut her head off!"

Jim motioned to Dick. "We are going to the door, Janine. You want Captain Williams to open it now, or wait till you get there?"

That was Shreeba's opening! With Janine's attention refocused for a split second, she grabbed the hand that held the knife with her left hand and jabbed her right elbow into Janine's stomach. Then her right hand grasped Janine's wrist below the knife. With a quick practiced move, she dropped to her knees and flipped the woman over her right shoulder. Janine hurtled through the air and slammed on her back in front of Shreeba. With a swift wrenching move, the knife was plunged into Janine's heart.

Dick leaped across the room to Shreeba, but it was all over. Jim holstered the Walther. "Where in hell did she get that knife?"

Dick was startled by the fierce look on Shreeba's face. He quickly scooped her into his arms and lifted her clear of the blood spurting from Janine's chest.

Jim opened the door and shouted to the guard: "Get the Doctor and the Security Officer up here, right away!"

Dick set Shreeba on the table. The fire was fading from her eyes. "Where in Allah's name . . . did you learn . . . to do that?"

A grin worked its way back to her impish face. "Bekaa Valley, Knife Fighting 101."

They were gathered for dinner in a formal hall at the British Embassy. Colonel Mackenzie of the Special Air Service sat at the head of the table, his MI-6 counterpart was at the far end. On one side, the Iranian guerrilla leader Admiral Toufani was flanked by Shreeba and Abrahim. Dick was seated next to Shreeba. Opposite him was Colonel Jim Conrad of the Royal Canadian Mounted. Next to him was the KGB defector, Yuri, then came Oberst Maximilian Weber of the Grenzegruppeneun Commandos and the talented Egyptian artist and *Purple* operative, Abood Nasser.

Their conversation seemed out of place in the elegant surroundings. The MI-6 Commander explained the afternoon escape of the four KGB officers from the headquarters of the Paris police. They had assistance from inside, and outside, the detention area. They had fled in a yellow Citroen and a black Mercedes. The only items still in police custody were the personal communications systems and side arms that had been confiscated last night.

Mackenzie asked Yuri: "What should we expect now, in terms of KGB effort?"

Yuri's pale blue eyes regarded the Beef Wellington before him. He sipped the red wine and carefully returned the glass to the table. "There is an unwritten code, Colonel. KGB officers who lose partners are authorized to seek revenge with the means available. Headquarters may, or may not, lend them additional assets. In this case, they will probably get support."

"How many agents will we be up against?" asked the MI-6 Commander.

"The four escapees, and perhaps another six. Our total force in Paris numbers over three hundred."

Jim Conrad's eyes met Dick's. Yuri continued: "However, less than one-tenth of them are capable, or equipped, to take part in the type of revenge operation this will involve."

"Thirty's still an impressive number," said Mackenzie.

"I would guess Headquarters won't assign more than ten," said Yuri. "Other than myself, their only interest is Captain Williams."

Yuri scanned the table slowly. "Colonel Mackenzie is in our files as a formidable SAS Officer, but that doesn't put him on our hit list." He looked at Jim. "I don't believe the pleasant fellow who has been taking care of me for the past month is in our files," he chuckled, "at least not in his present configuration." He glanced to his right. "Oberst Weber is in our files as a sharp thorn in the side of our terrorist operations, but that does not make him a special target at this time."

Yuri nodded politely at Abood. "I must say I don't know you, Sir. You have never been in my files." He smiled at the MI-6 officer. "You know you are on our list, Commander, but that does not separate you from the rest of your service."

He looked across the table. "I'm not familiar with your guests from the Middle East," he smiled at Shreeba, "but I'd certainly like to meet *you*."

Jim Conrad laughed. "Don't forget the video I showed you! Would you explain the KGB's interest in Captain Williams?"

"Yes, certainly. The file I originated on Ralph in '64, and which I reviewed before leaving Moscow, contains several photos of the Captain. He is identified as a participant in your Operation *Starlight,* and as a person who would have a score to settle with Ralph, if his betrayal of the operation was uncovered."

Mackenzie responded, "Well then, the bloody assassins outside this embassy are waiting for Captain Williams."

"Yes Sir!" confirmed Yuri. "He and I, and anyone they might have identified during your operation last night."

Max glanced at Toufani. "What about it Admiral? Could they recognize you, or Abrahim, or Ms. Shreeba?"

"Certainly not me," answered Toufani. "I was in the shadows. Abrahim and Shreeba were in close contact on the dock but were partially disguised."

Max grinned at Abood. "That was a hell of a disguise you had on last night, but you were up-close at the *Petit Palais*."

"Yes," agreed the Egyptian, "but only Ralph got a good look at me. Don't forget, I'm still in jail on drug charges."

"Yeah," Mackenzie chuckled, "and the bloody MI-6 fool sitting in for you looks better in that disguise than you did."

The MI-6 Commander addressed Mackenzie. "We have four people to smuggle out of here: Yuri, Captain Williams, Abrahim, and the lovely Shreeba."

Shreeba blinked her eyelashes at the Commander and smiled.

Mackenzie looked at Jim Conrad. "Got a plan, Colonel?"

"Yeah, but it will take some coordination."

"Are there material assets I should begin assembling?" asked the MI-6 Commander.

Jim turned to Dick. "What kind of a motorcycle did you say you towed behind your RV?"

"An '84 Honda V-6."

Jim looked at the Commander. He responded quickly: "Several dealerships in town. What color and when do you need it?"

"Tomorrow morning. Need to rewire it, and let Dick practice before nightfall. Don't worry about the color, but have someone with a light-colored helmet, who does not resemble Dick, ride it into the embassy."

The MI-6 officer looked up from his notepad. ". . . and?"

"Two agents who can rope a motorcycle."

"Okay, sounds like a lot of sport. You want those chaps before nightfall tomorrow?"

"Yes Sir," answered Jim. He looked at Mackenzie. "That's how Dick will get to the SHAPE airfield south of Brussels."

Conrad smiled at Shreeba. "You can probably ride a bike better than our ancient fighter pilot, but we'll transport you and Abrahim by air later this evening."

He again spoke to Mackenzie. "I want to make a series of fakes with Whisper. I'll take Abrahim first, and see what response we get from the boys outside."

"Jolly good! I've planned to back up Whisper's eyes and ears with a satellite." Mac looked at his watch. "Should be in position in about an hour. Midnight launch for Abrahim?"

"If that's okay with him," said Jim. When the Palestinian nodded his approval, Jim continued: "You'll have to travel light. I'll drop you at SHAPE headquarters. They will take care of you until the Admiral arrives by car tomorrow morning for his visit. Is that all arranged, Colonel Mackenzie?"

"Yes indeed." Mackenzie smiled at Abrahim and Shreeba. "You will be spending the night in Chief Air Marshal Frazier's underground quarters. His steward will meet you at the helo pad. Abood and I will pick Shreeba up tomorrow night enroute to the SHAPE airfield. We'll join Dick for a short flight to England."

Jim explained to Shreeba. "My helicopter only seats two. It will be about one-thirty when I return from delivering Abrahim. Could you be ready to leave at two-thirty?"

"Yes. Admiral Toufani, would you bring my things in your car tomorrow, along with Abrahim's."

"Naturally, my child," said the distinguished guerrilla commander. "We shall miss you in the mountains, but we wish you a wonderful life." He glanced at Dick, ". . . filled with many little blessings."

Dick grinned and looked at his plate. The others laughed at Shreeba's quick reply: "That is also my wish, Sir. Hope I don't have to play Scheherazade all my life."

Abood added, "All she had to do was stop telling stories."

Shreeba giggled. "Then my lips are forever sealed."

Changing the subject, Dick asked the MI-6 Commander: "Does Mildenhall know we're delaying Yuri until tomorrow night?"

"Yes. It will all work for the better. They found a Sematex bomb in the C-141 during pre-flight this afternoon. Fortunately, they were clever enough to keep it secret. We'll be doing a *fake,* as you call it, by escorting someone who resembles Yuri aboard that aircraft in a few hours. They will launch for Andrews, but land at Goose Bay. Your country has agreed to declare the aircraft missing for forty-eight hours. By then we'll have Yuri safely at Andrews, with a Nimrod that will leave tomorrow night."

The MI-6 Commander looked at Jim Conrad. "We have special orders from White Hall to continue that Nimrod on to the Philippines with you, Colonel Mackenzie, Captain Williams, Oberst Maximilian, Ms. Shreeba, and Abood."

Dick looked sharply at Mackenzie. The stocky one-eyed warrior ran his hand over his close-cropped red hair and smiled. "Yeah, Brown Bear, we'll get some of the KGB when they chase your Honda tomorrow night; but we're choosing our own battlefield to blast others who may be on your tail. Shreeba has asked for some time at our safe-house to think over her future, Abood needs a break before returning to Baghdad to paint Saddam's picture all over town, and the rest of us need a holiday for a week or two."

It was ten-thirty the following night. The heavy traffic on the

Champs-Élysées would give Dick the advantage on his motorcycle and help conceal the sound of Whisper.

The Honda had been rewired to allow Dick to turn the lights off while the motor was running. Jim had installed a homing device that would allow him to track the cycle, and wired a monitor for the chip in Dick's shoulder into Whisper's system. With the earphones installed in Dick's dark-colored helmet, he and Jim would be in constant communication.

They were taunting the KGB. Their morning stakeouts had surely seen someone with a light-colored helmet ride the bike into the embassy grounds. When they saw a rider with a different helmet leave late at night, they would be compelled to react. The object was for Dick to be pursued in a manner that gave *Purple* the edge. Reducing the number of KGB operatives and assets early in this high-stakes cat-and-mouse game of attrition was essential.

Abrahim and Shreeba had been safely transported last night. During his departures and arrivals, Jim had used Whisper's sensors to pinpoint several KGB stakeouts.

The official car that transported Toufani to SHAPE in the morning had not been followed. The same was true for Mackenzie and Abood when they departed in the late afternoon. The task remained for Jim to deliver Yuri to Mildenhall, while attriting the KGB assets they hoped would pursue Dick.

Dick sat straddling the familiar bike. The MI-6 Commander shook his hand and wished him well. "This is what a fisherman calls *trolling,*" he said.

"Used to do this in 'Nam," replied Dick, "to reduce the surface-to-air missile population; but we used F8 Crusaders, not Hondas."

He reached back to check the tie-downs on the case containing the M-16, checked the 9mm Browning in his shoulder holster, gunned the engine, and followed the Commander to the back exit.

"Hello Mountie, Brown Bear's underway," he called.

From the Whisper helicopter perched out of sight on the roof of the embassy, Jim answered: "Roger, Bear. Starting my engine. Wait for my signal before you catapult out of there."

"Wilco."

Dick stopped short of the small iron gate, which was designed for pedestrians. The MI-6 Commander waited patiently.

"Remember, Bear," called Jim, "take an immediate left and stay on that street until I tell you to head for the Champs-Élysées. The suspected KGB motorcycle's parked in a driveway about a hundred meters from you. He's sitting on the curb. Don't start too fast, give him a chance to get behind you before you accelerate."

"Are the goat-ropers in position?"

"Yes. You probably won't see their cable on the street. I'll tell you when you've passed it. Whisper's warm and ready, are you?"

"Affirmative. Ladies and Gentleman, Brown Bear's coming out of chute number one, on that famous old bucking horse, Honda."

Jim laughed. "Let's hope you can ride him." He lifted Whisper quietly from the embassy roof.

Dick saluted the MI-6 Commander. He swung the gate open. Dick turned on his lights, gunned the strong engine, laid down a strip of rubber, and skidded into the quiet street. Then he reduced power and watched carefully. Yeah, there was the KGB guy running up the driveway to his bike. Dick checked his speed at 50kph. He was about 40 meters past the driveway when the lights of the KGB's motorcycle appeared in his rearview mirror.

"Got a nibble, Mountie."

"Roger. He is telling the rest of his crowd to wakeup. They are responding from the same locations we briefed this afternoon. Okay, Bear, pick up speed. You're fifty meters from the cable."

Dick gunned the engine and picked up the cycle's nose, hoping the rider on his tail would see the acceleration. He pulled out to pass a small auto. As he did so, he saw the cable on the street.

"I saw the damned cable, Mountie."

"Roger that. Your tail's closing. He won't have those car lights to help him, and it'll be in the air before he gets to it."

Dick stayed in the left lane, watching the trailing motorcycle's headlight in his mirror. Then it appeared to fly into the air. He saw sparks as the somersaulting cycle bounced down the pavement.

"Nice timing!" shouted Dick.

"Yeah, one down and a dozen to go. Take a left at the next corner and get on the Champs-Élysées. They have a yellow Citroen paralleling you on the boulevard, but he has heavy traffic ahead."

Dick followed Conrad's instructions and was soon on the colorful street, heading for the immense traffic circle where the major highways entering Paris merged.

Like other bikes on the boulevard, Dick used the lane-dividing lines to scoot through traffic. Following the MI-6 recommenda-tion, he turned off his headlight. Paris cab drivers had a sadistic habit of flinging their doors open in front of bikes, when they saw them coming.

"The Citroen's about a hundred meters back, Bear. Take it easy so he doesn't lose you. According to my communications-locator, they have two cars tailing you and stakeouts on the major roads to the south, west, and north."

"It's a beautiful ride down here, Mountie."

"Roger Bear. Keep your eyes on the loose bricks in that road. If you go down now, I don't know you!"

Dick laughed at Jim's ages-old idiom from his college days.

The traffic circle was ahead. "Going into the circle, Mountie."

"Roger, have you bright and clear on my gadget. We're directly overhead at five hundred feet. The Citroen's still a hundred meters back--now his playmate's coming up behind. Get out the good china, grandma, we're gonna' have a crowd for dinner!"

"Bear's rolling out on A-1, heading north."

"Roger that. When clear of traffic, you'd better get some speed."

The lights of Paris were fading in the distance before the traffic began to thin. Dick was holding 150kph. The yellow Citroen and its black Mercedes companion were three hundred meters in trail.

"Why don't they try to close, Mountie?"

"They're going to cut you off at the pass, Bear. Sensors indicate an intercept vehicle twenty kilometers ahead. I have transitioned to fixed-wing and am accelerating ahead to check it out. I'm locked on the Citroen and will warn you if he tries to close."

"Traffic's clearing. Okay if I go to one-ninety?"

"Affirmative, Bear. Enjoy the life."

A few moments later, Dick heard Conrad's reassuring voice: "It's a Mercedes, Dick. Hate to mess up such a beautiful machine. He's on an entrance to the autobahn and will probably try to roll out in front of you. When he starts to move, I'll flame him. Could be some bright lights if he explodes, but don't slow down. The others are edging up behind you."

"Yeah, believe I've sorted them out in the rearview mirror."

"My gadget shows you two kilometers from the Mercedes, Bear. The others have told him exactly where you are. He's start-ing his engine. Standby for some fireworks."

Jim had transitioned to rotary-wing. He was hovering at two hundred feet over the autobahn entrance where the Mercedes was waiting. As the auto's lights came on, he locked Whisper's fire-control director on the windshield. Then he changed his mind and moved it forward to the engine compartment--no need to create additional KGB revenge-seekers! Jim dropped Whisper to fifty feet, and unleashed the fury of the 7.2mm miniature Gattling gun.

The Mercedes' shattered hood flew into the air. The engine's fuel system ignited in a ball of orange flame.

Dick was startled, but kept the speeding Honda steady as he flashed by the scene. "Any survivors?" he asked.

"Yeah, three guys running up the autobahn entrance. They're in no mood to shoot at you. Accelerate, Bear, the Citroen's closing! I'm transitioning to fixed-wing and will catch you shortly."

Dick pushed the Honda to 200kph. The cold night air tore at his leather-jacketed body. "Thank God for face-plate helmets," he muttered. "Hope no coyotes are roaming this road tonight."

"Okay, Bear, I'm back overhead. The Citroen and Mercedes are side-by-side, one-hundred-fifty meters back. Road ahead is clear for 25 kilometers."

"What are they up to, Mountie?"

"The Citroen wants to take you now, but the Mercedes guy is saying hold off. He says there's a stretch of rough road about thirty kilometers from the border. He figures you'll have to slow down or lose control. That's where he wants to take you. Wait a minute, yeah, the Citroen agrees."

"How far is that, Mountie."

"Sixty-five kilometers. Slow to one-seventy and save a little fuel. I'll let you know if they change plans."

The next fifteen minutes were pure enjoyment. Few autos were driving to Belgium at this time of night. Dick and his pursuers flew by a police car, but the Gendarmes could care less.

Unfortunately, the stress on his body began to take effect. Dick could feel the cramps coming into his right leg. He fought to focus on other things, scanning rapidly between the road ahead and the lights of his pursuers behind.

Jim was back on the radio: "Bear, the Mercedes has told the Citroen they're approaching the bad pavement. He wants to push you to at least two hundred."

"What's the plan, Mountie?"

"Nearest traffic is ten kilometers ahead. I'm dropping down behind them. I'll take out the Citroen first, then the Mercedes. Concentrate on the road, Bear."

Jim eased the fixed-wing Whisper into a firing position forty meters behind Dick's pursuers. The Citroen was slightly ahead of the Mercedes. He locked the night-vision fire-control on its trunk and opened fire. The vehicle's rear end erupted in a bright flash as the gas tank exploded. The brake lights of the Mercedes glowed. It swerved to avoid a collision. Jim attempted to lock on, but the Mercedes decelerated too quickly. He circled for another shot.

Dick saw the flash in his mirror. "Nice shooting, Mountie."

"Don't slow down, Bear. The Mercedes is four hundred meters behind you and accelerating. I'm rolling in for another shot."

Jim Conrad again coolly aligned Whisper, locked the fire-control on the Mercedes' trunk, and squeezed the trigger.

"Damn! My guns are jammed. Don't let this guy close on you, Bear. I'll swing around front and block him with Whisper."

"To hell with that, Mountie!" shouted Dick. "They're certain to have some heavy firepower. If you get down where they can see Whisper, you and Yuri are dead meat."

Dick saw the exit sign appear in his headlight. He pressed the rewired turn signal switch to turn off his brake lights, then he decelerated rapidly. "I am clearing the autobahn, Mountie. Get directly over them and illuminate."

"Wilco, Bear. I'm with you." The occupants of the Mercedes would not be able to fire directly above their car while moving. If Jim saw a door opening, he could extinguish Whisper's searchlight and quickly disappear.

Thirty feet up the elevated exit ramp, Dick skidded to a stop. He left the engine idling, took the M-16 from its case, and felt inside his jacket for the magazine. Whisper's brilliant searchlight illuminated the Mercedes.

"They're braking, Bear. They're going to stop."

Dick snapped the magazine into the rifle, switched to full-automatic, went to one knee, and steadied it on the Honda's hot rear tire. His target was skidding to a stop on the autobahn, only fifty meters away.

He saw the right front and rear doors opening and heard Jim's call: "Three people getting out, Bear."

Dick sighted carefully and emptied the M-16's magazine in one long continuous burst. He concentrated on the right front tire and the man at the front door, who was raising an Uzi in the direction of the searchlight. Then the scene went pitch black. Dick threw the M-16 into the ditch and leapt back on the Honda. His vision was very restricted, from having stared into the bright light. He rode carefully up the exit to the crossroad.

As Dick neared the top of the overpass, Jim was back on the air: "Got them all on night-vision, Bear. One's down near the right front door, one's bending over him, and another's running up the road toward your exit with a weapon. I see you on the overpass. Roll down a few feet so you're behind the hill, then turn your lights on and get the hell out of there."

Dick's vision was clearing. He followed Jim's instructions to the letter and seconds later roared back onto the autobahn.

The faithful Honda was soon at 150kph. "What's going on back there, Mountie?"

"Standby, Bear, be with you in a moment."

In the headlight, Dick saw the warning signs about the rough road. He began decelerating.

"Sorry, Bear, had to listen to what they were saying. They are changing the tire on the Mercedes. You hit the guy by the right door. He's in bad shape. The guys in the Citroen got out okay. One of them must be the OinC. He has ordered the Mercedes to come back and pick them up. They want to get out of there before the police arrive."

Dick laughed. "Put away the good china, grandma, dinner is cancelled."

"Yeah, looks like the entertainment is over. Yuri's sitting here beside me shaking his head. Says if Moscow had a Whisper, he would never have defected."

"Bear roger. This road's not so bad as I remembered. I'll be at the border in a few minutes."

"Better ditch that 9mm before you get there. Got your papers?"

"Yeah, and enough gas to get to my favorite Shell station in Mons."

"That's about it, Bear. See you at Mildenhall in a few hours."

Dick shifted gingerly on the Honda, trying to relieve the cramp in his leg. "Thanks, Mountie. Hell of a job!"

"Congratulations to an old Nebraska cowboy, who lasted those *eight seconds* again."

From the border, he took the shortcut he'd driven so often while stationed at SHAPE. He was soon sitting across the street from the country house where he had lived with Maria. Now, he had to put her out of his life. He could never forgive her angry betrayal that had resulted in Rita's death. Even if that were possible, it was abundantly clear that the remainder of his life would be on the run. He would be hunted by the KGB, and by Mirhashem.

He checked his watch and started the Honda. In his final glance at the comfortable home, he thought about the last night he had with Rita--that New Year's Eve by the fireplace three years ago.

He accelerated up the back road to the SHAPE airfield. Tears flooded his eyes. He raised the face-plate, they were soon dried by the sharp wind in his face.

16

ONLY GREAT AND BEAUTIFUL THINGS

"You may stay in your seats while we're refueling. If you decide to disembark, please take your carry-on articles with you. Thank you." The pert young Philippine Airlines stewardess returned the microphone to its hanger and smiled--again--at Dick. "Are you sure there's nothing I can do for you, Captain Williams? Would you like more orange juice?"

"No thanks, Angie. You have spoiled me enough already."

She touched him gently on the shoulder and left to continue her other duties. She had given him special attention, from the moment he'd asked her about Bebe Espano. She claimed they occasionally worked together and were close friends.

Dick had chosen this flight out of San Francisco with the hope of seeing Bebe again. Besides the physical thing, which he clearly remembered from their last flight together, she could have updated him on the political situation. As the Philippine dictator's favorite concubine, she had been a valuable source of information during Project Aura. She was a part-time stewardess and the girl friend of Jack Richardson. Jack had been elevated to Cultural Attaché at the embassy--the post reserved for the CIA Chief of Station.

Dick leaned back in his seat and closed his eyes. The last week had been very trying. After delivering Yuri to the CIA at Andrews AFB, Mackenzie had diverted the Nimrod to Denver, dropping Dick off before the *Purple* group continued to the Philippines.

Dick's mother was losing ground. Her Altzheimers was deepening, and she needed constant care. She had been living with his sister, but his sister and her husband both worked days. They took the decision to place her in a local home for seniors. The presence in the home of several old neighbors made their heart-rendering situation a little easier.

Mackenzie seized upon Dick's one-week delay to set up a sting operation at Manila International. As *Purple*'s newly appointed Field Supervisor for Southeast Asia, he was establishing a training center at the crater base that had been built for Project Aura. The

SAS Colonel needed to know if the U.S. Embassy could be trusted with sensitive information on the movement of personnel. Mac had directed Dick to contact him by Skyfone four hours before his arrival. He would be informed of his role in the sting at that time.

The refueling had been completed. Passengers were returning to their seats. Angie was again on the microphone, preparing them for takeoff, while smiling flirtatiously at Dick. He yawned, stood up momentarily, and stretched his body.

When Angie finished her announcements, he asked: "What time is it in Manila?"

She checked her watch. "It's one-thirty in the morning, Captain. You should be in bed." Her soft brown eyes and long fluttering lashes conveyed the rest of her message. Dick's smile acknowledged the invitation, and he asked her to wake him in one hour. It was a five-hour flight from Guam to Manila. He sat down, buckled his seat belt, and reset his watch to 01:30.

In an old shed on the eastern edge of Manila, teen-ager Juan Alvarez looked again at the radium dial of his Timex. It was one-thirty. He and his friend, Tony, were sleeping on the floor in the back of his brother's Jeepney. An elongated version of the American jeeps left in the Philippines after the war, Jeepneys were Manila's primary source of transportation.

Juan had been born in the poverty-stricken slums of Manila, and lived there for his first eight years. His mother died from one of the deadly illnesses that frequently swept through those slums. After her death, Juan's angry father joined a protest movement, trying in vain to improve the horrible conditions under which tens of thousands of Filipinos struggled to survive. He was arrested during a government "crack-down." He starved to death in prison, because the Alvarez family was not allowed to bring him food.

Enraged by his father's death, Juan's older brother, Pedro, joined the New People's Army--the Soviet-sponsored insurgency organized from the HUK terrorist groups of the fifties. He rose quickly through the ranks.

Pedro worked the streets near the U.S. Embassy. His alert eyes and ears provided valuable information to the KGB agent who had helped him buy the Jeepney. "Yuri" was so impressed by Pedro that he selected him to receive specialized training.

Yuri had taken Pedro to Libya, where he was instructed in the use of terrorist weapons. A quick learner, he was elevated to a special class studying the shoulder-fired surface-to-air "Strella" missile. When Yuri returned Pedro to Manila, by way of Mindanao, two of the missiles came with him. They were stored in his Jeepney, under a false floor. Yuri bought the old shed as a place to store the Jeepney, and a home for Pedro and Juan.

Pedro frequently instructed other NPA terrorists in the use of the potent weapons. Juan always assisted him, and Pedro considered him qualified to launch a Strella. When Yuri ordered Pedro to prepare to shoot a missile during the Philippine military's air show for the President, he named Juan as his assistant. However, the attack had been cancelled at the last minute.

The KGB official who replaced Yuri was arrogant and boastful. Pedro didn't trust him, so he and Juan used their savings to buy black market passports and visas to America. They made reservations on Pan Am, and had arranged to sell the Jeepney for enough money to pay for the tickets. Pedro planned to leave the Strella missiles in the old shed, for the KGB to find after their departure.

Pedro's dream had been shattered by a police raid in Quezon City. He and two other NPA regulars were captured. They were tortured to death--but they had refused to implicate others, or identify themselves.

Yesterday, Juan had seen Pedro's mutilated body hanging from a lamp post outside police headquarters. He dared not claim it, or he would soon be in that same position. He vowed revenge. He would use the missiles to shoot down a government aircraft.

Tony stirred on the Jeepney's floor beside him. He asked: "Juan, how soon do we drive to the airport?"

Juan again checked his old Timex. "It's two-thirty, Tony. Get some sleep. We leave here at four-thirty."

Angie bent over Dick and stroked his cheek. "Two-thirty in the morning, Captain. Time to get up and go home."

Dick woke up smiling. He turned his face quickly and brushed her fingers with his lips, then he sat up and stretched his body against the seat belt.

"How did you know what I was dreaming?"

She giggled. "You were smiling in your sleep, Sir. Would you like something to drink?"

"No thank you. I'd better shave first."

She opened the overhead bin and stretched her lithe body to reach his travel bag. She looked down, caught his eyes surveying her, and asked: "Am I in the same league as Bebe?"

He laughed. "I hope not, Angie. Her boss has fallen into disrepute. Her contract may be cancelled at any moment."

"Yeah, I know." She handed Dick the bag. "Maybe it's for the best."

As he squeezed past her in the aisle, she said softly: "Let me know if you need help."

In the lavatory, Dick removed his Skyfone from the bag and selected the scramble circuit for Colonel Mackenzie.

"Hello, Dick. Been waiting for your call."

"Hi, Mac. Did you get up early, or forget to go to bed?"

"Little of both. We've had a great week-long holiday. Jerry and Carla arrived from Honduras Monday. They've gotten acquainted with Shreeba and Abood, and Helmut. Richardson took us all to dinner at the Calamari last night."

"Jerry and Carla part of your new *strike team* concept?"

"Yes, and I hope to get Abrahim away from Toufani to team with Shreeba. Maybe you can fill in while I'm waiting. It's something we need, Dick. The GP-7 charter tasked *Purple* with infiltrating terrorist organizations, but we need an extra punch to take care of business. Rapid-deployment strike teams are one of the answers. The crater's the perfect base for that operation."

"Talking about *extra punch,* is Jim Conrad with you?"

"No, he's at the crater, setting up new facilities for us. Is your flight on schedule, Dick?"

"Yeah, we should be there by six-thirty. How's the weather at your end?"

"Heavy thunderstorm over Quezon City, but it's moving north. Should be gone when you get here. Did you wear your white uniform, like I asked?"

"First time I've had it on in three years. Getting a little tight in places, but the stewardess seemed impressed."

"It's perfect for our sting, Dick. We need something highly visible. After you land, General Matos will be waiting at the bottom of the ladder with a Constabulary car. I've included him in this test of your embassy's security. He's isolating his people from the test by driving you himself."

"Be great to see him again."

"He's not looking so good, Dick. Hell of a strain on him these days. He's leading a *Malacanang* group that's trying to convince the President to step aside. Helmut will be with Matos. They will take you to the VIP lounge, where you'll change clothes with him. After the switch, Matos will take you to Villamor Air Base. Jim will pick you up with a Wessex around seven-thirty. He'll have a Skyfone, if you want to contact him."

"What happens to Helmut?"

"An embassy limo has been requested to pick *you* up at the VIP lounge. The request was made through the embassy's classified channels--and that's our test of their security. It'll be a new driver, who doesn't know you. In your white uniform, Helmut should be mistaken for you by anyone trying to intercept you."

"If the embassy does leak, and if the KGB or Mirhashem decide to settle old scores, what's to keep Helmut from becoming mince meat? Why can't I do the job myself?"

"It may require more physical activity than your decrepit spine could withstand, Bear. Don't worry! Richardson will be in the limo with Helmut. He's the only embassy official in on the switch. He agreed to make the test in exchange for some equipment from *Purple,* which will allow him to listen to the KGB in Manila. If the KGB reacts, we will know about it and protect Helmut immediately--with an SAS team that happens to be in town on *holiday.*"

Dick laughed. "You conniving, old, one-eyed bastard! Were those guys in the Nimrod?"

"Yeah, they needed to get some flight time. Jim will take you directly to the crater, Dick. We'll be out later in the afternoon."

"Thanks, Mac. See you there."

Dick returned the Skyfone to his bag and took out his razor. A few minutes later, he returned to his seat. He checked his watch. It was two forty-five.

Angie came by to offer him a blanket. Dick declined and asked her to wake him in two hours.

Juan and Tony had been awakened by the thunderstorm. The fifteen-year-olds set buckets on top of the Jeepney to catch the rainwater leaking through the shed's roof. It also served as the boys' drinking and bath water.

Juan looked at his old Timex. It was two forty-five.

"You think that guy will be able to change the picture in your brother's passport?" asked Tony.

"My brother said he can do everything. He's the guy that made it for him. He will have it ready tomorrow, then we'll be brothers for life."

Tony grinned. ". . . and I'll be older than you. Do we pick up the passport before we sell the Jeepney?"

"No. We must deliver the Jeepney to Tondo at noon. After we get the money, we go to Makati and buy clothes for America. Then we pick up your passport and pay for the tickets at the Pan Am office in Ermita. Get some rest, Tony. Ask God to stop the rain so we'll be able to shoot the missiles."

Dick awoke with a start. A brilliant flash of lightning lit the western sky. Angie was speaking: "The Captain has turned on the seatbelt sign. Please return to your seats."

She was interrupted by another announcement: "This is the Captain speaking. We may encounter some light turbulence, but there's no cause for alarm. The thunderstorm in the west should clear Manila International before we arrive. If not, we have plenty fuel to wait it out. Lean back and enjoy an early morning coffee."

Angie continued: "We are beginning our breakfast service. I think you'll find our papaya juice delightful. We offer a full range of items to please you. Enjoy your breakfast."

Dick yawned, accepted the hot towel, and rubbed his face and hands vigorously. He checked his watch. It was 04:00.

Juan shook Tony gently. "Come, Brother. It is four o'clock. Today we avenge Pedro--tomorrow we're on our way to America."

The two teen-agers sprang from the back of the Jeepney. As he had done every morning for the last four years, Juan checked the screws in the floor plates covering the crates of deadly missiles.

Tony removed the water buckets from the Jeepney's roof. They each took a drink, and they were ready to go. Breakfast was a luxury neither of the boys had ever experienced. Their first meal of the day was usually a mango or papaya, offered by a customer in exchange for a ride in the Jeepney.

The rain had stopped, but they were greeted with a flash of lightning and a jarring clash of thunder as they opened the shed's door. Juan walked down the alley between the shacks to the main street. In a few minutes, he was back.

"The storm's moving north, Tony. There will be water on the streets. We'll go slow and pick up customers along the way."

"Where are we going, Juan?"

During NPA exercises, Tony had been to possible missile-firing locations with Pedro and Juan. Most of them were in shanty towns off the ends of Manila International's east-west runway.

"The wind is out of the east," said Juan. "We will head for the banana grove west of the runway. If the wind changes, we'll stop at one of the places near the eastern end."

The Jeepney's dependable engine roared to life. Juan skillfully backed it down the alley and into the main street. As they drove away, both boys looked back at the old shed they had called home. If things went as planned, they would sleep at the airport tonight-- in their new clothes--waiting for their morning departure for America on Pan Am. They had no items to take with them. Everything they owned was on their backs or in their torn trousers.

Within a few blocks, they began picking up their usual early morning customers. Thankfully, one of them was the middle-aged woman who always paid her fare with a mango. Tony cut it in two pieces with his rusty knife; and they continued down the street, eating breakfast as Juan drove slowly along. People stepped on and off the rolling Jeepney, giving Tony the small change they knew to be the fare for the distance they would ride.

When they arrived at the entrance to the highway that ringed Manila, Tony announced the Jeepney would be taking the main highway to Pasay City. All the passengers got off to wait for the next local Jeepney. Juan drove carefully into the early morning traffic. He stuck the mango in his mouth and chewed slowly, savoring its tangy flavor. He checked his Timex. It was four-thirty.

Dick took the last slice of mango from his tray. It was too bitter for him to enjoy, but it brought back pleasant memories of his days in Cuba. He recalled his first flight on Cubana Airlines, enroute to join his squadron at Guantánamo Bay. Landing at Camaguey in a crosswind, the pilot had ground-looped the old DC-3. After the chicken crates had been re-stowed and the new passengers had embarked--all of whom were Batista's soldiers--the pilot had taken off again, without so much as a glance at the landing gear.

Camaguey was Consuela's home town. Would she still be at the crater, or was she somewhere in a plastic-surgeon's office? Dick closed his eyes for a moment, remembering her lovely dusky face.

When he opened his eyes, Angie was bending over him with a pot in each hand. "Coffee, tea, or . . . ," she giggled.

Dick laughed. "You don't have time for the *or*," he said, then added softly, "but I wish you did."

She filled his coffee cup, breathing in his ear: "I did earlier, Captain Williams, but you didn't."

She was interrupted. "This is the Captain speaking. We are encountering some headwind, but we should be at the arrival terminal shortly after six-thirty."

Dick checked his watch. It read 05:00. Looking out his left-side window, he thought he saw a long shore line in the distance. Then he realized it was only the leading edge of the wing, becoming visible in the faint predawn light.

Juan and Tony drove slowly. In the Jeepney's dim headlights, they could barely see the muddy road around the grove of banana trees. During NPA exercises, they had been to this spot many times with Pedro. The KGB had planned to use the Strella missiles against a suitable high-profile target arriving or departing from Manila International.

Juan turned into the eastern end of the grove and came to a stop. The Jeepney was hidden from view.

There was a stiff breeze from the east. Juan's target, the Philippine Airlines flight from San Francisco, would be coming directly over them at six-thirty, during its approach to Manila International. The NPA had always provided Pedro with updated airport arrival and departure schedules. Juan prided himself in knowing them by heart.

Juan checked his watch. It was five-fifteen. He and Tony had plenty of time to get the missiles and launchers out of their crates, assembled, and ready for firing. Tony held the flashlight, and Juan began removing the screws from the Jeepney's floor plates.

Dick leaned forward and twisted his neck to look back. He wanted to have a clear view of another spectacular Southeast Asia sunrise, but it didn't seem likely this morning. It was 05:30, and sunrise was not until 06:20. By that time, the airliner would be at a lower altitude, approaching Manila International.

Juan and Tony had the first missile and launcher out of the crate. As always, they were going carefully through the step-by-step directions. Yuri had translated the original complicated Russian orders into easy-to-read-and-understand cards, complete with pictures and drawings.

They completed the assembly and were starting the system checks, but something was wrong.

"I don't believe the power-pack is working," said Juan.

"Maybe the batteries are dead," suggested Tony.

"They shouldn't be. The last KGB check was only a week ago."

"Maybe that guy didn't know what he was doing. He's not nearly as good as Yuri."

"Yeah, Yuri was fantastic." Juan went back to the check list. "Let's try it again, from the beginning."

"Do we have enough time? Maybe we should start on the second one."

Juan looked at his old Timex. "It's fifteen before six. We still have time to repeat the setup instructions on this one, . . . and get the second one ready. We will have a better chance of avenging Pedro if we fire both missiles at the same time."

Dick leaned forward and looked back at the beautiful light-blue horizon emerging in the east. There was something about a sunrise over the ocean that always inspired him. It seemed to be a promise from God, that *only great and beautiful things* could happen on this day.

"It's no use, Tony. This power-pack's dead. Let's get started on the other launcher."

"Maybe we should take the power-pack from that one and put it on this one? Wouldn't take so much time to do that."

Juan smiled. "Yeah, you're right. Shine the light down here, so I can get at it."

- 310 -

Tony looked up at the eastern sky. "It's getting pretty light."

"It's only six. We have a half hour before our target flies over our heads."

Colonel Jim Conrad was preflighting the Wessex helicopter on the hangar deck in the crater. One of the joys of his assignment with *Purple* was the opportunity to continue flying. At age thirty-seven, he would have reached the point in the Canadian military where he'd have been kicked upstairs to a desk job. The number of flying billets for senior RCMP officers was also very limited.

He strapped himself into the Wessex, gave the plane captain a thumbs-up, and smiled as he was towed into position on the elevator. He had made the right career choice.

The waters in the old volcanic crater parted, the roof panels opened, and the elevator raised the Wessex into takeoff position.

Starting the Wessex, Jim noticed the wondrous sharp horizon of the eastern mountains. It was a great day for flying. He'd planned a low-level route through the mountains and valleys, before swinging out to sea. As usual, he would report to Philippine air traffic controllers that he was inbound from a ship at sea.

He checked his watch. It was 06:15. He was on time to make his scheduled 07:30 pickup of Dick Williams at Villamor Air Base.

Juan and Tony were in position at the southeastern corner of the banana grove. To the south, a Philippine Air Force DC-3 was preparing to land at Villamor Air Base. Juan was tracking it with the Strella.

"How does it look?" asked Tony.

"Perfect!" exclaimed Juan. "That guy's got to be back on the power, and I'm still getting a good lock on his engine heat."

Juan fingered the trigger mechanism. "Man! I could blow him out of the sky right now."

"Yeah, but who would care," said Tony. "That old crate isn't worth blowing up. When we get our 747, the bastards who killed Pedro will lose millions."

"You're right, and the survivors of the three hundred Americans who are going to die will sue them for millions more."

The DC-3 had landed. With Tony's help, Juan took the heavy launcher from his shoulder and set it carefully on its crate.

"Keep watch to the south, Tony. When they're landing to the east, the airliners start their approach from there. The one we're waiting for should be here shortly."

"This is the Captain speaking. Please fasten your seatbelts and remain seated for the duration of the flight. We're beginning our final approach and will be at the arrival terminal in a few minutes. Thank you for flying Philippine Airlines."

Dick checked his watch. They were on schedule. He leaned forward to look across the aisle and out the far window. The air over the city was clear--one of the blessings from the rainstorm disappearing in the distance.

Angie was coming down the aisle for her final check. No one was sitting next to Dick, and she paused to lean over the empty seat. "Thanks for flying with us, Captain." She glanced at the Navy wings on his chest. "You're probably not used to going this slow."

Dick smiled. "I wish the flight could have lasted longer."

She pressed a small piece of paper into his hand. "Maybe it will." She continued down the aisle and took her seat at the front.

"Look, Juan! There it is." Tony was pointing at the 747 passing south of Villamor on a westerly heading.

"Yeah, that has to be it. No other flights are scheduled for another half hour. Come on, Tony. Help me get the launcher on my shoulder."

The right wing dipped as the Captain began his turn back to the east to line up with the runway.

Dick smiled. A bright slice of sun was clearing the horizon. He would see another Southeast Asia sunrise.

Juan balanced the missile launcher on his shoulder. As they had often practiced in this location, Tony was standing in front of him, peering through the small banana trees at the sky behind him. They could hear the roar of the 747's engines approaching. The giant aircraft would pass directly over them.

"Double check switches on!" shouted Tony.

Dick looked at the Manila skyline. He could see the Philippine

Plaza Hotel. Memories of Rita rushed to his mind.

The Captain added a little power. They were at three hundred feet, approaching the end of the runway.

Juan was centering the Strella's cross-hairs on the 747's left engines. The roar from the plane was deafening.
"Do you have a lock?" shouted Tony.
"Yeah, get down! I'm going to shoot now!"

Dick glanced forward at the airport buildings. The blazing sun was bursting over the terminal roofs.

"Shoot! Shoot!" screamed Tony.
"I can't!" screamed Juan. "The sun broke my lock!"

The Captain flared for landing. The deafening noise from the engines dissipated.

Tony was crying. "We missed him! Dammit, we missed him!"
Juan lowered the missile launcher and said calmly: "There will be another, my Brother. The 747 from Tokyo will be here in thirty minutes." He glared balefully at the bright sun. "By then the sun will be high enough for me to hold the lock."

Dick was overjoyed to see Helmut behind the wheel of the familiar green Toyota. He joined the Chief of the Philippine Constabulary in the backseat. They barely had time for a hand-shake before Helmut parked at the VIP lounge.

Dick and Helmut went immediately into the restroom to change clothes. They had precious little time for conversation.

"Why the hell does that white uniform fit you so good, when it was so tight on me?"

"Probably your life-style, Brown Bear. Thanks for stretching it for me. I've been putting on a few pounds also."

They finished the switch, and Dick walked quickly to the door. "I'll give your clothes back to you at the crater, Helmut. Keep your head down! I hope those KGB guys we were playing with in Paris don't show up here."

Helmut laughed. "That crazy SAS Colonel is hoping they will, along with a couple dozen Middle East terrorists. He has his team of trained killers staked-out on the road back to town."

"Take care, old friend. Look forward to speaking with you later." Dick hurried out the door.

General Matos was still in the backseat. Dick opened the front door. "Are you trusting me with your automobile, Sir?"

"Don't make me regret it, Dick," laughed Matos. "It's not by choice. The boys on the gate at Villamor would wonder what was happening if I was driving."

"What time is it, Juan? That next 747 should be here."

"Maybe he's late. Keep watching to the south. We want to be ready when he comes."

"There are people around that old farm building to the north."

"I'll keep an eye on them. It's been deserted for years. Let's bury the other missile and the crates while we're waiting for the flight from Tokyo."

Dick braked the green Toyota to a stop alongside the Villamor Air Base terminal building.

"I'm indebted to you, Sir."

"Don't worry about it, Dick. I'll get my money's worth out of you one of these days. As soon as our leader goes into exile in Hawaii, I'll be asking you to testify against his cronies--for stealing our money and smuggling it to the U.S. through your base banking system. Drop by and see me before you leave Manila."

"Be glad to do that, General."

Juan smoothed the last shovel of dirt. "Good job, Tony. After we fire the missile, there'll be nothing left here but the smoke."

"Wonder what happened to the flight from Tokyo?"

"Japanese are late for everything. I don't mind waiting to kill them. We'll be taking revenge for other Filipinos besides Pedro."

"More people are walking around that old farm, Juan. What if they decide to pick some bananas?"

"Don't worry, Tony. We can get out of here in a hurry."

Dick strolled through the small terminal and walked to the flight line. Amazing! He was in civilian clothes, unidentified, and he was walking beside military aircraft without being challenged. What easy pickings it would be for any organized terrorist group.

He checked his watch. It was 07:20. He took the Skyfone from his flight bag and called Jim Conrad.

"Hi, Bear, which hotel roof are you perched on?"

Dick laughed. "Those were the good old days, Mountie. You're not on the way in Whisper, are you?"

"No, just a big old lumbering Wessex. You are at Villamor Air Base, aren't you?"

"Affirmative. I'll be waiting at the end of the flight line."

"Okay, Bear. I'm over Sangley Point. Be there shortly."

"Take a look, Juan. Some of those people are coming."

Juan walked out of the grove to look at the old farm building. He returned quickly to Tony and the Strella missile.

"Yeah, a couple of them are heading this way. That's a very muddy field they have to cross. Must be hungry for bananas."

"What are we going to do, Juan? Maybe we have to choose between avenging Pedro and getting to the States."

"Help me put this launcher on my shoulder. It'll take them at least twenty minutes to get here. We'll shoot the next thing that comes along, whether it's an airliner or some General going into Villamor. It's all the same to me."

". . . and to me, Brother!" echoed Tony.

"Mountie, Brown Bear, believe I hear you coming from the west. Yeah, . . . think I see you now."

"That's probably me, Bear. I'm going off the air now. Takes two hands to land this thing."

"Roger that. Unless you want a rest, keep it running and I'll jump aboard."

"Okay, let's do it. Helmut's German beer at the crater is a lot better than the San Miguel in the Villamor club."

Tony was pointing along the south side of the banana grove. "Here comes a helicopter. Looks like he's going to Villamor."

Juan balanced the heavy missile launcher on his shoulder and moved carefully to the corner of the grove. He stood alongside the last banana tree.

- 315 -

As it approached Villamor Air Base, the helicopter was passing from right to left, about 3,000 feet away. Juan centered the cross-hairs. He saw the red locked-on signal in the sighting mechanism.

"Stand clear, Tony!" he shouted. "I'm going to shoot."

The big chopper began its flare for landing. The Strella's blast knocked Juan to his knees, but the trail of the deadly rocket was going directly for the helicopter.

Dick could not believe his eyes, but his reaction was immediate. "Missile at your six, Mountie!" he screamed in the Skyfone. "Get down! Get down!"

He was running helplessly toward the Wessex when the missile hit the tail rotor housing. It did not explode--*Juan had forgot to arm it*--but it knocked the tail rotor blades off the helicopter. The Wessex began to spin wildly. It plummeted toward the concrete apron of the aircraft parking area.

Dick was still running. He was fifty yards away when it hit the ground. There was no explosion, only the thud of a terrific impact. The helicopter split apart. He had twenty yards to go when the fire started in the largest piece of wreckage. In his last few steps, he spotted Jim--strapped in the seat.

Sharp pieces of wreckage tore at Dick's legs and arms as he lunged for him. The Mountie's head was hanging down. His shirt was soaked in blood. Dick unbuckled the seatbelt and harness, tore away the radio cords, and pulled him from the seat. Dick's back failed him--he fell to his knees in the wreckage--but he held on to the Canadian's body.

He looked up to see fire engulfing the wreckage. A heaven-sent burst of adrenaline gave him superhuman strength. He pulled himself erect, grasped Jim Conrad in his arms, and staggered away from the fire.

He was fifty feet from the wreckage when the ruptured verte-brae gave way again. He fell to his knees. The fire's blast was hot on his back, but the flames were not reaching him. He crawled on his torn knees, with Jim clasped tightly in his arms.

"Conrad! Jim Conrad! Can you hear me?" Dick screamed again and again.

When the Canadian weakly raised his head, Dick could see the source of all the blood. There was a horrendous cut on the side of

Jim's throat. Blood was gushing from his jugular vein. Dick's hands flew to the severed vein, trying to staunch the flow.

In the back of his mind, Dick heard the wail of a siren. "Hold on, Mountie! Help's on the way."

Jim's mouth moved, but he was unable to speak. The jagged metal that had severed his jugular had also cut his larynx.

Dick cradled Jim in his left arm--trying desperately to stop the bleeding with his right hand. The Canadian's head was tilted away from Dick, his arm trailed uselessly to the ground. Blood was flowing from his throat to his shoulder, down his arm, and running off his fingers onto the concrete.

Jim's eyes were open. He was staring at the blood dripping from his fingers. Very slowly, the Canadian Mountie began to move his hand. He was drawing on the concrete--with his own blood.

"Save your strength, Jim!" cried Dick. Tears were streaming down his face.

A bloody finger traced the letter *R* on the smooth concrete. "Rita, yes, Rita!" screamed Dick.

With incredible effort, Jim Conrad moved his arm slightly and began again. His bloody finger completed a circle, then drew a horizontal line in the middle. Dick saw the finger slowing, and knew his partner was dying. He pressed harder and harder, trying to stop the flow from the torn jugular.

With one last valiant effort, Jim drew a vertical line in the circle, adjacent to one end of the horizontal line--then his body went limp in Dick's arms.

Dick screamed, "Mountie! Stay with me! Hold on!" He saw men running toward them. He struggled to his feet, still holding Jim's body. Then something snapped inside him--he collapsed to the concrete--he felt himself tumbling into a bottomless black void.

EPILOGUE

Jim Conrad began life on the steps of a RCMP station house. He was only one day old when he was left there in the freezing cold of a Canadian blizzard. He grew up in a Catholic orphanage. A brilliant child, he was fluent in six languages when he graduated from high school. Athletically gifted, he went to college on a football scholarship. He ignored offers from professional football to pursue his first love--flying. He earned an advanced degree in Aeronautical Engineering and traded that diploma for a set of wings in the Canadian military. Enthusiastic, and a natural-born leader, he accepted the challenge of exchange duty with the Royal Air Force. He made two deployments, flying fighter aircraft from the deck of HMS *Ark Royal*.

While returning from his second cruise, he received word that the Mother Superior who raised him had been killed--an innocent victim of an FLQ terrorist bomb in Quebec. Fiercely loyal, Conrad requested an immediate transfer to the RCMP. He teamed with a former college friend, Ray James, and went underground inside the viscous FLQ separatist organization. They were too late to stop the attack on the Canadian Labor Minister, but they were instrumental in arresting the assassins. Ray James was killed during the arrest.

Ray's wife and college sweetheart, Rachel, entered the RCMP with her husband. After his death, she teamed with Jim Conrad. Their dedicated and effective work against the FLQ impressed the Canadian Prime Minister. He appointed them Canada's first representatives to the newly chartered GP-7 special security agency, labeled *Purple*. To protect her young son, Rachel changed her name to Rita Jay.

Ray Junior considered Jim Conrad to be his uncle. The little boy seemed to understand his mother's need to avenge his father. He willingly grew up under the loving care of his grandparents, Annie and Ollie Carlson.

He was only ten when the RCMP aircraft scattered his mother's ashes in the valley that she had called home. He often spent the twilight hours in the rural cemetery, by the stone engraved with the names of his parents. Ray came to love the family of wolves that lived in the pine grove above the cemetery. They seemed to be guarding the eternal flame that burned over his parents' graves.

Ray was fourteen when the body of his uncle was laid to rest next to his parents. Jim Conrad had often visited the small town. As a former friend of the town's deceased heroes, Rachel and Ray James, he was popular with the local citizens. A representative of the RCMP informed the local banker that Ray Junior was the sole beneficiary of Jim's will, that included the proceeds of a $250,000 life insurance policy.

The entire village turned out for Jim Conrad's graveside funeral. The neatly manicured green grass in the small cemetery contrasted with the surrounding pastures, where waves of grass were turning an early-fall brown.

The family of wolves awoke from their mid-afternoon nap. The six-month-old cubs peered curiously at the automobiles parking down the hill, below their lair in the pine grove; but they obeyed their mother's warning growl and stayed low. Only their inquisitive ears could be seen above the fallen logs.

The lazy circling of the eagles in the cloudless blue sky was interrupted by RCMP aircraft landing in the pasture north of the cemetery. The Otters' noisy engines shattered the peaceful silence as they taxied to the cemetery fence. When their propellers stopped, the tranquility of the valley returned.

The eagles again soared high overhead, while ten uniformed officers of the Royal Canadian Mounted disembarked from the first aircraft. They hurried to the second aircraft, opened the cargo door, and gently removed the coffin. It was draped proudly with the maple leaf flag of Canada. The Victoria Cross, England's highest military decoration, was affixed to the flag.

Six of the Mounties hoisted the coffin to their shoulders. Others lifted a wheel chair and its occupant from the aircraft. They formed a column and began a slow march to the gravesite. An honor guard of four Mounties led the procession. Close behind them walked the Queen of England's representative, the Governor General of Canada. The pallbearers and the coffin were followed by the wheel chair, bearing a United States Navy Captain in dress blue uniform. His face was concealed by dark glasses and the gold-braided brim of his hat. The wheel chair was pushed by a broad-shouldered, highly decorated Colonel from the United Kingdom's elite Special Air Service. The magnificence of his formal kilt uniform was enhanced by the black patch over his left eye. Next came a Colonel in the uniform of West Germany's famed Grenzegruppeneun Commandos. His icy-blue eyes stared straight ahead. The commando was accompanied by a small, slender, well-dressed man of Arabic descent. He pushed his gold-rimmed glasses back on his nose, to hide the tears whelming in his dark eyes. At the rear of the procession was the tall, ramrod-straight figure of an Air Chief Marshal in the Royal Air Force. Rows of decorations on his chest attested to his courage, but there were tears in the corners of his piercing dark eyes. Beside him walked a tall, imposing man in a gray suit and hat. The hat was pulled down to hide most of the stern features of his face.

The ceremony was brief. During his eleven years in *Purple,* Jim Conrad had fulfilled the ultimate provision of the GP-7 charter on five occasions. He had saved the Queen of England from an IRA bomb at a seaside resort. He had saved the English Prime Minister from an assassin's bullet. He had also saved the lives of two Presidents of the United States: one during a visit to London and the other during a visit to West Berlin. The Polish Pope had been saved from a terrorist sniper in the Philippines. Jim Conrad had personally unraveled the sophisticated German terrorist group, the Red Army Faction, cell-by-cell. His courageous and unselfish actions in the defense of freedom and democracy, and the GP-7 heads-of-state, were too numerous to mention.

Of course, none of these *Purple* actions could be mentioned at the funeral. All were cloaked under a blanket of secrecy, which was the only protection GP-7 afforded its trusted few. The eulogy was delivered by the Governor General. He could only describe Jim's service in the RCMP as courageous and exemplary. His death was attributed to an aircraft mishap, which occurred during the performance of a dangerous counter-terrorism mission overseas.

The sharp crash of the honor guards' rifles startled the cubs. They pressed tightly against their mother, she reassured them with a throaty growl.

The soaring eagles veered briefly away from the cemetery, but were back overhead when the Governor General accepted the flag from the honor guard. He presented it to Jim's acknowledged nephew, Raymond Edwin James, Junior.

The ears of the curious cubs stood erect as the sound of taps echoed from the cemetery. With tears streaming down his cheeks, the Navy Captain struggled to stand from the wheel chair. He was supported by the SAS Colonel, as the coffin of Jim Conrad was lowered into his final resting place.

The Governor General accepted the Victoria Cross from the honor guard. Without words, he hung it around the neck of the gangling fourteen-year-old. Ray Junior stood silently, his eyes closed in prayer. Then he walked slowly around the grave to the Navy Captain. He had recognized him as the man who had been at his mother's funeral four years earlier. He had provided the "eternal flame" and the gravestone, which now included the inscription:

COLONEL JAMES CONRAD
RCMP
1949-1986

The teen-ager took Dick's hand. He removed the medal from around his neck and gave it to him. Dick touched the honored decoration to his lips, then returned it to the boy's hand and whispered in his ear.

Ray Junior went to the gravestone. He touched each of the three inscribed names with the Victoria Cross, then he knelt down and kissed each of the inscriptions. Finally, he returned to the open grave. He lifted the medal to the sky, as if offering it to the eagles soaring high above; then he held it by the long ribbon, lowered it gently, and laid it on the coffin.

Somewhere above those soaring eagles, God had to be saying: "Greetings, Colonel Conrad. You were a courageous peacemaker on earth. I welcome you to heaven as one of my children."

Upon his return to the crater in the Philippines, Dick Williams was greeted by a neurologist and a psychiatrist.

The neurologist immediately placed him in traction and began infusions of medications to reduce the swelling in the severely damaged nerve bundles of his spinal cord. Dick dismissed the psychiatrist as unnecessary, but Colonel Mackenzie insisted they spend some time together.

During his third day in traction, Dick was visited by the crater's housekeeper. Mrs. Ramierez had also taken care of *Purple's* safehouse in Magallanes during Project Aura. She brought Dick the shoebox in which he had saved his personal notes from the project.

Mrs. Ramierez also handed him an envelope. Jim Conrad had instructed her--in the event of his death--to give it to Dick.

In the quiet solitude of the dispensary, Dick surveyed the lines of apparently random hand-written letters of the English alphabet that filled both sides of the single sheet. Only the last sentence was readable: "The Shadow knows!"

Despite his deep sorrow, Dick had to smile. During the lighter moments of their friendship, he and Jim had occasionally joked about the radio show, which had been so popular during their youth. Dick rang the bell for Mrs. Ramierez. He requested two pieces of cardboard, a straight pin, scissors, a tablet, and a pencil.

With those tools, he set about solving the coded puzzle which would reveal Jim's final message to him. He cut the pieces of cardboard into circles, one smaller than the other. Then he marked 26 equal spaces around the circumference of each circle and inserted the letters of the English alphabet in order. Finally, he centered the smaller cardboard on the larger and pushed the pin through the center. He spun the smaller circle around, stopping when the letters were aligned. As he remembered the Shadow's basic code, the letters on the outer wheel would spell the decoded message; while the letters on the inner wheel would come from the puzzle.

It took only a few minutes for Dick to discover that none of the 26 possible settings of the inner circle would yield a readable message. The first word in the coded puzzle was a single letter, which meant it had to be an *A* or an *I*. However, neither of those starting points produced understandable letter combinations.

Dick had refused the many pain-killers offered by the neurologist, his mind was clear. After a half hour of quiet deliberations, the process came back to him. One began with a match of the first coded letter with the letter *A* or *I,* then moved the inner wheel a certain number of spaces clockwise, checked the next coded letter against the letter on the outer wheel, and moved the wheel a certain number of spaces again.

The trick was to determine the sequence of numbers to be utilized in moving the wheel. Since the combinations of numbers were infinite, the code was unsolvable--unless the persons who were communicating knew the numbers in advance.

Dick took the tablet and pencil and began with birthdays. Four hours and half-a-tablet later he tried the date that he, Jim, and Rita had first met--the 23rd of June 1980, at Don Ho's club in Hawaii. Dick played at length with those numbers. It was after midnight when the sequence of 2-3-0-6-8-0 began to unveil Jim's message.

The first word was *I*. The next five words were: *am happy to tell you.* Remembering the *R* that the dying Jim Conrad had written in blood on the concrete, Dick's spirits soared and his heart began to pound.

"I am happy to tell you that Rita lives. Only Nelson and I, and now you, know this. She escaped by diving out the door before the first RPG hit the limo. She rolled into the ditch and crawled into the bushes along the airport road. She watched as Shepherd and his boys killed most of the ambushers. She saw Salah and Enrico escape. She walked back to the airport and hid in the crowd. When she saw the CCCP airliner take off, she knew she was still in danger. Two nights later, she knocked on my door in the Manila Hotel. We talked for a long time, Brown Bear, and finally decided on the funeral with the fake ashes to throw everyone off her trail. It was a very difficult decision for her! She loved you very much, but she realized you and I were the only ones aware of her mission from Berlin to Manila. There was a leak somewhere around you that was life-threatening to her. Nelson provided her with a change of identity, and she is following his recommendation to remain clear of her son until he is twenty-one. Until that time, only Nelson will know where she is--and he is sworn not to tell. Don't make it difficult for him, Dick. Remember, Rita could identify herself to you if she chose to do so; but she would then be back in the same dangerous situation. Her appearance has been altered. You would never recognize her. If you want to honor her, Dick, write about the sacrifices she made in Purple--ending the white-slave racket in Manila must head the list. Tell the world about it! I do not know how and when you might write the story of Purple, but promise me that you will do it someday. If you are reading this, I am already dead. I will not apologize for keeping you in the dark. You know I did it for the girl we both loved. You can be certain that, when I died, my last prayers and thoughts were to

bringing the two of you back together--whether on earth or in heaven."

Dick read the message over and over. Memorizing each and every word. When the therapist came into the room for his morning exercises, Dick sent him for a waste basket and matches. He burned the tablet, code wheel, and Jim's letter. That afternoon he began sorting the notes in the shoebox, in preparation for telling the story of Rita Jay, Jim Conrad, and *Purple.*

Printed in the
United States of America
by
Central Plains Book Manufacturing
22234 C Street, Strother Field
Winfield, Kansas 67156

Loyalty, Betrayal, and other Contact Sports (Charlie) is a work of fiction. Names, places,
and events are either a product of the author's imagination or are used fictitiously.